Tempting Olivia

An Oxford Romance

Tempting Olivia

Published by:

To Jayney

1

It should have been another perfect day for Olivia Sachdeva. It started well.

She checked her reflection in the brass plaque for Bentley and Partners, flicked hair from her eyes and watched it swish across her light-brown cheek into a flawless black curtain along her jawline.

She glided up the steps, past the sign that gleamed even in the March sunshine. Into the tall, stone, Regency terrace of Beaumont Street, Oxford. Chin up, back straight, weight on her toes, chic and fluid, as if she still took ballet lessons.

"Good morning, Zain," she said, as she breezed past the young receptionist at the entrance desk.

She was already halfway up the curving stairs before she heard the reply of, "Morning, Olivia".

Was Zain tired from a late night and only half functioning before coffee? She glanced back to see him rub his eyes and sip from a takeout cup. She smiled. Of course, she was correct. Because noticing the details and understanding people was part of her job.

The airy white interior of the building was quiet this early in the morning, and the click of her lock was sharp in the absence of chatter from colleagues as she entered the head of family law office on the first floor. A double first in jurisprudence from Oxford and an indefatigable work ethic had propelled her to this position before she hit mid-thirties, and she aimed her sights higher at managing partner.

The cleaners had left her room exactly how she wanted. Good. Large partner's desk at the end. A set of leather chairs and coffee table informally but precisely arranged between two tall multipaned windows. Although still a leafless early spring, the view into trees and rooftops at the back of the building was tranquil, ideal for sessions with emotional clients. Everything was placed in a relaxed position, which wouldn't be so relaxed if they weren't so accurately aligned. There was an artful method to informality which others didn't appreciate. Friends, awkward Charlotte and irreverent Millie, sprung to mind.

Following her routine to the letter, she hooked her wool coat behind the door, replaced her neat black trainers with high heels, filled the kettle in the corner and misted the potted ferns on the two generous window ledges. She plucked a couple of dead leaves away to restore perfection then sat at her desk with a glass mug of whole leaf white tea. The delicate scent of Darjeeling tantalised her senses and lifted her further, part of her routine and mental preparation to receive clients who arrived in all kinds of conditions.

Angered, despairing, resigned, composed but holding it in. Anyone in any state could come through that door, and she and her serene office were ready. Her job was all about helping imperfect people sort their mess, in a responsible and polite way to restore order to their world. Olivia would swiftly analyse and categorise her client to tailor her advice, and gently cut through the haze of human emotions to the heart of the matter.

Who did she have first? She flipped up the laptop screen and, while it whirred into action, she dabbed moisturiser on her hands and rubbed it into her supple brown skin.

A notification of 'Film night – Charlotte' popped up, and she allowed herself a distracted thought, because film night once a month with her best friend meant a chance to pander to Olivia's two weaknesses, no indulgences:

One – ice cream of all flavours, particularly coconut. Even better if she could get pistachio kulfi, which she would lick to savour its silky richness.

And two – Kate Laurence films. Because was there nothing the actor couldn't do. Comedy, romance, sci-fi, historical, she'd won awards for them all. And no matter how much Charlotte teased her about the aesthetic appeal of the honey-haired, rose-cheeked actor, it was her skill that Olivia admired most.

Kate would plunge Olivia into a vivid experience, with her suspension of disbelief complete, whether into the terror of a woman lost on an island or swept into a different era. Best was a Kate Laurence romantic comedy, guaranteed to soothe and melt Olivia even after the worst week, and a perfect antidote to daily work as head of divorce and family law.

She visualised the evening ahead. Charlotte would tease that she only watched Kate Laurence films. And Olivia would rebuff and refute that claim, citing numerous arthouse movie examples as evidence. Then with Charlotte's distraction and indecision, they would fall back onto the actress' work. It was a ritual. One she cherished. And she sighed.

"Are you ready for your first client?" Zain buzzed up. "Ms Woodhouse, your 8 o'clock, is here."

Of course, she was ready. She stood and smoothed her black fitted dress down her slim figure.

"Could you send her up, please," Olivia replied.

The schedule listed 'Ms K. Woodhouse' booked for an initial divorce consultation – a blank sheet for which Olivia was prepared with an open mind and deep reservoir of experience.

"Thank you, Zain."

She sauntered from behind her desk and mulled over which film Charlotte would 'choose' while she waited for the client to come upstairs.

Perhaps a historic piece and serious work of acclaim? But it was the end of a long winter and she craved sun and fun in the form of light-hearted Kate. Yes, a romance where the actress showed her comic timing, playful side and a smile that was sunshine. Her distinctive smile that set her apart from others and showed the uniqueness, sparkle and the soul of the character.

She was in danger of drifting, the only time she did. Charlotte, her best friend, mistook this for dreamy admiration of the actor behind the role. And this was absolutely not the case. Olivia was frosty about the accusation.

Never meet your heroes. Never check which political party a singer supported. And never, ever, read celebrity gossip about your favourite actors. Because knowing about the real person would break the spell. That wonderful breath of fresh air in *Encountering Evie* would be tainted by a divaesque outburst in public. The erudite heroine of *Finding Fossils* spoiled by a string of expletives thrown at photographers.

No. Any knowledge of the person that was Kate Laurence was banned, no matter how much her friend followed various social-media fan accounts.

Halfway across the room, pondering which film she would choose, a light knock on the open door interrupted her thoughts.

"Good morning," Olivia said, approaching the doorway. "Do come in."

Then she stopped. Mid-stride. She almost tripped. And Olivia never stumbled. Ever. But the only woman capable of causing her misstep came through the door.

"Good morning," said the mellifluous voice.

It had a depth and maturity that always compelled and was so recognisable. As recognisable as the honey hair that flowed in the suggestion of a wave to the shoulders. And the white skin, without the rose touch today. The beautifully shaped eyebrows, now with a determined crease between them. And the lips, which usually had an additional curve over other mortals, pinched in a tight line.

Regardless of the differences, for once Olivia wished she followed celebrity gossip. Because she might have been warned about what was happening in front of her.

All her favourite films and comfort fantasies were about to be turned upside down and inside out. Because it was the very human, likely very messy divorcee, Olivia's weakness number two – the actor herself.

"Hi," the woman said. "I'm Kate Woodhouse. You might have heard of me as Kate Laurence."

2

Yes. Olivia had heard of 'Kate Laurence'. And, considering her adamant disinterest in the aesthetics of the real woman, it was difficult to take her eyes off the actor.

She blinked, her considerable brain stalling, as if the cogs lost their purchase, fell apart and clanked to the ground. It was so marked it seemed audible.

How long did she pause? The statis stretched timelessly, enormous in Olivia's mind but hopefully a fraction of a second to the rest of the world. Hopefully.

Olivia opened her mouth. "Kate..."

Laurence. No Woodhouse. The client. Olivia blinked again while internally she gave her head a shake to focus on the persona here.

"Ms Woodhouse," she settled on at last, "please take a seat."

She gestured to the comfortable leather armchair, chosen to relax clients through their awkward circumstances. She wished she had the same, then spun on her heel and sauntered around the large antique desk.

She took a moment, with her back turned to the client, to let the wheels click together and her mind become the well-oiled machine it usually was. Olivia had remained composed. Good. This was a salvageable and professional situation.

Except, dammit, she hadn't shaken hands. She usually obliged the custom but didn't care for the unnecessary physical contact. It put people at ease, that expected exchange of pressing palms together.

Perhaps the client... Again her brain tripped over who stood here. Perhaps Ms Woodhouse hadn't noticed.

Olivia glanced over her shoulder. Still there. That world famous actor. Sitting incongruously in Olivia's office rather than on a screen.

She was taller than Olivia expected. She'd assumed the full-figured actor would be average to short, but when she walked in the door she almost matched Olivia's height. Now seated, the client maintained a strong physical presence. She wore tan leather brogue boots and dark jeans, snug around hips that were never slim on camera. The herringbone blazer and crisp white shirt, fitted and tailored into the waist, enhanced both her chest and shoulders. Olivia had followed her for years, and the actor's unapologetic and outspoken comfort in her curves was part of the appeal.

Olivia did a double take again at the actress. How could a person, shorter and softer on camera, be so physically present in real life? How did they do that? Although she'd seen some men insist on standing on higher ground for photos and guessed they did on film too.

Still, it was unnerving. And distracting. Her head spun at how the screen could tell a story and reality be so different. This would play hell with her comfort viewing.

Olivia sat, crossed her legs and assumed an elegant pose.

"Ms Woodhouse," she said. "How may I help?" Excellent. Her delivery was intact.

"Thank you for seeing me this early in the morning. I realise it's before your standard hours. I appreciate it."

The voice. It transported Olivia to a hundred viewings. Not the posh, high received-pronunciation of Olivia's, or the West Country of Kate's last period-piece, but a mature timbre with an informal estuary underpinning the RP. It made Kate relatable, said commentators, although still posh said others. Right now, it was reminiscent of other divorcees. Tired mainly.

Olivia nodded slowly, as if appreciating Kate's consideration, rather than her mind tumbling over a hundred different renditions of the actress.

"Truly, it's no bother," Olivia replied. "I'm happy to see clients at this hour."

Kate stared at her, a crease in permanent residence between her shapely eyebrows and full lips taut in a line.

"I hope Hugo didn't push me in front of others."

Kate knew the managing partner? Olivia's eyebrows rose. That was news to her.

"Not to my knowledge," Olivia said. "He hasn't mentioned you."

With her precise memory, Olivia would have remembered the managing partner bringing up a notable client. And the avuncular Hugo never kept his cards close to his chest.

"Good." The client nodded. "I wouldn't want to jump the queue. I'm his new neighbour and everyone has been welcoming and helpful."

Olivia twitched and the wheels turned. So, Kate Laurence had moved to Park Town, an affluent address in North Oxford, and it sounded for an extended time. The proximity to Olivia's work and home was another alarming intrusion into reality. Every personal and professional instinct said to turn this client away.

She must have mulled over the scenario for too long, because Kate added. "I know my career is high profile and people do me favours. I don't want to take advantage, especially if someone else needs the help more."

The actor showed self-awareness at least. Was she also aware of how hard it was for others to encounter her and keep a level head?

"You come highly recommended," Kate added.

"Hugo is very generous," Olivia replied automatically.

"I wasn't referring to Hugo."

"Oh?"

That was unnerving too. That the famous woman, with such a high profile in Olivia's conscience, had also heard of her.

"A friend suggested you, and another backed it up."

"That's..." Weird, frankly. Olivia felt rather exposed. "...pleasing to hear."

"My best friend said you managed her annulment sensitively and quickly. I could do with the same, because I'm getting a divorce."

The familiar face gazed at Olivia, chin raised, but not defiant or defensive. Long legs crossed, hands rested on the arms of the chair, broad shoulders relaxed. This was a woman at ease with her decision. It was almost regal, with none of the disappointment, shame or anger of many clients as they uttered 'I'm getting a divorce'. No. She looked reconciled to it.

"We had an on-and-off relationship for years," Kate continued. "We finally got married three years ago. Silly really. I knew it was over as soon as the honeymoon." The actor tilted her head in a way that suggested she was anything but stupid. "But we both agree it's time to draw a line under our relationship, for everyone's sake."

Olivia had the same intense reaction as when Charlotte shoved a social media snap of Kate beneath her nose. She wanted to push the gossip away. This was none of her business. She didn't want to know. Except the actress sat before her, insisting on telling her everything.

The photo flashed in her head. Kate smiling. A baby in her arms, an older child by her side. And some actor partner, her husband, with his arm around her. He was a good-looking man, she supposed, in that utterly unmemorable way men had for Olivia. Tall. Hair. Arms. Legs. A man.

"So I'm hoping a solicitor of your calibre can push the divorce through quickly and smoothly. Then we can all get on with our lives," Kate said, with the same powerful composure and lack of doubt.

Uncompromised. That's the film that reminded Olivia of Kate's manner. Where Kate played the adult daughter in an epic family drama, her features stronger and more vivid today. It was like they softened her face on screen. Perhaps Olivia's internal image was based on movies when the actress when younger. But Olivia enthusiastically followed later films, and she was sure the camera didn't bring out this imposing version.

Olivia watched as the actor spoke, gripped as if another drama unfolded before her eyes, Kate's physical presence demanding all the attention in the room. It drew Olivia in with unnatural strength beyond a common client, the spectacle resonating by association with poignant performances. Which was not a professional reaction.

Olivia sat up in her chair. The very human complications of divorce required empathy and understanding, but to a degree where she remained emotionally detached and level-headed. Olivia stiffened, determined to remain an effective lawyer.

"...Of course, my kids take priority. My workload will be less busy while I settle them in Oxford..."

Olivia's head turned again, finding it difficult to believe her eyes. Because this was Kate Laurence, nominated for Oscars so often it was newsworthy when she wasn't shortlisted. The actor sat in her own personal drama right in front of Olivia. It was so compelling, her mind flickered on an edge of disbelief, then riled with discomfort at being privy to inappropriate information.

Olivia struggled, her laser-like focus challenged, because she couldn't shake the dissonance of this being *the* Kate Laurence.

Enough. This had gone too far.

"Ms Woodhouse," Olivia said. She leant forward on the desk. "Before you explain any further, I should make some observations and offer my initial advice."

The actor twitched, as if taken aback, perhaps not so down to earth and humble to be surprised at pushback. Famously dark green eyes, with the amber ring around the pupil, stared back as clear as on a film poster.

"We have a good, and I believe deserved, reputation as a boutique firm with experience of what we term high-value clients."

The gaze returned was penetrating. Few looked at Olivia Sachdeva with that unflinching attention.

"However," Olivia continued, "we are a small partnership. Given your profile, you might be better engaging a larger practice with a dedicated PR team."

Still the gaze.

"Should the case become protracted, complex or shift into the public sphere, we might not be the best placed to handle the fallout."

"I have my own PR consultant."

"You would need it. And so would our firm if it escalated."

"But you handled the McKenzie divorce? Maria's my closest friend and another actor. She's the same."

So that's how Kate knew of her. Olivia maintained eye contact with the determined actor.

"With all due respect," and Olivia meant that, "Maria McKenzie, whilst being a respected artist, is not a multi-Oscar nominated global superstar."

"You have heard of me then," Kate fired back.

"Everyone," Olivia paused for emphasis, "has heard of you."

There was a lull, and neither seemed to blink. Perhaps she was getting through to the client. Because, in her experience, considerable even in her mid-thirties, this case could have tabloids camping on Beaumont Street with a bag of bad PR for the partnership.

Olivia breathed in, "Ms Woodhouse–"

"Ms Sachdeva," Kate countered, and the focus and sparkle in her eye nailed Olivia. Exhilaration thrilled inside. "One of my most trusted friends recommended you, and in my business real friends are rare. I'm convinced you're suitable."

But this highlighted another problem. The feisty response where Kate came alive, like she had in *Uncompromised,* had Olivia's heart thumping. That was far from suitable. And even though reminiscent of one of her favourite characters, she didn't want reality trespassing on her main comfort in life. Without films, she'd be left with only ice cream.

She watched the client reiterate the reasons for choosing Bentley. Its convenience near to the star's new home. The recommendation from several past clients and the managing partner. The fact that Olivia was honest about the practice's capabilities, which was a galling twist, all things considered.

Olivia closed her eyes. This was...challenging. And not in a good way, like stretching for another career peak. She wanted to run, because this trespassed over professional boundaries in a way she didn't want to explain to anyone.

She checked her watch as a diversion.

"We're coming to the end of this initial consultation," Olivia said.

This was a nightmare. A head-spinning nightmare. The woman sitting opposite embodying so many roles and characters, but also a distinct real human. Olivia tapped her index finger on the desk, her thoughts falling into order as she drummed the rhythm.

"Perhaps," Olivia paused, "you could mull it over and..." She almost suggested booking another early slot but didn't want to make it easy.

Kate considered. Green eyes flicked to a clock on the wall. "All right," the actor said.

"Good," Olivia replied.

And yet they stayed seated.

It was a little awkward.

Olivia rose first, this was her office after all, and she rounded the table determined this time to shake Kate's hand.

But when Kate got up, her physical presence was so powerful it forced Olivia to draw back. Yes, Kate stood nearly as tall, but broader and more full-figured, and Olivia felt less substantial in front of her.

See the thing Olivia had to admit was she'd admired Kate Laurence since she was seventeen years old and the actress was twenty-one. Kate shot to fame while in her teens, rising stratospheric by her twenties. And Olivia's seventeen had been young enough for admiration to bloom into a crush with enormous posters on her bedroom walls. Something she'd been mortifyingly reminded of by her mother, who kept her room intact like a shrine.

At thirty-four, she was beyond posters and movie-star crushes. But the actor held undeniable power, and Olivia didn't want to face the reality of that teen crush. Or examine the reasons for her comfort viewings. These things needed to stay separate. There were challenges to which she would rise. Then there was excruciating personal self-examination, which she wanted to avoid when mixed up in a professional setting.

Except that was difficult to do, especially when she offered her hand to say goodbye and felt the very real woman, vivid on her palm.

Kate's hand enveloped hers, slightly larger and warmer, but the difference perceptible and all-encompassing. So many meetings ended in a rough crush of a handshake that a softer touch was shocking. And doubly so here. She blinked. Because this was Kate Laurence, like she reached out of a screen. Olivia blinked again. No, a client.

"I'll be in touch," Olivia said, somehow evenly, then she squeezed the client's fingers. "Ms Woodhouse."

A pause. Those eyes. Those intelligent green eyes with a ring of hazel. Yes, actors had a script, and Kate always projected a keen awareness on screen, but it sparkled in real life too.

The actor gazed with calm confidence. "Thank you," she said, then politely, with an eyebrow raise that Olivia would have been proud of, "Ms Sachdeva."

3

Olivia sat stunned for all of five seconds before her brain whirled into action. She examined her issues.

First, the client was physically attractive. Olivia could handle that appropriately. She didn't let that kind of thing dominate her life, unlike other people. She very much had someone in mind. Two people, in fact.

But lancing suspension of disbelief and ruining her favourite films? The ones she rewatched so many times she didn't dare count right now. Oh, that irked her. A lot.

And worst of all, she might not perform her role to the highest standard if distracted. That was unsupportable.

Then there was the issue of Charlotte. On the plus side, her friend indulged Olivia's comfort viewing of Kate Laurence films, even though less interested in them herself. But with Charlotte being easily led, this wasn't surprising. Mention any kind of food and you could guarantee Charlotte would have a sudden craving for it. Same with films.

But Charlotte followed fan media on the film star and was forever flashing publicity shots in front of Olivia, thinking she'd be fascinated. Every time, Olivia would refuse to look at Charlotte's phone, fix her with a glare and reiterate, "For the love of god, Charlotte. How many times do I need to tell you? I'm not interested."

Through her impulse-control resistant friend, it was like Olivia had a parasocial relationship by proxy with the movie star.

At the end of the long day came a familiar knock on the door. One-two-three-four-five gentle knocks followed by an unnecessary, "It's me." And an even more unnecessary, "I mean, it's Charlotte."

"Come in," Olivia said, her usually silky voice tight with a snag in its threads.

Wavy, mahogany locks flowed around the door first, familiar long legs and fluid gait next. Although tall, Charlotte always stooped to gaze at the floor, as if she'd trip over a speck of dust.

"You finished for the week?" Charlotte said, looking up, with a rosy-cheeked smile that filled the room with sunshine.

Then she stumbled over less than a speck of dust.

"Oops," Charlotte laughed, coming to a rest in front of Olivia's desk. Then, "Oh, what's wrong?"

The beaming smile morphed into a puzzled crinkle at the top of her nose.

Olivia scowled and pressed her fingertips together, as if she held an invisible ball. She'd sat like this for an hour at the end of the day, mulling over her awkward situation. A whole hour wasted circling around why it was impossible to take Kate Laurence, no Ms Woodhouse, as a client. And she needed to call her Ms Woodhouse for vital distancing.

"Nothing," Olivia said, fingertips pressed together.

The puzzled crease deepened between Charlotte's brown eyes. "Your fingertips are almost white; you're pressing them so hard."

"What?"

"Your fingertips are pale."

So they were. And they'd turned numb. Olivia dropped her hands to the desk and rubbed her thumb over her fingers. She must be agitated for Charlotte to notice that quickly. Her intelligent friend wasn't always the most observant. In fact, frustratingly oblivious at times. Their one and only romantic evening years ago sprung to mind, where Olivia had to constantly remind Charlotte they were on a date, rather than out as friends.

"I'm preoccupied," Olivia huffed.

Still the concern. Still the crinkle at the top of Charlotte's nose.

"With a case," she added.

There, that should satisfy Charlotte and avoid further questions, because her friend was professional and respected client confidentiality. They worked in different areas of the firm and rarely needed to know each other's law business. And under no circumstances, none at all, did Olivia want her over-interested friend to hear that Kate Laurence was a potential client.

Could she keep this low profile within the office?

She'd wrapped up the McKenzie case with half the practice ignorant. She'd have a word with Zain on reception and firmly remind him that discretion was required. Liz, the office manager, would be professional and tactful. Hugo would be proud of the calibre of client but understand the need for quiet.

Hmm. It was more than possible and very desirable. Because if Charlotte knew, Olivia would never hear the end of it. Her best friend would bound around and beg her to take the client. And although Charlotte would respect confidentiality and boundaries, it would always be there. That bubbling excitement. The knowing smile. The knowledge that Olivia was meeting the real woman, which would force another crack in the wall between comfort TV and real life.

"Are you sure it's a case?" Charlotte asked.

Olivia whisked round, hair flying.

"Why?"

Charlotte tilted her head and bit her bottom lip. "You have a preoccupied look that's different."

"Oh?" Olivia replied, and raised her eyebrows with a nonchalance she didn't feel.

"When you're gripped with a case, you have a tenacious focus in your eyes...like a wildcat with prey."

Well, that was not flattering.

"In a dignified way," Charlotte added.

Olivia notched her eyebrows higher in accusation.

"You still look chic."

"Glad to hear it," Olivia replied.

"It's just," Charlotte tilted her head further, "you seem more affected than usual." Charlotte paused, as she often did, as if a tumble of thoughts stalled her mouth. "Well it's...I don't know." Then she beamed with a smile again. "Like you met someone exciting."

"Excuse me?" Olivia's eyebrows couldn't get any higher.

"You have a spark when you meet someone you click with." Charlotte grinned. "Or find a loophole in the law before anyone else."

Really? How unfortunate. That she had a tell, and that Charlotte knew her well enough to spot it.

"Honestly. It's just a case," Olivia dismissed.

Charlotte's face remained bewildered.

"A very," so very, "challenging one," Olivia emphasised.

"OK." Charlotte nodded at last. "I wondered if someone had asked you on a date."

What? Olivia remained quiet.

"Something about your eyes," Charlotte continued. "I can tell when you've met an interesting woman. Not every woman. But always a woman. You never engage with men in the same way."

How unfortunate and accurate. Olivia hadn't realised it was obvious on the surface too.

"Well," Olivia said, to give herself some time to ponder. "Something to be aware of," she finished.

As for Charlotte knowing about Ms Woodhouse, the client? Absolutely must never happen.

Olivia slipped her trainers on, swung her coat around her shoulders and escorted Charlotte downstairs.

"Hey Zain," Charlotte said. "How was your day–?"

Olivia grabbed Charlotte's arm and whisked them through reception, so quickly it snatched the air from her friend's mouth before Zain could chat. She would issue him with a firm reminder about confidentiality on Monday morning.

The moment she stepped out of the front door into Beaumont Street, fatigue hit. She'd been composed with clients all day but unravelled fast with only Charlotte for company. She shed any semblance of patience as they walked past the honey-stoned walls of Worcester College and north into Jericho.

How on earth was she meant to deal with this? She mulled over her problem as they strode beside the college walls. Charlotte wittered on midstream about an IPR contract. Olivia nodded, keeping track of Charlotte's issue while another part of her brain muttered 'Kate Laurence' over and over.

The visions kept coming. The real woman morphed with roles Olivia had seen multiple times. As they passed the grand stone columns of the Oxford University Press, a Victorian Kate sprung from memory. Further up the street, by the Jericho Tavern pub, Kate's glowing smile appeared from a contemporary romcom. Past the small historic cinema, the Phoenix Picturehouse, and Kate vividly stared at her from an art-house film. Literally stared at her.

Olivia faltered and gaped at the movie poster and a banner announcing a 'Kate Laurence Season'. What had she done to deserve this?

She must have sighed or growled, some slip in composure.

"What's wrong?" Charlotte asked.

Her friend stopped in front of the blue-painted cinema façade, with Kate peeping at Olivia from over her shoulder.

"You look paler," Charlotte said.

Actually she felt ill, but there was no way she'd tell Charlotte why. She used diversion tactics instead. Easy with Charlotte. She put her foot forward and asked, "How's Millie?"

"Millie?" Charlotte's face lifted and her eyes became lost in dreamy swirls. "She sends her love."

Of course she did. No doubt Millie sent it with a bawdy laugh and flirty challenge.

One of the most impetuous and annoying people on the planet, and Charlotte would have to fall in love with her. Millie only had eyes for men at college and had broken Charlotte's heart through unrequited love, then apparently broken her own heart by toppling for Charlotte years later. And now the two were insufferably happy together.

And you didn't get more different than Olivia and Millie. She did accept Millie may be good for Charlotte. Happiness was written all over her friend's blushing smile. But Olivia couldn't always shake the nagging doubts. Difficult not to when day-in, day-out she saw broken relationships. She was trying, however. Call it growth. Millie was still aggravating though.

"And." Olivia swallowed, making her voice as non-judgmental as possible, because she imagined all sorts. "Where is she this evening? Some wild party?"

Charlotte shot her a disapproving look. It wasn't Olivia-level disapproval, more like being swatted by a puppy. She was tempted to say something affectionate and encouraging.

"Millie's playing bridge with her old landlady," Charlotte said with gentle censure.

"Right." To be fair, Millie hung out with the retired professor most often. "Good to see she's behaving." Virginia would keep her on the straight and narrow.

But Olivia shouldn't have said that.

Charlotte gave her another puppy-level look of disapproval. "Actually..." Then Charlotte smiled, that distant pink-cheeked one when distracted about Millie. "I wouldn't put it past Virginia to play strip poker."

Olivia mentally rolled her eyes.

Charlotte drifted, bit her lip and blushed, clearly picturing Millie naked.

She let her friend daydream while they marched past chattering cafes at the heart of Jericho. They turned down a quiet side street and stopped midway, outside the narrow-terraced brick cottage and small front garden, a tiny square patch of lawn poking through with crocuses and daffodils in the early spring chill.

Her key turned smoothly in the yellow-painted classic door, and Olivia inhaled as she stepped into the hallway. Home and sanctuary at last. The weight lifted from her shoulders as she walked through the door. Even the light was soothing, the chalky pale paint chosen for this harmonious effect. She slipped off her trainers, arranged them on a rack, hooked her coat on the stand and placed her slim briefcase inside the front room devoted to a sofa, stove and bookcases lining every wall.

"Shall I get chopping?" Charlotte said, so familiar with Olivia's home that she led the way down the hall to the larger sitting room at the back.

"Please," Olivia sighed.

Another level of decompression hit as she stepped into the lounge. This was her inner sanctum and painted in a calm grey. The sliding glass doors at the end led to a small courtyard garden with ivy decorating the walls, and tall potted plants inside the doors gave the illusion of a continuous space. Her modern classic sofa and chairs balanced comfort with aesthetics and were arranged around an oak coffee table in the centre with matching sideboard at the side.

Her television hung unobtrusively on the wall, and she devoted the remaining space to framed movie posters where the sapphic influence was strong from *Summerland* to *Maja Ma*. But none featured Kate Laurence, thank goodness. Not on these walls at least.

Out of reflex, she reached out and straightened *Maja Ma,* to align the pictures. Who knew what made them fall out of line during the day. Life was an endless struggle of keeping chaos at bay and battling those determined to increase entropy.

Speaking of which:

"Do you want the oven on?" Charlotte called from the kitchen.

Olivia sauntered through the archway to the narrow galley kitchen. "Yes, I was going to heat samosas."

"Homemade?" Charlotte said, eyes brightening.

"Homemade?!" She tutted in disbelief.

Her nani said life was too short to make your own samosas, and Olivia was too busy. But she and her grandmother never objected when Olivia's mum, Geeta, insisted on cooking them. Although Olivia made them last, otherwise her mother would be round with batches every day.

"As in, Geeta made them?" Charlotte added.

Olivia nodded. She leant back against the kitchen surface alongside Charlotte who was chopping crudites for dips. Charlotte glanced at her so often she feared for the safety of her friend's fingers.

"What?" she said, arms crossed.

"You're grumpy," Charlotte replied, half laughing.

She heard it. Charlotte had wanted to say "even for you" but stopped herself. Miraculous for honest, effusive, tactless (thank god, she had a good heart) Charlotte.

"Even for you."

There it was.

Because Olivia's indulgence was ruined. Her weekend sanity scorched. The imagined perfection of every character had its roots in flawed reality now. She'd even run out of pistachio kulfi she remembered. Ugh. This day.

"Sorry, you're right," Olivia said.

Charlotte's jaw dropped and her expression blanked at a loss.

"Well, you are." Olivia shrugged.

Still the blank stare.

"I can accept when I'm wrong. We couldn't do our jobs if we didn't take responsibility for our mistakes."

Again with the blank stare.

"I'm not saying I like it when that happens. Or that it happens often."

Charlotte's eyes twinkled and her mouth snapped shut, obviously holding back words.

Olivia raised an eyebrow and Charlotte's face blossomed into a full grin.

"Now, let's get the snacks ready." She patted Charlotte's arm.

Sat on the sofa, Charlotte settled beside her with feet tucked up and a plate balanced on her hip. Crumbs from samosas, breadsticks and crisps were inevitable from her friend. Olivia had resigned herself to this and bought a hand-held dustbuster especially. There were few people she'd tolerate and accommodate like this, but Charlotte was one.

Her friend pointed the remote at the screen. "Which one are we having then?" Charlotte tapped and scrolled to a list of favourites.

And there it was. Plainly on the screen. Rows and rows of Kate Laurence staring at her accusingly. Particularly from the one where she played a gritty cop, intelligent eyes piercing, the curving mouth serious and beautiful. Olivia had idolised the woman for well over a decade, and it felt inappropriate now she'd met the real person.

She cleared her throat. "How about a new film this time?"

Charlotte shrugged. "We can search for one if you want, but we only end up with Kate Laurence after my indecision and your obsession."

Hmm. That was surprising self-awareness by Charlotte and excruciatingly observant of Olivia.

"I mean it," Olivia said.

"OK. We can do the usual routine." Charlotte grinned.

This was vexing. What a time for her best friend to be plain-spoken. Olivia squirmed under Kate's gaze from the screen.

"Seriously Charlotte, could we please choose something else?" Then she lost her nerve and pressed the remote off switch in Charlotte's hand.

"Oh," Charlotte said. She turned with surprise. "But we always...What...Why?" she said at last.

"I'm," Olivia breathed in. "I'm not sure it's healthy to idolise actors."

"What?"

"I confess, I watch too many of her films." She nodded graciously.

"But Kate Laurence chooses roles that resonate with you." Charlotte shrugged. "And me. What's wrong with that?"

"We should look at broader stories." She grasped for a reason. "Ones that are more realistic."

"But isn't it nice to have a dream?" Charlotte asked. "An image of what life could be?"

"Unrealistic romantic fantasy," Olivia snapped. "She doesn't even play that many lesbian lovers."

"I wasn't talking about idolising her as a romantic partner." Charlotte grinned.

Oh. That was a little humiliating.

"As a woman," Charlotte added. "A person. Doesn't it make you feel good to know how humans can be?"

Yes, that was a more comfortable framing.

"But then," Charlotte's face opened into a cheeky grin. "Remember, mere mortals aren't so perfect."

Olivia gave her a look. "What are you saying? That my expectations of people are too high."

"I'm saying exactly that." Charlotte laughed.

That was Millie rubbing off on Charlotte right there. Although it was good to see Charlotte bloom in confidence over the last year, it was aggravating when it caught Olivia out.

"And," Charlotte continued, "you're supporting films which change the wider narrative about what a woman is capable of and redefining the boundaries of how others respond to her."

That was definitely Millie coming out.

"What's the harm?" Charlotte said, crunching into another samosa and flakes sticking to her lips.

The harm was that the real-life woman was a client, who needed a professional and clear-headed lawyer to handle her case, not someone who wanted a perfect role model on the screen.

And no-one was unproblematic. Not Charlotte, who shared so much with Olivia. And certainly not Millie. Not even her grandmother, whom she worshipped as a child. People were disappointingly human. And sooner or later Kate Laurence would have an opinion that jarred with Olivia's preference and the magic would be gone. And, in a divorce case, it would be sooner.

Olivia cursed her idolisation of the characters on the screen, perfect and frozen on celluloid, digital and the streaming ether.

What had sealed her adoration, and for many queers, was Kate cast as a lesbian in a sapphic drama. Her status was later boosted by standing by the role in the face of homophobic critics. Even when people mocked her boyfriend, and tried to imply he was inadequate for Kate to be kissing girls on screen.

At that point, Olivia had switched off from news about the actor. From relentless speculation about the actress' sexuality, her right to play a queer character, demands to know how she identified, fans accusing her of queerbaiting, and others arguing as vehemently that she had a right to privacy.

Kate's image had frozen in time. A woman, a handful of years older than Olivia, who stood up and played a lesbian on film, with no shame about the role, when few did twenty years ago. And Kate had been one of the public pillars that supported Olivia coming to terms with her own sexuality.

Did she need to grow out of this? Was it time to put this comfort away?

"Perhaps I need to move on from–" she could hardly say the name. Then she nearly said Ms Woodhouse. Her heart fluttered at the near miss. Charlotte would definitely question that. "I should broaden my romcom collection."

"But she makes you happy."

Yes she did. Olivia needed these known worlds, with a perfect heroine to relieve her over-active brain and help process the daily fallout from her stressful job. Her mother had cooking and looking at the sunny side of things, her nani had sudoku, her father had work, which was how he functioned whether at home or the department. And she respected this. But when your work was divorce and family mess you needed a break.

There was something soothing about watching a favourite film. The anticipation of a treasured moment, the satisfaction when it played out just as perfectly as before. Olivia sighed. But no longer. Because the moments were now ruined, and she couldn't indulge.

"You choose," she said, pushing the remote away when Charlotte offered. It really was coming to something when she let Charlotte have free rein.

"All right." Charlotte grabbed the remote back. "Let's have *The Half of It*. I haven't watched that in ages."

And she immediately regretted it. Did Olivia need to spell out the brief? "That's not a romance." She tutted.

"But the ending," Charlotte gasped. "When her best friend runs after the train." Charlotte held hand over heart, as if she might burst. "She thinks it's a stupid movie thing – a guy running after a girl on the train. But it's her friend, and he completely supports her being gay, and he does this unmacho, dorky thing for her." Charlotte seemed flooded with feeling as if watching the film at that moment.

"It's not a romance," Olivia said.

"It feels just as good, and there's the possibility of love with the girl. There's hope." Charlotte gazed off into the distance.

"Fine." She clenched her jaw. "We'll have a film about a man and a failed lesbian love story."

Charlotte batted her arm.

"Did you...? Did you just hit me?"

"You're being grumpy still," Charlotte said. "I want the Olivia who goes all soppy over romance films."

Bless Charlotte for ever thinking that Olivia softened. Others wouldn't believe it.

"I don't go all soppy."

"By your standards," Charlotte added. "And friends are just as important as lovers."

Was Charlotte trying to tell her something? That they still had each other, despite Charlotte not wanting to be lovers and running off with another best friend, Millie. Because the woman wasn't subtle.

Charlotte peered at her with big brown eyes full of hope.

Olivia sighed to answer the question with exasperation. Of course, she got the message. Although a tiny part of her still wanted to be The One.

"All right, let's watch it," she relented.

Huge beaming sunshine smile, pink cheeks, so much good will it was like looking at fluffy chicks and kittens.

"Thank you," Charlotte said. "It's one of my favourite films."

Charlotte got to her eventually, every time. Impossible not to with her face so obviously full of genuine feeling. And because Charlotte was the most loyal, patient friend too.

"Go on. Put it on," Olivia said, and she reached out and squeezed Charlotte's knee.

She was rewarded with a bigger grin, because it was rare she strayed into physical affection. Charlotte smiled with a deep power and looked at her with obvious love.

Olivia nodded, and her heart went pitter patter, because it sometimes still did for Charlotte. And that was not a concern for someone with the self-control of Olivia, unlike certain other people. She was definitely thinking of Charlotte and Millie. She compartmentalised, one of her greatest skills. And she finally relaxed into the evening.

By the time Charlotte left, Olivia had composed herself. She sat in her sanctuary, under the low glow of lights with night outside. Her mind gained greater clarity. Compartmentalising and holding multiple opposing views in her head while seeing a way forward was her forte.

"Fine," she muttered to the empty room.

Time to shelve her Kate Laurence indulgence.

She got up and removed the older movies on DVD from the shelf by the TV. Deleted the streaming versions from her lists and libraries on the screen. She packed the DVDs in a box and hid them in the cupboard under the stairs. She brushed her hands as if covered in dust, which was impossible in a house that Olivia kept spotless.

There. She was ready. Her mind tidy again. And who knows, maybe the divorce would be as quick and simple as Ms Woodhouse predicted. Olivia was sticking with the name. This could be another role for Kate Laurence – Ms Woodhouse, the divorcee. And no, she didn't think this was the healthiest, but it would get her through a straight-forward divorce.

Then perhaps Ms Woodhouse's life would be neatly tied up with Olivia fixing the pretty bow, and the episode packed away. And Olivia could resume her creature comforts and retrieve the box from under the stairs.

Yes, maybe the real woman wouldn't be a mess. Perhaps she was bland and unproblematic and Olivia could stitch this divorce up in record time, and all would return to normal again.

4

Honestly, my life's a bloody mess," Kate said.

Emma Richardson, her film mother, nodded from beneath a parasol, lips pursed and mouth scrunched into a hundred faint lines. Her co-star's grey hair, which was curled and piled high, wobbled as she continued her slow, understanding nod.

Emma breathed in, then winced. "Oh fuck these corsets. I can't even dramatically sigh in sympathy for you."

Kate began to laugh before being throttled by her own costume.

"See?"

Kate grimaced in response this time. "I need a stable, normal life. The same home for more than a month. My kids at a school." She gave a wistful and very shallow sigh. "Things like dinner at seven o'clock."

"Really? Is your life not normal?" Emma stretched her face in wide-eyed hysteria. "We're pretending it's summer in winter, at 8 a.m. in the morning for evening, a century in the past, and acting like my skinny arse gave birth to this fabulous behind." She slapped Kate's buttock. "This profession seriously does a number on you."

"Tell me about it. I've dragged the kids around the globe, and between Harry and me being in the business and this latest fuckup, I need to things to be..." Ordinary. She didn't know what that was anymore. "Not this. Not playing..." she tried to grab her character's name from the air.

"Lady Arnold," Emma supplied.

"Lady Arnold!" Kate threw her hands up. "Look at me. I'm sinking. I don't even know what bloody character I'm playing. I should be ashamed."

"You could do this role with your eyes shut."

"I am doing this role with my eyes shut. Haven't you noticed how tired I am?"

"I sympathise darling. Couldn't have done it myself without a lovely stay-at-home husband." Emma groaned and arched her belly, her hands supporting the small of her back. "I think this corset has squeezed the last urine from my kidneys."

"*Au revoir* kidneys," Kate said, feeling her own.

Kate gazed around the stone quad they'd inhabited since five that morning. College buildings formed the square with the circular and domed Radcliffe Camera shining at the centre. Its rich walls glowed, a picture of a warm evening, a careful illusion under orange spotlights. It was a beautiful setting, when not crammed with film crew, equipment, trailers and lights. One day, she promised herself, she'd stroll through Oxford and enjoy being here.

"Why do we do this?" Kate said, wondering if she'd ever have time.

"For the glamour, darling," Emma replied.

"Hold on, Kate." The deep voice of the director came from somewhere behind a camera. "We need a touch up of makeup to cover that zit."

She looked at Emma. "So glamorous."

"Well, you can't go around being the tenth sexiest woman in the world with a spot on your chin."

"That's the tenth sexiest *older* woman."

Emma flashed her best wide-mouthed outrage. "Older than who? You're not even forty!"

"Apparently some define middle age as starting at thirty-five."

Emma said nothing.

"You're meant to say you're still young," Kate nudged.

"Well tough titties, you're not."

"I'm not old though."

"But that's middle age. The decades in the middle. It doesn't mean you're old."

"Fair enough." Kate shrugged.

"It's such bollocks though, isn't it." Emma tutted. "Do you know, I've spent the last quarter of a century categorised as an older actress, and I've arguably got another twenty-five years to live? It's bloody silly spending two-thirds of your life classified as old. You have all this to come, dear screen daughter." She patted her shoulder.

A makeup artist scurried from behind the wall of cameras and crew, and Kate closed her eyes to a flurry of makeup brushes wafting over her face. Feet scampered away and Kate blinked to find Emma smiling at her.

"You're only as old as you feel."

Kate glared at Emma, the weight of her tired eyelids spoiling the shitty look she was trying to give. "I feel eighty."

"But with those spots, you could pass for a teenager."

Kate dug deeper to summon the shittiest of looks for her friend.

Emma laughed. "That's the problem with high-definition, darling. Never used to have to worry with lovely old fuzzy film." She leant forward to squint at her chin. "You can't even see it with the naked eye anyway and they'll filter us to oblivion." Emma grabbed her arm and hugged it to her side. "Come on. Ready for another turn around the Radcliffe Camera, daughter?"

"What is this? Take twenty-three? My feet are killing me on these cobblestones."

"You should have worn trainers, dear."

"What?"

Emma swished her long folds of dress away to reveal white trainers with lights blinking on the soles.

Kate gave a theatrical gasp. "Do you always wear those?" They'd co-starred in several films in different eras as sisters, another mother and daughter pairing, and adversaries, which had been the most fun.

"Whenever I'm inhabiting early nineteen hundreds England." Emma grinned.

"You would never know," Kate said in awe.

Five more takes and Kate was done. She rubbed her eyes as she stepped inside her trailer.

What day was it? Were the kids still asleep? Was someone with them? Was she meant to be on-set again today? She couldn't remember.

Her phone beeped on the dressing table and flashed up several reminders, including that she had a lovely appointment with her frosty lawyer.

"Christ."

She slumped in her tiny trailer chair in front of the dressing-table mirror.

"I would just like a quiet, peaceful, vaguely predictable life," she murmured to her tired, ludicrously coiffed reflection.

It seemed no-one in her life would let that happen. Movie studios, agents, directors, exes, her family who, god love them, had no idea how busy she was, even with assistants. And the lawyer looked as if she disapproved too.

Kate's phone glowed again with a call. She tapped on the speaker and unpinned her hair.

"Hi Maria," she said, as the locks fell around her face.

"Hey you!" her best friend burst back.

"You're far too perky for this time of the morning." Kate smiled though.

"It's ten darling! Are you still in bed?"

"I've been up since..." Yesterday it felt. "For hours anyway. I'm about to leave set."

"How's life?"

"Still an absolute bloody shambles," Kate replied.

"This is why you need a lawyer like Olivia Sachdeva," Maria said on the other end of the phone. "She'll have this sorted in a blink."

"Hmm. I have my reservations." It came out strained, as she wiped off makeup.

"Are you meeting her today?" Maria asked.

"We were introduced last week. This time it's a proper appointment to go into detail."

"Oh my god," Maria gasped. "You've seen her already. Isn't she glorious." Maria drew out the last word.

Kate stopped mid-wipe. "Maria!"

"What?"

"Every time you mention her, it's like you have a massive crush."

"I'm allowed. Straight girls can have a sapphic soft spot."

"On their divorce lawyer?"

"Why not?" Maria laughed. "Ed was the same. Honestly, we would have done anything she asked. We sat there like besotted pets, a couple of Labrador puppies, while she sorted out our lives."

And it had resulted in an amicable divorce. Their kids were happier too. If anything, Ed and Maria got on better than ever, and Kate wondered if reconciliation was on the cards.

As for Kate, as soon as she wrapped up this divorce, and had her youngest settled at nursery and nearly teenage boy at high school, her romantic plans were to never, ever, and she meant absolutely fucking never, go near another human being again.

How had she managed to have only three serious relationships and it be so complicated? But this was the story of her life. The most level-headed, responsible, organised and respectful actor surrounded by utter chaos and people who threw a whole toolkit into the works.

"Sorry, the kids are yelling something. I'd better go," Maria said. "Good luck. Trust her. She's brilliant."

"Will do. Call you later," Kate replied, smooching her mouth to end with a kiss.

She tapped the call to a stop and remained not exactly reassured, because she had the impression the lawyer disapproved of her. Her lawyer's chilliness had an edge at times.

Maybe it was all on Kate, and her underlying anxiety about low grades and leaving school early when filming disrupted her A levels as a teen. Then the accusations that her face got her roles other actors deserved who understood the challenging material better.

She couldn't be more different from Olivia Sachdeva, with her Oxford education and prestige law firm. Olivia struck her as a person who knew her stuff though, that her Oxford education came with real world understanding and professional credibility.

Kate had checked Bentley's website and a gallery of grinning lawyer faces, all but Olivia Sachdeva who looked as if the photographer had said some insensible shit to make her smile. Kate might be projecting from her own experience of some photographers, but it had won her respect with a flurry of quiet amusement.

So, she dressed for the twenty-first century, jumped in a studio car and headed to Bentley again with an open mind.

5

The guy on reception sat to attention and seemed ready for Kate. When she'd arrived for her first appointment, his eyes had shot wide with recognition. But this time, he leapt from behind the partition and swept her up the stairs as if his life depended upon it.

When they reached the open door to Olivia Sachdeva's office, he sighed with relief.

"Come in please," came from inside in that smooth RP.

Her lawyer's voice was precise, in a way that somehow demanded high standards. Kate smiled and obediently entered the room.

"I'll be with you in a moment," said the woman on the other side of the desk. She sat with perfect posture, elegant fingers tapping over the keyboard and silky black hair neatly tucked behind her ears.

Kate smiled again. Olivia Sachdeva, discreet family solicitor to A-list folk who valued their privacy, was as composed as the first time they'd met.

Except in that first meeting, Olivia had sauntered from her desk with a hand stretched out and deep brown eyes projecting experience, intellect and capability. Then something odd happened. Like someone hit pause. Nothing as obvious as a double-take. Kate saw startled second glances all the time. But there was a pause with a subtle severity, somehow extraordinary in the elegant lawyer. Just a fraction of a second, then someone flipped a switch and the impeccable Ms Sachdeva resumed motion as if nothing had happened. Like a single ripple disturbed a deep pool, then became smooth as a mirror again.

For the rest of their first meeting, Olivia had been as serene and authoritative as a headteacher over a teen, and her silence pulled details from Kate quicker than anything else.

"Good morning," Kate heard again, and Olivia approached with the same saunter, but without the pause today.

Olivia offered her elegant hand, and when Kate took it, the handshake was quick, smooth and businesslike.

"Do sit down," Olivia said, before turning on her heel.

And Kate's body obeyed without thinking. Yes, this was exactly the kind of person she wanted handling her divorce.

"Before we go any further," Olivia started, "are you certain of our suitability to represent you?"

Unflinching dark eyes gazed at her, again businesslike and patiently waiting for Kate to answer.

"I'm sure," Kate said. She was too tired to pitch for another lawyer as well as go through a divorce.

"Should you wish to change your mind, I'm happy to recommend alternatives," Olivia said. She raised an eyebrow as if nonchalant about a client leaving.

"Ms Sachdeva." Kate wanted to kick herself, because she'd lapsed into mirroring the lawyer's formal style, but she was irritated. "This is my second divorce."

Another eyebrow lifted.

Kate's irritation ratcheted up, because people loved to frame her as a chaotic, irresponsible, bohemian artist.

"Yes, I had a messy first divorce." And so public. All over the papers fourteen years ago. "So I was more prepared the second time."

The solicitor remained unmoved, her elegant arms leaning on the desk, long fingers entwined. God, the woman knew how to make a client talk by presence alone.

"I had a prenup signed," Kate carried on, "and we've been separated now for two years. I wanted to make sure we're happier apart. I knew straightaway but thought a cooling off period was best."

Still the solicitor listened.

"My privacy, and my family's, is important to me. Friends and colleagues have respected that, and my PR agent tells me it's avoided the gossip threads."

Yes, there was the odd cryptic reference sometimes, but there always was about her love life. It usually mixed with enough far-fetched fiction to make it all sound incredible.

"My accountant manages my finances. I take a salary from my assets, and they manage the rest. And, although my ex and I were involved for years, our marriage was short and we kept many things separate. It should be a straightforward divorce. My accountant tells me that if I had to handle the application myself, they'd be ready."

The lawyer blinked. "Your accountant thinks you should handle the divorce yourself?"

Bugger it. That was not what she'd been getting at. She didn't want to give Olivia wriggle room and turn her case away.

"Ms Sachdeva," Kate sighed.

Where to start? It took all her energy organising family life, with the kids shuffling between her and their father.

"To give you an idea of my schedule, when I'm not even leading a major film this year: on Monday, I woke up at 5 a.m. covered in my four-year-old's vomit. I cleared the sheets while telling my twelve-year-old to get out of bed for school for the tenth time. I helped him with homework about the difference between Buddhism and Islam, and was still covered in sick when my assistant arrived at 7 a.m. By 9 o'clock, I was in makeup and squeezed into a fake whalebone corset. My agent sent me three projects to read. My PR company emailed head shots to approve. My son's school reminded me that I'd missed an appointment with the year head, and then a journalist who'd got my personal address accused me of lying about winning an Oscar, which was filmed when I received it. My mother sent me a message saying that she knows I'm busy, but could I please send my cousin a birthday card. I already had, but then needed to reply to my mother as well. There's a reason why the bags under my eyes look like sacks of coal. My life is complicated and sometimes a fucking mess. So no, I do not intend handling this myself. I need help. I won't be DIYing a divorce. I pay for someone to clean my house, take my child to nursery and sometimes tuck her into bed, which makes my heart ache. So, I am damn well going to pay for the crappy stuff like divorce." Then hopefully she could get on with life and see her children instead. "I am determined to get a professional to handle it."

The lawyer looked at her and blinked, almost lazily, but also in a considered way that was ultimately derisory. Honestly, how did this woman think that Kate could handle the divorce herself?

"Ms Woodhouse," the lawyer addressed her, "I don't think for a moment that you should handle the divorce yourself."

"Oh," Kate said. Then she laughed. She couldn't really add anything to that.

"I'm only surprised that your accountant did," Olivia said, with a perfect balance of disapproval and enough restraint to sound polite.

"Oh." Again.

It annoyed her, but she also liked that her serene lawyer had Kate tying herself in knots. And telling her exactly what she thought of her accountant's advice without directly saying he was an idiot. That might be useful in negotiations.

And was that a flicker of a smile on Olivia's lips at Kate's laugh? A glimpse of the person Maria saw perhaps? Kate was suddenly curious about the woman beneath that smooth surface.

"All right," Olivia said, moving them on, as if aware Kate watched her. "Tell me about your first divorce, please. I need to know if you have any remaining legal ties and obligations. Arrangements regarding children for example. Those kinds of matters."

Kate allowed herself a smile at children being 'those kind of matters'. She had the feeling Ms Sachdeva wasn't fond of kids.

And god, for someone who was the most responsible and reliable among her actor friends, she couldn't think how to describe her life without it sounding stereotypically dissolute. None of the changes were her choice.

"OK," she started. "My first marriage ended up a nightmare in the courts. You might have seen the press coverage a few years ago."

All over the papers. *It's a steal. Slick hubby takes Kate's millions.*

"It got so messy that I had to stop filming abroad to attend court, then got slapped with a lawsuit by the studio for interrupting filming."

Fun times.

"But I went for a clean-cut deal," Kate continued. "I gave him more than his fair share, so he'd agree to waive rights to royalty-based fees on a couple of films and a series I made while we were married."

And that had been a savvy decision. The series became iconic, and the residuals gave her a reliable income, which allowed her to choose work and take risks on interesting projects.

"But children?" the lawyer nudged.

"We didn't have children together. Their father is Harry Shaw." Kate paused to let the household name sink in.

The lawyer inhaled, her nostrils flaring slightly, and breathed out. The reaction didn't say recognition, more exasperation.

"And did you and Mr Shaw get married?"

"No. We are..." What were they? Friends, lovers, then friends again. *Fuck buddies* she heard Harry say lasciviously in her head with that charming smile of his. She only let him get away with it because they both knew their relationship was firmly friends-only. She left it at, "No. We didn't marry."

"Right," the lawyer said in a way that implied many thoughts. "But you got married again, to someone else?" A raised eyebrow. A stress on the *again* and the *someone else.*

Kate closed her eyes, overwhelmed by her current mess and the takes people had on it. That bohemian actor lifestyle, falling in love with co-stars and whirlwind affairs and marriage, then children with a different man.

She'd married once. Had children with a good man afterwards. And had planned to stay with the love of her life. Three significant relationships at thirty-eight years old. It wasn't exactly dissolute. But the press made it sound dramatic and, when she opened her eyes again, her lawyer had raised one of those beautifully shaped eyebrows.

"It sounds worse than it is. I have a great relationship with the kids' father. Harry's a very different person to me."

He got to be fun, while Kate had to be the sensible one and rein it in sometimes.

"We make a good team. But it was Natalie who was the love of my life. And I thought we'd finally got our act together, living on the same continent for once, and we married three years ago."

And it was a disaster. They'd exhausted that relationship without Kate realising until the honeymoon. She'd looked at her wife and realised that the woman she'd adored on set at twenty, and fallen in love with again at twenty-five, and still loved at thirty-two, even when Natalie would leave for another film, wasn't there anymore. They'd worn it out long ago, and it had just gone. Two strangers in a young marriage of hope over sense.

Kate sighed, as the realisation settled over her again, as true as the first day of their honeymoon.

It was quiet.

Very quiet.

Kate looked up.

"Did..." the lawyer paused and shook her head a little. "Excuse me, did you say...." And again. "Did you say Natalie?"

"Yes."

"You're married to a woman?"

"Yes."

She'd kind of assumed the lawyer knew this before, given the frosty reception at their first meeting. The lawyer always looked at her like a degenerate client in a tangle that needed her professional skills to untie. And even though her marriage had kept a low profile, she wondered if some of her friends had slipped up. She was looking at Maria accusingly here.

But this genuinely seemed news. The subtlety of Olivia's expressions was extraordinary. But she had twitched. And her eyes had widened. Was there even a flush on her flawless brown cheeks?

"Is something wrong?" Kate asked. She stared at the elegant lawyer, who sat as still as a sculpture.

And there it was again. That almost imperceptible but significant pause as Kate watched a single ripple disturb the lawyer's surface.

6

Olivia stared at her laptop screen, her finger hovering over the touchpad, jaw dropped, staring and staring while the warmth that had flushed on her cheeks evaporated. Words refused to form.

This was definitely a moment she couldn't hide, the kind that had film editors splicing in tumbleweeds and lonely church bells. Her heart didn't thud. Perhaps it had stopped completely. And her body tingled with a stunned coolness.

"So, you say you're married to a Natalie?"

Good. The sentence came out evenly. But she felt so detached from herself it sounded distant. It was like an out-of-body experience, watching herself stare at the screen and hearing her voice as if someone else spoke.

"Do you have a problem with that?" Ms Woodhouse said in a familiar and powerful voice.

Olivia turned her head, slowly and deliberately.

"Problem?" she said, in the same detached way. Her eyebrow arched by itself, and right now she was glad it became sentient and made its own way up her forehead, because she had very little control.

"That I'm bi?" the client said, her eyes narrowed. "Pansexual?"

Kate emphasised the middle syllable, then pinched her lips into an annoyed smile, the accentuated bow shape so characteristic of the actor. The eyebrows too, another dip beyond ordinary players. The chin raised in the kind of restrained power-move that struck audiences silent. That she was free of makeup only made it more compelling. Olivia was tempted to clap, if only she wasn't on the receiving end of it.

"That I have a 'same-sex marriage'?" Kate shook her head. "I thought you'd handle plenty."

Olivia remained staring, eyebrow still striking out on its own.

"Because," Kate said, "there's frosty detachment and clinical professionalism, Ms Sachdeva..." She emphasised the name with such potency, another time it would have given Olivia goosebumps. "...Then there's outright homophobia." A pause. Sparkling defiant eyes. A magnetism that was inhuman. "And I will not stand for it."

It was a delivery that made people bow at her feet in films. Olivia blinked and her thoughts tumbled into place.

So. Kate Laurence. Ms Woodhouse. The client. She was one of these late-awakening bi women then.

She pictured Millie with knuckles on generous hips and a barbed profanity on her lips. Olivia mentally raised her hands and acknowledged she'd been closed-minded about that before, and that Millie had genuine feelings for Charlotte. Olivia broadened her mind to acceptance. There, she was growing, and her image of Millie disappeared in a puff of smoke.

"Indeed, I've handled many cases."

Thank goodness her voice was her own at last, steady and clear.

"And I don't have a problem with it. In fact," Olivia elaborated, "I have a friend who came out as bisexual in her thirties. It's still remarkably common, especially for women." She gazed at Ms Woodhouse. "Apparently," she couldn't help adding.

"Oh, I always knew I liked women," Kate said.

Olivia's other eyebrow shot up.

"I had girlfriends first," Kate continued. "I was surprised when I liked the odd man too and realised gender doesn't restrict who I love."

A tumbleweed rolled past. Then another. Olivia's mouth dropped open and there really were no words.

"Why?" Olivia heard herself saying.

"Why what?" Kate blinked and wrinkled her nose.

"Why on earth bother with men, if you'd already found women?" Olivia blurted.

She couldn't stop the words. Olivia's professional life depended on her grasping all kinds of perspectives and grey areas. But this? Utterly beyond her comprehension. And the instant incredulous thought was out of her mouth before any professionalism filtered it.

Kate raised her eyebrows, apparently as capable as Olivia at asking a question via a quirk. The eyebrows said, had her lawyer really blurted that? A personal judgement that had no business being aired? Kate stared at her unrelenting. Actor versus lawyer, lawyer clearly in the wrong.

But wasn't there another factor here? Olivia froze. Because not only was it inappropriate, but her outburst said a lot about her private life too. Would anyone, but a lesbian, have said that?

Disbelief on the actor's face slowly morphed into realisation and amusement too. A lick of the lips. A glance to the side. Then a steady gaze right back into Olivia's eyes.

It was an obvious and loaded moment. Was there any chance Olivia had not blurted out her sexuality?

Kate's smile curled wide.

Absolutely none. Not one tiny strand held on to the privacy of that information.

"Forgive me," Olivia said, fluidly coming back into herself. "That is none of my business and a personal judgement I shouldn't have made."

Kate nodded slowly several times, accepting the apology. "Thank you," she said, the tone censorious.

But the amusement wordlessly remained on Kate's lips and the revelation about Olivia thickened the air with intrigue.

"Excuse me a moment, while I take down the details," Olivia said, turning to her laptop.

Because they'd covered a lot of ground already, and she needed to record the basics. And yes, it was totally an excuse to cover her fumble and recover her poise.

She tapped away at her keyboard, the words flowing across the screen as she touch-typed. She glanced to the side, to see if Kate had let the revelation go.

No. Still looking. Olivia snapped her gaze back to the laptop.

"I won't be a moment," she said, to cover herself.

"Take all the time you need," Kate purred.

And internally Olivia sighed, because that delivery. And internally Olivia also died, because Kate had her sussed.

She took a deep breath. Time to regain her professional credibility.

"So," she turned back, dispelling any hint of embarrassment, "I find it useful at an early stage to discuss priorities. Every situation is different, and I will clear decisions with you." This was going well. She was in her groove. "But so that I know the general emphasis, please tell me what's most important for you."

Kate blinked, so Olivia continued.

"For some, amicability with their spouse is paramount, even if that means slowing down the process. For others, retaining their assets is the priority. And others again–"

"My kids," Kate interrupted.

Olivia paused in question.

"I have enough money, Ms Sachdeva, even if Natalie takes half of everything. But I want to protect my kids. They need stability."

A deep determination became rigid in Kate's features, and she didn't doubt the actor was honest about her priorities.

"This marriage was a mistake for my children." Kate paused and swallowed. "Especially when they need to be settled. Whatever makes this quick and quiet, then I want to do that."

It was the most perturbed she'd seen the actress. There was always some kind of pain. Brutal and raw in some divorces. Excruciating embarrassment in others. No-one endured the whole process with equanimity. But this was the most affected Kate had been.

"Could I ask," Olivia said more gently. "Does your wife have any legal standing with the children?"

Kate looked at her.

"As a default, she doesn't have parental rights via the marriage. But did you arrange anything beyond that? A parental responsibility order or adoption for example?"

"No." Still the same serious expression. "It's just Harry and me. We have full rights."

"Thank you. That should make things easier." She made another note. "And are you pursuing a no-fault divorce?"

"Yes." Kate perked up. "We both think the marriage was a mistake and we want an amicable divorce."

"Again, that will make things more straightforward."

An alert blinked on Olivia's screen.

"Our time's at an end." And they hadn't covered enough. "We'll look at finances next time, but before you go, may I offer some advice?"

Kate nodded.

"This might be too late, but please consider renting rather than buying a house until after the divorce. Property and home are emotive areas where proceedings get acrimonious, especially if you want stability for your family."

"Thank you. I already heard similar advice. I'm renting the house I'd like to buy eventually."

"Excellent," Olivia replied, also pleased with her own professionalism. "We'll need to go into finances next time. Until then," she stood and sashayed around the desk, "please inform your accountant to release details to Bentley, and we can proceed from there."

She offered a hand to the still seated actor. Ms Woodhouse took a moment to rise. Deliberate almost. Then she rose purposefully and stepped forward to gaze at her. It was as if Kate knew she wanted her gone from the room before her professional veneer cracked.

Kate tilted her head. Perhaps she was just perplexed by Olivia's behaviour, which was far more revealing than she ever displayed with a client.

"Thank you for your time," Kate said.

Warm, soft fingers enveloped her hand. Did time play with her again? Did it slow, so that the ordinary compression of a handshake became something extraordinary. The physical contact was so much more vivid and expansive than the first handshake. She was undeniably aware of Kate as a real, living human being surrounding her.

Olivia swallowed. "Ms Woodhouse," she said to cover her reaction. Then when Kate didn't respond, she raised an eyebrow.

"Ms Sachdeva," Kate said, mirroring both the formality and the eyebrow. "Thank you for your advice."

And the release of compression was almost as exquisite, leaving her hand tingling.

She dropped the client's arm and crossed the office to open the door, acutely aware of her fingers the whole time, not daring to move them and lose the physical intimacy. She turned the brass handle with her left hand to save the sensation and opened the door. She checked left, right. All clear.

"Goodbye, Ms Woodhouse," she said, standing aside to allow her client through.

"Goodbye, Ms Sachdeva," Kate replied.

And although Kate cleared the doorway without touching, she felt the actor pass from the top of her forehead, down her chest, all the way to her toes.

She watched Kate descend the stairs and disappear out of sight into reception. Not once did the actor turn around, and with a relieved sigh she closed the door behind her. She sauntered back, drew her chair up to her desk, entwined her fingers and became thoughtful.

So this case? It might be as straightforward as Ms Woodhouse claimed. Perhaps she'd handle it as quietly as the McKenzies', with newspapers, media and Bentley associates unaware of it until finalised.

For Olivia personally? She closed her eyes and felt the warmth drain from her body. This had mess written all over it.

Kate Laurence, the actor she'd plastered over her walls as a student, was queer. This revelation was momentous. An earthquake rumbled. How could she ever watch any of Kate's work in the same way again?

Those early films, that had her hanging enormous posters on her wall, morphed in her head. Those feelings of admiration and acceptance in the wider world were suddenly a simple crush on a queer woman. It all churned in her mind, heart and stomach.

"Yup," Millie, of all people, appeared in her conscience with a cackle. "That completely fucks with your cosy comfort cinema."

Olivia was sure Millie had become her internal voice of guilt recently. Which was aggravating because she didn't even know about her indulgence on Kate's films. Charlotte was sworn to secrecy on this matter.

Then there was Charlotte. Sweet lord, her best friend must never know that Kate was sapphic. Imagine how Charlotte would react. She'd be ecstatic, and Olivia would never hear the end of it. Her heart cantered.

Why hadn't Kate come out publicly? What was that about? Years and years of lesbian friendly films and she was sapphic all along? Honestly, coming out was the least she could do to prepare people.

Oh god. This woman. This mess. Only years of restraint and decorum had Olivia resisting letting her head drop on the table and repeatedly thudding her forehead on the desk.

Charlotte must never, ever hear of this.

7

So, her frosty lawyer was a lesbian. Kate had not expected that. She laughed at her own surprise, then covered her mouth.

She drew her coat collar around her neck and pulled a beanie down over her ears, attempting to avoid the attention of a small group of tourists and the odd postgrad. At least it was easy to blend in on cold days.

Also easier without makeup. Not the recognisable face of an actress 'at the height of her powers', according to a review sent by her agent. Or who had suit and watch makers clamouring for her to model products now she exuded beauty and experience in her late thirties – her agent's feedback again. She looked like a plain mum picking her kid up from nursery, which was where she was headed.

She strolled up St Giles, past the stone buildings of ancient St John's college, and the Eagle and Child pub on one side and Lamb and Flag the other. She took the Woodstock Road fork by the church towards Somerville, where a neighbour had found Bea a place at the college nursery.

She shook her head. She had not read her intriguing lawyer at all.

"Shit," she muttered. Where was her gaydar?

Screwed up by fatigue and her messy life, she answered herself. And perhaps switched off permanently, because she had no energy left for people beyond family and obligations.

Interesting though, the information out there now and changing her perspective. Kate knew Olivia was blunt, but the lawyer had been impartial and proper up to that point. And the very personal and revealing opinion had shot out of the blue.

Kate's lips curled again. There was nothing vague about Ms Sachdeva's opinion, or blurry about where she drew the line with her sexuality. No, it had been absolutely fucking definite. Kate loved it.

After the outburst, Olivia had returned to typing, and Kate had smiled to herself and looked at her watch. She'd wondered how her lawyer took the new information, that Kate was married to a woman. And she'd glanced up, only to find Olivia peeping towards her, and Kate twitched away, just as her lawyer did the same.

A certain understanding had melted into the room and a fresh set of sensibilities overlay them both.

Gone was the possibility of Olivia's husband in a suit, and in its place perhaps a high-powered girlfriend or wife? Maybe the successful lawyer was single, and Kate imagined a clinically clean and organised home for Olivia.

Ms Sachdeva was intimidating though, in her perfect Regency office with lofty classic ceilings. And with her prestigious degree and confidence, always opening the door and suggesting Kate could leave for another solicitor.

But Kate was stubborn enough to stay, even while she had reservations about her lawyer's attitude.

Tempted to call Maria, she imagined another onslaught of comments about 'divine Olivia', 'she of brown eyes and classic jawline' and 'lashes to die for'. Kate rolled her eyes. Yes, Olivia was clearly beautiful. But there was no bloody way Kate would tell her about Olivia's slipup. Not with Maria's girl-crush, her friend on a happy high of hormones and lusty because she flirted with Ed again.

Whereas Kate.... She yawned. After that day she needed a nap, having been actor-Kate since before dawn, divorcee-Kate in the afternoon and now returning to Kate and kids. She tried to shrug off the weariness and slip into being mum.

"Hey, baby girl," she said, when Bea appeared at the college nursery door on the hand of her favourite minder.

Her wee girl scowled in response, bottom lip dribbly and protruding, little brow crinkled in tiredness and frustration. Bea fussed about her hair usually, and brushed her blonde locks before nursery, but it twisted in curls of paint, food and maybe a bit of mud. If she hadn't insisted on cleaning it, then she was stretched beyond tired.

"Home time," Kate said, acknowledging Bea's silent protest.

"She ate well," the bubbly minder said with a smile. "Finished all her lunch. No accidents. And we made cupcakes today, didn't we Bea?"

Bea was not fucking impressed and scowled some more.

"Show Mummy," the minder said.

Bea thrust a blue paper towel towards Kate with something mangled inside.

"That's lovely," Kate said. "Let's eat that at home."

Please god, make her forget. Then Kate wouldn't have to eat it and live on the toilet for a week afterwards with another nursery tummy bug.

"Carry," Bea said at last.

Too tired to say all of "carry me". Too tired to take another step towards Kate. She imagined that by the time they got back, Bea would be plunging into exhausted meltdown.

"Come on, lovely," Kate said, crouching, and Bea all but fell into her arms. "Let's get you home."

Then she winced, because Bea didn't think of Park Town as home yet, and Kate didn't have the energy to handle that. But this time Bea was too tired to quibble.

After carrying child on hip through the college quads, she put Bea on top of a wall, then hoiked her onto her shoulders. Small hands gripped her forehead and, as she cut through a narrow street, Bea started humming to self-soothe in her overtired state.

No point asking how Bea's morning was or if she enjoyed nursery. Best to get her straight to bed for a nap. Then maybe later she'd talk, when the pressure was off and her young brain unwound.

Kate's phone vibrated against her chest from her coat pocket.

"Excuse me, sweetie," she said, holding tighter to Bea's left knee while slipping out her mobile with her right hand. One of the film production assistants called. She slid the phone between her ear and Bea's arm that was clamped around her head.

"Hello?"

"Hi, Kate," said the enthusiastic assistant.

She missed the next part, as a couple with grey hair scowled at her walking by. The disapproval might have been for many reasons. The nudity scenes when she was young, the nudity scenes now she was older, the lack of nudity scenes in another film, her private life, a dress she once wore. Who knew?

Then the man muttered, "Mothers are always on their phones these days."

They hadn't recognised her at all. Just ordinary shaming. She was tempted to ask when the hell else could she answer the phone, when the kids might be awake and needing her twenty-four hours a day.

"Sorry didn't catch that," Kate said.

"Checking that you received the updated schedule? We hadn't received confirmation from you or your PA."

"Oh." Fuck. This would throw Bea's routine again. "No sorry. That's slipped through the cracks." There were too many these days. Even with her reduced filming obligations this year.

"Script changes have affected three of your scenes," the studio admin continued. "I've sent the latest version and you're needed on location in Oxford every day this week."

"Could you take your finger out of my eye?"

"What?"

"Sorry, not you. My daughter's on my shoulders."

Tiny fingers had slipped over Kate's brow, Bea finding a good grip there.

"Bea?"

Kate squeezed one eye shut to avoid injury, hunched her shoulders to lock Bea in place while hanging onto her phone. She walked slowly with the small window of vision focussed on the pavement.

God, she must look a sight to people like the passing couple and her lawyer, perfect Ms Sachdeva. Kate had this lingering impression that Olivia didn't approve of the list of marriages, and children, and who knows what else.

"OK, got it," Kate said through gritted teeth as she strained in the awkward position.

"Thanks, Kate," the chirpy assistant signed off.

"Well, sh..." Shit, arse and fuck. "...shame," Kate finished.

Bea craved stability. She needed the same people, routine and bed, more than Kate's son who'd thrived on travelling the world with other film kids from actors and crew.

Kate tucked her phone into her pocket and grasped Bea's legs.

"Let's get you home, tiddler."

And Bea was so sprawled over Kate's head, she might even fall asleep before they reached the house.

With full vision back, Kate stomped along the pavement. If her agent could see her, he'd wince and moan that she'd never get glam dresses for red carpet events if she walked like that. Tough shit. That's how her big bones and curves travelled this Earth, in a very ordinary walk.

She crossed Banbury Road into the quiet enclave of Park Town, the sound of traffic and people receding in the streets of large Georgian houses and grand curving terraces. She unlocked her door, bundled into the hallway, up the steep stairs, ignored all the unpacked rooms and stepped into Bea's small bedroom before the grizzling peaked into wailing.

"Here we go," she murmured, easing Bea from her shoulders and onto the bed.

No time left for changing into PJs.

"Let's take off your jacket and lie down for a nap, sweet pea. Come on poppet," she whispered, trying to slip away the coat while Bea gripped hers.

Bea was beyond words, but her clutching fingers said stay.

"OK, I'll cuddle you for a minute."

Kate curled up in the short bed next to Bea, her little fingers still gripping Kate's lapels.

"Made it," Kate sighed, as much to herself as Bea.

She closed her eyes in relief. Then stretched them wide again when her head swirled with fatigue.

She must not fall asleep. She had a schedule to update. New lines to learn. And if she drifted, curled up and awkward in this four-foot bed, she'd have a crick in her neck for a week.

A warm hand, clammy in a way that made it even softer, rested on her cheek. She listened to Bea's breathing fall into a relaxed rhythm, the soundtrack into dreams. Kate's head spun with the cosiness and smell of her child near, the mix of dribble, banana and a bit of dirt from the garden, the most soporific concoction on Earth. The softest hair flopped and soothed over Kate's cheek, still that fine fluff of a toddler.

Kate's head lurched. She really should get up. What would her lawyer think? So much to do.

But small hands on her cheek, and her heartrate slowed. And warm breath on her eyelids, so relaxing. The unparalleled comfort of her child.

She must not fall asleep...Must not...Learn lines...Must...Sleep...

***

What did Olivia think?

It was rare she uttered expletives, but it came close, because Charlotte had just messaged:

"OMG!!! Look at this." With many more exclamation marks. "What do you think?"

Beneath the message shone a picture of Kate Laurence from a fan feed, about to pull a hat over her head. And behind? A very familiar shade of stone wall.

"I swear that's Beaumont Street!!!"

Olivia sat rigid on her grey sofa. Her beating heart filled her chest, terrified at photographic evidence of Kate's proximity to the office. Also, she was irritated by Charlotte's punctuation, naturally.

She tapped into her phone. "That could be many places; Bath perhaps?"

Because Olivia typed out her messages properly. And while impulse-control resistant Charlotte was an exclamation mark kind of person, Olivia would construct a controlled question.

"Post says Oxford."

"Might they, perhaps, be mistaken?"

"Don't spoil it!" So many exclamations. "Let me think she walked straight past our office." Many, many, laughing faces.

This was a very Charlotte thing, who was an exclamation marks kind of person in real life. Whereas Olivia refrained and indulged in an eyebrow-raise kind of punctuation and emotional tell.

Olivia closed her eyes. How long would she get away with this?

"That would be so..." very close to the truth "...funny." Olivia typed back.

Did her head spin? Was she quietly and elegantly hyperventilating? She didn't know if she was about to keel over and pass out.

"Got to be Oxford!!!" Charlotte replied.

"It could be anywhere in the Cotswolds with that limestone."

It wasn't. Olivia recognised the distinctive black pattern on the stone, which tinged the golden street like a biscuit burnt at the edges and was definitely two doors down from Bentley.

"Anyway. Exciting!!!" Charlotte messaged.

That was not the word Olivia was thinking of.

It was late at night and Charlotte fell quiet, likely distracted by something, also likely Millie, which Olivia didn't want to think about.

She inhaled deeply through her nostrils, then slowly out of her mouth.

This subterfuge didn't sit well, but it was necessary to do her job. She must compartmentalise and remain professional. And Charlotte, who leaked her thoughts and emotions everywhere, must do the same by remaining ignorant.

Ugh. This case. Why did it have to be this actor? This apparently queer actor. And why did the managing partner have to introduce her? The one person she couldn't turn down without damaging her career prospects. How was she going to keep this under wraps?

8

Olivia broke. She called her client before eight o'clock.
She'd woken in a cold sweat after dreaming that Charlotte and Millie told Kate everything about her film obsession. And they all sat, naked, on her sofa. Her lovely, grey, exquisitely designed sofa.

There was the hygiene element. And the compulsion to clean the furniture, even though it had been a dream. But mainly the utter heart-pounding humiliation of the revelations laid bare.

And the people laid bare? Clearly she was feeling vulnerable if her subconscious conjured everyone naked. That was why, surely.

She called. It really was too stressful, and it detracted from her effectiveness as an adviser. If she worried about Kate bumping into Charlotte at every turn, she wouldn't perform her best.

Kate answered.

"Hello. This is Olivia Sachdeva. I was wondering, with your busy schedule, if you'd prefer me to come to you today?"

Kate's response cut out halfway through a word and a cry from a small child.

Then the call came back to Olivia. Video call. A bit immediate for this time of morning, but very well. She answered it.

"Sorry, I'm all fingers and thumbs with my hands full," Kate said. Literally, it seemed, because one arm held a child before it wriggled and scampered away. "You were saying?"

Olivia pondered. "I wanted to offer you an in-home appointment today."

Kate appeared a little blurry and moving like a confessional video, rather than high-definition movie star.

"That's kind of you, Ms Sachdeva." It always sounded as if Kate mocked her when she addressed her by name. "But I don't want special treatment."

"It wouldn't be." It would be a colossal favour to Olivia and keep Kate a mile from Charlotte.

"I know your manager, Hugo, booked me in, but I'm happy to come into the office. You mustn't go out of your way especially."

Olivia stared back. This awareness and consideration were annoying. "Actually," she confessed, "you'd be doing me the favour." She puzzled for a reason and failed. "It's more convenient for me this morning."

"Are you sure?"

"I am sure."

"OK." Kate nodded.

"Good," Olivia replied.

Kate opened her mouth, then paused. "Do you like having the last word, Ms Sachdeva?" She tilted her head with a smile.

Olivia considered. "Very possibly, but you asked me a question."

"Fair enough. Actually, I'm in chaos here, so it suits me too."

"The appreciation is all mine," Olivia said.

Kate pursed her lips. "You're welcome."

"Likewise," Olivia added. Apparently, she did like having the last word.

"All the same," Kate started, still with that smile, "it's appreciated."

Olivia raised an eyebrow.

This made Kate laugh out loud. "Did you just eyebrow your way into having the last word?"

She was inclined to raise another, but stayed the second.

"Until later then, Ms Sachdeva." Kate lifted a finger towards the screen to end the call.

And Olivia couldn't help confirming, "Until later," before the screen went blank.

Well. That was strangely aggravating and satisfying at the same time. She rather enjoyed the push and pull of their conversation, if only the whole scenario wasn't so fraught. And although still unnerved by people being inappropriate on her sofa, she'd got what she wanted.

***

Kate's choice of home was faultless. Olivia coveted Park Town with its pair of curving stone terraces, traditional lampposts and the central communal gardens behind railings. It was only a few minutes' walk from Olivia's home, but several times more grand and expensive.

She took a moment at the foot of the four-storey terrace and stared at the glossy black door to Kate's home. This was not her preferred approach with clients. They tended to behave better in her precisely controlled office, where everything from the light and temperature to the smell of tea was under Olivia's control. Everything predictable. Nothing too jarring for her sensitivity.

She reached up to knock.

As soon as she touched the cold brass knocker, the door opened and wrenched her from the chilly morning. Kate's blushing face appeared in the doorway within a cushion of warmth from the heated house. The fresh scent washed over Olivia so that she had to close her eyes a moment, pleasantly overwhelmed by the woman.

"Hi," Kate breathed out.

The actor stared at her with bright eyes, flushed cheeks and chest heaving from exertion beneath a black hoodie, so immediate and vivid, that it filled her every sense. The honeyed "Hi", a delicate sonorous assault to her ears. The client's makeup-free face blooming from exercise, visual perfection. And the enveloping warmth and fresh perspiration with a subtle edge of citrus from light perfume, dizzying.

Olivia opened her mouth to repeat back the greeting. But she tasted the woman as she inhaled so that "hi" would have issued as a wordless gasp. She swallowed. And regrouped.

"Good morning," she said, words thankfully precise.

"Come in." Kate beckoned and led into the hallway and down a short set of stairs. "I've just run back. I'm on the lower-ground floor. I saw you at the door from the lightwell."

The space downstairs expanded into a long kitchen and dining area, a lightwell on the roadside and sun-filled double doors at the other end. A view opened onto a patio and steps up into a glowing green garden.

With the low ceiling of the basement, it was difficult not to feel surrounded, like the house engulfed her, in the same way Kate's aura did at the door.

Kate marched ahead to a large dining table in the middle, her trainers quiet on the wooden floor. She shed her hoodie over the back of a chair to reveal a black running crop top beneath. She turned, scooping up her hair into a loose bun, with her bare arms tensing into shape.

Olivia stood at a loss about what to say. It was all a bit personal.

"You exercise?"

For the love of god. What was that? Of course, the woman exercised. The evidence was right there in front of her.

Kate rested a hand on the table, the other on her hip.

"Ms Sachdeva." Always with the ironic formality. "You're surprised. Are you suggesting that I'm not in shape?"

Her gaze descended Kate's body. Not what Olivia did by habit, but it was difficult not to when Kate brought attention to it.

"Not at all," Olivia said automatically.

She stole quick second glances at Kate's physique: the broad bare shoulders, not taut with muscle but shapely beneath soft skin; the curves of her tall, hour-glass body and generous thighs, clearly firm in tight running bottoms.

Her brain ticked over the evidence that Kate obviously exercised regularly. Then reviewed it, which was most unlike her. It was difficult not to be overwhelmed by the immediacy of everything. The house. The woman. As if being plunged into a Kate experience. It was rare she had this reaction. Tight clothing, nudity, partial or otherwise, was everywhere, and it didn't bother Olivia, so long as people didn't do it near her.

But with Kate? Was it an unfortunate reaction to her as a film star? So used to staring at her on screen? Actually, Olivia didn't think so. Because she'd thought of her as 'Kate Woodhouse', the woman who needed her professional expertise. And it had been shocking that the client was so vividly human and immediate at the door.

This was a lot. And probably a mistake. Yes, they were safely removed from the office, but the home and this encounter were very personal when Olivia was already juggling several compartments.

"...which is fine by me," Kate finished.

Olivia raised both eyebrows. There had apparently been talking.

"Ms Sachdeva?"

Olivia opened her mouth.

"..."

Rare again that Olivia was lost for words.

"Ms Sachdeva?"

Kate's face twitched with confusion? Amusement?

It was both. Olivia, used to reading subtle body language and nuanced conversation, imagined Kate was likely irritated at the topic turning to her body. It so often did in the media. And she was also likely amused that Olivia, for once, had missed a snippet. Because she never did that. She was razor sharp, on the ball, memory the clarity of finest crystal. But she'd completely missed what Kate said.

The parts of her brain, which were finely tuned to the industry of work, started to turn again.

"I'm...a little warm," she said. "Is there somewhere I could hang my coat?"

Did Kate raise her eyebrow at that?

Olivia stalled again, too shocked to respond.

Kate ambled closer, her figure blocking the sun from the window. Olivia's vision blanked for a moment before her eyes adjusted, and slowly came into focus and colour on the very close and detailed woman in front.

"Let me take it for you," Kate said, her voice softer now it no longer echoed around the kitchen space and the edges were rounded by the intimate distance.

Olivia set down her slim briefcase and looked Kate in the eye all the way. Because, although Kate stood with an appropriate gap, she felt the closeness with every atom in her body. Olivia raised her hands to her coat but paused with her fingers around the lapels, the movement somehow suggestive in the heightened tension. As if she undressed in front of Kate.

Kate with flushed cheeks. Kate still recovering from running, with heaving chest that slowed and deepened in a very evocative way. Olivia licked her lips.

Oh god, had she really licked her mouth?

She maintained eye contact like she walked a tightrope. And when she passed her coat to Kate, she did it with the precision of a surgeon. Because the last thing she wanted was to touch her.

"Thank you," she managed evenly.

"You're welcome," Kate replied. "I'll hang it up," she added nonchalantly.

But then her tongue, the tender tip of it, graced her bottom lip and all Olivia could do was stare at the pink perfection. She swallowed, or tried to, because it was suddenly difficult without being loud and filling the quiet residence.

Maybe Kate realised the movement was provocative, because she pursed her lips shut and smiled.

Olivia twitched. "Thank you again."

Kate gazed at her. "Always with the last word," she murmured, the pause filled with gentle humour.

Olivia waited, to ensure she had complete control over the next words in this balmy pocket of intimacy.

"Always best to sum up last," she whispered.

And the creases by Kate's eyes deepened as her smile grew. Kate looked away, for the first time in the exchange, rocked slightly to one side, then walked off.

Olivia stared at where Kate had been, vision filled with the blur of green through windows on the far wall, the chill of Kate's absence vivid down her whole body. She reeled from head to tingling toes.

But she'd made it. She breathed in deep. Then inwardly groaned, because it had been horribly audible.

9

The soft, black material in Kate's fingers still held Olivia's warmth. It was a surprising and vivid connection between them. She paused, took the coat and hung it over a hook in the stairwell.

She was used to physical contact from makeup artists, assistant directors shifting her body into place and other actors in intimate scenes, all choreographed moves, repeated over and over, until it was difficult to embody the character with any freshness.

But with this lawyer. This restrained lawyer. After only fleeting handshakes, she had this heightened awareness. Was it because she was home and had lowered her guard in the familiar surroundings, when in fact she attended a professional appointment? Perhaps she wore the wrong robes and character.

She peeked over her shoulder into the kitchen. Olivia stood in the same place, gazing towards the window, unreadable and impenetrable, although sometimes Kate had peeks beneath the surface. Like the slip about her sexuality, and the times she caught her considering Kate, then the odd flutter of humour between them, like a flurry. It was intriguing.

She knew how to act this and channel the story through a character so it came through her fingertips and every expression. But she rarely felt it as herself.

Funny. She breathed out a laugh. Curiosity for her lawyer, of all people.

She bet her pristine solicitor was tetchy about Kate racing to the door and sweating in her sportswear.

"Sorry," she said, striding back into the kitchen. "I've been rushing around with my youngest this morning."

Olivia spun towards her, with a neat twirl on her heel. The haughtiness returned and disapproval pinched her expression.

"She's home?" The solicitor asked. But before Kate could reply, Olivia answered herself. "I suppose you can keep her occupied during our appointment. Do you have one of those," Olivia gestured in the air, "child prison contraptions?"

Kate burst out with laughter. She quickly shut her mouth to trap it, although it ached in her cheeks. "Do you mean a playpen?"

"Exactly."

Kate tried not to laugh again.

Ms Sachdeva might often be puzzling, but here she was transparent. The woman did not like children. Maybe she didn't dislike them either, but they seemed unimportant or unfamiliar to her.

"No, you're safe from my daughter today."

Olivia raised a velvety eyebrow in question.

"I'm desperately trying to stay in an ordinary routine." And they were getting there, little by little. She'd helped Ralph with his homework before sending him off to the bus. Then dressed to sneak in some exercise after dropping Bea at nursery, which took so long she only managed a dash across North Oxford to get back for her appointment. "And I eventually persuaded my daughter into nursery," with gentle persistent work on an understandably reluctant Bea.

Her lawyer still looked at her, perhaps disapproving of Kate's life. And honestly, Kate wasn't fond of the current chaos either.

"So, I'm sorry that I'm sweaty and..." she gestured to the pile of toys by the back door and the breakfast dishes piled on the worktop.

Again, an impenetrable gaze.

Kate didn't know what to add. And when she failed to respond, Olivia tilted up her chin, blinked in that disdainful way, and said, "Shall we make a start then?"

Kate smiled, a little on the outside, much more inside. Because although none of the words mentioned it, her lawyer's disapproval was voluble.

Olivia took a seat halfway along the kitchen table, slipped a laptop from her briefcase, and sat with perfect posture. Back straight, shoulders aligned, tailored black dress with short sleeves exquisite and fluff free. Slim brown arms reached for the keyboard and elegant fingers touch-typed a password, so the screen flashed into action. She was a picture of organisation in Kate's hectic kitchen and life.

Kate reminded herself, this was exactly why she wanted Olivia as her lawyer, and she'd cope with a bit of disapproval.

"Would you like a tea or coffee?" Kate asked.

"What kind of tea do you have?"

"Erm..." Kate faltered on the way to the kettle. She had no idea. A box of non-brand. "Tea...tea?" She found herself saying. "Actually," she shook an empty box, "I've run out, but I have decaffeinated?"

"Then no thank you." And Olivia turned back to the screen.

Oh.

Olivia had looked at her as if she offered sweepings from the kitchen floor.

"Sorry," Kate said, feeling inadequate about her tea choices. "I have a decent coffee machine though and freshly roasted beans. Would you like a mug?"

A beautifully arched eyebrow demanded more detail.

"I have Colombian, mid-roast. Kenyan, which is quite fruity, some-"

"The Kenyan please," Olivia said without pause and went back to typing.

This was a woman who clearly knew what she wanted and was unwilling to compromise on it. Kate found it both annoying and admirable.

Again, the intrigue tickled inside. She couldn't resist her fascination with Olivia, so different from her friends and people she worked with. Who was she kidding? She worked with all her friends, in an insular world she'd inhabited since her late teens. Not even her family extended beyond it. Her mother worked as a drama teacher and ran school productions and the local pantomime.

Kate placed a small mug of rich, dark coffee on a wooden coaster next to Olivia, together with a jug of milk. She had a feeling Olivia might be particular about how much she took. She thought better of leaving the sugar bowl, because of a suspicious trail at the bottom, the width of a small, dribbly finger.

"Thank you," Olivia said without looking.

The lawyer eventually paused, picking up the petite, gold-rimmed mug, held it under her nose, took the tiniest of sips, then opened her mouth with a quiet gasp of appreciation.

"Very nice. I will have it black and without sugar."

And Kate felt a silly pride that the coffee was satisfactory.

Olivia aligned the coaster with the back edge of her laptop, set down the coffee, and spun the mug so the handle pointed to four o'clock, the arrangement as perfect and neat as the woman herself.

"Right," Olivia said. "We need to look at your property and finances."

Kate's stomach dropped.

"Your accountant has sent over several spreadsheets..."

Oh no, no, no. Kate took a deep breath.

She was not good at this, even with all the time in the world. Finances. She had incredible tenacity when drilling down into a story to find her character or refine her movement and get exactly the right nuance on film. But to focus on a financial statement?

Gah. It made her uncomfortable, like she wanted to jump out of her own skin and run. Her interrupted education bit her most here, at a sensitive part of that Achilles heel. Organisation? Logistics? She was great at those. Anything that involved numbers and her mind turned to cotton wool and panic struck. She started pacing around the other side of the table.

Olivia glanced up from the screen, and those fine eyes travelled back and forth with Kate's movement.

Kate stopped. "Sorry, am I distracting you?"

"Yes," Olivia said, before returning to the screen, "and you need to come and check these items with me."

Her body complied, walking around the table and plumping down on a seat. It was funny how obedient she was with Olivia. That, she realised, she also rather liked. It was that authority in her lawyer that she trusted and wanted, even though the woman clearly didn't think highly of her.

She shuffled on her chair.

"Ms Sachdeva," Kate said uncomfortably. Then "Olivia." Because she needed to be honest, and not play whatever they usually indulged in. "I have to admit something."

Olivia waited, staring expectantly.

Kate breathed in again. This was a big admission to make to Olivia, with her prestigious education and skills in language, law and finance. Kate didn't want another of those judgemental looks about this. It was too sore an issue.

"I'm not good with finances," she said quickly. "And maths. Anything with numbers. I'm horrible at it."

Olivia slowly blinked, as if Kate were stupid. "Why should you be? That's why you pay lawyers and accountants."

Oh. Kate smiled with surprise. She hadn't expected that.

"No-one's good at everything," Olivia said, "and you've spent your time at the pinnacle of your profession. Why on earth would you worry about being good at maths?"

Was that a compliment even?

Kate's cheeks twitched and she let herself grin.

"What?" Olivia said, eyebrows shooting up.

"You..." Kate had to consider carefully here, "puzzle me." Then she added, "Ms Sachdeva," to keep in line with their formal back and forth.

Olivia blinked, beautifully and disdainfully.

"I'm just trying to work you out," Kate added.

"I am not complex, Ms Woodhouse."

Really? Kate didn't believe a word of it. Not of this elegant woman with the epitome of refined behaviour. What hid beneath that controlled exterior?

"I am a predictable perfectionist," Olivia said. "And I acknowledge it may be irritating for some who are...." She looked as if she had someone particular in mind. "...perhaps less organised. But, yes, I assure you I'm most straightforward."

But not straight, Kate laughed to herself.

This self-contained, impeccable, chic woman both impressed and amused her. She felt horribly out of her league as a human being.

"Now," Olivia said abruptly, making Kate snap to attention like a student. "As I was saying, you pay professionals for work." Then after a pause. "If only your accountant and your wife's solicitor would do some."

"Oh?"

"How shall I put this?" Olivia started. Kate bet it would be politely but not positively. "They are less than quick responding to my requests."

"Right," Kate found herself saying.

"But I have some information we can go through."

OK. Kate prepared herself. She stretched for a black case from the pile of things on the table she used often, but never had a tidy place for. She snapped open the box and slipped on a pair of glasses she needed for fine detail. The grid of spreadsheets came into terrifying focus.

She shuddered. Then it fell quiet.

"What should I be looking at?" she said, confused, then turned to her lawyer.

Ms Sachdeva was very clear, and their closeness suddenly apparent, her hairstyle not a continuous shape, but luxuriously thick straight black hair, curled neatly behind an ear. The detail and clarity were compelling. The smooth eyebrows that said so much. The flawless brown skin. The mercilessly long eyelashes that Maria always sighed over. The deepest brown eyes. The pleasing shape of cheeks, the straight nose and the full dark lips.

Was she only now seeing Olivia clearly? Literally. She blinked and hated to admit that Maria was right about how beautiful she was.

Kate came to, with those dark eyes boring into her.

"You should be looking at the screen," the precise voice said.

"Of course," Kate replied. "As I said. Numbers are intimidating for me. Sorry if I drift."

True in general. Right now, totally an excuse.

But for a moment, Olivia's expression had become less severe. Kate could have sworn every feature on Olivia's face softened when Kate put on glasses.

She didn't dare check though, and she stared at the screen and focussed so intently it felt like her eyes bled.

She concentrated on everything Olivia said, her brain aching with accounts, until later and it was Olivia's turn to become distracted.

The lawyer peered at something over Kate's shoulder, in the corner of the room. "Is that...?"

"What?" Kate followed her gaze.

"Is that," Olivia stared at her with utter fucking judgement, "the most prized item of your profession," a beautiful eyebrow arched, "left rolling around on the floor?"

Her Oscar?

Kate slipped her glasses down her nose and peered towards the garden doors. Oh. One of her Oscars. Yes, there on the floorboards was a golden statuette, together with a squish toy, cereal box and Duplo figures.

It looked totally fucking disrespectful. Especially to someone like Olivia Sachdeva. The number of actors who'd performed to inhuman heights and had deserved the accolade, and she left hers kicking around on the floor.

"Ralph," she said, and inhaled through her teeth. "My son must have got it for my youngest to play with."

It was her first award. The one that had been dropped numerous times, because her energetic son wouldn't keep his hands off when he was little, no matter where she hid it. Bea was the opposite. Tell her in enough detail why something was necessary, and she would follow rules to the letter.

Her lawyer opened her mouth, and Kate braced herself to be politely but devastatingly reprimanded.

"Could I..." fine brown eyes flicked to hers, "...have a closer look?"

Kate pushed her glasses up her nose to check her eyes didn't deceive her. Genuine interest flickered on Olivia's face.

Well, well, well. Did Ms Sachdeva have an interest in film?

"Of course," Kate said, and bit her lip. She rose slowly, surprised by the lawyer's interest, and strolled to the corner.

Oscar wore a pink checked dress, which Kate removed, then wondered if she should have left it on, to hide the dust and scratches.

"It's heavier than you think," she said, passing the weight to Olivia who stood beside her.

"They're made of bronze, I believe," Olivia said, carefully taking the award, and reverentially supporting the small man's back.

Kate winced as Olivia turned the statuette over in her hands, every tiny scratch clear.

"I meant to get it repaired," she said. But it always fell to the bottom of a long to-do list. "That mark there," she pointed, "pretty sure that's from my son gnawing it."

"Really?" Olivia said, appalled and stunned. "A child's teeth did that?"

"They're razor blades when little. They're not worn and blunted like an adult's."

Olivia looked at her with an expression that questioned why people had these small animals with sharp teeth.

This happened sometimes. That she had these glimpses into Olivia Sachdeva, who was becoming more real to her. Always fascinated by human behaviour, wanting to read it, copy it and channel it, someone as controlled as Ms Sachdeva intrigued her most.

She smiled, and actually so did Olivia, which made her smile more.

Olivia handed the heavy prize back with the same reverence as before.

Had she seen any of Kate's films? She'd fleetingly wondered at an earlier appointment when Olivia seemed surprised at Kate being queer.

"I won it for *Divine Friends*," she said, the film that put her on every lesbian's radar, according to Nat.

Some gossiped about her sexuality because of it, others rallied against Kate for taking roles from gay actors, which muddied the waters.

"About fifteen years ago," she added. God, it was more than that now.

A whole discussion came up when she acted lesbian characters. And Kate agreed queer actors should get more gay roles. But sometimes the public discussion became polarised, and actors were forced into coming out, or bi actors became classed as unacceptable too. It had her privately despairing, her manager in a conniption fit about it sinking her career, and her girlfriend warning she'd leave if Kate came out publicly.

Because people would assume the worst if they were spotted together. And that her girlfriend phrased it that way should have been a warning sign. So, Kate had stepped away, hating that she had to.

She looked at Olivia.

Had her lawyer watched the film? No. She imagined Olivia Sachdeva priding herself on elevated taste beyond the lesbian romcom that landed Kate in hot water. Although the sapphic historical might have appealed. Again, she had an image of refined Olivia reading poetry in several languages.

The lawyer simply looked at her. She hadn't a clue what Olivia thought right now. What went on behind the sharp brown eyes that saw things so quickly and understood concepts beyond Kate. Some high-flown musings or perhaps something to do with law?

"Sorry," Kate said. "We should get back to finances."

***

All the questions Olivia wanted to ask. Her brain exploded with curiosity about every single facet of that movie. The locations. How the role came about. She craved every detail about her favourite films now she knew Kate. How had she got her first roles? She'd been a late teen at the time. And why on Earth didn't Kate come out back then, when she'd been queer and defended lesbian cinema anyway?

She stared at Kate, who held the Oscar and freely talked about the film, and Olivia barely restrained the torrent of questions.

"Yes," she swallowed. "Back to finances."

Because these weren't billable hours for Olivia to ask questions of movie stars. And because this messed with her head and its tidy boxes and categorisations, the actor's image as dented and scratched as the once pristine Oscar.

Worse was the immediacy of the real woman. Olivia had fallen into an immersive Kate environment, as if suddenly plunged into warm water, with constant vivid drops of personal information. Like Kate didn't wear perfume, just a naturally scented bodywash because perfumes irritated her family. That she wore stylish geeky glasses that made Olivia go soft inside.

It was too much, and dangerous for compartments, and impossible to keep a logical mind.

And oh my god. She checked her watch. They'd run out of time again. She deflated on the inside while maintaining the outer shell.

"We seem to have reached the end of our appointment. We'll have to continue next time," she said.

She gathered her laptop, then coat, and they climbed the stairs. Kate opened the front door ahead of her, and Olivia stepped outside into the cool sobering air. She turned round and paused.

Dammit. She couldn't believe she was going to suggest this.

"I will need time to prepare the financial agreement. There are many loose ends from your wife's side and your accountant's. But when it's further along, could you come into the office to review?"

The office was better. Riskier with Charlotte lurking. But she couldn't balance a clear head and sympathy in this visceral world of Kate.

"Yes, please," Kate said. She looked tired, perhaps as drained by finances as Olivia was by keeping up her lawyer mask.

"I need you to go through them with me," Kate added. "I'm sure you appreciate why after patiently explaining everything to me today."

"I'm happy to run through at any level you need," Olivia replied. "You are the client and pay for my time."

"Thank you," Kate said.

"Until next time," Olivia nodded, almost too tired to have the last word.

And Kate closed the door.

This was a lot, Olivia admitted as she walked around the crescent, back straight, chin up, a picture of decorum. She had no control over this environment. And in the office, she had limited control over the other occupants. Vexing. Most vexing.

She needed to decompress. Lie in a darkened room. Forget that people, especially certain people, existed. What she really needed was a soothing movie night with a favourite Kate Laurence film. Except she couldn't.

"Argh," she silently screamed in her head.

And she marched home, stabbing the pavement with her heels.

10

Several days later, Olivia was back in her groove, composed, professional and handling annoying people with her usual finesse, the managing partner, Hugo Bentley, included.

"I need to ask a favour," Hugo said, sat at the head of the meeting room.

He pulled his waistcoat straight, smoothed his grey hair and rested his clasped hands on the long table. A smile lifted his white and ruddy face, always the agreeable avuncular sort.

But alarm bells rang. Hugo asking for a favour was a sign the favour was inadvisable, and that deep down he realised it too.

On the other side of the table, Liz Oduwole's eyebrows rose above her gold-rimmed glasses, almost hitting the line of her greying curls. She puffed out her rich black cheeks, clearly suspicious too.

Hugo shuffled and straightened his waistcoat again. This was definitely going to be inadvisable.

"I know Richard had trouble settling into the ethos of the firm last year..."

Olivia cast Liz a look. Liz returned said look.

Because this Richard was someone who valued his own knowledge and well-being above all others, all the time. Young, arrogant, skilled, but with an inflated opinion of those skills. Hugo saw a young bull of a man, turning on the charm whenever the managing partner entered the room. Liz and Olivia were more present when the mask dropped, and Richard left everyone else to do the work and clear up his mess.

"But I still believe he has a valuable contribution to make," Hugo said, apparently earnest.

"Hmm?" Liz rumbled, impressively. The sound came from deep within her chest and questioned the supposed value of the contribution.

"He has an ambitious drive that's essential in business..." Hugo continued.

If only that drive wasn't solely for his own benefit. Liz crossed her arms, resting them high on her bosom, clearly thinking the same.

"...so I want to accommodate him in some way."

"Uh huh?" Liz rumbled again.

Oh, this was seriously inadvisable. Olivia had an inkling where this was going.

"I'll come to the point," Hugo said at last. "Richard has expressed an interest in changing specialities."

Hugo had to be kidding. Olivia suppressed a roll of her eyes.

"He's not the best fit for the IPR and tech group."

Olivia tilted her head. Liz tilted hers. Hugo straightened his waistcoat.

"We thought perhaps a spell in a different team might be good."

"Did we," Olivia said flatly. "And which team did *we* think Richard suited?"

"Well...funny thing is...we wondered..."

Here it came.

"Perhaps family law?"

Across the table, Liz closed her eyes in despair.

"You see," Hugo blustered. "I believe in giving people second chances. And to give him credit, he realises it would require retraining. It shows a sense of humility." Hugo nodded along to himself.

Olivia cleared her throat, the purpose two-fold: to register her displeasure and for Hugo to hear her loud and clear.

"I am looking for another associate for the family law team," Olivia purred, "but I wanted to offer Alec Gooch a permanent part-time position to fulfil our current obligations."

"Hmm." Hugo stared at the ceiling, giving it some thought. "Do you consider him a better candidate than Richard?"

"Yes," Olivia replied simply.

"Does he have enough presence to front awkward cases in court?"

Olivia summoned a mental comparison for due diligence. On the one hand, there was Richard – apparently some found him good looking. He was tall, white, arms, legs. Olivia mentally shrugged. He was knowledgeable and presentable, but his arrogance struck her most.

Someone who registered more favourably was Alec Gooch, a friend of Millie's, for his sins. Short, white, thinning hair, arms, legs, and a generous and flexible mind which sought the most suitable solutions. Because while Alec was confident in his own abilities, he knew when other people were better for the job, and he listened to second opinions.

"Alec is experienced and has a self-awareness that impresses me," Olivia said.

"Actually." Hugo beamed. "You might need to hire both, given the high-value clients you're attracting." He clearly referred to Kate and the McKenzies.

She looked to Liz out of reflex, someone she found experienced and level-headed, and her ally so often. The office manager shrugged as if Hugo had made a valid point.

"If we're going to expand," Olivia said, "I'd prefer a different skill set."

"Please would you have a chat with Richard though?"

Olivia stared at Hugo. He took this as acceptance and continued.

"He might surprise you. I know he's had issues working with others..."

By others, Hugo meant Charlotte. And if Richard clashed with her, there was no hope for him. Charlotte bent over backwards to consider other people's points of view. Olivia sometimes assumed she didn't have her own opinion and saw it as a weakness, but it made her friend a great mediator. Which underlined how little hope there was for Richard if he couldn't work alongside her.

"He hasn't found the level he excels at yet," Hugo continued, "but he has a lot of potential."

More alarm bells rang.

"Changing departments can be seen as retrograde step," Hugo began, "but changing my speciality twenty years ago gave me a broader preparation for my role as head of Bentley."

Loud alarm bells.

"So, could you have a chat? Please?" Hugo at least begged.

Olivia gritted her teeth. "Of course."

The chances of the chat ending in a job offer, she put so near to zero it didn't register at all.

"As I said," Hugo added, his cheeks more ruddy than usual. "I do believe in giving people second chances." He stood. "Right. Thank you both. I'll leave it in your hands."

And Liz and Olivia watched Hugo walk to the door. That his shoulders rose showed he felt their gaze the whole way.

"Well," Liz drew out with a sigh.

Yes, it was creditable that the managing partner gave people second chances. Olivia opened her mouth, but Liz got there first.

"God grant us the endless second chances of a mediocre man like Richard."

"Quite," Olivia replied.

They checked towards the door in synchrony to ensure it had closed.

"And," Liz continued, "if Hugo's grooming Richard for managing partner, he'll have my resignation so fast he won't know what hit his arse."

Olivia was glad Liz said that too. They both knew that Olivia eyed that role as her ambition. She'd come straight to Bentley from qualifying with a top degree and had worked hard since, bringing credibility and a reputation for excellence with her. What did Hugo think she lacked, to consider others?

Liz rose from her seat and pointed a finger in the air. "I'll be having words with Hugo. There are second chances, but there's also damage limitation. And I can't see Richard responding well to a short leash and a supervised role."

Thank god for Liz. She saw it all instantly.

As for Olivia, in her 'chat' she'd clarify that any new role would be junior until he proved himself.

"Alec though?" Liz said on her way out. "Does he have the presence to front cases?"

Olivia paused, because she always considered what the experienced practice manager said.

"In a different way to Richard, yes. But most importantly, Alec would admit when he was out of his depth, whereas Richard would wade on to the bitter end."

And Olivia had no intention of seeing Bentley dragged to that conclusion, whether or not she headed the boutique partnership.

They both sighed.

Olivia paused on the way to her office across the hallway from the meeting room, as voices came up the stairwell. She peered over the rail and down the steps onto two heads below, one pale with thinning hair, the other thick and slicked back.

"Overrated though," Richard's voice boomed up the staircase.

"What...Why?" Alec's voice replied.

"Come on, she's the same in every role."

"But isn't she known for her grasp of accents?"

"Only by people who can't tell the real thing."

Olivia hesitated, heart beating perceptibly. Perhaps because Kate was her current client, or she thought of her anyway, but were they talking about Kate Laurence?

"What are you saying?" Alec asked.

"That women use their feminine charms to get roles," Richard said with mock delicacy. "Whereas men have to prove themselves."

"What?" Alec stopped on the stairs.

"She slept her way to the top, Alec. That's what I mean."

"I understood what you're implying, but that's a very sexist assumption."

Yes, Alec was her man.

"Like it doesn't happen," Richard dismissed. "And how many Oscars has that Laurence bird been nominated for?"

Her heart leapt again. They definitely talked about Kate. Was news out that she was a client? Olivia would have to leap on Charlotte and throw a bucket of water in her face to keep her calm.

"I'm saying," Richard added, drawing closer and towering over Alec, "the commitment for a man to bulk up for a role and perform the stunt work himself, that gets my respect. But the Laurence woman looking sexy for a couple of hours?" Richard gloated. "Come on."

Alec shook his head. "Different roles have different challenges, surely, and she performs a broad range. They're filming a historical piece at the Bod."

Perhaps word wasn't out. Maybe they'd passed filming outside the Bodleian Library. She felt an urge to go and see. Either way, the two men resumed up the stairs and Olivia dipped into her office.

Just making it to her seat, an obscenely loud knock reverberated on her door.

She gave herself a moment, before pitching her voice to say, "Come in," in a tired and dismissive tone, because it was obvious who demanded attention.

"Olivia," Richard said, striding into the room. "Do you have a minute?"

He sat on the client chair and drew it to her desk without waiting for an answer. Then flexed his arms, so biceps bulged in his tailored suit jacket, and launched in.

"I might be jumping the gun here, but Hugo said he wants me to help the family law team."

That was quite an interpretation and spin on it, and not what Hugo had suggested.

"Really?" Olivia said.

She sat back, crossed her legs and rested her entwined fingers on her lap. This should be interesting.

"I've had a useful spell in the Tech and IPR team and I want to further my skills and range." He planted his feet wide apart. "So, to kill two birds with one stone, I'm here to offer my services to your stretched team."

As if adding a new person to a project late, especially one who'd need additional training, ever helped meet a deadline.

"Go on," Olivia purred, maximising the opportunity for Richard to bury himself.

"I'll level with you, Olivia." He leant on her desk like it were his and he graciously interviewed her. "My skills are more useful in other areas of law."

He had some gall. Olivia was known for being fair-minded and impartial, ruthlessly so. She'd never give her best friend, Charlotte, an unfair advantage at work, for example. Compartmentalisation again. But for Richard to approach Olivia, after he'd clashed with Charlotte last year, and had to be diverted to separate clients? That was quite something.

"Yes?" she said evenly, leading him further.

"I'm eager to capitalise on my interpersonal skills in a way that's underutilised in detailed technical projects." He stroked his chin, massaging his square jaw. "I can bring a powerful presence to the team, as a strong, confident advocate when required."

Sometimes a court case did need that. But to suggest they lacked that steady presence when she was sitting right there? Illuminating.

"I imagine you're very busy."

Yes, she was.

"So, how about we discuss it over dinner?"

There. That was her opening.

Olivia blinked lazily and slowly. Perhaps she came across as charmed. "Dinner?" she said, her voice silky.

"Dinner," he nodded. "And maybe a drink or two later."

"Hmm," she purred.

He curled a lip in a smile.

"You're not," she paused, just to reel him in a little further, "trying to use your masculine charms, are you?"

He laughed as if she joked, or flirted. But something must have clicked into place, an echo from the stairwell conversation finally making it through.

"Dinner and drinks only," he said, leaning away. "That's all I'm implying. A social evening between two colleagues who are busy during the day. Only if it's tempting for you."

He was about as far from tempting as possible for Olivia. In every single way. Perhaps he didn't know she was a lesbian. She hadn't dated in the year and a half since he'd started at Bentley. But really? Had he no idea at all?

"Richard." She gazed at him. "I'm not tempted."

And she let the words sink in to answer all his questions.

The silence was significant, and Richard leant back little by little, Olivia milking every awkward moment of it.

He rallied at last. "Thank you for your consideration. One of the other partners can benefit from my skills instead."

Richard took his leave. He shut the door forcibly. Olivia sighed as she relaxed in her chair, the situation managed.

And it was rare she indulged, but she allowed herself a private pronouncement of, "What an insufferable arse."

11

Olivia checked her watch, and the corner of her laptop screen, and the classic round wall clock. Because this was cutting it fine with Kate's next appointment to be having lunch with Charlotte at her desk.

But she'd got this. All under control.

Charlotte had been on time, with quiet alarms prodding her friend through appointments, so even when deep into technical contracts she surfaced for lunch.

Olivia sat straight-backed by her desk and dipped a roti into the bowl of chana masala she'd bought from Gloucester Green market, the flatbread soaking up the spicy sauce.

"If that was me, I'd have chickpeas on the floor and sauce down my dress," Charlotte said, looking longingly at Olivia's lunch.

She thought it best not to say anything, because Charlotte was right. Crumbs already sprinkled her friend's black shirt, and no doubt the carpet.

Charlotte rubbed her fingertips together and hovered over her own lunchbox of multiple compartments with wonder on her face.

"Millie's packed me lemon muffins."

She lifted a round golden sponge from a compartment, paused, then retrieved a folded note that must have hidden below.

Olivia rolled her eyes. She'd never thought the salacious, curvy woman from college would be so soppy to pack love notes into lunchboxes, but here they were.

Charlotte's lips moved with a faint whisper as she read the note, eyes darting along the lines, her cheeks rising with every word. Then she stopped, and pink flushed on her face. She bit her lip before carefully folding the message and tucking it back in the lunchbox.

Charlotte was so utterly readable and, of course, Millie would write a love note that turned rude. Charlotte drifted, no doubt, in a sexy dream about Millie. Her clever friend was particularly dippy these days, with her brain addled from sex. Olivia could see it in Charlotte's face as she munched her muffin, staring into the middle distance, coming to with a blink and a blush, then becoming distracted again in a smile.

And just as predictably, there was a pang in Olivia's chest. Because she wasn't the one to make Charlotte blush like that.

She always knew Charlotte would fall for Millie.

As a fresher at college, Charlotte charmed third-year Olivia, with her unassuming smile, and attention to every word of wisdom from Olivia, with a little crease of concentration between her eyebrows. But Charlotte's romantic heart always longed for the fireworks and irreverence of Millie. And that crashed and burned at the end of college, because Millie only wanted men when it came to sex.

Even when Olivia waited five years before suggesting they date, it wasn't long enough for Charlotte to be over the blonde bombshell.

Olivia had planned their one date with aching precision. A rose for Charlotte when they met. Dinner at the five-star Le Manoir aux Quat'Saisons. Then Charlotte kept lapsing into their usual chat before remembering, "Sorry, we're on a date aren't we", over and over. Olivia's eyes had wanted to roll so hard, she almost had to grab her eyeballs.

They did kiss. They did jump into bed. They excused the clumsiness with so many reasons. But the explanations killed passion on both sides, so they'd sat awkwardly in bed, naked, arms crossed, Olivia frustrated and Charlotte with pink cheeks. Until Charlotte turned melancholy and Olivia knew her mind went to Millie.

"Can we forget this, please?" Charlotte had whispered, and Olivia's heart had lurched at the sadness descending. Charlotte didn't need to say the rest. That she didn't want to lose another best friend.

As if guilt stirred Charlotte now, at their past and mentally tumbling around in bed with Millie, she twitched alert.

"So...So...Any dates recently?"

Utterly transparent.

"What about Jaipreet?" Charlotte added.

Olivia's ex of four years and her most significant relationship.

"She's in London," Olivia replied.

Jaipreet had moved for a promotion, and Olivia had understood. She'd also understood the increased distance and workload would end them at some point, but it still hurt when it did.

"Any chance you'll get together again?" Charlotte asked with strained hope lifting her eyebrows.

"She got married."

"Oh." The eyebrows collapsed. "Did I know that?

"Yes, you did."

Charlotte's memory so often brimmed with the most immediate thing. Olivia had noticed this. And that immediate thing was usually Millie.

"What about," Charlotte started again, "Annie, the events officer at Worcester College?"

"We've never really sparked."

"What about...Who is there?" Charlotte frowned. "I can't think who's left."

She forgave her friend's terrible memory, because Olivia had lived in Oxford a long time, and dated all those tolerable, and everyone else was married.

"Are you sure there's nothing with Annie?" Charlotte looked desperate.

"Positive. I'm perfectly happy being single. It's far preferable to being with someone inappropriate for the sake of it."

"But." Charlotte paused.

Olivia knew what was coming.

"Perhaps she might surprise you? Even if she doesn't check all the boxes? Maybe...?" Charlotte ran out of steam, or the thoughts bottlenecked. Her friend regrouped. "Are you being perfectionist about it?"

"I don't insist on perfection," Olivia replied. "We're all human and make mistakes. And no-one completely agrees with another. But I need a good reason to look beyond imperfections and spend significant time with someone."

What she didn't say was that Charlotte possessed those good reasons: loyalty, honesty, intelligence, and a sunny personality. Because even though Charlotte could be grumpy like everyone, she usually forgot what she was grumpy about, then out came the sunshine again. And not much lifted Olivia like that beaming smile.

Unfortunately, it had always lifted Millie too. Even though she'd not been romantically interested in Charlotte at first, something special had always been there. Olivia distinctly remembered Michaelmas term in her third year, sitting on the college lawns by the river, trying to ignore the loud fresher. The curvy short woman, with blonde curls and an estuary accent, spoke on her mobile.

"I hate it here, Mum," Millie had said into her phone. "I don't belong. They're all bloody stuck up. Loads of them are private-school students, and others pretend they row, or speak Latin, or whatever, to fit in with that bunch."

Millie's mother must have reassured her that she'd find friends.

"Yeah, there's this one girl..."

Maybe it was Olivia's retrospective interpretation, or the memory was accurate, but Millie paused, as if realising it was important. It had an inevitability about it now.

"There's this goofy girl called Charlotte who's really friendly. She's the opposite of me. Tall, long dark hair, quiet and well spoken." She laughed and it was obvious her mother did too.

Then the girl herself wandered nearby and Olivia wished she'd been quicker and intercepted her. Because Charlotte waved to Millie with a huge grin that held nothing back.

"Actually, she's here, Mum," Millie had said. "Yeah. I'll give it a bit longer. See how it goes. Love you."

And Millie had leaped up and wandered over to Charlotte with a sassy sway in her hips and a grin that meant mischief.

That was when Olivia lost Charlotte, her chance gone. And it would take another fourteen years for the silly pair to get together. But that was the moment it became impossible for her and Charlotte.

Olivia gazed at Charlotte across the desk over a decade later. Yes, she still had that tug on Olivia's heart sometimes. With those large brown eyes, blushing olive cheeks and the most genuine of smiles. Olivia lived for glimpses of human perfection to restore her faith in humankind, when mostly it disappointed, and Charlotte's smile was one such treat.

Unfortunately, her table manners were not. Olivia passed a tissue.

"What a mess I've made," Charlotte said, wiping her lips and brushing crumbs off her shirt. "Do you have...?"

But Olivia was already passing over a mini dustpan and brush, purchased specifically for this eventuality, which she kept in a drawer of her partner's desk.

"Thank you. I don't know why I'm so messy," Charlotte said, taking the set. "Well, I do. I suspect at least..."

Charlotte bent down, bum in the air, and mahogany curls tumbling to the floor.

"Shall I set you up on a blind date?" Charlotte said to the floor, muffled beneath waves of hair.

They were back on Olivia's love-life, apparently, Charlotte's brain leaping here and there.

Olivia crossed her arms. "I cannot think of another method more intolerable or less likely to find me a partner."

There was nothing worse than meeting a stranger with the expectation of physical intimacy in the air. The thought of going from unknown to stripped naked in a single leap filled her with abhorrence. She didn't understand how people such as Millie enjoyed it. Shaking hands and hugging all and sundry were bad enough.

Charlotte stood up, face pink and hair billowing like a lion's mane.

"Hard agree. Some of my worst memories are from dates and other people's expectations. I can't find people physically attractive that quickly." Charlotte shrugged. "Others do, and that's great for them, but I'm not made that way."

Charlotte bent down again to finish sweeping, then, "Oh!"

She stood up straight, crumbs from the pan scattering. She pointed the brush at Olivia. More crumbs flew. Sometimes she wished Charlotte wasn't quite so consumed by every emotion.

"Oh! Oh! Oh!" Charlotte said again. "I can't believe I forgot to tell you this."

"Well, what is it?" Olivia said.

"It's Kate!"

Her heart rate rocketed. She blinked and swallowed carefully before saying. "Kate?"

"Kate Laurence!" Charlotte cried. "She's filming in Oxford! Alec saw a film crew outside the library." Charlotte dropped the pan, and the remaining crumbs, and snapped up her phone. "Look!"

The screen thrust in front of Olivia showed an Oxford news article and a zoomed in picture of Kate dressed in Edwardian costume and a parasol resting on her shoulder. She looked as pale and tired as she had in Olivia's office. And nowhere near as pink and blushing as the time she appeared at her front door in Park Town.

Olivia took a moment as the memory washed over her, as vivid as Kate's scent when she'd opened the door.

"Well," Olivia said. "That's interesting." She twitched. It was difficult to deliver indifference right now.

"They've moved on," Charlotte continued. "I checked on my way to work this morning and it's empty around the Bod. But apparently, they're filming at Christ Church too. We should go." Charlotte grinned at her, nodding.

Olivia stared. Well, this...She took a deep breath...This was unfortunate.

"How many times do I need to say this? I'm only interested in her films, not her private life."

It sounded hollow, knowing she'd meet the real woman in a few minutes, and had charge of the actor's messy life right now. It was difficult enough shoring up the barriers between film adulation and professional responsibility and she didn't need Charlotte blundering in and blurring those boundaries.

Olivia glanced at the wall clock. Her heart pounded again. This was cutting it very fine, because in less than fifteen minutes Zain would buzz up her client.

"I know you're not into her," Charlotte said, her shoulders dropping. "But this is about making movies." She grinned and waited expectantly.

"It's not just the woman. I avoid the whole behind-the-scenes business."

This was a lie. An out-and-out lie. Olivia loved the makings of films and hearing directors' thoughts.

"Really?" A crinkle appeared at the top of Charlotte's nose. "Oh."

Olivia felt very bad about lying to Charlotte. However, it was also very necessary.

She cleared her throat. "I need to prepare for this afternoon's appointments." She stretched out for the brush and pan.

"Sorry," Charlotte said, coming to. "Of course."

She handed over the set. Olivia tidied in a matter of seconds, dispensing the crumbs into the bin and the brush and pan into her drawer.

"But." Charlotte tilted her head, lost in memories that would contradict what Olivia said. "Haven't we watched behind-the-scenes stuff before?"

"I'm sure we have," Olivia replied, heading for the door and encouraging Charlotte from the room.

Her friend followed, ambling excruciatingly slowly across the office.

"What about...?"

This was not the time. "Let's talk about it tonight," Olivia said, taking Charlotte's elbow and escorting her through the door.

"Didn't we watch a background episode on *Finding Fossils*?"

They had.

"Didn't you enjoy it?"

"Perhaps," Olivia tugged her friend to the stairwell and up the first steps, "I appreciated the palaeontology?"

"Really?" Charlotte said, still confused.

Nothing wrong with that field of geology, but that wasn't the main appeal. Who was she kidding? Not even Charlotte.

Charlotte stopped and spun round on the stairs to the attic offices.

"But...?"

Olivia froze, fingers clenched, anxiety about the imminent appointment creeping up her spine.

"Good afternoon, Zain," came from downstairs.

That voice. So recognisable. And with Kate only just in their conversation, Charlotte would recognise it too.

"What about the making of *The Silence*?" Charlotte said.

Get. Up. The. Stairs.

"Did you finish the Taylor contract?" Olivia said, so desperately it came out as one word.

Charlotte gasped, "That's not due, is it? Better dash and check. See you later." And her friend turned and ran up the stairs.

Olivia felt guilty, unprepared and nowhere near as composed as she needed. Why didn't some clients like Zoom, she thought, as she spun round. No travel involved. No need for handshakes. No pink-cheeked, glowing actors appearing at the door and stripping down to figure-hugging clothing. Perfect.

Olivia took neat rapid steps into her office, across the carpet, twirled into her chair, tapped her laptop alive, and hit the phone to tell Zain she was ready.

She inhaled deep, several times, to recover her breath. Warmth filled her cheeks. Never mind. Maybe it wouldn't show.

She relaxed her shoulders and straightened her spine, in time for a knock on the door and to say, "Come in."

12

Her frosty lawyer glowed.

Kate paused when she stepped into the room. Although Maria banged on about it, and Kate had appreciated Olivia's beauty before, it hadn't grabbed her attention like this. She couldn't miss it right now. Olivia's long eyelashes and deepest brown irises, always penetrating but shining today. Her velvety black eyebrows, so expressive. The defined jaw, slim neck, glowing brown skin, chin tilted up, almost defiant. And Olivia's lips pursed slightly, as if about to kiss disdainfully.

Yes, Ms Sachdeva made an impression. Kate smiled because Maria had likened her to a sexy headteacher. And yes, Kate liked the cool haughtiness.

The admired and expressive eyebrows asked a question, because Kate stalled in front of the solicitor's desk. She couldn't hide it, and she didn't want to explain her inappropriate hesitation either.

So she said, "Good afternoon."

"Please sit down, Ms Woodhouse," Olivia said.

Curt and to the point, Olivia gestured to the chair, as if to prevent Kate getting stuck between here and there. None of this dispelled the headteacher impression.

"How are you?" Olivia asked.

"I'm very well, thank you," Kate rattled off automatically.

Her lawyer smiled, with just a curve at the corner of her mouth and a deceptively languid blink of those long lashes.

"Are you in a good state to look at the financial agreement?"

Ah. It was a real question. "Yes, I'm good," Kate replied. "I'm not looking forward to it." She wished she could delegate everything to her lawyer.

"As an aside, you mentioned that maintaining your assets was important because of the precarious nature of your profession. In which case, you might benefit from private client and tax advice and a more varied portfolio."

Kate squinted, assessing what her lawyer implied. "Are you saying you're not impressed with my financial advisor?"

Ms Sachdeva blinked slowly again. "I'm saying it's beneficial to hear another perspective from time to time."

Ms Sachdeva was so not fucking impressed.

"OK," Kate said. "I'll follow your advice."

"Good. Now." Ms Sachdeva leant on the desk and entwined her fingers. "One thing your accountant did notice..."

The emphasis was on the *did*. Definitely unimpressed with her financial advisor.

"...were discrepancies in your joint accounts prior to the marriage. Also, a lack of clarity in your wife's assets."

"But..." Kate's head ached already. "We have a prenup. Isn't it clear from that?"

"Yes, you have a prenup. It's not as tight as I'd like, although it largely follows current guidelines when splitting property acquired during the marriage. But..."

Her lawyer paused. Kate didn't like that pause.

"I'd like to hire a forensic accountant to gain a more accurate picture."

"I..."

"Your wife and her lawyer are evading some of my queries."

Kate's brain stalled. Oh god, she didn't want to think about this. "But Natalie doesn't have much money. Not a significant amount anyway."

Ms Sachdeva considered her, then considered her words, and so obviously with regret said, "I strongly suspect she has comfortable funds."

Her stomach dropped again.

Olivia continued, and she listened as the solicitor explained that the prenup had been one-sided favouring Natalie, with the assumption Kate had the bulk of the wealth, with subtle clauses and phrasing that protected Natalie's. Then she outlined the reasons for her suspicions.

Kate had pushed Nat so far from her mind that this intrusion shocked. Always another disappointment with Natalie. She thought she'd seen the last of them. It hurt, and it was embarrassing that Natalie cheated her where she knew Kate struggled – that weak spot with numbers.

All the times that Natalie had looked at her with big eyes, wishing she could come on that holiday, or join that party, or take a chance on a part. And every time, guilty Kate with the lucrative roles coughed up for Nat. And all along, Natalie had her own money.

Fuck.

She stood up and wandered to the nearest window, not wanting to look the clever lawyer in the eye and feel bloody foolish. Kate breathed in and out, her stomach cold and hollow, and the glass pane misted in front of her. The fog slowly receded to reveal a grey sky, punctuated by dark spires, and she closed her eyes to shut it all out. Her second divorce, and caught out again, taken for a ride with finances.

It was quiet.

"Are you all right?" her lawyer asked, gently this time.

Kate blinked and realised her cheek warmed with a tear. A pulse thumped on her forehead, and she frowned, trying to stop herself from sinking into shame and despair. Everything felt like one step forward, two steps back, at the moment. Bea making it to nursery one day, then being so clingy she'd miss the next two. Ralph raving about school one night, then sullen the rest of the week. And that was before juggling work or sorting this stupid divorce, for a humiliating marriage that shouldn't have happened.

"I..."

"Come and sit down," Olivia said from behind, her voice soothing. "Have a more comfortable chair."

Kate turned to find her elegant lawyer pulling out one of the informal seats around the coffee table. Olivia gazed at her, hands rested on the padded back, patiently waiting for Kate, her expression professional and kind.

"Maybe now would be a good time for a cup of tea. Would you like one?"

Kate nodded. Fatigue blunted the movement, but it was clear enough for Ms Sachdeva to understand.

Kate dropped into the seat and stared into the middle of the room. She sat, half aware that a kettle bubbled somewhere in a corner with a gentle sound that lulled, of the quiet movements and Olivia preparing tea before she arranged a glass teapot and two china mugs in front of her.

"It's black Darjeeling. Do you take milk?"

Kate nodded again, with her mouth hanging wordlessly open.

Olivia sat in the chair beside her, always elegant and knees together. She leant forward to pour them both tea with milk, the delicate fragrance a balm at this moment.

"Sorry." Kate shook her head. "I thought I'd handle this better. I didn't expect..." She turned up her hands. All this shit and more regrets. Loss hit her again.

"Comes in waves, doesn't it?" Olivia murmured. She tilted her head and neatly stroked her hair behind an ear. "It's like being battered by a surge. And more waves come, but they get smaller and happen less often. It can take years before complete calm. Decades for some."

"Have you...?" The understanding sounded personal and the flicker of regret in her lawyer's features suggested an empathy from experience.

"I've never known a client handle divorce with equanimity."

Olivia gazed at her, and Kate realised how much she expressed through her eyes. She wasn't prone to large displays of emotion, no loud bursts of laughter, but her eyebrows skewered fools or softened with great sympathy, like they did now.

"People can rage," Olivia said gently, "or think they're over it, to find something like this rakes up everything. Regret underscores even the most amicable of divorces – that it didn't work when it should have done. It's an emotive undertaking and I've found no way to escape that."

Again, Olivia looked at her with deep understanding, sympathy without pity, professional and reassuring, and made Kate feel completely normal.

She imagined Maria and Ed in these seats, with Olivia guiding them through their divorce. She appreciated Maria's perspective now and Olivia's gentle support.

Kate sipped her tea, steam breathed on her face, the fragrance refreshing and the taste such a familiar comfort that her body succumbed. Olivia also knew her teas. It was perfect.

"I really thought I was over it." She looked at Olivia with foolish contrition.

"It never is for anyone at this stage," Olivia replied.

Kate curled her fingers around the cup, the warmth soothing, and her shoulders hunched as if on a cold day. She took a sip and the balance of muscat flavours and nip of tannin consoled.

"I..."

She was exhausted, as if she'd sprinted for months and come to a sudden halt, with all her fatigue descending. She sat reeling from it, her divorce clearer now she stopped and looked back.

"I reconciled to us splitting long ago. If I'm honest, perhaps since before we married. In retrospect, it was a last-ditch attempt to be together. And it was clear almost immediately that we can't."

She'd committed to her wedding day though, at the small ceremony in front of select guests. She didn't hold a single thing back and leapt in with both feet. Then they'd sank in unison and surfaced apart.

"I was twenty when we first met on a film set. She's an actor."

Olivia nodded.

"Neither of us were out publicly yet, so it was very clandestine."

And so exciting and heated because of it. Was that what fuelled the chemistry for so long, its illicit nature?

"I wanted to come out but didn't. We're talking over fifteen years ago. Things still weren't great for queer actors, even though there are many behind the scenes. At the same time, I was under pressure to come out because of my roles."

She checked towards Olivia.

Her lawyer indicated for her to continue. Of course, not every lesbian had seen those queer films, and Olivia might not know them, but they'd become iconic.

"Then we split up and went our separate ways. I met Harry. Then we broke up. Then I seemed to start this cycle with Natalie then Harry on separate films, starting a relationship, only to split up yet again."

She looked toward her calm solicitor.

"It sounds a silly habit. But the thing is, you get wary in this business. It's difficult to let anyone new in, and it was too easy to pick up with someone familiar who I trusted."

So, she'd find herself back with Natalie.

"Finally, Nat was happy to risk being outed, and we decided to give it a proper shot, got married, then..."

Away from working on set and stolen moments, the reality of Kate having kids seem to hit Natalie. And it was clear they were done the day they married. Even more so on the short honeymoon. Nat wanted to party all day and night, but Kate needed to check in on the kids by phone, Bea not yet two years old.

"It wasn't that she ignored my kids. They're very particular people who I adore, and I don't expect everyone to love them. But she didn't recognise I had obligations and bonds to others. I can't be with someone like that, even when the kids are grown."

Their love turned to ashes as soon as Natalie had to share Kate's attention, which was sobering and left a chill. And Kate's love evaporated too and left her feeling like she'd been conned.

They'd barely had any contact since. A good thing it turned out. And it was finally over. With her friendship and parenting with Harry stable, and her cycle with Natalie exhausted, Kate was out of trusted partners. It felt dire and a relief at the same time.

Except, it turned out Natalie wasn't someone she could trust after all. And the con cut deeper.

"I'm sorry," she murmured.

"All normal." Olivia sat elegantly at the table, attentive but calm, her eyes blinking slowly in a hypnotic way.

Kate sighed. "I wasn't expecting this."

"People often see a side of their spouse they weren't expecting." Olivia's voice stayed a light, silky massage that dissipated Kate's tension. "There's grief, anger, loss. Something different for everyone, and sometimes all at once."

Olivia's expression softened, staying both steadfast and reassuring. It worked because Olivia was clearly excellent at her job. And they sat, Olivia not pushing, but remaining attentive.

"What do we do?" Kate asked quietly, placing all her trust in Olivia.

"It's a serious legal matter if she has undeclared assets. We can pursue that."

"But it'll take time," Kate said, as much to herself as anything.

"Yes, it will," Olivia murmured.

Kate welled up inside. She sat, staring at nothing, aware of little except her burning eyes and breathing, lifting high and sinking deep, like she drifted at sea. In and out, until the humiliation and grief subsided, and the last wave passed, settling Kate on the shore, watching it travel back out to sea. She blinked, exhausted but ready to get up.

"I don't want to draw it out," Kate said. "I don't want to complicate things."

"You can proceed with the current financial statements and prenup. It may end up a similar division of assets either way."

"Yes, I want to do that," Kate whispered.

"May I suggest," Olivia began gently, "that a forensic accountant checks the finances in the background? It's costly, but if complications occur, we'd have the full picture at hand."

"That," Kate sighed with relief, "sounds a good plan."

"You can have a break for a while," Olivia said. "We can proceed with the financial disclosure from here. You'll sign off the agreement, but I need to prepare it first." She not so much smiled, but looked at her with warm assurance. The eyes again. So very expressive.

Olivia had the situation under control, like a cushion taking the blow for Kate and metaphorically holding her hand. To be honest, at their first session, Kate wondered if that hand would give her frostbite. She'd relaxed that opinion over their meetings. And when Kate sank today, Olivia had been there, reliable and steady, until Kate surfaced. It was powerfully reassuring.

"Thank you," Kate said. "For everything today."

"That's why I'm here," Olivia said. "I'm glad I could help." She said it sincerely, as if there were no doubt.

Olivia put out a hand, cordially this time, less brusque and business-like than before. And Kate took it. She wasn't icy to the touch at all.

"Ms Woodhouse," her lawyer nodded goodbye.

And Kate smiled. Still the formality. Still the professional propriety.

"Ms Sachdeva." She nodded in return.

***

Olivia watched Kate walk down the stairs and out of sight into reception, with no-one but discreet Zain to see her. She returned to her office, pushed the door to, leant back and closed her eyes.

She'd made it. The bulk of the work to submit the divorce completed.

Olivia had compartmentalised and professionally supported the client, Ms Woodhouse, Kate. After these important sessions, she wouldn't see Kate for a while, if all went as planned. If this Natalie had her head screwed on, she wouldn't make a fuss and would let that ill-prepared prenuptial agreement do its work and proceed quickly.

Kate had looked nothing like her roles today. Nothing like an Oscar-winning actress receiving her award with a sparkling smile. And nothing like the woman who'd welcomed Olivia at the door in Park Town.

The new information had blown Kate away, and the actor had sat drained and expressionless, the toll of the relationship clear. And Olivia had forgotten all about her comfort films and Kate's messy life ruining her indulgence.

She'd wanted to say thank you for those early movies, which had Olivia plastering posters on her wall at seventeen of Kate at twenty-one. For standing steady and putting queer characters into the world that became a reassuring presence on many a sapphic's wall. For risking her career. For still respecting her partner, while deep down frustrated and ashamed of not being out in public.

For the company of those stories. For the characters, their lives, and other people who loved them. It made the world feel more hospitable and provided a cosy corner to recover when life turned antagonistic. Because there were people out there, all watching those films with Olivia, and it built a safe place for a while.

Olivia wanted to say everything to Kate Woodhouse. But a lawyer shouldn't tell her client any of that.

She did what she needed to instead, and the reason she compartmentalised all along. She'd kept her solicitor head on, shifting perspectives to understand the client, her wife, the technicalities of law and specifics of their divorce. Then she'd paused when Kate became upset, understanding how people experienced loss in different ways at different times.

By the end of the day, when she'd listened and understood the situation, with respect and sympathy, her client received the support and divorce that she needed.

It was done. The dangerous part was over. And by some miracle, Charlotte hadn't found out. A couple of issues needed straightening then, if it all went well, it was a matter of waiting for the courts to process the divorce.

Olivia almost slid down the door in relief.

13

"You look like shit," Harry said, enveloping Kate in a hug.

"Tell me about it," she replied. "I feel like crap too."

His cuddle thumped the breath from her body, then he released and held her at arm's length.

Harry, however, looked great, with his auburn hair, short at the sides and tumbling into longer waves on top, and biceps and pecs filling his snug jumper. She bet he had buns of steel in those jeans.

"You're fit as fuck," she said, jealous of his energy.

He pulled a ridiculous muscleman pose, while pouting his lips, and made her laugh.

"I'm bulking out for this role," he said, relaxing. "Can't wait to be a weedy little shit again after this. I'm sick of bloody protein shakes."

He stuck his hands in his jeans' pockets, stepped back into the quiet road and gazed around the curving stone terrace.

"This is a seriously nice pad," he said, gazing up.

"I love it," she replied.

It was a beautiful compromise, somewhere away from the centre and traffic, in exclusive Park Town, not shut off behind walls, but private for the kids.

"You do look bloody knackered though," he said, stepping towards her again. "Shall I take Ralph and Bea next weekend too?"

"No," she said. "Thanks for the offer. Let's keep them in routine if we can." Because acting schedules made a mess of it already. "It's been full-on with the divorce and everything."

"I'm not surprised. Let me get the kids off your hands," he said. "Are they ready?"

"Maybe?" she winced and raised her shoulders.

Bea had grumbled all morning, wanting to stay home after several days at nursery. Kate had wrestled her into a bath and into a dress. Bea hadn't said it out loud, but obstructed every step of the way, from rejecting breakfast and every possible outfit. Then there was her boy, her nearly teenager, who already towered above her and whose voice dropped an octave below.

"Ralph's packing his own bag," she said.

Because no matter how badly he did it, whether he filled it with trading cards, tablet, phone, anything but clothes and a toothbrush, he was Mr Independent now and she needed to take a step back and trust him.

Harry shrugged with a nonchalant grin. "It's only a weekend. He'll survive with the shirt on his back."

"You think he dressed?" Kate raised an eyebrow, and Harry laughed before he focussed behind her and a smile softened his face.

She turned to find Ralph at the doorway, almost as tall as Harry, but still with the narrow shoulders of a boy, rucksack on and a tuft of stripy underpants sticking out of the zip. In his arms he carried Bea, a little rucksack on her back, arms around his shoulders and a smile on her face. Because nothing softened her grouchy baby like being picked up by big bro.

A rush of love and relief swarmed up her chest, and the pride almost knocked her over.

"Oh fuck," she whispered, turning to Harry. "I'm going to cry. Don't let them see. They'll both stop if I make a big deal of it." She swiped at her eyes several times.

"Mate!" he cried, putting his arms out. "Bumble Bea!"

Harry pulled the kids into a hug.

"Come on," he said, drawing her in too. "Family cuddle."

Kate nuzzled into Bea's soft hair. "You have a lovely time, sweet pea." She slipped her head between her kids. Bea's supple cheek on one side, Ralph's on the other, not as smooth and with the beginnings of fuzz. Harry squeezed them all together in comforting warmth.

Yes, this part worked, thank god. She breathed out and some of the weight lifted from her shoulders.

"Go do something," Harry shouted from the car as they left. "Leave the house! Leave it all behind! Take the day off!"

"Sure!" She waved off his suggestion.

When the hell did she have a day without obligations?

But the kids were happy with their dad, divorce proceedings ground away in the background, most of the rooms were unpacked or would wait another day... Perhaps she'd walk to the Radcliffe Camera, gaze beneath the Bridge of Sighs, stroll around the art exhibition for which she'd optimistically picked up a flyer in the reception of Bentleys.

Glasses propped on her head, hair tied in a loose low bun, she walked with those destinations vaguely in mind and gravitated towards the centre of town. The weight lifted again as she wandered past the University Parks, alongside ancient colleges and the gothic Natural History Museum.

There were looks, but not many. People didn't expect her to walk around the streets like everyone else. Some dismissed her as looking similar to that actor, 'Kate Whatserface', as a teenage lad called her once, before grinning and asking for a selfie.

The town centre was busier, and she nipped down a side street into Modern Art Oxford. She paid for the exhibition and wandered through empty, white-walled rooms with hushed awe. She sighed and closed her eyes. Still early in the day, the quiet galleries were blissful, and the stress evaporated from her shoulders into the air, leaving her light.

Distinct, precise but languorous footsteps echoed nearby, and she opened her eyes. She peered around the corner of a white wall, then did a double take, because it was Olivia. She did another double take, because the woman looked almost exactly as she did at work –

elegant black dress, this time with her slim brown arms bare to the shoulder, a coat neatly folded over her arm, shorter heels on black shoes, but in the wrong place and without her briefcase.

It was odd seeing her impeccably polite, not as icy as she'd first thought, lawyer out of context. Kate had imagined her joined to her laptop with figures and contracts day and night, and it shifted something, realising that of course she existed beyond that world.

She wondered if Olivia came with anyone today, a girlfriend or wife, but no-one appeared with her. Was there someone for Olivia? How would she know, when they'd only talked about work and Kate's messy life? It only added to the woman's intrigue. First icy, then sympathetic, always professional and never a doubt about the excellence of her service, but with moments where Kate glimpsed deep undercurrents. Blink and you'd miss them, but they were there.

Olivia studied a large canvas of broad, dark brushstrokes, which formed a voluptuous nude; an ordinary woman sitting in bed, light-brown skin vivid against white sheets, eating a piece of toast. It seemed too everyday for Olivia Sachdeva, whom Kate imagined admiring high art. But the lawyer was entranced. Olivia gazed at the painting and reached forward with relaxed fingers, as if she forgot herself. Then slowly she let her hand fall, while remaining captivated by the picture.

What moved and motivated a woman like Olivia Sachdeva? Kate stared until realising she'd become as captivated by the elegant lawyer as the woman had by the picture, her own fingers tingling in empathy as she watched.

She should leave Olivia to her private moment outside office appointments, because Kate had sympathy and respect for time away from work. She stepped back, but it was a dead end in the labyrinth, and she couldn't avoid walking past her lawyer.

With best stompy foot forward, she approached. "Ms Sachdeva," she said, playfully.

She lapsed into their familiar formality, but especially in the informal surroundings and out of office hours, it seemed absurd and made her smile.

Olivia turned and blinked. The slightest flicker of confusion passed over her features, Kate recognising ever more subtle expressions now. Then came definite engagement with the eyes. Pleasure? Perhaps that was too much, but acceptance at least.

"Ms Woodhouse?" Olivia said. Was her crystal-cut accent smooth around the edges today? Then the slightest change overcame those fine features, and Olivia's face glowed and softened. "Good morning."

"Sorry to surprise you," Kate said. "I bet you thought you'd seen the last of me for a while."

"I had assumed." One of those magnificent eyebrows rose. "But it's not unwelcome."

Kate almost laughed at her presence being 'not unwelcome'. She kept it to a smile. "I would have left you in peace, but there's no other way out."

Olivia nodded, although the eyebrow stayed aloft.

"It doesn't surprise me you're an art lover though," Kate carried on under interrogation from the eyebrow.

"That's quite a presumption," Olivia said, tilting her head, playful but careful. "I might be here for the café."

"True." Kate paused, wondering if Olivia could cope with a gentle tease, or whether that was pushing 'unwelcome'. "I hope they have superior tea?"

"Indeed, they do." Was that almost a smile?

"None of that dusty decaffeinated stuff."

Yes, there was a smile. Even a hint of pearly teeth.

Kate asked again, because she'd seen Olivia admire the painting with such immersive enthrallment, that Kate knew she admired art, or nudes. "Are you though? An art lover?"

"Depends on the artwork." Still the raised eyebrow.

"Same." Kate smiled.

"I imagine you have original works on your walls upstairs?"

So, Olivia assumed she had fine taste too.

"You're right," Kate said, continuing their formal to and fro. "I'm not sure how much value you'd place on the works or artists themselves. One is an abstract prodigy at four and the other does darker work at twelve."

The beautiful eyebrow descended in realisation, and amusement curved lips into an attractive bow.

"Your children."

Kate nodded. "My kids."

"Are they...?" Oh. A little frown appeared in the elegant brow and a side eye shifted around the gallery. "Are they with you?"

Olivia Sachdeva definitely wasn't a fan of ankle biters.

"No, they're with Harry this weekend. Their dad," she added.

"I assumed you meant Harry Shaw."

Her lawyer remembered. Of course, Olivia must keep an enormous amount of detail in that brain of hers.

"Are you...?" Olivia hesitated, perhaps cautious about stepping outside their professional bounds. "Relaxing and having a break?"

"I am, thank you."

"Good. I think you probably need it." And she gazed with a gentle concern, those fine eyes fascinating and fascinated, as if she took in every detail of Kate in the same way that Kate keenly observed too.

That warmth in her expression? Playful, intelligent, engaged. Had it always been there, or did Kate read her better? Or was it something new since their last appointment, when she thought they broke through a barrier in some way?

Then Olivia checked around the gallery, eyes darting and taking in every corner, and back to Kate.

"I'm sorry." Kate straightened at Olivia's discomfort, although didn't know where it came from. "I'll leave you to enjoy," she couldn't help glancing at the large nude, "the artwork."

Olivia's lips parted, as if she were about to continue their conversation, their fullness more apparent with this expression. But she only said, "Enjoy your weekend."

Kate turned and ambled to the door, with that peculiar pull at her back again. She'd felt it at home when the lawyer visited. It was so strong this time, she narrowly resisted the temptation to turn and look.

She paused. Silly. She must be craving company. She didn't want to return to the empty house, even though she'd been desperate for free time. But it wasn't just any company. It was that familiar tug towards the intriguing Olivia. And this time she didn't resist, and she peeped over her shoulder, the lawyer now looking at her phone.

She wondered at them both, and their careful conversations. Were they the same? Both acutely aware of others, their behaviour, motivations, the way they expressed themselves down to the slightest twitch of an eyebrow and curl of a lip. To understand, mimic and live for Kate, and understand and advise for Olivia.

Whatever it was, the curiosity about Olivia tantalised more than ever. Could she invite Olivia to join her for a coffee?

No. She answered herself. Stupid. This wasn't a session that Kate paid for. Clients were probably the last people Olivia wanted to see at the weekend. She should leave her in peace and move on somewhere else.

Something like regret pulled again as she slipped out her phone to search for the nearest museum.

14

Olivia stared as Kate strode through her weekend like in a film scene, the actor mesmerising as she retreated through the white rooms, but peculiarly real and ordinary at the same time.

Warm and tingly, that's how she'd felt with Kate up close. Perhaps she came near to talk without disturbing others in the quiet space, but Olivia glowed from the proximity.

She'd looked unlike anything Olivia remembered, in appointments or on the screen. Relaxed. Happy. Tired still. But her eyes had glistened as they talked. And her smile? Sigh. Kate had a vivid charm today. That must be what the cameras caught in her films, and she was sure the actor switched on charm at will.

And glasses. Olivia really liked her in glasses. It brought a geeky side to her that Olivia had never seen on film, and was all Kate Woodhouse, not Laurence.

Olivia straightened, uncomfortable that she'd slipped into daydreaming, and musing that, while she'd become more comfortable in the actor's presence, no way did she want her to bump into Charlotte.

Oh god, Charlotte. She'd be here any minute.

Olivia tapped into her phone, "I've already checked out the exhibition. Let's meet somewhere else."

Message seen. Dots bounced. Then stopped.

Dammit, Charlotte. Don't get distracted. This was a pressing concern. Charlotte must not trip through the gallery and bump into

Kate. Not after all this time. Not after Olivia had navigated the divorce this far.

She peered after Kate at the other end of the gallery. Another day, and she wished they'd talked more, her draw to the actor always strong.

Dots on her phone started bouncing.

"Already?!!!!!" Charlotte replied.

Olivia winced at the number of exclamation marks, then tapped, "Well." Olivia checked the time. Dammit. Charlotte was nowhere near late. "Where do you want to go instead?" she said, glossing over the issue.

Charlotte was going to say the Ashmolean.

"How about the Ashmolean?"

Olivia rolled her eyes. The Albright-family favourite pulled her in different directions, a more complicated prospect. The spectacular artifacts from around the world fascinated her, and she'd gaze at them for hours. Her mother, Geeta, took her round as a child, but many items were gathered by antiquated men with their colonial categorisations.

Olivia replied, "Fine", because she supported the organisation's introspection, expansive and diverse exhibitors, and because it put the British Museum to shame with the restitution of objects with illegal provenance. She had many thoughts on the latter trying to hide behind the 1963 British Museum Act.

A few minutes march down ancient side streets and past colleges, Olivia climbed the broad white stone steps to the museum. Charlotte came into view, gazing up and spinning around beneath the columns of the entrance.

"No Millie?" Olivia said, approaching. She intended it nonchalantly, but her delivery always tightened when pronouncing that name.

Charlotte came to a halt, with blushing face, mahogany waves flowing, and an instant smile for her. Olivia paused. It worked, every time, that bit of magic, so that Olivia's cheeks rose and she relaxed.

"Morning you," Charlotte said, her long arms swinging. "Millie might not make it, so it's just me for now."

Good, Olivia almost said. An even better prospect.

"What do you want to see?" Charlotte said, falling into step beside Olivia.

Honestly, she didn't care, but they'd deliberate for hours if she let Charlotte choose. Charlotte's 'faff spiral of indecision' Millie called it.

Sometimes Olivia wondered how her friend achieved anything. But somehow, when it came to the crunch and all possibilities focussed into the few, Charlotte's acuity became razor sharp and she hyper focused like a super lawyer, where time seemed to slow and she saw everything, blitzing contracts and alleviating complex situations with clients.

"How about we wander the ground floor in a clockwise direction?" she suggested.

"Yes, let's do that," Charlotte said.

Even by Charlotte standards, this was amenable.

"You know, I haven't stopped to appreciate the exhibits for ages," Charlotte said, spinning though the long gallery of Greek statues that lined the entrance hall. "I always dash up to the restaurant to meet my mother."

They stopped at a pedestal of red marble with a serious Roman bust. 'Claudius', Charlotte read, before losing interest and spinning around again, so much that Olivia feared for the remaining limbs of the statues.

Olivia sauntered in a straight line, coat over her arms, while Charlotte travelled all directions like a pin ball, one with relaxed momentum and dodging a handful of tourists this early in the morning.

"Goodness, look at this one," Charlotte said, reaching back to Olivia. "Imagine how long it took to sculpt."

"It took Michaelangelo almost three years to complete David, so proportionally less than that, I imagine."

Pitter patter went her heart because Charlotte beamed at her in a sudden flush. She often did that, as if plunged into an emotion.

"Of course, you'd know that," Charlotte said, smiling, "And-"

Then the smile vanished as quickly, replaced by a smack of shock and her mouth stretching into glee. Really, could the woman not stay in one thought for more than a second?

Charlotte pulled closer.

"Don't look now, but..."

Alarm bells. Loud clanging alarm bells.

"That woman over there..."

No, no, no. Surely not. Not here.

"I can't believe...Oh my goodness...."

There was a specific excitement about Charlotte that meant it was one person only.

"...but, she looks like Kate Laurence."

Not possible. Olivia had just left the actor across town. She couldn't be here too.

"Don't you think?"

"No," Olivia said.

"But you haven't even looked."

"You said, 'Don't look'."

Yes, she was in denial.

Charlotte grinned. "You have to see." Could her eyes get any bigger? "Please."

Agitated hands travelled towards her shoulders as if Charlotte was about to spin her round.

"Please have a peek," Charlotte pleaded.

Olivia blinked, preparing to turn with every semblance of nonchalance. "Where?" she sighed, spinning about.

She needn't have asked. The actor, in those lovely and studious, black-rimmed glasses, she really did look nice in those, stood reading a guide at the far end of the gallery, as stoney still as the statues lining the hall.

"There!" Charlotte said, shooting out an arm.

"Don't point!" Olivia hissed. That wasn't nonchalant. She gathered herself. "Let's try not to watch so obviously. And also, not shout."

Charlotte hovered over Olivia's shoulder. Good. Perhaps her friend would continue in a hushed tone.

"There, coming out of Egypt," Charlotte said in the loudest whisper known to humankind. "She's the image of Kate Laurence."

"You have the actor on the brain at the moment," Olivia muttered.

Like she didn't, with Kate as her client and having just bumped into her, and her presence so great she'd lingered in Olivia's mind since.

She turned her back to the actor to find Charlotte's glaringly obvious face.

"Stop staring, Charlotte," Olivia whispered.

Charlotte leant closer but gazed with wide eyes over Olivia's shoulder. "What did you say...? Oh." Her brain clearly caught up with the words. "You said don't stare." And Charlotte broke into a grin, before rubbing her brow, in a clumsy attempt at casual and to peep from beneath her fingers.

"No-one." Olivia tutted. "And I mean no-one, is fooled by you hiding behind your hand."

"Will you look?" Charlotte pleaded with huge brown eyes, like an adoring puppy. "Please. She's filming in Oxford, so it might be her."

"But the glasses?" Olivia pointed out.

Charlotte wrinkled her nose.

"Well, have you ever seen Kate Laurence wear them?"

It was worth a try.

"What difference does that make?" Charlotte curled up a lip. "It's just Kate Laurence in glasses."

Oh. That only affected Olivia then. Charlotte was apparently unfazed by the loveliness of a bespectacled Kate.

"Just remember," Olivia said, refusing to check behind, "that theoretically, in the unlikely event that it is the actor, don't start shouting about me being an admirer...of her work."

Charlotte stiffened, straight and serious. As serious as puppies looked. "I am respectful of your love for her work." She raised one hand. "I have taken notice."

"And while we're on the subject, may I remind you to never, *ever*, tell Millie."

Charlotte made a motion to zip her lips, then unfortunately unzipped them. "Because what would Millie say about you innocently admiring the performances of one of the sexiest women in the world?"

Dammit. Olivia closed her eyes for several seconds. When she opened them, Charlotte was beaming from ear to ear.

Her friend raised two uncoordinated hands in the air. "Sorry. Being respectful of your admiration for her work."

This was impossible.

"I'm whispering anyway," Charlotte said.

Olivia leant forward, so their noses almost touched. "Charlotte," she said, in a whisper worthy of the word, "it's about as subtle as a foghorn in a telephone box."

But Charlotte wasn't listening.

"She's gone," Charlotte said, eyes searching. "I bet she's in Ancient Cyprus." And she peeled off.

"Charlotte!? Where are you–?"

Oh, my god. Charlotte lolloped off, in an absurd impression of someone secretly following. This was excruciating.

"Charlotte!" Olivia hissed.

Her friend turned back with glee, beckoning for her to follow. "We can catch her if we nip through the Aegean."

Olivia launched forward, tiptoeing across the polished floor, if only to stop her friend from waving so unsubtly.

"I'm sure it's her," Charlotte whispered.

"So what if it is?" Olivia prickled.

"Because this might be our only chance to see her." Charlotte nodded. "A multi-Oscar-winning actress and superstar."

Olivia paused with the incongruity. Because that multi-award-winning actress was familiar as simply Kate. And she'd had many chances to meet her, even been to her home. Was privy to her sexuality. Had a professional view of her finances. Knew her kids' names. That she preferred coffee to tea. That she feared maths, but was razor sharp in other ways, and looked the most intelligent and beautiful woman in those glasses.

"She'll be getting away," Charlotte said. "Come on."

Dammit, she'd paused too long.

She scuttled after Charlotte, who peeped into dark galleries in no way inconspicuous. This was a nightmare. Past China, with a glimpse at India, and Charlotte loped into Rome.

Any moment now, Charlotte would crash into Kate, because coordination wasn't her friend's thing. Olivia and she couldn't be more different in this respect. And it would be awful.

Then Olivia stopped. What was she doing? Kate didn't know Charlotte. She wouldn't realise why this goofy woman furtively peered around a sculptured gluteus maximus in the cast gallery.

If Olivia quietly retreated and later claimed she'd lost her friend, it would be fine. She took a careful step back, watching Charlotte getting further and further away. One more quiet step, and she could turn and walk from the room.

But she backed into something. Something she swore wasn't there before. And froze.

It might be a priceless statue? That would be bad. Perhaps an irreplaceable cast? But it wasn't. It was much, much worse.

Because statues weren't soft. Or warm. Or wore a subtle scent like zested grapefruit. She reached back. Yes, definitely warm and soft. Quite lovely in fact. And the soft thing was apparently her height, given the cushioning pressed beneath her shoulder blades.

"I lost her," echoed from further along the gallery, accompanied by loping strides and footsteps. "I think she must have changed direction and–"

Charlotte squeaked to a halt on the polished floor. "Oh, my god!" Her tone hid none of her surprise. And whipping a hand to cover her gaping mouth didn't help on the subtlety front either.

"Hi," said the soft bump behind Olivia.

It was a voice she'd heard in a hundred films, in several accents, and unmistakably belonged to Kate.

She pictured the actor behind. A white shirt and jacket, a loose scarf casually but perfectly thrown around her shoulders. The dark jeans and tan boots she'd admired on the retreating actor less than an hour ago. Because what lesbian wouldn't admire boots like that. And don't forget the studious, black-rimmed glasses.

To the front, Charlotte pursed her lips so tight they paled, and the whites of her eyes grew so they encircled deep brown irises. Could they get any bigger? Apparently so, because Charlotte's brow crept higher and eyes stretched wider.

Olivia took a breath and prepared to turn round. Because regrettably, this was happening. The meeting she'd so expertly avoided for weeks, through timing, vigilance and thinly veiled threats, was happening, in broad daylight, right now, in public.

She spun neatly on her heel and came almost nose to nose with Kate. Their closeness an immediate and lovely whisper on her face. Whatever words Olivia planned, she lost them. Yes, it was Kate as expected, but although Olivia had seen her an hour ago, she seemed changed again.

The glow of her cheeks, the brightness of her eyes, the plumpness of her lips. Because Olivia failed utterly to stop her gaze from dropping to her mouth.

And the smile she found. There were curves to that smile, reminiscent of the most knowing of heroines. Ms Woodhouse really had a god-gifted charisma. That wasn't makeup or good lighting.

All those appointments where the actor appeared pale and fatigued, Olivia wished for those. Because the last thing she needed was Kate Laurence, turning up right here, right now, looking like that. Because...because...Well, Charlotte clearly. Nothing to do with Olivia's vivid reaction. Because her friend might blurt something out, and with Kate Laurence standing there, looking that good, it would be:

"Incredible," Charlotte sighed.

Charlotte's outline moved into Olivia's side vision, while she stared resolutely ahead at her client.

Was there any way Olivia could extricate herself from this position? Might she apologise and Kate graciously nod and move on without a word?

Those full lips opened. "Ms Sachdeva," the lovely voice said. "I've disturbed your weekend again."

There it was. The elephant that had sat in the corner of the room for weeks trumpeting its presence, so loud even Charlotte couldn't miss it. Olivia closed her eyes for a second, then stepped back, ready to face the music and Charlotte's reaction.

"You...? You...?" Charlotte's nose tried to wrinkle. "You know each other?"

Emotions played over Charlotte's expressive face. Confusion that so often lived there. Also, surprise. A little hurt, perhaps at the secrecy. But rising glee threatened.

"We..." Olivia started. Well, this was awkward. Very imperfect indeed.

She turned to Kate. "I should introduce you. This is my best friend, Charlotte, who works at Bentley, in a different department."

Perhaps turning attention to Charlotte would distract her long enough for Kate to leave and avoid a humiliating outpouring from Charlotte about Olivia's cinematic tastes.

"But you know each other?" Charlotte insisted.

Apparently not distracting this time.

"Ms Sachdeva is being diplomatic." Kate spoke with a low voice, pitched to avoid travelling the room. "I'm her client."

There was that, and Olivia was grateful to Kate for pointing it out, client confidentiality being all important.

"You?" Charlotte managed. "Client?"

"Yes." Kate smiled. "Olivia's being tactful, but she's handling my divorce. I don't mind another Bentley lawyer knowing."

A grin unfurled. Charlotte's surprise relaxed into realisation, her eyes flicking from Kate to Olivia with excitement.

"I can't..." Charlotte started. "I can't believe it."

What would Charlotte say? Olivia really needed to put a lid on this excitement.

"That's amazing. I mean, I'm sorry you're getting a divorce."

Kate shook her head. "We split up a long time ago."

"Good. But it is amazing," Charlotte burbled, attention darting from Olivia to Kate and back again. "Because..." Charlotte took a deep breath.

Oh god, what was coming? Oh, sweet lord or whoever was watching over this, because Olivia was an atheist, but prayed for divine intervention right now.

"Because," Charlotte burst, "Olivia is the bestest. I mean the best. She's really terrific." Charlotte shook her head in delighted incredulity. "If I was getting divorce, which I'm not, I would want..." And the smile on Charlotte's face glowed while she lined up her words. "You couldn't have chosen a better lawyer." And Charlotte's beaming face turned to Olivia with so much hero worship, she was touched.

"I've heard great things about her," Kate said.

"And so you should. She's very clever. Cleverest. I mean I went to Oxford, but Olivia is," Charlotte blew out her cheeks and pointed skywards. "Highest first. Law prize. And that's...Very brain... Really, all the things."

The fluster died to silence. It left Charlotte blushing at meeting Kate Laurence and gazing at Olivia with such obvious pride it made her heart pang again. Usually, she avoided Charlotte's mangled hero worship. It was like a less coherent version of her mother. But it touched her this time.

"Thank you, Charlotte," Olivia said quietly, because her voice would wobble any louder.

"Sorry. I'm burbling." Charlotte stood up straight. "And interrupting your relaxing Sunday."

"Yes. Just a peaceful morning, raving about my divorce lawyer," Kate said drily.

Kate checked towards Olivia at last, with a tilt of the head and a generous expression that suggested Charlotte rattled on, but she found it amusing.

"And I can understand why Olivia didn't tell me you were a client," Charlotte said.

Where was she going with that?

"But it's amazing to meet you." Charlotte stuck out an arm, in that slightly clumsy Charlotte way, to shake hands with Kate.

Perhaps this would be it. Maybe Olivia had got away with it. Kate might leave the museum and Charlotte unravel privately beyond earshot. She finally breathed out in relief.

But rapid footsteps clipped the floor and shattered the air. All three of them turned in the quiet gallery, as another voice intruded. Not the mellowed RP and estuary of Kate Laurence, but distinctly more London, more irreverent, and a horribly perceptive voice.

"What the fuck is going on? Swapping museums like it's a bloody treasure hunt?"

It could only be Millie Banks.

"I've been tracking Charlotte for ages, trying to find you."

A short woman, all curves and bluster, with a head of bouncing blonde curls, came closer. Phone out and eyes down, she headed for them with a horrible inevitability.

Millie rounded the last statue, lifted her face, came to a stop, dropped her weight onto one hip, didn't even blink, and said with a grin, "Well, fuck me. You're Kate Laurence."

15

Kate couldn't help laughing.

A short, curvy woman with extraordinary chutzpah beamed at her, hands on hips, chest out and blonde curls in motion.

"Honestly," the woman said, spinning to Charlotte and grinning. "I turn my back for a minute, and you're chatting up hot actors."

Kate had wondered if there was something between Olivia and Charlotte, and if 'friend' was an understatement. The two, towering, Oxford graduates clearly knew each other well, but then this woman burst on the scene and blew that away.

It was silly how much glowing was going on. Both had pink cheeks and hearts in their eyes, the shorter one more confident and outgoing, but just as infatuated.

"My girlfriend," the blond said, "knows a ridiculous amount about your films. It's like I've met you already."

Charlotte didn't look embarrassed by it. She hardly took her eyes off her partner.

"Millie Banks," she said at last, thrusting out a hand with neat tapering fingers.

"Kate." She shook her hand. "Nice to meet you."

Kate's cheeks ached, smiling at several things. At goofy Charlotte's outburst, at this charismatic woman who'd sashayed up and announced Kate's presence to the world, and Olivia standing by, cool and chic.

The rest of the gallery was quiet, with only a couple at the other end who'd looked up for a moment.

"Since when did you greet people with a proper handshake?" Charlotte asked. Her face still shone at her partner.

Millie sidled up and bumped Charlotte's thigh with a curvy hip. "Since I started dating posh lawyers." And she winked at her. And Kate didn't think it possible, but Charlotte gazed at Millie even brighter.

She'd wondered about Charlotte's eagerness and hesitated in case she was an over-excited fan. But Charlotte showed more enthusiasm about Olivia's skills. The respect was touching – a bit of hero worship of Olivia there, and she could see why.

But Charlotte's outright adoration was reserved for her girlfriend. This enthusiasm must simply be Charlotte, who filled with emotions like someone poured her full of sunshine one minute, then doused her with ice the next. And all in a blink of an eye, like another whose thoughts were transparent and immediate – one of Ralph's friends with ADHD.

"Well," Millie said, turning back to Kate, "given how I've heard nothing about you from these two. And how uptight and responsible they are. I'm gonna take a wild guess and say you have personal business with Bentley's best, and lawyer to the stars, Olivia."

"Got it in one." Kate smiled. This Millie came across all bubbly but was as sharp as the other two.

"You're so much quicker than me," Charlotte said, deflating.

"Rubbish," Millie replied, and she bopped Charlotte on the nose.

"I take twice as long to realise anything and...ten times longer to get the words out. I can be so stupid."

Millie cupped Charlotte's cheeks and gazed at her with reassuring tenderness.

"My dear Charlotte. Your brain is anything but slow. Yes, you get distracted. But you have a thousand thoughts whizzing around in there, and only one mouth to tell them. You have traffic jams. The last thing you are is stupid, my big-brained lover. Sometimes you take a while to get in gear, but then there's no stopping you."

And the way they looked at each other, there was no-one else in the room.

Olivia cleared her throat and raised a beautiful eyebrow. "Millie overstates my credentials."

Was she a little frostier than usual? The refined grump of the trio?

Either way, Olivia's statement sobered the couple, who pulled themselves from each other's magnetic gaze. Although when Millie turned, her eyes still swirled, drunk with love.

Millie sighed, then perked up and directed her bright blue gaze at Kate. "Fancy a cuppa then?"

Kate smiled, because outgoing Millie suggested it so easily, like a young extrovert aunt who forced her introvert family to speak to each other. She wondered if Millie would be dragging the two refined types into trouble for the rest of their lives.

"I shouldn't." Kate said, because definite tension came from Olivia's direction. "I don't want to take up Olivia's free time."

Millie wrinkled her nose. "Oh, don't worry about Olivia. She always looks pissed off when I'm about." And she flashed a grin towards her.

Olivia raised another patient eyebrow, and her lips tutted when she opened her mouth to speak.

"You are welcome to join us," she said. "Because Millie is correct. The look is all about her, not you."

Millie burst out laughing and it echoed down the chamber.

So, there was history here, but also friendship between these two? Complicated maybe, but friends?

"I..." Kate started.

"Please," Charlotte begged, without artifice.

She hadn't planned on going to the café, too recognisable and approachable on her own. But a group shielded her. And what was the harm? When had she hung out with anyone lately, purely for pleasure? She'd become guarded about people, used to them having an ulterior motive. But proper and professional Olivia would be responsible and discreet.

It was a sad situation, when you only trusted your lawyer for company, but that was the truth of it.

"Actually, I'd love a coffee."

Charlotte beamed, then gazed lovingly at Millie. They snuggled together and set off in front. Olivia rolled her eyes but fell into step next to Kate.

"I'm sorry I've crashed your morning," Kate said. She pulled closer to Olivia and their thighs momentarily touched.

"Not at all," Olivia said politely. She walked with perfect posture and coat neatly draped over her arms. Then she dipped her chin and muttered, "Because really, what's there to crash with Millie and Charlotte so engrossed in each other?"

She had a point. The pair in front lost themselves in long looks and giggles, with the odd glance back. Maybe they chatted about bumping into her.

Olivia sauntered on, resigned to it, perhaps used to being the third-wheel singleton. It was tempting to ask.

"I'm guessing they're a new relationship?" Kate said.

"Yes, and no. New, but it took them over a decade to get here. But here is less than a year old, so..." Olivia gestured to the pair who were euphoric with sapphic intoxication.

She envied them. Finding someone and everything feeling right and heavenly in a real way. Until it didn't. Over and over again for her and Natalie. Her heart sank, not at losing Nat, but that she had no-one.

Her lawyer... No, Ms Sachdeva. What were they today, beyond the office and contracts? Kate had never walked so close to her. Those inky eyelashes really were to die for, and those intelligent eyes watched her too.

"So, Ms Woodhouse?" A silky eyebrow rose. A classic Olivia move, Kate recognised now. Intimidating she bet for some, but she loved it. "Are you enjoying Oxford?" Olivia finished.

It was so obviously polite small talk, that she wanted to laugh. But she also wanted to talk to Olivia.

"Very nice, thank you, Ms Sachdeva," she responded in kind, and a similar smile curled at Olivia's lips, acknowledging the play. "I love Park Town, but I haven't explored much further, between settling the kids and work commitments. How long have you lived here?" She imagined Olivia stayed after university.

"All my life," Olivia replied though. "Born at the John Radcliffe, grew up in Iffley Village, applied to university here, and Bentley was my first choice for practice."

Kate paused. "Didn't you ever want to try somewhere else?"

"In theory." Olivia shrugged. "But I can visit. Oxford is home."

"You can build a home anywhere."

Olivia tilted her head. "But I don't want to."

Kate did laugh this time. It was so adamant and matter of fact. It commanded respect but also, and she was surprised by this, affection too.

She'd wanted the opposite, to devour the world and never live in the same place for long. But it caught up with her, all the travelling to yet another film location, and with the kids it became exhausting.

"Some people thrive on change and novelty."

Kate perked up at Olivia talking without prompting. "Millie, for example," Olivia added, with a twitch. "And I do like the challenges of different clients, or the excitement of a new piece of art or book. But that's on top of a bedrock of home. And for me, that's Oxford."

And that is that, Kate also heard. Again, it amused her while also seeming a deeply personal admission from Olivia. Did it strike at the core of who she was? Surprising from the woman who was so opaque the rest of the time.

"Honestly," Olivia continued, "it's one of the finest cities in the world. Why would I want to live anywhere else?"

And there was that superior quality about Olivia. Perhaps it aggravated her friend Millie, but Kate couldn't resist it. There was something appealing about the certainty and superiority of Olivia.

Maybe because it had a solid basis, the lawyer being fantastic at her job and extremely clever.

Still Olivia gazed at her, without a flicker in her conviction. Perhaps that's what it was – refreshingly reliable and predictable after Kate's work life and colleagues, who changed with the winds from character to character and from location to location. From flimsy sets with no backing, built one day and gone the next. It was like Olivia was as steadfast and dependable as the ancient walls of the colleges. It had an odd appeal, wanting to challenge it while also respecting it.

"You have strong opinions, Ms Sachdeva," Kate said.

"I do, Ms Woodhouse." Olivia smiled, clearly enjoying the formality and parrying they engaged in.

"Are you careful how you make those opinions?"

"I'd like to say always, but sometimes I can be as judgemental and shortsighted as everyone else."

Kate laughed. "You're very honest."

"I have plain-speaking friends who enlighten me at every opportunity."

Olivia's gaze flicked forwards to Millie with annoyance, the other woman walking ahead and adoring her taller girlfriend, unaware of the censure. Amusement tempered Olivia's expression though. A dry humour lay beneath the surface, far more playful than Kate imagined at first. It was enticing, always.

"And is this a typical weekend for you?" Kate continued.

"In what way?"

Did she know Olivia well enough to tease a little? Ms Sachdeva didn't seem the type to blush at this.

"Wandering through Oxford?" Kate started, as they passed a curvaceous sculpture which caught Olivia's attention. "Looking at nudes..."

That got her a side eye.

"And bumping into people?"

Olivia nodded. "Yes, I meet up with friends–"

Then Olivia turned in a smooth movement, her black hair swishing along her jawline, eyes doing that lazy, disapproving blink.

"No, Ms Woodhouse, I don't, under normal conditions, actually bump into anyone."

It was delightful and butterflies tingled in her belly.

"Just me?"

"Just you, Ms Woodhouse."

Kate paused. Perhaps it was time to acknowledge that pull. She'd said she would never act on it again, and she had no intention here either. But she'd be lying to herself if she didn't admit that Olivia gently backing into her had been the highlight of her month. Especially when she'd reached back and touched her thigh.

This was her lawyer. Her frosty, disinterested and disinclined solicitor. But Kate hadn't had this much fun in harmless, playful conversation in months.

"Good to hear." Kate grinned, and they politely sauntered on.

Yes, her safe lawyer, who'd be the last person interested in her.

16

Well, this was odd. And more than a little tense. But also undeniably pleasant. Another complex situation in Olivia's life.

They settled in the grand basement café, beneath the vaulted ceilings and at an alcove table between large supporting pillars. Millie and Charlotte sat opposite and Kate beside her, leaving Olivia stuck between her screen idol and the one that got away.

This was in no way perfect. She would have to process this later, because frankly it was a lot, even for someone compartmentalised.

This was also potentially disastrous. Would Charlotte ever read the room or a social situation? Or at least, after focussing long enough to read the room, not blurt out something anyway. Then there was Millie, who loved to stir things up. How had Olivia ended up friends with a woman who wore secrets on her face and the world's biggest troublemaker? Although, this dreaded collision of worlds was not as bad as expected. So far.

And with Kate? She'd become more used to her very physical presence, for it to not overwhelm today. Not even the warmth of her thigh, almost touching Olivia's. Or the subtle scent from her citrus bodywash, mixed with something that was distinctly her. Another small step into her comfort zone, from someone increasingly familiar.

Olivia turned to Kate and was privileged with a close-up of the actor, a front seat to the smooth detail without the jagged harshness of high definition. She gazed over the mix of blondes and browns in Kate's hair tucked behind an ear, and the laughter lines that burst like stars beside her eyes. She wanted to prompt a smile and see them deepen, because she knew how they'd look.

Olivia cleared her throat. "Charlotte says you're filming in Oxford," she said, to fill the silence and stop herself from appreciating lovely lines.

"Just a bit part, really." Kate smiled, those lines deepening. "I have a couple of pages of dialogue to learn, then I'm in the background for most scenes. After this, I'm going home to re-read the book and adjust to the story again."

"For a small role?"

"It is small, but everything counts in a scene. From the detail on a dress, to how an extra stands in the background." Kate turned her shoulders to face Olivia. "Everyone needs to pull the same way, for even a few seconds to work. The sound quality, the colour palette, the slightest flicker in an actor's expression. The hours that go into producing a minute of footage on a period film like this are enormous."

The expression on her face. Sigh. Kate was immersed in what it took to create movies, and her awe and keenness to make Olivia understand consumed her.

A fluid fuzziness settled inside Olivia, that sensation when she found something pleasing. An exceptional artwork. Preventing a client falling through a loophole. And now Kate appreciating the effort to make a film, how the layers of attention and expertise all added to the whole, unnoticed by many but appreciated by some. It tickled Olivia's brain in an enjoyable way and satisfied inside like warm oil.

She gazed at Kate for too long.

"Like if a brushstroke was out of place on a masterpiece," Kate continued, perhaps thinking Olivia paused because she didn't understand. "That's all you'd see – that flaw. Everyone must play their role well for the whole piece to work and the main characters stand out. If I don't get my minor part right, I'll catch the eye even more. I'm not being arrogant, but I have a high profile, which means I draw attention. So, I have to hit it perfectly, and that means being understated sometimes."

"I didn't take it as arrogant," Olivia replied. "And I admire your respect for your colleagues."

Was there a blush to the surprise in Kate's face? Pleasure? Her eyes sparkled.

"And of course," Olivia carried on, "you shone even in *Devolution*."

That pleased face dropped. "Oh crap." Still the shock. "You saw *Devolution*?" Then Kate smiled and shook her head. "I don't believe it. Tell me that's not the only film you've seen of mine."

"No." That was an understatement.

Kate breathed in. "What did you think?" And she dramatically held that breath while waiting for an answer.

Olivia considered for a moment, always striving for tact but balancing honesty.

"It's," she started, "a truly awful film."

Kate burst with laughter, and Olivia found her own cheeks rising. Because that was the one. The smile where Kate's deep green eyes shone. What were they like? Emeralds Olivia was tempted to say, but the colour shimmered too vividly for a cold jewel. More like a glistening rainforest then. And those laughter lines? They were very, very appealing.

"Do you know," Kate said, swinging her body around to Olivia and enthusiasm pinking her face. "I still have a lot of respect for that movie. I see how much skill it takes to make even what reviewers dismiss as a shitty film. And I admire something in every single one. I learn from every actor I work with, and every piece I see, whether it's acclaimed or not."

That fuzzy feeling flowed again inside her belly. Because generosity together with excellence, Olivia admired even more. It was humbling and inspired fondness. The heights Kate strived for earned Olivia's admiration, but the accompanying humanity had a glow tingling.

She rested her hand over her stomach, half appreciating the warmth that kindled there, half to stop it.

She sat up straighter, the movement catching Charlotte's attention. But not Millie's. Because the latter already observed with an interested focus. That was not a perceptive gaze Olivia wanted to meet right now.

"How long are you in Oxford?" Charlotte said, leaning on the table towards Kate with the energy of a big puppy.

For once, thank god for Charlotte's impulsive randomness.

"I'm staying for at least a year," Kate replied. "I've been on the road too long and my kids need to be settled. And after the divorce, I want Oxford to be our home."

"You've probably guessed this." Charlotte beamed. "But I'm a huge fan of your work."

"Thank you," Kate nodded. It came easily and practiced, Kate being gracious and comfortable with people.

"I've always wondered when Charlotte watched those films."

Olivia twitched because it was Millie who'd uttered the observation, with a suspicious tilt of the head.

"Hmm?" Charlotte replied, eyebrows shooting up in alarm.

"When on earth do you see Kate's films?" Millie asked. "I haven't seen any since we started living together."

Deliberate or not, Millie dug in a dangerous place. Olivia's pulse fluttered in her neck. Because Charlotte did not excel at carefree deception.

"Well...? I...?" Charlotte froze like a deer in headlights. "Because..."

Please don't look this way.

"When would I have seen them?" Charlotte squeaked at Olivia, a plea that was hopelessly revealing.

She took a moment, waiting for her heartbeat to calm. "Perhaps," Olivia said, grateful for the nonchalance in her voice, "at any point before then, given Ms Laurence's long filmography?"

"Right!" Charlotte nodded. "Yes!" She turned to Kate. "I remember *Divine Friends* coming out. So excited. I got the DVD and watched it ten times on my laptop in my bedroom."

"Did you now?" Millie said, with innuendo.

"What?"

"Watching it in the privacy of your bedroom?" Millie purred.

That was so typical of Millie, full of rude suggestion. It was aggravating, for Charlotte's sake, of course.

"Oh god, no." Charlotte put her hands up towards Kate. "Not like that. Honest." She turned back to her partner. "Millie, that's so naughty. There were no..." she lowered her voice, "...no sex scenes or anything."

Millie only grinned, damn her.

"It, it, it..." Charlotte took a breath to line up her words. "My mother didn't support me being gay. So, DVDs and my laptop were a lifeline to queer media growing up."

"I understand," Kate said with a generous smile.

Perhaps Kate was practised at handling reactions to her work, but Olivia swore she was genuinely at ease, and she wasn't often wrong.

"You're making me feel old though," Kate added.

"But," Charlotte wrinkled her nose, "you're only a few years older than us?"

"I started out young, I suppose. That was my," Kate gazed at the ceiling, recalling, "I think tenth major film at twenty years old." She shrugged. "Seems like I was older, because that's the first time I met my wife."

Charlotte nodded along to Kate's response. Then the penny must have dropped, because the nodding slowed with realisation.

"Did you...?"

Charlotte stared at Kate with an open mouth. Then at Olivia.

She knew exactly what Charlotte was asking but wanted no part in this conversation.

"Olivia's handling the divorce with my wife." Kate clarified.

You could see the cogs turning, the realisation clicking into place. It didn't take someone as observant as Olivia to spot that this was momentous for Charlotte.

"Oh," Millie said, getting there quicker. She circled a finger in the air. "So, we didn't realise about the one-hundred-percent sapphic nature of this gathering yet?"

There were calculations and machinations behind Millie's gaze. This was not good. And the delight in Charlotte's face grew colossal.

"You're... You're queer?!" Charlotte said.

"Queer as fuck," Kate replied.

Could Charlotte's grin get any bigger? Olivia wanted to close her eyes, but she daren't miss what unravelled in front of her.

"Goodness," Charlotte spluttered. "I mean, I'm such a fan of your films, but...Oh my god..."

Charlotte stared at Olivia with rampant enthusiasm. Anyone could tell what she thought. Olivia raised an eyebrow that could kill, or at least clearly told her friend to stop looking at her.

But Charlotte didn't notice, or failed to rein in her thoughts, because out popped, "I cannot tell you how much that film meant to some lesbians."

And the way she stared at Olivia implied which ones.

"So many lesbians I know."

Gah.

"I mean, we *adore* that film."

For the love of god, please stop looking at her.

"And it means even more now. Because we thought...You're...Wow." Charlotte sighed, then stared at Olivia. Again.

"Thank you," came at last from Kate, her voice a wave of calmness. "That's really lovely to hear. It meant a lot to make that film and play someone queer, and it's always incredible to hear when it helped someone else."

And Charlotte beamed so much it snuffed out her words.

Would that be the end of it? Would Olivia's admiration stay private?

But at least Charlotte got to say it. Thank you for the representation, when there'd been almost none. Fondness glowed in her belly again. Knowing more about the actor only increased her respect for her work, and she appreciated the personal cost for Kate behind the scenes now too.

"Can I ask you about when you made *The Ocean*?" Charlotte moved on with her questions.

And Kate generously answered, the two leaning together over the table in conversation.

Millie's gaze didn't leave Olivia though. While Kate and Charlotte chatted about movies and current projects, Millie's scrutiny remained unrelenting, and Olivia flicked through a museum pamphlet to avoid engaging.

After coffee, they managed to tear Charlotte away from Kate. For someone who took time to get going, Charlotte had gathered momentum. But Kate wore a genuine smile when they said goodbye outside the St Giles entrance, Kate leaving to return a missed call.

"Queer then," Millie said with suggestion, as they ambled towards the town centre. "Who knew?"

"Indeed," Olivia replied. She itched to watch Kate walking in the other direction to Park Town.

"Did you?" Millie asked.

"No," Olivia replied curtly. "Not before the second appointment."

"And you didn't tell Charlotte you were representing one of her favourite actors?" Millie narrowed her eyes.

"Respecting client confidentiality, as you can appreciate Millie."

As an ex-lawyer she should.

Millie's tongue stuck out as she licked her lips. She stopped, shifted her weight to one side, and put her hands on her hips.

"I admire your restraint, Olivia," Millie said with a ridiculous smirk.

She was ignoring that and prayed Millie hadn't guessed her film habit. Because the blond would handle that admiration in the crudest way. And this was already trampling over boundaries and throwing the contents of Olivia's tidy boxes up in the air.

Millie mused. "She seems very happy for a divorcee."

Now what did that mean?

"And hanging out with her lawyer is *very* friendly."

That was too far.

"That's grossly inappropriate," Olivia hissed.

She wouldn't tolerate that kind of gossip. Client relationships were forbidden, and she had her reputation as a lawyer to protect. And she'd be mortified if Kate overheard the suggestion. As if Kate Laurence noticed Olivia beyond politeness and her role as a solicitor.

"What are you two talking about?" Charlotte said, waking up from distraction on her own.

"Nothing," Olivia snapped.

"Nothing," Millie said airily.

It reminded Olivia of a past realisation between them. Again, with Charlotte oblivious in the middle. Olivia narrowed her eyes back at Millie, wondering if she was getting back at her.

"I won't say a word," Millie sang.

"Because there's nothing to say."

"Of course." Millie grinned. "Doesn't mean I won't enjoy this though."

That smile – naughty, wicked – and Olivia had to admit, she probably deserved some comeback from Millie.

The trouble was, she'd been thinking about how good Kate looked, so much better and healthier than when she'd first walked into her office. And how engaging she was as a real person, from their own to-and-fro, but also when she chatted with her best friend.

And that sometimes, while Charlotte and Kate chatted, she'd found Kate regarding her.

She'd caught it before, that intelligent sparkle in the actor's eyes on screen. But in real life, she couldn't tell what went through her mind.

"I can't believe we met *the* Kate Laurence," Charlotte sighed. "And she's your client!"

Charlotte grabbed her arm in excitement, and she was too stunned to flinch.

"She's so nice!" Charlotte beamed. "And down to earth, and respectful, interesting, observant, insightful. And my goodness, she looked good today."

"Yes, she's," Olivia stumbled over her words for once, "very agreeable," she conceded.

And she did agree with all those things Charlotte said and had more compliments too. Because the actress had so many intriguing sides to her.

She glanced over her shoulder. Then her heart tumbled over the misstep, because she found Kate looking back.

Well, that was unfortunate. And unprofessional. Some reorganisation of those compartments was due. Then she couldn't help herself and peeked over her shoulder again.

Dammit. Still looking.

17

The child stared at her.

Olivia wondered who was more unnerved, her or the girl. They sat on either side of her desk, both sitting properly, Kate having stepped outside the office to take an insistent call.

While Kate dressed in a casual style, in shirt, jeans and tan boots, her daughter was impeccable with neat blonde hair, a dark pink dress and patent leather shoes in which you could check your reflection. The slightest speck of dust spoiled the shiny left shoe, and the child reached forward and brushed it off with small fingers, finesse only tempered a little by childhood clumsiness. Then she sat up and stared at Olivia again.

Kate mentioned that her daughter, Bea, was five in September. But something in the child's eye suggested somewhere between fifteen and fifty.

Olivia opened her mouth and, in a rare failing, said nothing.

She peeked at the tote bag of books, drawing paper and soft toy on the floor. Kate had left it for Bea to play with.

Should Olivia suggest that and encourage the girl?

Although normally her greatest fear with children was the loud wailing, and not knowing which of tired, hungry or missing mum ailed them, she had the impression the child might disapprove. And she had no idea what to do with that.

So instead, Olivia said, "One moment please," and picked up the phone. "Charlotte, could you come to my office?" and she ended the call.

As she rose from her desk, the child watched her every move. She paused. "I will be back presently," and, after no comment from Bea, continued her saunter to the door.

She opened it to find Charlotte loping towards her and scooping a wave of hair over her shoulder. Millie followed a step and a bound behind, hips swaying and blonde curls bouncing. The two were so inseparable, Millie sometimes called in for lunch.

"Sounded urgent," said Charlotte, as she wiped a lunchtime crumb from her mouth. "What's up?"

"I have an issue in my office," Olivia said, and gestured into her room.

Charlotte and Millie poked their heads round the doorway, then turned back to her with huge grins.

"Well, well, well," Millie said, bustling up. "The mighty Olivia Sachdeva defeated and calling for reinforcements in the face of what looks like a four-year-old."

"She's nearly five," Olivia said. Then mentally tutted at how pathetic that sounded and braced herself for what was coming.

"Watch out, Charlotte." Millie grinned. "Do not underestimate the issue. The girl is nearly five."

Charlotte smiled at Millie before saying, "Is she Kate's daughter? Is she around?"

"She had to take a call. And I have no idea how to interact with the child." She gestured into the room.

Charlotte and Millie gazed at her, the former with kind indulgence, the latter with hand on hip.

"Well, I'm not good with children," Olivia added.

People like Charlotte might not mind being pawed and crawled over by random children, but it was most unnatural for Olivia.

"Have you tried using her name?" Millie suggested. "That might help you relate to her, rather than referring to 'the child'."

"I believe she's called Beatrice but responds to Bea."

"You make her sound like a pet," Millie said. "I hope you didn't play fetch."

"No, I didn't. But is that worth a try?"

Millie stared at her. "Are you serious?"

"Maybe a little?" She shrugged.

Millie stared again. "Do you really not have any experience with kids?"

"Of course I do. I was thirteen when my mother gave birth to my brother."

"And how did you find that?"

"He was very annoying."

Millie threw back her head with laughter.

And he was noisy and aggravating. Especially when she'd been studying for GCSEs and A levels. And the hygiene. God, children were messy, if they were anything like her brother. She remembered his first four years as revolving around food, whether it was going in or coming out. Inevitably, all conversations about children turned scatological at some point, and that's when Olivia definitely wanted to be absent.

But with this one? She didn't know where to start.

"Well, this isn't helping," she said at last to Millie, who was having too much fun at her expense.

"But you're not hopeless with kids," Charlotte said more kindly. "When my sister dumped my niece and nephew on me, you had them laughing and doing chores. They had a brilliant time."

"It's easy to tap into highly competitive children. But I'm not sure what this one wants. She just stares at me rather disdainfully."

"Is it like looking in a mirror?" Millie said, tongue sticking out between smiling lips.

Olivia lifted an eyebrow. It came naturally and often when she interacted with Millie.

"Come on," Millie said. "Can't be that bad." And she took a step towards the door, then, "Wait!" She put her arm out to prevent them following. "Did the mother say if she bites?"

"Oh," Olivia halted. She peered into the room at the small child in the large leather seat. "She didn't mention it. Do you think it likely?"

She looked at Millie. Millie looked at her from beneath eyebrows.

"Oh. You're joking," Olivia realised, and she drew herself up and stroked flat a non-existent crease in her dress.

"Yes, I'm joking." And Millie tutted before she bustled into the office, squatted on the floor in her tight jeans, crossed her legs and beamed up at the girl.

"Hello, I'm Millie," she said.

The girl stared.

"Are you looking at my curls?" Millie asked, shaking her head so the short waves spun.

The child, Bea, seemed mesmerised and reached out. See, this was the thing with children, no sense of personal space.

Bea paused.

"It's OK," Millie said, "you can feel how soft they are, if you want. Some people wouldn't want it, but I don't mind."

Of course, Millie would be at ease with kids, and of course, the child was grabbing handfuls of hair and letting it fall through her fingers in fascination.

Charlotte gazed at them, a soppy smile on her lips.

"Don't say you're going soft on children," Olivia said, giving Charlotte a gentle nudge.

"Me?" Charlotte turned to Olivia, the smile for Millie still making her expression silly. "No, my niece and nephew put me off for life."

But the smile rose again on her friend's cheeks, always with adoration when Charlotte gazed at Millie.

"Now, you know who's amazing at reading stories." Millie's voice reached them. She flicked through a picture book. "That lady over there." And Millie returned the same loving glance to Charlotte.

"She does all the voices. And look," Millie pointed at an illustration, "there's a wicked queen in this one. We'll get Olivia to read that part." And she grinned at her.

Olivia raised an eyebrow. "Very well," she said, inhaling through her nostrils.

And Millie grinned wider.

***

"Eddie, I've got to go," Kate said, glancing up the stairs again. They'd taken almost the whole appointment when she was supposed to be approving her financial agreement.

"Bye for now, darling," her agent rang off.

And Kate pocketed her phone in her jacket and launched up the steps. Just when she'd dispelled the flaky actor image with her lawyer, then this happens.

She'd glimpsed respect in Olivia Sachdeva at the museum. And when Olivia said she admired her professionalism and regard for other actors she'd been so surprised and flattered she needed every acting skill to suppress a blush.

She liked having her lawyer's respect. In fact, it made her giddy, for the first time in a long while.

Then today, she'd rolled up to her appointment with Bea on her hip and a bag full of kids' stuff on her shoulder. Bea had been clingy after the weekend away and sometimes you needed to relent and give Bea a break; one step back so they could take two steps forward tomorrow. Olivia had blinked in that slow way, where she took it in her stride, but wasn't exactly approving.

And after Kate had weathered that, her bloody agent rang in the middle of the appointment, five times. Kate had to leave the room and talk him down from wanting to sue someone for what someone else said about Kate and her agent. She assumed it should be the other way round. But Kate had sorted the matter, and the situation was now in the orange rather than deep red.

How were Bea and Olivia handling things? She'd left Bea with a book, paper and pencils and a frosty lawyer. She wasn't sure who'd handle things worse.

She rounded the corner to Olivia Sachdeva's office and inhaled to say, "I'm really sorry about the interruption–"

But she froze in the doorway, her mouth open and words snatched away by the sight that greeted her.

Her very particular, really quite grumpy – there was no way to avoid acknowledging this even though she adored her tot – daughter was happily sitting on Charlotte's knee. Bea's face was a picture of contentment. Millie sat on the floor, while Bea pawed her head and curls and looked at the book Charlotte held between them. And Olivia sat, elegant as ever, in a black dress on a seat beside them.

"You fools," Olivia said in character. "You'll regret this."

Kate covered her mouth to silence a laugh.

"The end," Charlotte said, shutting the book. She grinned at Bea, whose eyes sparkled back.

So, this is what suited her daughter. Not bubbly, soft nursery folk who were there with a song and cuddle all day long. But lawyers.

Kate watched, stunned.

"I'm not a fan of the ending," Olivia said, her curtain of black hair swishing along her jawline as she turned her head with sharp disapproval.

"Well," Charlotte considered. "The villagers had a point. She wasn't exactly patient with them."

"I think she's misunderstood," Olivia continued. "If they'd listened to her in the first place, they wouldn't be in such a mess."

Bea frowned, giving the conversation some thought, and flicked through the book to look at the illustrations.

"What do you think, Bea?" Olivia said, and Kate had to restrain herself at her lawyer's matter of fact tone with Bea, as if she were another adult.

She must have caught Charlotte's attention, who slipped Bea off her knee and onto the chair. The tall woman strode towards her, leaving Millie, Bea and Olivia with opinions around the book.

"Hi," Charlotte said quietly, beaming as she approached. She turned back to gaze at the trio as she stood next to Kate. "Your daughter is lovely."

That wasn't what people usually said about Bea.

"She sat on my knee, made herself comfortable, and we've read all the books from her bag."

Charlotte crossed her arms as she gazed at Millie, Bea and Olivia, who all still had opinions.

Kate felt the weight lift. God, it helped when people just went with it when it came to kids.

"Thank you for pitching in," she said. "Sorry if you've missed your lunch."

"No worries. Millie popped in with sandwiches and we'd finished anyway."

Charlotte's partner was clearly at ease with children too, peering into the book while Bea clung to her head and fistfuls of hair.

"Do you have kids?" Kate asked.

"Me? Us? No." Charlotte paused in thought. "Though Millie... No." She finished. Her mouth pulled into a flat smile.

Kate found it easy to warm to this woman. She was so transparent that Kate saw every feeling, and it encouraged quick trust towards her.

"It's complicated," Charlotte added needlessly. "And I've never wanted my own."

Kate had guessed at the private complexity. "They're not for everyone."

"I don't know how parents cope, to be honest," Charlotte said with wide-eyed disbelief. "I've only just got to grips with looking after me."

A distinctive alarm call went off from Charlotte's phone. Then another.

"Sorry," Charlotte said, tapping at the screen. "I have alarms and reminders for everything."

Kate recognised the app. "My son's friend with ADHD uses that. He says it's brilliant."

"Oh..." Charlotte's face fell and pink flushed on her cheeks. Her eyes darted away for a moment, before settling on Kate's with more confidence. "Turns out I have a few ADHD traits." She gave a reticent smile. "I think that's why I've taken so long getting to grips with adulting, or at least understanding how I work."

Kate nodded. "Makes sense."

A crinkle bothered at the top of Charlotte's nose. "Actually, I have a lot of ADHD traits," she admitted, breaking into a grin that Kate couldn't help returning, because her smiles did that.

"Millie suggested it and...err...I have other traits too. I never thought about having ADHD, because I'm not particularly hyperactive, but oh my god I'm inattentive." She shook her head. "I kind of always knew, and got frustrated with myself, but," she lifted her phone, "now I've got a better idea about my brain, I'm trying new strategies to help me keep on top of things."

"Do they help?"

Charlotte considered. "No, not very often," she said with open honesty, and they laughed.

"Sometimes though, thank goodness," Charlotte said, and they turned to the trio, who were rising from their seats.

It was funny, looking at them all. She was going to miss her lawyer in the airy, light building and the sure hand of Ms Sachdeva managing everything, right down to her grumpy child it seemed. With the glimpse of Olivia at the museum, and seeing her again with friends today, Kate wished she'd met them another way, so they could keep in touch.

Millie bounded over, then slowed into a sway and cosied up to Charlotte.

"Right, sweet cheeks, I need to get a shift on back to work."

"Me too," Charlotte replied. And there they were again, beaming at each other, like there was no-one else in the room.

Charlotte flinched as if remembering other people did exist. "Sorry. It was lovely to see you, Kate."

"See ya, Kate," Millie said, and they both floated out the room on a cloud of dopamine.

When she turned, Olivia and Bea were still seated, Olivia holding open the bag and Bea neatly inserting her books inside.

"This seems rather heavy," Olivia said. "Shall I give it to your mother to carry?"

Bea understood perfectly and nodded.

They stood in synchrony and strode towards Kate, Bea with her chin up and back straight as if emulating elegant Ms Sachdeva.

"I'm afraid we've overrun," Olivia said, handing over the bag.

"Sorry. My fault," Kate replied.

But Olivia didn't seem disapproving. She spoke formally as always, but her tone increasingly warm, more like their conversations at the Ashmolean than their early appointments. And her eyes just now, the way they regarded Kate, the subtlest of differences.

"I'm heavily booked, but I have a slot late Thursday. Do you want to come in then?" Olivia said, with a flicker of an eyebrow.

Kate liked these quivers her lawyer indulged when she talked, her body language such restrained elegance that these accents spoke volumes.

"Um," Kate started. Was she acting on her temptation to see Olivia and friends more? Maybe, but she said it anyway. "I'm going to sound a complete diva here, but could you come to me? I'm shooting that afternoon."

Olivia tilted her head.

"We're filming at the Botanic Gardens. I'm on set all day, which usually means waiting for hours between makeup and takes."

And she kind of hated that Olivia's opinion of her films was based on *Devolution*. She had this urge to impress her educated lawyer at this prestigious law firm. Perhaps erudite Olivia might be impressed by the Edwardian story she filmed instead.

"Do you fancy a peek behind the scenes?" She found herself tilting her head too, mirroring Olivia. "I could give you a tour?"

Her lawyer paused, like Kate had seen on two other occasions, as if her clever brain tussled with multiple problems. Then Kate realised she made assumptions. Movies might not be Olivia's thing, and film wasn't life to everyone.

"Sorry, if you're not interested in behind the scenes–"

"Yes," Olivia said quickly. Then she blinked as if she'd not meant the word to shoot out. "I'm able to come out to you," she added with her usual control, a hint of a smile surfacing. "I will add that to my schedule."

"Great," Kate said.

"Thank you for asking me," Olivia nodded.

"Looking forward to it." Kate couldn't stop grinning.

Was it relief that Olivia had accepted her friendly invitation? Yes, she'd overstepped the mark and was glad her lawyer didn't mind. But was there excitement too?

"I love sharing everything about film," she said to excuse her enthusiasm. "And I'd love to show you round. Tell me if you get bored though, because I can rabbit on all day about the story, the techniques, everything." She clasped her hand into her waist to stop it waving around.

Another pause from her perfect lawyer.

"I will," Olivia said softly. "Thank you again for the invitation."

"Great," Kate said.

She'd already said that.

"OK," she added for variety.

She reached for Bea's hand as much as a lifeline for herself as for Bea. "Come on, sweet pea," she said, turning for the door. Her daughter stared at her with confusion bumping her little forehead.

"Goodbye," Kate said, waving over her shoulder.

Was she nervous? God, this was silly. She needed to stop talking.

They turned down the bright stairwell. With every step, she fought the temptation to look back because her face would blaze if Ms Sachdeva caught her flustering over nerves. It was one thing to check along St Giles to the three friends by the museum, another to gaze back for approval from the singular Olivia.

"Tell me things, Bea," she squeezed her daughter's hand. "Tell me all about stuff."

Because she had butterflies.

18

Did Olivia need to see Kate in person? Did this last clarification warrant an appointment, especially when difficult to arrange given Kate's schedule?

No. Not at all.

Did she *want* to see Kate in person?

Olivia skipped past the issue, because it would be rude to turn down the invitation. And regardless of what Olivia said to Charlotte, behind-the-scenes filmmaking fascinated her.

Quicker than usual, in her neat slip-on trainers, black to match her dress, she marched past college buildings to the far end of High Street, slim briefcase at her side and alert for signs of filming at the Botanic Gardens.

A crowd gathered opposite Magdalen College and the chapel tower. The number of tourists had grown, now it was further into spring, and groups peeked over the hedges of the closed gardens. Security stood at the gates and at the head of the lane running down the side, filled with trailers and a bus.

She drew out ID, ready to say her name and business, and was waved through the iron railings and down into the garden entrance.

The chatter of tourists and students whizzing by on bikes faded as she descended towards the rich stone walls of the entrance, with its two grand wings and arched gateway in the centre. And there, under the arch, in a halo of evening sunshine and vibrant green garden in the background, stood Kate, as if she'd stepped out of the nineteen hundreds.

"Ms Sachdeva," the actor said, walking towards her, the generous length of her skirts flowing around her legs. "How delightful to see you." She'd tightened her voice up a class and back a century, the formal interplay underscored by her costume.

Olivia had to fight a beaming grin which wanted to mirror the actor's, because Kate smiled at her with the full works. Twinkling eyes with creases beside them, the extra curl to her lips, the mature shape of her cheeks, more sculpted and distinctive than on her teenage poster.

"Ms Woodhouse," Olivia nodded her head, "you look particularly fine this evening."

"Why thank you. You are most kind." Kate curtsied.

She stopped herself from blushing with a quick intake of breath. Kate had understood the play, but Olivia felt silly now. Inappropriate.

"Shall I escort you around the set?" Kate offered her arm with an ostentatious flourish.

And again, Olivia became caught up in the play. She blinked in the low sunlight that haloed the actor. She gazed at Kate's arm, fingers curled around a soft inviting cave, the pads beneath the fingertips a tender teardrop. Olivia reached forward, and the anticipation of touching those teardrops with her own smoothed the moment, like she moved through warm water. It was as if she watched a film vignette, but real sunshine burned her black dress, tantalising spring air kissed her cheeks and golden light surrounded the woman more vividly than ever.

"Sorry, Kate," a deep voice boomed.

Olivia twitched away her arm and into reality.

A man in shorts, with hairy legs, headset and tablet in his hand, rushed up. "We've fucked up the recording. We didn't get it."

"Sure," Kate said without hesitation.

But she didn't take her eyes off Olivia, and the moment lasted a fraction longer so that Olivia succumbed to its pull again.

"Sorry about this," Kate said gently, dropping back into her usual accent, although the smile and honeyed tones remained. "Happens a lot. Something always comes up. You OK to wait a few minutes?"

"Of course."

Should she stay here? And try to recover from the moment that slowed and oiled her body so perfectly she seemed ethereal.

"Come and see," Kate said, that best smile curling again.

And Olivia followed without thinking, the afterglow easing her into the garden like she floated on a cloud.

They filmed beyond the main walled garden, on a peaceful tip of the island, across the river from playing fields of the private school on one side and Christ Church Meadows on the other.

"Everything's still in place," the man said to Kate as they walked the central path. "It was the last closeup."

The pair looked incongruous, the man in shorts and trainers and Kate hitching her Edwardian dress from the ground. They stopped by a large stone urn on a pedestal, where a crowd gathered with cameras and sound equipment hovered above.

"Come closer," Kate murmured, beckoning to encourage Olivia to stand behind a camera operator.

She had a clear view. Kate took the place of a woman who'd stood by the urn and a man primped Kate's piled-high hair.

"It's good for continuity," another woman said from somewhere within the group.

Kate checked her feet, lining her toes along a line of scuffed sand on the path.

"OK, ready," she said.

Activity ceased, and a hush descended. Olivia's attention flicked between a screen closeup and Kate a couple of metres in front.

Kate's whole form changed. The strong shoulders rounded, her face fell into grief, and the shine in her eyes eclipsed, as if a cloud passed overhead.

She took a step forward and whispered, "Stop."

The single word pulled Olivia into the scene, an entire story in that line. Kate filled the syllable with helpless desperation, and her expression became a fading force that understood it was futile. Maybe Olivia was still caught in the intensity of her personal moment from before, but she believed Kate conjured this for everyone. Barely a few seconds of filming and Olivia knew she'd watch this movie over and over.

She stared at Kate, hooked by the emotions that gripped every muscle, and only when everyone shuffled and mingled, did she realise someone must have called "cut."

Then Kate met her eyes and transformed, filling up again and becoming herself, like the keen greeting at the gate.

"Remarkable," Olivia whispered.

"Isn't she!" the authoritative woman in front said. "Thank god some of us are professionals. Thanks, Kate. Double check it please."

Kate waited on her mark while Olivia gazed on, captivated by the woman and impressed by the professionalism of the actor.

It was fascinating seeing the preparation for filming, then the drop of magic, which was all Kate. That was the take. Olivia could sense it. She'd been immersed in the scene, the cameras faded away, with Kate exuding the character in a shift in body language and subtlest movement in her face. It didn't seem possible from the exhausted woman in Olivia's office. And she'd delivered the single line with deceptive simplicity, imbued with emotion while nuanced enough that it sounded real rather than performed.

At work on a film, her client, Ms Woodhouse, no Kate, was as phenomenal as Olivia could have ever imagined. And although she hadn't watched her films in weeks, this wouldn't spoil them.

"That's it," someone called. "Thanks everyone."

And Kate walked towards her, eyes sparkling again, the bow of her mouth sublime.

That smile. It caught in her chest. It was funny how Kate didn't have a typical movie star smile. It was too crooked and naughty, and her lips curled around it untrained, a perfection in its own way.

Olivia's heart went pitter patter, and a glow radiated. And that wouldn't do. That didn't belong in the real world. That was for evenings only, with delectable ice cream and fictional heroines when she relaxed without restraint. Not here. Not...

"Do you agree?" Kate said.

"Excuse me?" Olivia managed.

Kate laughed. "I wondered if you'd drifted off."

Olivia raised her eyebrow. "Ms Woodhouse. I do not drift."

Except she had. She so had.

***

Well, well, well. The behind-the-scenes tour entranced Ms Sachdeva. Kate smiled. Olivia was clearly hooked.

"How do you do that?" Olivia said with a shake of her head.

"What?" Although Kate knew. She absolutely caught Olivia immersed as she'd finished the take.

"Throw yourself into a role, like you blink and are someone else. And I was right there with you the moment before."

"Practice, understanding the character and wanting to make it real," Kate said, and she'd wanted it badly today in front of Olivia.

Olivia stood taller, eyes keen, while they strolled around the garden. They watched another scene being setup and blocked. And Kate revelled in her cool lawyer being impressed.

"I couldn't do it," Olivia said.

"I couldn't do your job."

Anxiety twinged in Kate's chest just thinking about the language of contracts and spreadsheets. "I don't know how you understand obscure words, and complicated finance, and manage all that in a human context."

Concern pinched Olivia's forehead.

"I missed out on uni," Kate explained. "I didn't pass many GCSEs or A levels. Filming commitments were partly to blame, but I get insecure about it sometimes."

Particularly when shamed by directors for not having an English literature degree to prepare for prestigious roles. And why she'd never done Shakespeare again, after some reviewers used it as an excuse to sink their teeth into her early classic portrayal.

"I didn't know that," Olivia said. "I can only say that I find you highly articulate and perspicacious."

Kate laughed. "OK, I read pretty widely, but I have to guess the meaning of perspicacious."

Olivia nodded, "I didn't mean to be grandiloquent or imply–"

"Grandiloquent you say?"

And Olivia's eyes flashed, amused at being caught out again. She was about to respond when her attention caught on something else. "Is that...?" Kate followed Olivia's gaze. "Emma Richardson?"

Now was that admiration, at the grande dame of British cinema?

"Yes, it is," Kate said. Amusement tickled inside.

Olivia's cheeks flushed. "Does this ever feel normal for you? I deal with well-known clients, but being surrounded by celebrities, is that your daily life?"

"They're simply colleagues after a while, especially on set. There's a lot of waiting around, then bursts of filming. And Emma and I have worked on several films together."

Olivia nodded while gazing towards Emma across the garden. "Like *Finding Fossils*."

Oh. Now that was a succulent little detail from Olivia. Kate bit her lip to hold back a smile. So, her lawyer had seen more than the disastrous *Devolution*. Perhaps she'd watched it for the historical story and actors like Emma, but it still thrilled, seeing polite, imperious Olivia Sachdeva wide-eyed with interest.

"Do you want to say hi?"

"God no," Olivia snapped. And the curt disapproval made Kate laugh.

"Why not?"

Olivia stopped and looked at her. "I don't want her to be disappointing."

"But she's nice."

"I enjoy her films, but knowing the personality behind the performance might spoil them."

Kate paused. "Hinders the suspension of disbelief?"

"Exactly." Olivia seemed pleased that she understood. "Is it the same for you?"

"Kind of." Kate considered. "But I don't get lost in films often. I get distracted looking for tips, or by an actor's technique, or wish they'd edited the film differently. So many things. But I do understand not wanting to spoil the experience by seeing the reality behind the camera."

"Besides," Olivia added. "After a day of work, I'm not keen on meeting new people."

Kate lifted her chin in question.

"Or anyone, if you must know."

Kate laughed. She'd kind of guessed this about Olivia already. "Is it the fear of finding them disappointing?" she asked.

Olivia pondered a moment. "More the actuality."

Kate laughed louder at her lawyer's bluntness. "So, you find people disappointing in general?"

Olivia inhaled. "Yes, immensely."

"And more specifically, say, with actors?"

Olivia looked at her, as if Kate shouldn't press. "My experience has mixed results."

"Should..." Kate began, failing to resist this nugget of information, "should I take that as a compliment, Ms Sachdeva?"

"If my opinion means something to you, then yes, Ms Woodhouse."

"OK." Kate smiled, and they carried on walking. "OK," she said again.

She didn't push. Because though the compliment was careful, she liked it coming from Olivia. She liked it a lot.

And although Olivia's limited patience for people was exhausted, her fascination with scene setup, cameras, lighting, explanations of post-production, makeup and wardrobe seemed endless.

They watched Emma film a scene outside the rose cottage, Olivia rapt, and Kate trying to rein in her smile at Olivia's awe. She hadn't been this excited about work in a long time, with the divorce and being downright bloody tired. But showing Olivia around reminded her how much she still loved this business.

Olivia's intense interest never wavered, attention captive the whole time, and Kate kept telling her more, just to keep her company.

They moved on when the director called the final take on Emma, before the older actress had a chance to approach. When Olivia turned away, Emma threw Kate a quizzical glance, followed by a salacious look up and down at the lawyer over her glasses.

"Stop it!" Kate mouthed at Emma over her shoulder, and she hustled Olivia away.

They were both beaming when they walked out of the garden-wall side gates towards Kate's trailer in the lane.

"I have a couple of hours before I'm due in wardrobe for the night shoot," Kate said, climbing the steps into her small trailer. "Should we finish the agreement?"

There was a pause, and Kate turned. Close by, Olivia regarded her with a radiance still lingering in her eyes from the tour.

"I wondered," Olivia said, quietly, "how much have you seen of Oxford?"

"Hardly anything, apart from the day I met you."

"Would...?" A pause. "Would you like a look behind the scenes by river?"

"I...Yes? Now?"

"A small diversion? To repay you for your tour behind the camera?"

There was an excitement wound up in Olivia's elegant stance, always the composed deportment, but sprung tight right now.

"OK?" How could she refuse when Olivia's deep brown eyes shone so keen.

Olivia turned to go. "Meet me by the greenhouse bank. I'll be a few minutes."

"Wait a sec." Kate said. "Could you?" She pointed over her shoulder at the buttons down her dress. "Save me getting the wardrobe guys out?"

She turned her back, tilted her head forward and bared her neck while she leant on the makeup table.

There was a pause, and the silence thickened with expectation.

"Of course," Olivia whispered.

And the atmosphere thickened again as Olivia stood behind, the closeness of her body landing like a warm shadow. It lingered, vivid yet not touching, and Kate wondered if her fine neck hairs standing in anticipation were obvious.

Seconds passed before the top of her dress gently tugged. Olivia must have attempted the top button without touching her skin. She pulled, but it didn't give.

"Sorry... I'll need to hold the neck of your dress," Olivia said quietly, and Kate would have given anything to see her face.

Soft fingers stroked inside the hem, and Kate closed her eyes to the sensation between her shoulders. Such a small contact, but it touched her whole body. Loop after loop, fingers circled down her back, a light touch every time, before the rouleau loops gave over pearl buttons, the suggestive movement trailing lower.

"There," Olivia whispered. "There," gentler again. And the warm shadow dissipated, leaving Kate's back cool. "I think you can reach it from there."

"Thank you," Kate murmured. "I'll...erm, just be a minute."

"Meet you by the river."

Olivia's footsteps on the gravel receded. Kate stood a moment, breaths deep and slow, wanting to luxuriate in the sensation a little longer, Olivia's residual touch tender and lovely.

Had she made Olivia uncomfortable? Should she apologise to her self-contained and restrained lawyer, whose handshake was the fleeting limit of physicality.

Kate was used to her body being the landscape of someone else, makeup smearing her face, wardrobe prodding and squeezing, her lips devoured by other actors. But Olivia carefully unfastening her dress felt personal. It hadn't been the everyday push and shove of the profession.

But it would be awkward if she made a big deal of it.

She shrugged the nagging issue away to get changed, while her back still hummed with intimacy.

19

Where had Olivia got to?

Kate waited on the path by the glasshouses and threw a light canvas jacket around her shoulders. She ran her fingers through her hair and teased it from its Edwardian styling.

The setting sun, low in the spring sky, bathed her in rays and lit up the river as a shining gold ribbon. Upstream, below the stonework of Magdalen Bridge, a man tied a raft of punts away for the evening, the long, low, rectangular boats clunking together. Downstream into playing fields and meadows remained quiet.

Water stirring caught her attention and Olivia glided into view from beneath a white wooden bridge across another tendril of river. Clear of the ornate crossing, she stood from her crouching position at the back of a punt. She dropped a long pole in the river until it hit the bed, pushed against it to propel the boat forward under her feet, then let the pole trail in the waters like a rudder.

Her slim arms tensed as she moved the boat. The outline of muscle rippled clear and appealing as she handled the heavy pole, with water running down her arms and dripping from her fingers. Kate hadn't appreciated the athleticism of the woman before. Her apparent strength, the balance on the boat, her elegance in a black dress and neat trainers. And Kate stared at a loss for words.

Olivia cut a circle in the stream, sending ripples spiralling, and brought the punt to line up against the wall, perfectly executed, of course. Lightly travelling the bottom of the boat to a platform at the front, Olivia trapped the punt between pole and wall, and stretched her fingers towards Kate.

She'd been tempted to apologise for asking for help with her dress. But, floored by this appearance, she stayed quiet.

"Would you like to go on the water?" Olivia asked. Her expression held polite appeal, excitement and the reassurance of an expert, always with Olivia. And perhaps worry that Kate might say no?

Kate only hesitated because her cheeks flushed, and it wasn't from the evening sunset.

She laughed and sat on the wall, her feet dangling over the water.

"Sorry, it's a bit of a drop," she said. It was nothing to do with the drop. All about wanting to stop glowing so damn much.

"To be fair," Olivia replied, "it's higher than I remembered."

"Where did you get the boat?" Kate said stalling.

Rows of punts floated below Magdalen Bridge further up the river, but the trader had gone for the day. She met Olivia's gaze. "You didn't steal this, did you?"

Olivia raised an eyebrow, although her mouth curved and said she was nowhere near serious. "I'm sure you appreciate my respect for laws. No, I borrowed one from my old college. I had a quiet chat with the porter."

"Did that involve bending the rules a little?"

"No comment," Olivia said.

And Kate laughed.

She liked this side of her lawyer. Olivia was aware of exactly who she was and was humorous with it. Someone's ability to laugh at themself was a quality Kate always fell for. Having self-respect, but with that release of not taking themselves too seriously. Harry had it. Charlotte had it. And though more considered than those two, so did elegant Olivia. And it struck her that Nat didn't. She laughed plenty, but only at others.

She stared at Olivia's outstretched hand. Should she be thinking about the potential fall into the river, or about what she was even doing here, or why she'd invited Olivia this evening? But she didn't want to.

She took the hand. The coolness of water on Olivia's fingers shocked. As did the squeeze and surprising strength afterwards, followed by warmth as they held onto to each other – like comfort and fire at the same time.

The boat wobbled beneath her feet, and she dropped into a crouch. The thrill didn't sober her or hide that she was more agitated than Olivia.

"Come and sit down," Olivia murmured, kneeling with her face close to Kate's.

Kate sat back in the boat's bottom on a set of cushions and leant against a partition. She didn't want to meet Olivia's eyes, because she hadn't felt this flustered in a long time. She shuffled the cushions, and waited for her confusion to settle, before breathing in deep and turning back to elegant Ms Sachdeva, tall and slim in her dress and standing ready to go.

Her breath caught again. "Don't you, erm," she pointed behind, "stand on this platform?"

Olivia pushed them away from the wall and downstream into meadows. The punt glided into the middle of the water, with not a flicker of doubt or imbalance from Olivia.

"If you're in Cambridge, you stand on the platform," Olivia said.

"And?" Kate replied, puzzled.

Olivia looked at her. "We're not in Cambridge," she said drily.

Kate laughed. "Is there a reason apart from than that?"

"No."

"Really?"

"Honestly, people follow this rule more religiously than some acts of parliament. They get very tribal about it."

Kate smiled and licked her lips, wanting to work Olivia out. She never knew what to expect, although every discovery thrilled.

"And you?" she asked.

"I follow the rules."

"I expected nothing less."

Kate was pleasantly put in her place by the same authority Olivia showed in her office, when she was sure of herself but reassuring to others. It was sexy, Kate realised with another blush. That knife edge balance that said Olivia would call you out if you said something foolish. It had a frisson but safety to it, a sense that Olivia would do the right thing, and she trusted her as a lawyer and person.

Olivia watched her, obviously sure of herself, from the pressure down to her toes, the elegance of her stance, the surety of the steer and the unblinking focus on Kate's eyes.

Kate forced herself to keep looking, against a weight of reluctance and fear at what she felt.

"You know," she said, tilting up her chin, "you can be very intimidating sometimes, Ms Sachdeva."

Olivia didn't even blink. "I do know."

Kate laughed again. There it was, that confidence. Yes, she found it sexy.

"And so can you," Olivia added more gently.

And her gaze pulled at Kate inside. It shouldn't have done, not that strongly, but it did.

***

The unbuttoning of Kate's dress, parting the material to reveal the paleness beneath, taking in the smooth texture of her skin, the smell of hairspray or some product to keep her hair piled in the right style, but always with the essence of Kate vivid to Olivia who was sensitive to aromas – bad and too good.

Olivia pushed into the riverbed again and again. The cold water dripping from her hands, as she tugged the pole from the Cherwell, kept the memory at bay of her fingertips lightly brushing Kate's back. The sound of the water drowned out the blood thudding in her ears, as she recalled pearl buttons slipping through her fingers. And spring scents mixed with her memory of Kate's whole aura.

The actor reclined in the boat's bottom, white shirt lazily open at the top, one knee up in her loose jeans, the other leg straight on the cushions. Kate gazed up at the trees that shadowed the river with bright new leaves, the sun flickering through them. Then sometimes Kate turned to watch Olivia.

The evening was too present for her to dream about undressing Kate – the air whispering past her face, sun warm on her body, and the sound of the boat cutting through the water mingled with a couple's laughter in the distance.

"This is a treat," Kate said, eyes keen on Olivia's and a satisfied cat smile on her lips. "A rare one." She lay relaxed under the spell of the tranquil river and dropped her hand over the side to trail a finger through the water. "A little bit of peace," Kate sighed, "in between shooting, and divorce, and the kids."

Olivia stayed quiet, leaving her to enjoy the respite.

"Where are we though?" Kate asked.

"We're between college and school grounds. Christ Church Meadows are over there and," she turned, letting the punt drift, "across the playing fields, you can see St Hilda's."

This was the reason for their outing. She'd had the compulsion to show Kate something of her world, having seen hers.

"That's where I went to college. It was all women at the time."

"Of course, you'd choose an all-women's place." Kate smiled.

Olivia nodded. "Naturally." She couldn't help returning a small grin.

She remembered applying. Her mother had sat her down at the kitchen table, in the house they still owned in Iffley Village. Her kind mother. Because she did recognise Geeta as an extraordinary human being. It was just that Olivia was done with being mothered and Geeta could never quite stop and treat her as an independent person. She knew this. Her mother knew this. And yet they were stuck in this rut, unable to resolve it and move on.

Olivia had been working hard at school, and Geeta was worried, which was mortifying.

"You don't have to score the top mark every time," Geeta tried to reassure her. "Have a break from studying sometimes. You don't actually have to go to university. Something else might appeal to you. Be free to do anything you want."

And Geeta had gazed at her, despair flickering behind that kind smile. But Olivia wanted respect, not mothering. And back then, she wanted to go to Law School and nothing less than Oxford would make her happy.

"But I like scoring well," teenage Olivia had said. She genuinely enjoyed lessons, daily reading wasn't a chore and she looked forward to ending her day in a book.

"You're such a bright girl," Geeta had said, reaching out her arms but remembering to stop short of touching her. "You could do anything. Go anywhere," she implored and celebrated at the same time. Then she dropped her hands with a sigh. "But you want to study law."

Olivia had shrugged and rolled her eyes. "Yes." Because she'd been certain for years.

"OK," Geeta had said, beaming with acceptance, which irritated Olivia just as much.

Kate watched her with a smile and tilt of her head.

"You drifted," she said.

"Sorry. I was thinking of my parents when I went to college."

"Do you get on?"

"My father and I are very similar. He's a university department head and we love our jobs. We probably spend too much time at work. My mother is... Well, we're different more than anything else. I can see that."

"Do they support you being gay?"

"My mother couldn't be a bigger ally and wave the flag more proudly. I..." And again guilt gnawed at her. "Charlotte thinks I'm ungrateful and take my mother for granted. Because..."

Geeta hadn't batted an eyelid when Olivia put posters of Kate, and others, on the walls. Or voraciously read every sapphic novel she could get her hands on. Geeta even took her to watch a Pride march as a young teen. Her mother clapped and cheered the line of queers, while Olivia quietly observed, taking it all in, becoming comfortable with it, although she didn't quite see herself in the noisy parade.

"I realised so early, and she was so supportive, that coming out was largely academic. By the time I was sixteen and had a girlfriend, we both knew I was unequivocally a lesbian."

Kate sat up a little. "She sounds amazing."

"How about you? Are your parents supportive? Did they always know you were bi?"

"They didn't blink. They're theatre types. Mum wanted to be an actress and taught drama. We always had industry folk running through the house, so I grew up surrounded by queers."

Something they had in common then, both completely at ease with their sexuality.

"We're both lucky," Kate said.

"Charlotte would agree. She says we should swap mothers, and I don't think she's joking either."

"Do Charlotte and your mother get on well?"

"Very well. And I enjoy talking to her mother, who is a King's Counsel barrister and phenomenally intelligent woman. She's been a source of advice for years."

Kate frowned a little. "Charlotte said her mother didn't support her being gay?"

The observation, and that Kate had remembered, took her by surprise.

"I think it's more complex than Charlotte says. I can't imagine Nicola being simplistic about anything."

"It sounds like you've known each other a long time."

"Yes."

Olivia was going to elaborate, but suddenly didn't want to, because it was complicated. "We've been friends since college," she said simply.

"And do your mothers get on well too? Are they friends?"

"Good god no."

She said it so vehemently that Kate laughed.

"They are," she tried to phrase it delicately, "prickly around each other."

"So, the warm and frosty dynamic doesn't work for them?"

"I don't think it's–" She stopped and narrowed her eyes. There was no doubt Kate thought of Charlotte as the warm one. She let the boat bump into the bank. "Did you just imply I was frosty?"

Kate's gaze didn't flinch. Her cheeks tensed, holding in amusement.

"I'm going to ignore that," Olivia said, lifting her chin and staring over Kate's head.

And Kate laughed out loud.

She pushed on, then met Kate's eyes again, because she liked the gentle tease from her. And because Olivia knew how she came across.

She smiled, with the low sun glinting through the trees. Because this was the most pleasant evening, with Kate lying in the bottom of the punt, hair cascading, arms behind her head, shirt open a little.

Her heart beat stronger, and Olivia was aware of not feeling frosty at all.

20

"Someone's happy."

Kate twitched to find Emma's reflection looking at hers in the makeup trailer mirror.

"Hmm?" Kate replied.

Emma drew back her chin and looked over her glasses. "Someone's glowing in fact."

Kate folded her arms and gave the older actor's reflection a stern stare. "What are you implying?"

"Nothing." Emma chuckled and pouted to put on lipstick.

Because nobody put lipstick on Emma; one of the things you could insist on when you'd been top of your industry for several decades. But Kate had starred in too many films together to be as overawed as the makeup artist.

"Like fuck, it's nothing," she said.

Emma's gaze flicked between her own smirking reflection and Kate's. "You've got a spark," she said with popping lips.

"A spark?" Kate mocked.

"Yes, dear. You've been dead behind the eyes for months, but the glimmer's back."

"What?!" Kate said, stretching said lifeless eyes wide.

Emma shrugged.

"Jesus," Kate's voice leaped up an octave. "I've been borderline bloody depressed."

"Well..." Emma considered a moment, "yes to that too."

"A little sensitivity wouldn't go amiss."

Emma turned in her chair to face her properly. "Would you like a hug?" she said in a mock mumsy voice. She stretched out her arms, fingers beckoning.

"I'm not asking for that."

"Would you like a hug," Emma looked over her glasses, "with your lawyer?"

"You–" She tutted and spun round. "You bugger."

Emma cackled and her face wrinkled into a hundred naughty wrinkles, proof she'd been teasing Kate for decades.

"No. I..."

She tripped over her words, because the image of her elegant lawyer stretching out to help her from the boat played in her head: soft hand holding hers, leaping onto the grassy bank beside her in the sunset, and the vivid wish that Olivia would hold her body against hers.

"Shit," she spat. "Yes, I'd like a hug with my lawyer."

"I knew it!" Emma shot her fists in the air with an enormous grin.

"Dammit." Kate covered her face, then swore again because she'd smudged her cheeks, and makeup would have a fit.

What on earth was she doing?

She inhaled. "I've got a bit of a crush," she said. "A tiny, silly crush."

Yes, she finally succumbed to Olivia Sachdeva's fine eyes, and haughty manner, and luscious eyelashes. She'd never admit this to Maria though, who'd recommended Olivia.

"Well, it's nice that you're smitten with someone else." Emma smiled. "You've been bouncing between Nat and Harry for too long."

"Harry and I were done at accidental-pregnancy thirteen years ago."

"Really?"

"More or less."

"The second child says 'more'."

"The second child...Bea was..." This was a lot of detail. "...via donation."

"Good lord. I didn't know that."

"I wanted another baby before Ralph got older. Nat never stayed around, so Harry and I settled into co-parenting."

"Then Nat turns up again and throws everything in the air."

"Yes." She closed her eyes.

She knew it then. She knew it ten years before. And she knew it right at the start. But sometimes you had to go through it all, to truly believe it was never, ever going to work. Thank god, she was there now. Nearly there, she reminded herself. This divorce wasn't over yet.

"Anyway," she said, gazing at the foundation she'd rubbed onto her fingertips. "Just a crush."

"Are you sure?" Emma said, nudging her. "Nothing else?"

"Yes," she said, firmer. "We're completely unsuited."

"You looked a fine couple to me."

"Stop it." Kate threw her a pissed off glance, but her mouth insisted on smiling.

"Why?"

"Because it's not respectful to Olivia. She's..." Kate breathed in. "She's intellectual, restrained," undeniably part of the attraction, "and," very importantly, "has no interest in children whatsoever. And they are my life. So there."

"Really?"

"Honestly, I think she'd insist Bea sign a contract before playing a board game. It's that level of interaction."

"Hmm." Emma nodded in consideration.

"And there's no getting away from: she's my lawyer."

"Your divorce lawyer."

"My frigging divorce lawyer."

What the hell was, whatever part of her, thinking. Body, mind, soul. She wasn't sure which was lighting up for Ms Sachdeva. Maybe the woman appealed to them all.

"But you do like her?" Emma said more seriously.

"It's a tiny crush," Kate said emphatically again. "It's bound to happen sometimes. Doesn't mean I'm looking for anyone. And I don't have time for another fuckup of a relationship."

"Right," Emma said.

Because Kate was done. No more relationships. She and Nat were finally over, and she didn't want anyone until her kids were happy, well-balanced human beings, who'd left home and... Oh God, that was a long time.

It stretched out in her head. An age to go without flirting, stolen glances and moments to enjoy being herself, beyond work and being a mother.

She rubbed her hands together to get rid of the makeup. "Do you think...I mean..."

Emma smiled with gloating patience. "Spit it out."

"Do you think it's against some law to, you know, date a lawyer representing you?"

"Just out of interest?"

"Purely theoretical."

Emma's expression fell serious. "Actually, I imagine she'd lose her job and ability to practise."

Well, that was sobering. And reassuring that her crush couldn't lead anywhere, because another relationship was the last thing she needed.

"And of course," Kate added, "there's a flaw to your innuendo. Ms Sachdeva is the least easily impressed person I've ever met. She's not the slightest bit interested in an actor with four GCSEs."

Emma turned to her. "Ms Sachdeva is a red-blooded woman, and entranced by the face that launched a thousand sapphic memes. You seriously underestimate your allure."

"What?" Kate spluttered. "Now? With my mum bod?"

"Your curves have never been better." Emma slapped her thigh. "Besides, are we really talking about the Ms Sachdeva, who scampered away to return with a punt, and took you on a romantic trip along the Oxford tributaries at dusk?"

"I..." Emma had a point there. "She was being polite and showing me something in return for the film tour."

Emma looked at her.

"That was it." Kate nodded.

Emma still looked at her. "I haven't heard anything so delusional since you accepted a role on *Devolution*." She shook her head.

"Stop it." Kate slapped Emma's thigh in return.

"Such a god-awful film."

"Cult favourite, don't you know."

Emma peered over her glasses. "People watch that film to laugh at it."

"But they still watch it."

"You are not that desperate for approval."

"Bloody am."

Emma laughed, then sighed. "Aren't we all."

Kate leaned back when makeup came in, who tutted at them both for smudging their foundation, and at Emma for making a hash of her lips. Kate waved her apology, sat back and closed her eyes, while makeup rattled through a case at the back of the trailer.

"Fine," she said at last to Emma. "I admit I have a sizeable crush on my cold lawyer."

"Your hot, cold lawyer," Emma added.

Her clever, beautiful, increasingly charming lawyer.

She didn't deny it, because she'd spent too long watching Olivia guide them through the narrow rivers and under the trees, getting a little wet, but never less than elegant. Who could be frosty, but very human on the inside.

Every peek of Olivia tempted Kate to look more, and this evening revealed another tantalising layer of college and family. Kate felt privileged at the insight Olivia had shown her, which seemed personal and intimate.

It turned out, when you looked beneath the surface, that Olivia Sachdeva was spectacularly lovely. Especially in the twilight, when Olivia's beauty glowed, her eyes dark and lips accentuated, like Kate could feel her by simply looking. It made her want her, and fear wanting her at the same time, because she ached seeing someone that beautiful. And that hadn't happened to her in a long time.

21

A spring fog kissed Olivia's cheeks, as she clicked her heels through nighttime Jericho. Lights from café windows glowed into the mist, people darted into the warmth of pubs, and her footsteps echoed in the quiet street. She wore a black cape over her shoulders against the chill of fog and an evening dress beneath, also black but with a hint of darkest ruby as a concession to frivolity. She stretched a carnival mask over her head, teased her hair over the fine elastic and adjusted the velvety front piece – blood-red like her mood.

It was the weekend, much-needed recovery time from people, but instead she was here, in front of the portico of Freud's. Its grand ionic columns supported the entrance to the rectangular Greek revival building: once a church, now an arts café and bar. Worse, it was a private masquerade party for Hugo Bentley's sixtieth birthday, which meant the most egregious of events – a work social.

Hugo invited too many clients for her to relax this evening, as well as every solicitor in Bentley. And right now, climbing the pale golden steps, she was distracted too.

She hadn't finished reviewing the final statements with Kate, and several other issues nagged at her. Except work had flown straight from her mind when she watched Kate on set.

And in her trailer...Olivia paused. She remembered with overwhelming clarity the softness of Kate's neck on her fingertips, and the enticing glimpse beneath the material. She'd seen Kate undress in films, but this was real and vivid on all her senses. The sliver of naked back, the undulation of her spine, the patterns of her pale skin, tiny downy hair which Olivia craved to touch, even though they'd be too fine and beyond perceptible. She wanted to lean down and breathe on them, and she closed her eyes, because the memory of Kate's scent came to her instantly.

Stop it. That was nowhere near the line of appropriate.

She opened her eyes and forced her mind into gear. Olivia had to be perfect and attentive at a work event. She was in no position to behave unprofessionally, no matter how informal everyone else believed the evening. Not with who she was, and where she wanted to be. Richard might get away with too many drinks, but not her.

She waved her gold-embossed invitation at the attendant. As she stepped through the blue double doors and into the cavernous warm space, the fog that tingled like pin pricks turned humid on her cheeks. Strings of soft lights overhead lit the bar on the left and classic looped-back chairs and tables lined the edges of the room beneath shadowy stained-glass walls that held a faded elegance.

The centre of the floor and the apse at the far end were left clear for, she shuddered, dancing. How long could she avoid Hugo's friends pulling her into a mortifying clinch? She'd have to snag Charlotte for a dance, even though she'd tread on her toes.

The echoing chamber filled with chatter and music played in the background. Despite the event being a masquerade, she recognised Hugo in the middle of the throng – tall, in black-tie, a silver half-mask covering his eyes with greying fair hair above.

"When are you going to retire then, old man?" Another man slapped him on the back, an easily identified college friend of Hugo's. And Richard, ugh, laughed with them.

Charlotte was there, her luxurious mahogany waves unmistakable around an orange mask, and leaning down to hear what a curvy, short blond said. Olivia would have guessed Millie from the scarlet, from mask to pointed heels. And another white woman in a satin green dress and mask chatted with them – Hugo's daughter, who had organised the event.

And Liz. Thank god.

Warm inside the building, Olivia handed her cape to an attendant. She joined the office manager at the bar, who sat adjusting her black and grey curls around a gold mask.

"Good evening," Olivia sighed, coming alongside.

"What can I get you?" Liz said with a broad smile. "And then I have news," she purred. She shuffled closer, bending her head conspiratorially.

"Wine perhaps." She'd have only one.

"I'll get Champagne because Hugo's covering the bar." Liz grinned.

The bartender placed two tall flutes on the top and the pair clinked glasses before Liz crossed her arms and leaned on the counter. "Richard," she rolled the R, "is leaving."

"What?" Olivia peeked over her shoulder towards the loud braying in the middle of the room.

"Handed in his notice on Friday."

"Why now?" Olivia said, turning back to Liz.

Just when everyone was chivvying Hugo about retiring, she thought Richard would pounce.

"Timing," Liz said. "Hugo's mulling over stepping down, but Richard's nowhere near senior enough to jump into his shoes. I think he's betting elsewhere will be more lucrative. That and every partner turned down his offer of 'assistance'."

"What? No-one wanted his wonderful expertise that he offered to more highly qualified staff?"

Liz pursed her lips, but they curved in a smile. "Apparently not."

"Good," Olivia said. "Finally used up all his lives at Bentley."

"Off with the gloves tonight then?"

"I'm pleased for Charlotte," Olivia said. "No wonder she looks relaxed this evening." And she glanced over at her friend, who beamed like sunshine from the dance floor.

"Hugo's disappointed," Liz said. "He had some notion of preparing him long term for seniority."

Olivia had suspected as much.

"And although I'm fond of Hugo," Liz added, "he can't see past his own image when looking for a successor. Even one with as many failings as Richard."

She was glad Liz saw that too. Maybe her path to the top job was clear again, without upstart Richard. She took a small sip of dry bubbling Champagne.

Then she felt it. Perhaps something caught her eye that her mind failed to grasp. A movement. A sound. But awareness stole over her shoulders and tickled up her neck. She twitched her gaze over the crowd. Nothing.

But she knew what, who, she felt. She pushed the realisation down without saying her name, wanting to deny the increasing presence within her subconscious.

"I should do the rounds," she said to Liz.

She sauntered further into the building, fingers curled around her glass. She nodded to clients she recognised by face, stopped longer with those she knew better, all the while wanting to search the room.

"Good evening, Patrick," she said to one of the oldest clients, a friend of Hugo and private wealth client to another partner.

"Olivia, splendid to see you," he said, raising his glass. "I wanted to talk to you. A friend's in a spot of bother, a family matter."

She half-listened to his query, which angled for free legal advice, while she caught snippets and impressions from around the room. Richard moving on to a larger firm, London, more opportunity, bigger. Hugo sorry to see him leave. A burst of laughter as another partner entertained with family stories. The receptionist recommending hot nightspots.

The volume of the party rose, the temperature became hotter, the air thicker.

"I'll let him know, thank you," the old client said about her advice. "Always the expert on these matters."

She nodded. "You're welcome. Excuse me, I should talk to a few others."

"Of course."

She spun away, but only took one step before she stopped.

It may have been a moment, not even a second, that the crowd parted, a natural movement of the room so that a view opened. A black suit appeared, the flow of the trouser material and subtle sheen on the jacket lapels suggestive of quality. The crisp white shirt pristine. The loose bow tie descending over a curving chest. The hands relaxed in trouser pockets and weight confidently dropped on one hip. She wore a black mask around the eyes, but the golden hair, the curve of the lips, the shape of cheeks, everything about her figure was so visually familiar that it would always steal Olivia's attention. And Kate looked straight at her, as if the distance between them was nothing.

Olivia blinked, the space shifted, and Kate turned to Hugo who cut in to talk to her.

She breathed in. Ms Woodhouse in Edwardian costume was a remarkable and admirable actress. Kate in a tux? Another prospect entirely and absolutely compelling.

Olivia made for the bar and ordered another Champagne, just to stop herself from staring at Kate across a crowded room.

She sipped quickly, one after another, while she stared at blurred strings of lights and bottles behind the bar. As if this would slow her beating heart and take the heat from her cheeks.

"Evenin'." A voice sidled up in unmistakable, flirty, London tones.

She turned her head, not in the slightest surprised to find a short blond in a scarlet dress, arms crossed on the bar.

"Good evening, Millie," Olivia said, then nodded, "Charlotte," to her friend behind.

"Isn't this an amazing party?" Charlotte beamed. She raised her glass, probably sparkling water, but she still spilled a bit.

This evening was many things. Noisy, vexing, frustrating that she had to be here, yet nothing would pull her from the building while her attention sought Kate. Even now her back tingled, aware of her somewhere in the room.

"Kate's here," Millie said. Her eyes fluttered through her mask, making those two words horribly suggestive.

"I know." She sipped too quickly at her drink so that bubbles fizzed in her head and made her blink.

"She looks good," Millie said, drawing out the last word indecently.

"Really, Millie." She snapped her head round so fast, her hair spun. "Should you be noticing that kind of thing when you're with Charlotte?"

"She could wake the dead in that suit." Millie laughed. "Seriously, I bet long-gone lesbians are rising from the grave for Kate in that tux."

See, this is what bothered her about Millie. Always. Eyes wide for anyone attractive.

"That isn't respectful of Kate or Charlotte," she said in a harsh whisper, so it wouldn't carry beyond the group.

"The woman is indisputably hot."

Olivia glared at her. It was an embarrassment and beyond belief that Charlotte put up with talk like this. Wasn't she even slightly troubled?

"Charlotte!" Olivia despaired.

"Hmm?" Charlotte gazed at her with a blank expression.

"Well?"

Millie grinned. "I was telling Olivia how hot Kate looked this evening."

"Oh my god," Charlotte spun round, spilling her drink again. "Yes. Totally hot."

Olivia tutted. "That's not what I'm getting at."

Millie smirked and leaned back to Charlotte. "She's looking for your affirmation that I'm libidinous and disrespectful."

"Oh," Charlotte said. "Yes, Millie absolutely is, but Kate is drop-dead gorgeous."

For the love of god. "Will you two–"

What was the point? Charlotte gazed at Millie like she walked on water, and Millie undressed Charlotte with her eyes.

Millie rested her elbow on the bar. "Don't get your knickers in a twist, Olivia. You can still appreciate someone sexy and gorgeous without it detracting from the one you love."

"Can you?" Olivia growled.

It made no sense to her. Finding someone sexy took time to grow and was a powerful and personal connection, not something she could feel for many at the same time. Whereas Millie seemed to rub sexuality in people's faces, with her extravagant sensuality, her physicality and the intimate way she interacted with everyone. The woman could have won an Oxford Blue for flirting at college. She had others duped and intoxicated, and yes she meant Charlotte, with people all over her in a way alien and uncomfortable to Olivia.

"Kate is unequivocally sexy. Who on earth doesn't think so," Millie said. "Gorgeous face, fabulous figure, tits to die for."

It jarred as if a church bell crashed to the floor. Every sinew in Olivia's body tensed hard like cold steel, then clanged as if someone cracked her with a hammer.

"Must you do that?" Olivia said, her shoulders rigid and hands squeezed into fists. "Can you stop objectifying people, just for one minute?"

"What?" Millie curled up her lip. "Pretend we're not in a room full of tits, dicks, clits and messy orifices covered in posh rags?"

Again, it clanged in her head and crawled over her body. She closed her eyes and composed herself. Millie had a talent for turning things vulgar.

"Do you have to be so crude?" Olivia spat.

"Do you have to be so puritanical?" Millie chanted back.

Olivia growled, "I am not–"

"Oh, stop it, Olivia. We're different people. You do you and I'll do me," Millie shrugged, "so to speak."

Olivia's cheeks flamed.

"Seriously." Millie shrugged again. "We're never going to agree on this. Why try? I always noticed men across the room and jumped into bed at the drop of a hat. Whereas you need courtship starting in prehistory. I do not exaggerate."

Olivia breathed in, ready to counter.

"We're different in the way we speak," Millie rolled on, "feel, fall in love, and honestly, most of the time, it doesn't bloody matter. It's not like we're dating. God forbid."

But the thing was, they had to spend time together because of Charlotte. This had always been the trouble. And although they showed each other more understanding and patience than ever...

"We're still going to piss each other off sometimes. And I'm not going anywhere because Charlotte is my everything," Millie said, as if reading her thoughts. Because the woman missed nothing and was as bright as Olivia. She had no illusions about that. Millie Banks ran rings around them all.

"I will, however," Millie said, "apologise and rein it in about Kate."

Olivia glared at her, her mask probably hiding none of her fury. Because damn it, the woman had homed in on exactly why it annoyed her so much today. She didn't like Millie's gaze, no matter how she claimed it was superficial and meaningless, especially on Kate.

"It..." Olivia uncharacteristically stuttered. "It doesn't matter who it's about."

"Really?" Millie shook her head. "Like I said, sorry. I'll cut the crude crap about Kate."

"You're...you're delusional. How much have you had to drink?"

Millie stared at her. "I'm up to my eyeballs on paracetamol and stone cold sober."

22

Kate relaxed, hidden behind her mask.

Hugo and his daughter had introduced her to others as simply 'Kate, our neighbour', before she fell in with Charlotte and Millie anyway. It was the least on show she'd been in years.

She had intended turning down their invitation, planning a quiet evening in with Bea and Ralph. But as soon as Hugo said they had a child minder for his grandkids and a limitless supply of pizza, Ralph had dropped her and left her standing on the doorstep without an excuse. Even Bea skipped off without a glance back, and Kate wondered why she ever worried about spending enough time with her kids.

So, she came and planned one polite drink. Except she had another, and a third, because Olivia's presence lured from wherever she circled the room, and Kate didn't go home.

She spotted her, talking to the shorter curvy Millie. She should say hello then leave, because three drinks shouldn't mix with a crush. And because Olivia in an evening dress which wavered subtly between black and deep ruby and left her beautiful arms and long legs bare had an edge over office Olivia or even romantic-punting Olivia.

She should catch her now, while less dangerous with Millie there. But when she approached, Millie peeled away and left her no option but to talk to Olivia alone.

"Good evening, Ms Sachdeva," she said, quickly reverting to their playful style and grasping for safety in their old back and forth.

Olivia whipped round, eyes flashing beneath her mask. "Ms Woodhouse," she said, hand flying to hip and whole body emanating irritation. "Good evening."

Whoa. Firey Olivia.

"Sorry," Kate breathed out a laugh. "Am I disturbing you?"

"No more than anybody else this evening," Olivia said. Then relenting, "Probably less so."

Was that another polite compliment from the exceptional Ms Sachdeva?

"Ms Woodhouse," Olivia tilted her head. "You look..." The words died somewhere. Somewhere interesting. "I wasn't expecting to see you here."

"I look?"

Olivia raised an eyebrow. "You..." Again she hesitated. "You must be aware that you look good tonight."

Looking good was a complicated thing.

Yes, she'd liked her reflection before leaving for the party, hair dark and golden in the evening light, shapely in her tux, comfortable with the lines by her eyes. Didn't mean she wasn't flattered down to her bones that Olivia thought so.

She smiled, because while Olivia complimented her, she also seemed annoyed about it.

"You look good too," Kate said. Too good. "I hadn't planned on coming out this evening." She moved the conversation swiftly on, skating over how attractive Olivia was.

Olivia flashed another glare. "You just threw this on last minute?" She gestured down Kate's body.

"I wore it to a premiere once, and it was handy."

"Of course, you would happen to have a..." More gesturing.

"Yves Saint Laurent."

"...An Yves Saint Laurent tuxedo hanging about, ready for a party."

It did sound ridiculous now Olivia said, although Kate wasn't sure why she was so annoyed.

She paused, then simply said, "Yes."

The wind seemed to abate from hurricane Olivia and her hand dropped from her hip.

"I'm sorry," Olivia said at last. "You didn't deserve that. I'm taking out my irritation with someone else on you."

Kate bet on Millie in scarlet.

"Anyone in particular?" Those three drinks were too curious.

"Actually several." Olivia considered further. "In fact, almost everyone."

Kate laughed and found herself licking her lips. It was difficult not to be flattered by Olivia implying she was better company.

"Can I get you a drink?" Olivia asked more gently, with a hint of one of those delicious Ms Sachdeva smiles, rare and divine.

Kate should say no.

"Why not?" she heard.

Olivia passed a Champagne flute, pinching its stem so Kate had space to take it without their fingers touching. The coolness of the glass surprised, now she didn't find Olivia the coldest part of the room. That time had long gone.

The music had become louder and Kate stood closer so she didn't need to shout. And because she liked this privacy with Olivia.

"So, you're not a fan of social events, or just this one?" she asked.

Another curl of dark lips, and eyes still flashed with fire beneath the blood-red mask. "I think we've established that I'm not a fan of people in general."

"We have." Kate grinned and sipped the wine, the bubbles pleasant and making her heady. "So, how do you spend your weekends?"

"I read. Sometimes I work. Perhaps catch up with a friend or two. I do like company." She gazed at Kate. "The right company."

Kate leaned in, wanting to be the kind Olivia sought.

"And watch films, of course. I am a fan of cinema."

"But not actors," she quipped.

Olivia pursed her lips. "As you know, I try to avoid those, although it turns out some are very pleasant."

And a smile accompanied it, one of those delicious expressions that held pleasure and teased a little. Really, how had she ever thought of Olivia as cold.

"I'm glad to hear it," Kate said. And she couldn't hide her delight even if she tried.

A burst of laughter drew their attention to the centre of the room. Dancing had turned more raucous than the polite swaying at the beginning of the evening. The Bentley receptionist, Zain Ahmed, she always remembered a receptionist's name, was dipping and waving his shoulders, then patting his heart, to show an older woman the move.

"Liz, the practice manager," Olivia said, pointing with her raised glass, "and a good friend of mine."

Charlotte joined Liz and Zain in the middle of the room and attempted the moves too.

"How about you?" Kate asked. "Do you dance? Is that also part of your weekend?"

Because, even though her friends did, she wasn't surprised Olivia stayed refined on the sidelines.

She realised Olivia hadn't answered and turned from watching the trio having fun on the dance floor to Olivia, who looked decidedly unfun.

"Yes, I dance," Olivia said in a way that should have withered. Except Kate liked the edge now. And the fire in Olivia's eyes which flamed through the mask.

"Oh?" Kate said. She couldn't stop grinning.

"I took ballet for years as a child."

Kate could believe it, the way Olivia held herself with fluid elegance, back straight and head always centred.

"My misguided mother took me, in an attempt to make me comfortable with my body and around people physically."

"And did it help?"

"I always felt comfortable with my body." Olivia raised her chin. "I just didn't want other people touching it."

Kate laughed because Olivia said it with so much self-awareness and that dry sense of humour. Olivia also seemed pleased that she'd made her laugh.

"But actually, I loved dance," Olivia relented, taking a relaxed sip of her Champagne. "Ballet, bhangra, then Latin and ballroom at college."

"Really?" Kate said. "Isn't ballroom a lot of unnecessary touching?"

"But there are rules. I knew what to expect and I enjoyed refining the movement. There's a pleasure in perfecting a routine so that it flows."

The thought of pleasure from Olivia made butterflies circle.

"Did you dance with a woman? A girlfriend?" And those drinks were too curious.

"No, a man."

"Really? And how did you find that?"

"Adequate." Again the smile.

Kate spent too long gazing at those lips, and blushed when she found herself licking her own.

"And the touching?" she couldn't help asking.

"Respectful," Olivia said, then added, "He was very, very gay."

"And I suppose you were...?"

"Also very, very gay."

Kate laughed at Olivia's perfect deadpan delivery. She loved it, because it was so Olivia. That flawless smooth surface, with the occasional ripple disturbing with hints of what lay beneath. Deeper and deeper she wanted to see. She wondered, though, about polite waltzes between Olivia and a male equivalent, the steps of both impeccable, and whether she'd be the same with a woman.

"And you?" Olivia said. "Do you dance?"

Kate considered Olivia, and the answer. "A bit." She was reticent suddenly. "I had to learn a few sequences for a film."

"*The Ocean*."

Oh. That was a surprise.

"Yes, it was *The Ocean*." Her cheeks ached, trying to restrain her glee. And she couldn't help adding. "So, you have seen more of my films, other than those with Emma Richardson and my 'truly terrible' one."

Did Olivia blush? It captivated Kate, while wanting to ease the embarrassment at the same time.

"To be fair," Kate said, giving Olivia a reprieve. "*Devolution* did only score ten percent."

Did she dare ask outright what Olivia thought of her dancing in the other film? No, she didn't.

"When I learned for *The Ocean*," she continued instead, "a ballroom champion taught me a few classic steps. It was rigorous training." Days and days, hours and hours, until her feet ached, learning the moves to link a waltz, cha-cha or tango, perfecting it until it appeared smooth as silk, for less than five minutes of film. "Of course, they filmed it carefully to make it look polished." Focussing on the top of her body, the circling camera enhancing the spin of the waltz. "But I was proud of my work."

What was Olivia thinking? Did she hold back judgement on the film and dancing, too polite to say Kate hadn't succeeded?

"Care to show me?" Olivia asked, with a tilt of the head.

"You want...? I mean, I still remember..." She shouldn't do this. "Do you want to dance?"

Olivia curved out her hand. "Ms Woodhouse?"

Elegant fingers offered and it was irresistible.

"Ms Sachdeva, I would be delighted."

Kate beamed at their play and took the hand, suddenly aware of nothing but Olivia's soft fingers in hers, being pulled through the crowd, the rest of the party blending into shapes and music and laughter, all blurring except the vivid contact of this woman, the sway of her hips, the elegant dress, her profile looking back, the expectation.

Butterflies. Butterflies. Butterflies.

Olivia spun, so they came face to face, hands outstretched offering to dance and nudging Kate's stomach. It stopped them from standing too close, when Kate would have welcomed more intimacy, but the contact lit her up inside.

"Do you want to lead?" Olivia asked.

Kate took up the double hand-hold. It didn't feel like she was leading whatever this was. Oh, it was fun though.

"OK." She grinned.

Those butterflies.

"A cha-cha move?" She started a one, two, three and four in her hips, and Olivia slipped into the rhythm, mellifluous as honey.

"You know your timings." Olivia smiled.

Was that approval?

One, two, three, cha cha. Olivia light on her feet and body swaying fluid to the music. Kate easing forward then falling back. Finding her flow and muscle memory now so that she turned her partner in her arms, and Olivia spinning, as smooth as a hot knife slipping through butter.

The way Olivia moved. Kate sighed inside.

"Nicely done, Ms Woodhouse," Olivia said, peering back over her shoulder, then spiralling again so they faced.

It was like how they'd talked for weeks. Kate pushing forwards and Olivia pushing right back, a give and take that Kate was more than willing to indulge.

She dropped her right hand to Olivia's waist, collapsing the distance between them. Legs intertwined, hips swaying, neither of them missing a beat. While pretending politeness with her left and lightly clasping Olivia's fingers out at shoulder level.

"I'm glad you've seen that film," Kate said, then her heart leaped because she so obviously craved Olivia's approval.

Olivia looked into her eyes, body in perfect motion beneath Kate's palm. "I've seen it several times."

"Oh," Kate said. And she smiled. Too much.

Olivia said it without mocking or recalling films with ten-percent ratings. She gazed at Kate, and something changed between them and the way they moved. It was moments before Kate's mind registered the switch in song and beat, long after her body had slipped into an ever-closer hold. Gone was the upbeat tempo and they fell into something more intimate.

"I'm...pleased. I'm proud of that one," she murmured. That was all it needed to carry to Olivia's ear now.

"You should be," Olivia said. "You learned to dance well too."

It swelled in her chest, that approval and flattery, surprised at her own admission and heart leaping as she realised how much Olivia's opinion meant to her. Leaping again because they pressed so close. She couldn't say anything, only stare into Olivia's eyes, flashing bright, even though the anger had long gone. Rhythm seduced their movement, ebbing and flowing, and Kate's hand slipped further around Olivia's waist so they moved as one.

Olivia swallowed. "It doesn't surprise me that you dance well," she said, so near that her breath tickled over Kate's cheek with the sweetness of Champagne.

Her heart beat strong. "I take my work seriously."

"I've noticed," Olivia whispered. "It's something I admire about you very much."

Kate had to gulp down butterflies and hope they didn't explode in her chest. "And you?" she said. "You kept up ballroom and Latin?"

"Occasionally." She didn't miss Olivia's gaze flick to her lips for a second. "When my old partner needs a stand-in."

"And..." Kate shouldn't ask, with the evening turning flirtatious. Had it been there all along, their to and fro, back and forth, all the while bringing them closer. "...do you dance like this?"

Olivia's breath caught. She recovered and her eyes lifted again to Kate's.

"No."

Did the temperature rise with the acknowledgment that this wasn't how Olivia always danced? Without thinking, she stroked down Olivia's spine and up the rise of her behind. She pulled them low and tight, the heat of them together extraordinary.

"And is this OK?" Kate murmured, her cheek against Olivia's. "Close like this?"

Olivia didn't answer. But in their raised arms, fingers keenly wrapped around hers.

She risked the question again. "Do you mind this...contact?"

Another thrill from Olivia's body. Kate couldn't miss it.

"Quite the contrary," came the same formal phrasing from Olivia, but none of the calm delivery. The words trembled. "I do find physical contact intense." A pause. "But sometimes deeply pleasurable."

Kate's body stayed in rhythm while her head hummed, the moment loaded. She felt it in her chest, their breasts snug together and her heart pounding. Did Olivia find her attractive? Did she feel the same as Kate when they drew near each other, with that warmth and sensitive awareness of exactly her proximity and its capacity to thrill?

She tilted her head away to see Olivia's eyes, and they burned beneath the mask.

"When it's the right person," Olivia murmured.

And Kate's mind was too loud.

The music had changed once more, her body realising again before she did. She held Olivia close, everything else a blur and inconsequential, her eyes never leaving Olivia's so that when Olivia's dropped to her mouth and lingered, she saw it at once. Unmistakable.

Olivia spun in her arms, so she faced away, but their hold stayed heated. Kate's curves fitted into those of Olivia's back. She rested her hand on Olivia's belly, feeling her warm muscles undulate and tense, her fingers stroking over hers, in a way so evocative, as if she wished they slipped lower. And Kate felt it like hot oil.

Is that what she needed? The careful contact, the achingly slow approach, the powerful suggestion. Kate luxuriated in it. Is this what her body had craved, and Olivia had unknowingly given her? Kate drank it in, as intoxicating as it was soothing, while she lived through every sense.

As if conscious of the rising desire and their hands stroking lower, Olivia spun back. They fit so tight that when Kate's chest rose and waned, she didn't know if her breathing moved them or Olivia's.

"I..." Olivia started, then her gaze fixed on Kate's cheek. "Your mask."

She stopped dead and Kate loosened her hold.

It was an uncharacteristic impulse from Olivia, perhaps from the physicality of the dance, but she reached towards Kate's face without hesitating.

"Is that uncomfortable?" Olivia's hands rested around Kate's face, fever emanating from her fingers.

Gently the mask lifted from Kate, an edge tugging at skin on her cheek in a thrill. The piece rested on her head, while Olivia gazed beneath her eye. Then a fingertip, stroked there in an arc.

"It's left a mark," Olivia breathed, her eyes captivated and never leaving Kate's face. And she traced the line back again.

Kate didn't know if she was more transfixed by Olivia's expression, or the sensation of her finger trailing her skin.

Did Olivia feel this? Did she sense this moment too? Was there more than one crush hiding here?

Kate reached up and tentatively held the edges of Olivia's mask. She paused, checking there was no objection to the reciprocity, and slowly raised the blood-red cover.

Beautiful, deepest brown eyes stared at her. And she recognised the expression. The same desire shocked her own face. Kate gulped as neither looked away. She couldn't move, so present right now, that it weighed heavy and light at the same time, and her heart thudded.

"Olivia..." she whispered, and they hung subsumed in the same want.

Bright lights intruded, and only then she realised the music had stopped. Chatter broke all around them and the world rushed in.

Olivia blinked in the illumination, her expression collapsing into many things. And Kate still couldn't move, from the power of her attraction and alarm she saw on Olivia's face.

Olivia looked around in panic.

"Do you...?" Kate started.

"I need to go home," Olivia gasped.

"I–"

"Good night, Ms Woodhouse." And Olivia turned, struck out into the crowd and disappeared.

23

Olivia sank into her beloved grey sofa.

What had she been thinking? She even went so far as, what the *hell* had she been thinking? She'd asked herself this every time she woke in the night, and multiple times this morning. She broke into a sweat and covered her face with her hands, even though there was no-one to hide from.

The sun shone with annoying cheerfulness through her window, like it had a child-drawn smiley face. It lit up the new foliage of the vine and ivy in the courtyard garden and added to the warm humiliation on her cheeks.

She'd seen too much of Kate. It had filled her head with fantasy. This was unprofessional, inappropriate and wildly unhealthy for her. Weeks ago, she'd put her film fixation in a box, and a real-world tension had sprung up in its place, palpable in their badinage and spilling out onto the dance floor. Kate came face to face with it, and Olivia hadn't been able to hide a thing.

And Kate's face as she lifted the mask. Olivia breathed out. Had there ever been a more beautiful expression on the actor's face? The concern, the careful hesitation, the pink blush of her cheeks, the full lips, the burning eyes. All for Olivia. It intoxicated and swirled her head.

She stood up, uncomfortable. She couldn't fall for this. Whatever Kate felt last night, after too much Champagne and being swept up in the dance, Olivia was sure would be gone in a headache this morning. Which left Olivia horribly exposed for her own feelings that were getting out of hand.

Because the actor was charming, and challenged her, then revealed vulnerabilities which had Olivia relenting like a sap, wanting to sweep her off her feet when they danced, and taking her on romantic punting trips at dusk.

Oh my god, how had she let this happen? This was a disaster.

She needed to get out. She needed to exercise this whole feeling away, so by their next appointment she could act professionally. Because any hint of a relationship with a client was career death for Olivia, and Kate didn't need the implication mid-divorce either.

Dammit, what a mess. She required a complete change of scenery to ground herself again.

She paused. She knew just the place. Ugh. It was annoying but needs must. It would distract her, and in fact drive her beyond distraction.

She changed into a cycling top and bottoms and put on a helmet, all black with a concession of visibility strips. She lifted her bike from the ivy-covered shed and wheeled it out the rear gate into the narrow Jericho side street.

She paused in the daylight, the presence of Freud's too near to block out. That dance. Kate's chest had curved into Olivia's back. Her hand had fluttered around her waist and fingers down her belly. Their movement, fluid and slipping into the music, had resonated so pleasingly it thrummed through her. And all the while, Kate had wrapped sensually about her.

It had been one of those moments where everything flowed, the perfection of it sweeping Olivia up, so that she'd stroked Kate's cheek without thinking. She'd experienced the most vivid sensation on her fingertip as she touched the red mark left by Kate's mask, their whole connection concentrated there. She imagined the tiny, tender ridges on the pad of her finger again, and her entire body hummed with the intensity of it.

Enough. She needed to burn these memories away.

Across Jericho, along the canals, past narrow boats, she pedalled until her thighs burned, then pushed harder again. Wishing to see as few people as possible, she stuck to the river past Osney Island, her bike bumping over the uneven path and obliterating puddles. And she didn't stop as she powered away from Folly Bridge in the centre of town. Past meadows and boathouses, and the countryside Isis pub, she came to Iffley Lock where she dismounted covered in sweat. She negotiated the Mathematical Bridge, the lock, across the three narrow islands in the river, and pushed her bike up the narrow path up into Iffley Village.

Snug between a stone thatch cottage and a larger house, she pulled her bike through a gateway in stone walls, up to what looked like an unassuming bungalow.

She knocked on the door, then squared her shoulders as a shape approached through the frosted glass panels. The door opened.

"Well, hello," the voice said, with a guilt-inducing level of surprise.

Her mother, in a T-shirt and jeans, dusted with flour as they so often were. Shoulder-length black wavy hair streaked with grey now she hit mid-fifties. Shorter and curvier than Olivia, who took after her tall, slim father. And cheerier, more effusive and instantly likable. Olivia knew this.

"Well, this is a lovely surprise," Geeta said, warmth in her voice.

She spoke, not in Olivia's clipped tones, but in a relaxed RP with hints of Birmingham where she grew up. The hints would become the strongest Brummie when she fell in with old school friends, laughing and joking so that Olivia hardly recognised her. Then, just as quick, Geeta would slip into Nani's accent when they chatted in Punjabi, the two mixing in English so fluidly they didn't seem to realise they talked in two different languages. They'd sometimes forget that Olivia had never been fluent, and by now she'd forgotten all but their most frequent phrases.

"I was out for a bike ride. I thought I'd call in," Olivia said quickly.

Her mother beamed, pleased. Too pleased. "It's lovely to see you," and Geeta spread her arms out to offer a cuddle.

Olivia put a hand up to refuse. "I'm very sweaty."

Her mother nodded, accepting. "Come on in," Geeta gestured. "Have a shower if you like."

"I will. I brought a change of clothes."

Geeta paused in the hallway with an indulgent smile. "Because you can't be too prepared, when out for a bike ride and might want to drop in somewhere."

Geeta wasn't stupid. Yes, she had this...Olivia struggled for the words...earth-mother quality, which was all generous hormones and less detached analysis, but the woman was still quick and clever.

"My lovely girl. You always were prepared," Geeta said, giving her a reprieve.

Olivia blinked, trying not to get irritated by the endearment.

Because while best friend Charlotte found Geeta's effusive love a joy to behold, Olivia wanted to be treated like a responsible grown up. Granted, she'd insisted on this from the age of seven and Geeta, quite rightly, had been cautious. But that was a long time ago. As was the time she'd moved out for good after college holidays.

Still the smile, blooming with motherly love, as if she were seven years old.

Charlotte never seemed to grasp that Olivia preferred the mentor-like role of Nicola Albright, who offered advice while respecting her abilities. Olivia talked to Charlotte's mother as a peer and colleague. Meanwhile, Geeta clung onto a younger version.

Speaking of which, she needed to remind Geeta, yet again, to clear out her old room, including film posters. More than ten years was enough time, surely, for her mother to come to terms with her leaving. She wished Geeta would throw everything in the bin, especially at this moment, with a memory of glowing cheeks and green eyes gazing at her. She flinched and stepped into the house.

School photos lined the hallway, her brother Adam on one side and Olivia on the other. They chronicled every year from the long black hair past her shoulders in primary school, to the shorter styles in secondary until, by sixth form, she found the style she'd kept ever since. Really, what was the point in changing if you found something perfect?

The expressions in the photos were constant though. She had a memory of her teen brother gleefully running down the hallway, goading and pointing to each photo.

"Disdain, disdain, grumpy, disdain," her brother had joked.

And Geeta had tried very hard not to laugh. Her annoying brother took after her annoying mother.

Olivia showered in the downstairs bathroom, her old room across the hallway nagging at her the whole time. She glared at the closed door afterwards, knowing what lay in there, her mother having left it pristine from Olivia's teenage years, including those damned posters of Kate.

She swiftly turned away from the guilt-inducing past, pulled on a cream sweatshirt, which she only wore because Nani gifted it, and followed the smell of cake to the back of the house.

It opened into a large extension of open-plan kitchen, seating area and dining room with floor-to-ceiling windows to the garden. Geeta stood by the counter on the right, cutting up fruit.

"By the way, Nani," Geeta pointed a knife towards the wall, indicating the lounge on the other side, "wants you to take her to Handsworth for Bandi Chhor Diwas."

"Very well," Olivia replied, standing beside her. She hadn't accompanied her grandmother to the gurdwara and celebrations for a couple of years.

"Thank you." Geeta nodded.

Neither were religious, but Geeta's mother still was.

"She probably wants to show you off to aunties," Geeta said.

"I don't mind," Olivia replied. "As long as they don't want to introduce me to men."

Geeta smiled. "Of course. Here." She passed a plate of mango. "Could you take this to her? I need to check the chocolate cake for your father's department meeting."

Olivia sniffed the plate out of habit.

"I know," Geeta said, an edge to her voice. "It smells of nothing and the flavour is weak. They're never good enough for her. She knows it's impossible to buy decent mangoes in Oxford."

It was unusually snappy from her mother. But Olivia appreciated how irritating mothers were, Geeta being a case in point.

"If you take it, she won't moan because it's you." Geeta added.

This was true, because Nani indulged her, and Olivia idolised her in return.

Taking the bowl, she found her grandmother sitting on the sofa in the lounge. Olivia remembered Nani as a busy solicitor, always in a business suit, after taking a law degree as a mature student. The same sharp eyes spotted Olivia coming in, although more relaxed these days and dressed in Punjabi suits, now she was retired and enjoying familiar comforts from her childhood.

"I didn't know you were here!" Satinder put down her sudoku and threw up her hands.

"A surprise visit." Olivia beamed. She leaned down to let Nani kiss her, one of the few privileged to do this.

Olivia sat beside her and passed the bowl.

"How's work?" Satinder said.

"Fine as usual."

Apart from the transgression of flirting with a client. But Nani was the last person she'd want to tell this.

"Hugo retired yet?" Satinder asked, taking a bite of mango. Her face wrinkled, and she shuddered. "Oh, that's tangy." She lifted her chin and shouted over Olivia's head. "They're not ripe! There's no flavour!"

Geeta poked her head around the door.

Olivia tasted it too. "I agree. Very one-dimensional."

Geeta threw her hand in the air. "Look, neither of you cook or prepare food for me, but you analyse my meals as if you're professional critics."

Nani shrugged. "Just because I don't like cooking doesn't mean I can't appreciate food."

"It means you could be more polite though!" An edge crept into Geeta's usually agreeable voice, and she disappeared into the kitchen.

Olivia looked at Satinder in question.

"The change," Satinder said with the wave of her hand.

"For god's sake. It doesn't take being menopausal for you to be annoying!" Came from the kitchen.

So, that's what was making her easy-going mother tetchy.

Satinder raised an eyebrow. It was very like Olivia's.

"And I know you're raising your eyebrows at me," came again.

Olivia did take after Satinder more than her mother, right down to the career. Olivia always looked up to Nani, and she looked at Olivia with triumphant pride when she got into Oxford to study law.

"You know," Satinder nudged Olivia and took another bite. "I think I might prefer them this way. Like a healthy Tangfastic sweet."

Olivia peered at her. "Perhaps you should tell her."

"Maybe." Nani shrugged.

Maybe Geeta should clear Olivia's old room. Maybe Satinder should tell Geeta she was happy with her food. These things dragged on for years, like a familiar and perpetual thread of annoyance tying them together.

"Is Dad around?"

"Course not. He's in the department."

Another familiar situation, but it had worked for them. Olivia's parents had been married for thirty-five years, a source of constancy like those annoying threads, which reassured Olivia about the world, when her job oversaw so much of it falling apart.

She still peeked into his study though. The small room overlooked a patch of garden that ran beside the house before tumbling down towards the river. It remained largely the same since her last visit, when she'd found it largely the same as all the years before, the computer screen the only significant evolution over the years.

The same radio sat on the bookcase for Radio 4 and the cricket. Same desk and chair. A sofa along the side wall and plenty of cushions, all neatly arranged. She'd hidden in here away from her noisy baby brother as a teen, and her dad didn't have to tell her to straighten the cushions afterwards, because they were so alike.

Because much as though she wanted to take after Nani, she resembled her father too – a tall, slim, elegant man with a ferocious intellect and focus, often sat in his office, with everything in a particular way.

"I was about to have a mug of tea by the river and a chocolate muffin from the spare mixture," Geeta said when Olivia returned to the kitchen. "Do you want one?"

Of course, even though Geeta offered ordinary supermarket tea. Because when her mother made it, the water, strength and amount of milk was childhood perfection.

They wandered down the grassy slope of the garden, hidden from neighbours by large shrubs and small trees. The informal landscape had been another peaceful escape as a child. They strolled down to the riverside where a garden table and two sofas sat. Geeta threw off the covers and hid them beneath the seating.

"Nice with the sun out," Geeta said.

Olivia didn't reply because, really, what could she add about the weather?

Her mother gazed back at her and smiled, and Olivia nodded instead.

They sat next to each other, cradling their mugs, Olivia's the same she always had at home. The tea didn't taste right in the others. Geeta might be someone who drank tea with wild abandon from any old vessel, but she appreciated that Olivia didn't.

"You can talk about anything, you know," Geeta said, looking over the river.

Olivia should have known. Of course, her mother suspected something was up with this out-of-the-blue visit.

Olivia nodded again. She took a bite out of the chocolate muffin.

"This is delicious," she said.

"Thank you," Geeta replied.

And they stared at the river some more, over the islands and upstream towards the Isis Tavern.

Strangely, it was tempting to talk, sitting there just the two of them with no expectation from Geeta, who was used to Olivia telling her nothing.

Olivia opened her mouth, not sure what was going to come out. Then closed it, because of precisely that. There was nothing to say about it all, except Olivia wanted to vent frustration somehow. She opened her mouth again, then:

"Is that Charlotte?" Geeta said.

Olivia huffed, unfairly, that she'd been interrupted. "Where?"

"Across the river on the towpath."

Olivia couldn't see around the bush Geeta pointed towards and waited for whoever to come into view.

"It is Charlotte." Geeta's face lit up and she waved.

Olivia wanted to roll her eyes at her mother's adulation of Charlotte, but if her friend wanted to play surrogate child and keep Geeta company she shouldn't complain.

"Who's that with her?"

She couldn't see. "Millie most likely." Olivia tutted out of habit.

"No, it's a taller woman with a young child."

Olivia stared at the river, about to take a bite, chocolate muffin poised in front of open lips. It couldn't be. Surely. She closed her mouth, muffinless.

"What did you say?" Olivia squeaked.

"Rather glamorous woman, in a casual kind of way."

No, no, no. Charlotte wouldn't.

"Actually," Geeta nudged her, "she looks a bit like that movie star you fancied."

Apparently, Charlotte would.

"Mum..." Olivia began.

"It's the hair, and sunglasses and figure." Geeta laughed. "Charlotte!" she called.

"Mum!" Olivia hissed.

"Charlotte!" Geeta leapt to her feet and waved. "Come over for a cup of tea! The side gate's open! Bring your friend!"

"Oh my..."

Olivia closed her eyes. God damn her friendly, gregarious mother. And while god was at it, damn her friend as well.

What the hell was Charlotte doing spending Sunday with Kate? For once, she wished Charlotte was rolling around in bed with Millie instead.

"I'll go and meet them," Geeta said. "You coming?"

Olivia paused and squeezed her eyes tighter shut. If she had to sit through this car crash, she could at least spare one of her senses.

"Fine," she growled.

What had she done to deserve this?

24

Hello!" Geeta cried, as they walked up to the house.

Charlotte loped around the corner from the side gate, all smiles and blushes, apparently ignorant of the devastation she was about to unleash.

Olivia didn't know what to do with herself. She smoothed down her loose cream sweatshirt over her yoga bottoms, out of sorts in every single way. This was worse than being dropped unprepared into the middle of court.

Charlotte enveloped Geeta in an easy hug, wavy hair billowing, and holding hands afterwards.

"Millie not with you?" Geeta asked.

Was her mother now buddies with Millie as well?

"No." Charlotte's shoulders sagged, and her forehead crinkled into concern. "Period started."

Geeta groaned in sympathy. "Endometriosis flareup?"

Oh. She didn't know that. It made sense and explained why Millie sometimes turned pale and disappeared off the face of the Earth. More surprising was Charlotte sharing this information with Geeta, but not her.

"She's knocked out with painkillers and snuggled up in bed," Charlotte continued. "I'm heading back soon to give her a cuddle. But we'd organised lunch with Kate at the Isis, so we're out for a walk."

"Oh yes, your friend?" And they peered back towards the house.

Olivia breathed in and braced herself.

Kate's daughter played with early flowering clematis woven through the hedge and tree, the pale flowers incongruous over the shrubs they climbed, and Kate smiled and encouraged her towards the others. The two were a picture of delight. It was horrifying.

Olivia didn't want to look. If only she could pause this moment and rearrange them to face the door, so when she pressed play they walked back out again. But the moment kept on coming.

Kate ran her fingers through her hair and shook her head so honey locks flowed away from her eyes. Perhaps if she kept her sunglasses on there was an infinitesimal chance her mother wouldn't recognise her? But no. The glasses were coming off, now out of the public eye, but not away from her perceptive mother's. Dammit, dammit, dammit.

Kate pocketed the sunglasses in her blazer and her movie star face shone flawless today. The proud cheeks, the sparkling green eyes, the beautiful curving lips. All so utterly and unmistakably recognisable.

Olivia tensed every muscle. Here it came.

Geeta inhaled so loud the neighbours must have heard. Then she clapped her hands together and pressed praying fingertips to her mouth, as if to stop herself from speaking.

"Oh, my goodness," they failed to stop her saying. "I can't...I don't believe it." Geeta whipped her head round to Olivia, eyes wide.

Stood rigid, Olivia failed to even raise an eyebrow. She wished she could feign awkwardness and look down and scuff the grass with her trainer, she wanted to avoid her mother's gaze so much. Instead, she inhaled through her nostrils and tilted her head in defiance. That was her limit.

Geeta's shock relaxed as their eyes met, and her mouth rose in an indulgent smile.

Yes, her mother understood. This was why Olivia visited, out of sorts and skulking home. Because even if Geeta didn't have the details, she knew there were issues here.

It was excruciating, the whole situation and Geeta's quick and complete understanding of her, as if Olivia would never escape being a transparent child to her. She wanted to turn on her heel, march to the river, scream over the entirety of Oxford and plunge into the water. She made do with crossing her arms like she was fifteen again, which was also unbearable.

Geeta recovered and turned back, covering her heart with her palm. "Goodness me, what a surprise. You must be Kate Laurence." Geeta offered a hand.

Kate smiled, an expression Olivia recognised as genuine, if a little distracted, and shook hands.

"Are you called Kate? Or is that a stage and equity name?"

"Yes, it's Kate, although a different surname."

"I can't tell you how many films..."

Oh god.

"I'm sorry," Geeta stopped herself. "You must have this all the time. And hello," Geeta said, lifting her voice, as she turned to Kate's daughter.

The child scowled. Olivia empathised.

"My daughter, Bea," Kate offered. "She's tired, so might not be chatty."

"Come and sit down by the river then?" Geeta said, spreading her arms. "I have some C. A. K. E. if that would help?" She raised her eyebrows.

"That would be lovely," Kate replied. "Thank you. She didn't have much at lunch."

Geeta dropped to her knees, face glowing and welcoming. Which was excellent. Yes, talk to the child.

"Hello, Bea. I'm Geeta, Olivia's mother. I'm assuming you've met Olivia?"

The child nodded and scowled some more. Olivia didn't blame her.

"I wonder, are you like my daughter and have a soft spot for chocolate cake?"

There was nodding from the child. Which was good. But also allusions to Olivia's childhood. Which was not.

"It was Olivia's favourite."

Please stop.

"She always insisted on it, every single birthday."

Someone kill her. Her or Geeta. She didn't mind which right now.

"I make them very chocolatey with lots and lots of icing. Would you like a piece?"

The change in expression was instantaneous. She swore the child's eyes grew to twice the size. Was Olivia as readable as this to Geeta? Ugh. Of course she was.

Bea checked up at Kate, who nodded with indulgence.

"I'll get your mum a slice as well," Geeta said. "Would you like to show me just how big a piece you can eat?"

A grin spread on the girl's face, the first Olivia had seen.

"Charlotte, would you mind helping with tea?" Geeta said lightly.

"Of course," Charlotte said, spinning around.

The two retreated into the house with Geeta, happy and relaxed and oblivious to being expertly manoeuvred. And it left no doubt about how transparent Olivia remained to her mother. Gah.

Their voices faded and then stopped completely at the bump of the sliding kitchen door. Then it was just Olivia and Kate.

"I am so sorry." Kate came towards her, stopping a pace away and raising her hands in apology. "I had no idea. Charlotte was chatting about someone called Geeta, and I assumed she was a friend. I didn't realise she was your mother until we came through the gates."

Green eyes searched Olivia's. No embarrassment, no hangover, no dismissal of the night before. That tension built again. Olivia didn't miss it. She wasn't like Charlotte, who needed a sign, like a billboard, to spot these things. Although Kate's expression may as well have been one today.

It was there. A definite attraction between them. Their bristling back and forth had grown through curiosity, softened into friendliness, and here they were, the air so thick between them, she prayed she didn't reach across without realising.

"I might kill her," Olivia said quietly.

Kate's face broke into a smile so large it eclipsed the sun. Those lines. That sparkle. Olivia's heart went pitter patter, and she inhaled audibly.

Kate heard, and Olivia didn't try to cover it, and they both gazed at each other.

"This is..." Kate started, "probably not ideal is it?" she said, eyes glistening although pleading concern.

"No," said Olivia gently. "Not the best."

"I mean, today, but also..." Kate turned up her hands.

"I know," Olivia said.

She was OK with this, talking around the issue, so they didn't face it full on, because they couldn't. It shouldn't exist at all. They both knew what they avoided and why and that was enough. If they didn't spell it out maybe they'd get through this.

She imagined both had been attracted to people they shouldn't be. One such person chatted in the kitchen with her mother for a start.

"I'm sorry..." Kate said again, this time biting her lip. A very lovely, full, attractive lip.

Olivia swallowed.

And Kate smiled, because she saw it all.

"So," Kate said, straightening up. "Have your parents lived here long?"

Polite. That was good and suitable. Olivia breathed in deep with relief, and to push herself out of their intimacy into normal conversation.

"Nearly all my life."

"You grew up here?"

"Yes, my room..." Oh god her room. She didn't want to face that full on either. "Yes, I grew up running around these gardens. I used to have a den by the river."

"That's adventurous?" Kate tilted her head, perhaps disbelieving.

"It was for reading and escaping from people."

Kate laughed. "Same. I always liked acting, but it was the immersion in stories I craved. I was a huge reader."

"Really?"

"Still am."

They gazed at each other again.

This was the thing. They were two people who shouldn't spark, who had incompatible lives, and yet, these connections kept happening. These moments of warmth that insisted on drawing them together.

"Come and sit down," Olivia said. "My mother won't let you leave without several cups of tea and two slices of cake anyway."

They turned and wandered down the slope, Kate taking in the garden, the sun shining in her hair, then catching Olivia's eye, and both turning away, because neither should be looking at the other like that.

They sat by the river, relaxed enough to sit on the same sofa, but a careful distance apart. Olivia drew up a knee to her chest and threaded the other beneath.

"You look very nice, by the way," Kate said, staring over the water.

Olivia quietly laughed. "In my baggy sweatshirt?" she said, in disbelief.

Kate turned and held Olivia's gaze. "In everything."

Butterflies and regret leaped in her chest. Olivia blushed and pulled at her top, before admitting, "Same goes for you."

And Kate pursed her lips, as if butterflies were melancholy with her too.

Rapid steps drew both round and Bea thundered down the garden and threw herself onto the sofa between them.

"Geeta said I should sit down then I can have some cake," Bea said with red cheeks and in such quick fire even Olivia laughed.

Geeta came, laughing too and holding out a tray of cake. Of course, her mother had Bea under her spell. And Charlotte followed behind, just as spellbound. Under her mother's influence, Olivia almost forgot herself and patted Bea on the shoulder.

"Here we go," Geeta said, putting the tray down on the low table.

Bea grabbed an extraordinary slice of cake, surely bigger than her tummy, and pinched icing between her fingers. Geeta offered a fork and Kate put up her hand to refuse, both beaming at the girl engrossed in her cake.

"So, are you in Oxford for a film?" Geeta said. Now that everyone had tea, she sat on the next sofa beside Kate.

"Originally yes. We finish location filming soon, then it's studio work over the summer holidays. But..." she glanced at Olivia. "I'm hoping to stay here. My oldest loves his school. And Harry, who I co-parent with, lives only a few miles away."

"Oh?" Geeta said lightly. "A great place for you to settle down then?"

"Yes, it is."

"Hmm," Geeta said, nodding. "Interesting."

She could see her mother's mind ticking over. Sometimes Geeta was transparent too. Stop it, she wanted to say. Stop analysing Kate for suitability, because that wasn't going to happen. Despite this attraction. Because...well... Olivia strained to make it sound ridiculous. Kate was a movie star, but it didn't seem strange anymore. Because she was Kate. Familiar Kate. But it was still an impossible situation. Not because she was some distant movie star, but because she was a client.

"And do you have someone to settle down with?" Geeta said, nonchalantly placing a forkful of cake into her mouth.

It was not subtle. Olivia rolled her eyes.

"I'm actually in the middle of a divorce."

"Hmm," Geeta said, nodding and swallowing her cake. "From your...wife?"

No. That was impossible. Her mother didn't have a better sapphic sonar than her. She refused to believe it. But Geeta had spotted Olivia growing up, hadn't she.

"That's right," Kate said.

"I hope that's going smoothly for you." Geeta took another nonchalant nibble.

"We've been split up a long time."

"Good." Geeta nodded. "Good."

"Bea doesn't really remember it."

They looked at Bea, who had no idea the world existed beyond chocolate butter cream. Geeta and Kate continued chatting, but she missed what they said because Charlotte stood up from behind her mother and strolled over. She beamed at Olivia.

"You're living on the edge with a pale jumper next to chocolate cake."

"Bea's eating tidily," Olivia said. More neatly than Charlotte, in fact.

Bea glanced up with chocolate smeared like thick whiskers on her cheeks. Maybe not then. Olivia rose from her seat and peeled away with her friend.

"I was going to give you a ring this morning," Charlotte said, "to invite you to lunch, but things got chaotic."

"Is Millie OK?"

"Yes. I mean no. It's a bad flareup." Concern furrowed Charlotte's brow.

Olivia was tempted to send her love, because that would trip off her mother's tongue, but Millie might not appreciate it from Olivia. "I hope she's better soon," she said instead.

Charlotte nodded. "Hey," she said, lightening a little. "Did you have a nice time last night?"

Olivia stiffened. "Yes. Very agreeable." Because while Kate and their attraction heated the room, Charlotte was often oblivious.

"I saw you leave to dance with Kate but didn't catch you after that."

Completely oblivious. What a relief.

"And Richard's leaving," Charlotte said, brighter again.

"Thank god," Olivia started with sympathy, before movement caught her attention.

Geeta sat down next to Bea, talking about cake, but in the space where Kate had been seated. Where had she gone?

"Mum?"

"Yes, darling." Geeta glanced up.

"Where's Kate?"

"She popped back to the house for the loo." And Geeta turned back to Bea.

"Mum?" she said, more desperate.

"Yes, darling." Geeta frowned this time.

"Which loo?"

Because this really was important.

"I said it didn't matter. Whichever she found first."

But it did matter. Because Olivia didn't want Kate exploring the house, and opening every door, especially the one opposite the main bathroom.

"Excuse me a moment." She shoved her teacup into Charlotte's hands. "I just need to..."

She started walking up the garden, then marched, the vivid image of her room flooding her mind. Her neat bookcase beneath the window, university law books arranged by subject, and novels by genre, size, and spine colour, revealing her fastidious nature. A mortifying matriculation photo on the wall of student Olivia. Old stuffed toys, which Geeta insisted she'd regret throwing out. But most of all, two huge film posters with Kate prominent and unmissable in both.

She broke into a run. Could she catch her?

She slid the full-length glass door back with a thud and jogged into the kitchen. No-one there. She peeped around at Nani, still alone and asleep. The small loo by her father's study was empty. Her heart rate leaped again as she raced along the hallway, because one glance at those posters would reveal her cinematic adoration.

Every door remained closed, and she sprinted to her old bedroom, bursting into the room and coming to a halt at the foot of the bed.

It was gone. Her bookcase, wardrobe, stuffed toys, all gone. Her single bed was now a double, the sheets turned back from someone sleeping there.

She spun around. The wall was redecorated in a calm sage green, and a painting of Iffley church hung where she'd displayed her infatuation with Kate Laurence films. It was all gone.

"Olivia?"

And the real Kate stood in the doorway.

Olivia panted from her run and panic.

"Are you OK?" Kate pressed, stepping into the room.

Olivia shook her head and stared at her. "I erm..."

She needed a moment, disoriented by the change. She blinked, letting it settle, and willed her head to stop spinning. Everything slowed and stopped in focus, Kate still there, staring at her.

"This..." Olivia breathed. "This used to be my old room."

Kate watched but said nothing.

Olivia swallowed, and the dryness caught in her throat. Her cheeks burned and Kate must realise something bothered her. This felt wrong. Not that Kate intruded into her personal life, but that everyone apart from Kate knew about this. Lovely Kate, friendly with her mother and best friend, a superstar but vulnerable and real. Everyone except her knew Olivia's secret.

"I..." Oh, she didn't want to do this. Her stomach dropped. Would Kate ever look at her the same again? Would she ever have that respect for her skills? Or show that admiration that had clearly grown? Olivia stared at that beautiful, concerned face one more time before the revelation would change it.

"I have a confession," she started, squeezing her fingers into her palms. "I haven't seen a couple of your films. I've watched tens and tens of them. Some many times."

There. It was out. She confessed.

Kate gave away nothing although her silence asked for more explanation.

"Some are comfort things for me," Olivia said quietly.

She'd never felt so shy. Such a simple admission, perhaps trivial to some, but it hit deep for her. A silly film indulgence, but it stripped layers of protection and history.

"They're a perfect escape. Somewhere to hide or recover when everything else is difficult," she whispered, feeling exposed as she peeled back to the truth. "I loved the stories you chose, ever since your early films, and I found it easy to root for someone who'd played a lesbian."

Kate still watched, without a word or hint of what she thought. But Olivia had started now and she needed Kate to know.

"I liked being swept along in a story by an ally who wouldn't disapprove of me and my life. I could let myself go, idolise the character on the screen, wish for her happiness or success, knowing it was safe to support you. Letting go completely, that's..." she paused "...not something I do very often."

Her breath caught in a shudder as she waited. Everything hinged on what Kate would say next.

Kate shifted her weight over her feet and stared at the floor. "Is this why," she lifted her eyes to meet Olivia's, "you didn't want me as a client?"

God, it sounded superficial and insensitive now. "Yes," Olivia whispered.

"Not wanting my imperfections to intrude on your suspension of disbelief?"

She heard her own words back at her. She nodded.

Kate frowned and looked away.

"I've always respected the roles you chose," Olivia said. "And your performance, even when cast with less-than-ideal partners. And yes," she did need to admit it, "I thought you stunning on the screen."

The distance they stood apart charged with a very different tension from before. Kate stayed silent. And Olivia deflated.

"So now you know." Olivia didn't have the energy to shrug. "I was a huge fan."

Kate's face remained stoney and Olivia couldn't tell what went on beneath the surface. Such a perceptive reader of people, and she didn't read anything here, just when it was most important.

Kate glanced up, a frown deepening between her eyebrows. "If it's any consolation," she started, "I'm used to being different from what others imagine or want."

"That's not–"

"I've seen the disappointment a hundred times." Kate cut her off, an edge to her defensiveness. "That I'm not as sexy, flawless, witty, whatever qualities you liked in those characters."

"It's – "

"I'm used to being a letdown, Olivia. One woman can't live up to all the roles I've played."

Olivia's heart sank again. "That really isn't it," she whispered.

"I'm very human, with many failings, and someone who's made mistakes, not all correctable in a burst of heroism."

Olivia paused this time, because Kate described Olivia's first impression, disapproving of the actor with multiple marriages and children. Kate had seen through her attitude immediately when they first met. All of it.

"But you're incredible," Olivia murmured. She didn't realise she was going to say it, until it was out. She paused, afraid to let words like that have free rein. "I've always respected your talent as an actor. But now, with everything I see, every new thing I find out, I respect you even more."

Did Kate soften at that?

"The way you prioritise your children. I may not have my own, but I value responsible parents. I admire your honesty. Your professionalism and skill. The way you show patience to my friend and mother, in fact, to anyone you encounter. Far more than I do."

She prayed this got through to Kate.

"And I find you," Olivia swallowed, "as an actor, a professional, as a person...I find I like you." She stopped, because her feelings began to tumble. "I like you a lot."

It sounded nothing, but Olivia felt everything. Did Kate realise how much she admitted here?

"It's funny that," Kate said. She stepped further into the room, her expression softening into quiet despair. "Because I like you too. Very much, in fact."

And the distance collapsed with warmth.

Kate paused, eyes never leaving Olivia's. "I will respect your professionalism. But please let me admit that I'm stunned by you, as someone I find beautiful and clever, and who scares me a bit." Kate's eyes sparkled at that. "Who scares me in a good way."

Olivia breathed in several times before she could speak. Then she realised, "We need to stop talking now."

She tried to smile, while being pulled in different directions. Relieved that Kate still looked at her that way, but devastated that she shouldn't.

"Because that liking you business." How her heart thudded. "That liking you a lot. I can't. Not this much." She pleaded with Kate. "Because there can't be feelings like that. You are my client. And this has to stop."

Kate nodded, sadness shadowing her face as she considered Olivia. "This really isn't ideal, is it?" she murmured, echoing what they'd said in the garden.

"No," Olivia replied. She shared the same sad smile. "Nowhere near the best."

25

All frostiness gone. The clipped voice softened with confession. Vulnerable and revealed. Kate's heart swelled, wanting to handle Olivia with care now that she understood. There was little more compelling than Olivia Sachdeva opening up to her like that.

They both stared in shock as they ambled back to the river. The day must have taken its toll on Olivia, this very private and restrained woman having the personal ripped open for scrutiny. Kate's hand twitched. She wanted to reach out and squeeze Olivia's for comfort, her own too, except she shouldn't, and Olivia kept her arms crossed.

"This day," Kate said, "it's a lot, isn't it?"

Olivia glanced up, eyes heavy. "It really is."

And Kate's heart ached hearing the tremble in Olivia's voice.

She tried to smile to ease the tension for Olivia. She wondered what distressed her most. Their growing attraction, inappropriate for client and lawyer? Kate was too involved and impartial to address that right now. But she guessed at the films too, a huge admission from someone so reserved. Kate didn't want to dismiss it or draw on a trite line from a script.

"You know, I used to watch Emma Richardson movies on repeat," Kate offered quietly.

"I can see why. She's an excellent actress and always projects intelligence and empathy."

Kate heard the defence as Olivia's own, maybe reassuring herself and Kate about the reasons she'd watched so many.

"I thought she was attractive too," Kate couldn't help adding, with the gentlest teasing smile.

Olivia laughed. It really was beautiful. Leaping out of her unrestrained, a rare, wonderful sight and sound. Then she looked at Kate, those imperious eyebrows rising in heartache this time. Too close. Too soon.

"And..." Olivia hesitated. "How did you find her when you met in real life?"

"I kind of hoped she'd be a horrid human being." She cast a glance to Olivia as they walked, "But I still have a bit of a crush on her."

Olivia stopped and laughed out loud again. She wiped away a tear. And Kate beamed, because it sent her high, making Olivia laugh and being able to break the tension for her.

"Actually," Kate added, "we know each other too well for a crush. We say things that might sound flirty to others, but it's just familiarity and keeps us entertained."

Olivia recovered and tilted her head. "Are you saying this to make me feel better?"

Was Kate trying to say they'd get over their attraction? That they'd get through this?

"I think I'm saying," she paused, considering Olivia, tender from the confession, beautiful as always, alluring beyond anyone else. "I'm used to things being complicated."

Which left everything wide open, and her heart thudded.

They carried on walking, neither looking at the other. And although they didn't talk, as they wandered the long garden to the river, Kate hated that their time ended.

"You OK?" she whispered as they approached the others.

"Yes," Olivia murmured. "Thank you." And with one last glance she let her arms drop by her side, eased back her shoulders, and elegant Olivia returned.

Kate did the same and shifted into a different version of herself. But she missed the open vulnerability she'd shared with Olivia before she'd pulled the layers over again.

"Oh, there you are," Geeta said, turning round with a smile.

Kate didn't miss the glare Olivia gave her mother, or Geeta raising her hands and mouthing, "I'm not saying a word."

"Hey, sweet pea," Kate said to Bea, pretending not to catch them.

Her daughter and Charlotte sat cross-legged, making a daisy chain between them.

"Shall we head home?"

Bea stood on the sofa and furrowed her brow in concentration, always something Kate adored. She lifted the flowers to Kate's head.

"Oafuff!" Bea said.

Kate blushed at hearing her own cut-off phrase that crept out when frustrated.

"It's not big enough," Bea said, and the necklace of flowers rested on top of Kate's head.

Geeta laughed, then covered her mouth, picking up on what Bea said.

"Oafuff?" Charlotte asked.

Bea looked at her as if she were a fool. "It's what you say when something's gone wrong."

"Is it?" Charlotte wrinkled her nose.

"Really?" Olivia purred. She crossed her arms, elegant fingers drumming on her bicep, her poise recovered. Kate was glad to see it. "Oh for f...goodness sake?" she suggested, beautiful eyebrow raised and soft smile curling her lips.

It was dreamy. Far too dreamy.

"That's the one," Kate said, completely won by Olivia's expression.

Geeta approached. "It was good to meet you, Kate," she said, putting out her hands and squeezing Kate's between them.

"You too," Kate replied.

Because it was. Another slice of Oxford life, of people she thought wonderful and craved as company. Another glimpse of Olivia, and a deeper insight into who she was.

But it was too good to be true. Time to go.

She turned with regret at leaving these people. The welcome of Geeta, the unassuming friendship of Charlotte, and Olivia who was many things. None allowed to be part of her world. She lifted Bea into her arms, glad of the hug, because she needed the comfort right now.

"Does it look good as a daisy crown?" Kate said to Bea. "It's not what you wanted, but can we enjoy it as something else?" she said lightly.

Bea frowned at her. "No."

Oh. So much for that life lesson. And her heart hurt.

She set Bea on the ground, and the group headed towards the house.

"Come on." Charlotte beamed. "I'll take you back by the river."

Bea took this as a prompt to take an adult's hand and surprised everyone by reaching for Charlotte's. Bea was choosey about her grownups, but even she swayed with the warmth of these people. Kate's heart hurt a little more at that. And again, when Charlotte glanced round, mouth a perfect 'o' and eyes glistening in besotted surprise. Charlotte covered her heart, touched at being the chosen one, then walked with Bea up the garden, stooping and chatting.

They reached the front of the house.

"I'm heading back through town," Olivia said, her words clipped.

Cutting their time short, Kate realised.

"OK," she replied.

"I will...erm...see you at our next appointment," Olivia added. She drew herself up into the familiar lawyer, the surface hardening, eyes avoiding Kate's, returning to how they were meant to be.

"OK," is all Kate could say.

Olivia held her bike seat with one hand and carried her helmet with the other.

"Goodbye," Olivia said, the last word between them. And she didn't look back as she pushed her bike along the road.

Kate watched Olivia walk into the village, heavy and rooted to the spot, unable to tear herself away. When Olivia blinked out of sight, she slowly followed Bea and Charlotte towards the river, aware of the woman receding further and further behind her.

Yes, Kate was over that tiny crush on her cool lawyer. The one with an Oxford first, who could slice up a dancefloor with sharp steps, and spin with heated precision. The one who lounged elegant and delectable in a soft jumper. Who said, simply, that she liked her, and it meant so much.

Yes, Kate was over that, because the day had blown it wide open into something else. Something much harder to recover from.

26

Olivia made a mocha coffee in the galley kitchen at work and hugged the steaming mug.

"What a gloomy day," Liz grumbled next to her, stirring a cup. "I'm resorting to adding hot chocolate too."

Through the end window, the sky spread grey over the city of spires and Olivia deflated, every bit as overcast.

"One ray of sunshine for you though," Liz sidled up closer. "Hugo is planning to go part time soon." The office manager's eyebrows did a dance. "The timing is excellent. You," Liz elbowed her gently, "are perfectly lined up for promotion. He wants more involvement in tech cases, and he can't do that and head the firm on fewer hours."

Liz checked towards her and grinned. "Everyone was talking about you landing these high-value clients before Kate Laurence, and as soon as that leaks out, well," she waved a hand, "it's come at exactly the right time."

Olivia hugged her mug tighter with both hands. She should be excited, but other thoughts tugged at her.

"Perfect. Simply," Liz drew out the word, "perfect."

She needed this case done, and Kate out of her mind, to focus on the job she'd always aimed for.

"You OK?" Liz said, lifting her chin.

"I'm a little distracted," Olivia replied. "Sorry."

She had been all week, and every day her distraction only seemed to grow.

"This isn't like you?" Liz said.

"No, I…"

She needed to sign off with Kate before submitting the financial consent order. If that went smoothly, everything should slip through until the divorce was final, with minimal input from Kate. Then Olivia could push this fantasy from her mind, the one that had a very real-world presence and was due in her office.

"I'll be fine," she said. "Soon."

Liz smiled. "Good, because your time has come. Right," she shoved off the counter with her bottom and marched out of the kitchen with a, "catch up later," and a wave over her shoulder.

Olivia wandered to her room, closed the door and leant back against it. What was wrong with her? Her energy had disappeared, leaving her despondent and aching.

She knew why. And who as well. But what was the point of it? Craving a woman she could never be with?

God, it was remarkable though, that Kate Laurence was attracted to her, and she pictured the beautiful actor with her intelligent expression and presence on screen. But the image fogged, and the sense of Kate came through stronger. A woman she knew, and who was so much more wonderful, with an unshakable impact.

But a woman whose life was incompatible with hers, Olivia reminded herself. An actor, busy with family, and whose job demanded she travel all over the globe. It made no sense. She'd be gone in another phase and film. Although Kate had the best intentions to settle in Oxford, her world clearly took turns she didn't expect, and that was the antithesis of what Olivia needed. And who was at this moment, a client.

Time to put everything in its place and back in the right compartments. Because this could go no further. Her career and self-worth depended on it.

She put down her coffee, spinning the square coaster to align with the desk front. She turned, trembling a little, more nervous about this meeting than any before.

"Ms Woodhouse," she practised saying. It wavered.

"Ms Woodhouse," she said, steadier this time, although her insides dropped like a cold stone at treating Kate as a distant client.

She was ready. Her fingers shook. As ready as she'd ever be.

A knock came at the door. She crossed the room to open it.

Immediately Kate's presence washed over her, blasting away any clarity or logic. Here they were again. Kate stood in front of her wearing similar clothes to that first meeting, and Olivia's feelings couldn't be more different.

She opened her mouth to say, "Ms Woodhouse," but nothing came out.

Kate looked at her, desperate to stay impassive, her expression flickering on an edge but eyes holding firm. Then a single, quiet word from her.

"Olivia."

It obliterated any semblance of neutrality and they gazed at each other, eyes yearning, a sad smile of regret apologising.

"Come..." Olivia looked away, "please sit down." Because she couldn't stand that close to Kate and do what she had to do.

She sat at her desk and tapped her laptop into life. Although she stared at the screen, her whole attention pulled towards Kate. The actor with legs crossed, the boots, the jeans, the shirt open at the top. Olivia saw it all clearly even though she focussed on dry letters. The slight tan on her white skin from spring days. The curve of her lips, with tension at the corners. Those beautiful green eyes, clear and full of too many things.

Olivia raised her hands from the keyboard, took a breath to gather herself, then settled them again.

"There are a couple of minor changes..." and she paused, staring at the screen.

Because she needed Kate to come closer, to show her the agreement and clarify it in terms that made sense to her. And Kate would sit near, her scent and warmth bathing Olivia. And, with just as much familiarity, Olivia realised Kate would say "OK" too soon, because she avoided looking at numbers.

"I have to..." Olivia struggled.

Kate stayed silent. She remained in the same position and Olivia knew she watched with unflinching intensity. And although Kate said nothing of their attraction, it hummed between them.

Two items. That's all they needed to check. Just two more.

"These amendments..."

The words stuck again, and that stone dropped deeper inside with realisation. Olivia dipped her head and let the regrettable understanding sink, down and down.

"I want to tell you," she said quietly, "to push back against your ex."

She stared unfocussed, the lines on the screen blurred.

"Your wife's been unfair and dishonest every step of the way, from the prenup to the financial agreement."

She shouldn't be saying this.

"I think she takes advantage of your generosity and your fear of figures. And your accountant is lazy and depends on that too. I want to beg you," she paused because she felt it so strongly, "to get another financial adviser, someone you can trust to manage your income. And yet, I know you want this done quickly."

She swallowed, the realisation sinking further.

"And a part of me wishes you free from this too. And that's the trouble."

Olivia's shoulders sank. Because it was already too late.

"I'm emotionally invested with you."

She was in way over her head.

"And I can't tell if I'm advising you appropriately anymore. With you, I don't even know what detached and impartial is anymore. When you're in the room, my heart beats too fast and my mind spins. It doesn't matter that we're not involved, because I'm overwhelmingly attracted to you, in so many ways, and I can't advise you with a level head."

It was all too late.

"I'm sorry. I let myself get carried away and I've let you down."

She stared, the letters and figures blurring to nothing. What had she done?

"Olivia," Kate whispered.

"I should," she swallowed quickly, "I should have advised you to seek representation elsewhere, right from the start."

"Olivia–"

"I can't represent you," she said sharper. Then, "I shouldn't," more gently, as she deflated. Because she'd failed to do her job.

"I trust you," Kate said, as if trying to reassure her.

"It doesn't matter, because *I*," Olivia said, emphatically, "don't trust me." She glanced at Kate, not daring to linger. "You cannot have a lawyer who feels like this about you. Because you're just sitting there, doing nothing, and I can barely think. I know where you are in a room. Always. I might take my eyes off you, but my mind is still where you are." She breathed in. "I am inextricably drawn to you." She gasped again. "I cannot control this. I cannot compartmentalise this. I have failed utterly here."

The guilty admission sank deep. She'd hardly put a step wrong her whole life. But she had tripped and tumbled weeks ago without even realising. "What must you think of me?" Olivia whispered.

"All kinds of things," Kate murmured, "because I've been thinking of you all week."

Olivia's inhalation shuddered, because Kate's voice bled seductive regard and concern. Another wave of realisation washed over her, of how much this woman's appreciation affected her.

"I'm struggling here too," Kate said quietly. "But I understand you need to finish this."

Olivia turned to her, Kate's features soft in the overcast afternoon, the corners of the office already in shadow. They gazed at each other, neither saying a word, until Olivia's screen blinked dark and the shadows fell further.

"I wanted to call you," Kate whispered.

She sounded closer as the light failed outside, and more intimate in the darkening room.

"I wanted to call you too," Olivia heard herself whisper. She didn't move, her fingers still resting on the keyboard but tingling and dissociating in the dying light.

"All I can think of is how your hands feel," Kate murmured.

And her fingers thrilled with the attention.

"I imagine you taking my hand and pulling me through the crowd again, and I ache to dance with you."

And Olivia couldn't help falling into reminiscence, Kate stroking around her belly, body pressed behind. She'd indulged so many times, reliving the sensation of being surrounded by Kate with her breath balmy on her cheek.

"Do you know how often I recall that moment," Kate said, "you lifting my mask, touching my face and looking at me like that?"

She sensed Kate's lips turning up with fondness and heard the desire in her hushed voice. And she nodded because she'd imagined it all too.

"I want to hold your cheek," Kate whispered. "I want to kiss the corner of your mouth, down your neck, along your collarbone."

Imagined lips caressed everywhere that Kate's words lingered and with the sound of Kate swallowing, the sensation only deepened inside.

"I can feel it because we've danced close enough for me to imagine. I know how your body fits into mine."

Olivia closed her eyes.

"I want to touch you."

Her breath hitched.

"I want to kiss you."

And her head swirled.

"I want all of you."

And the desire almost hauled her across the room.

Olivia opened her eyes, and her hand nudged the laptop into glaring light. The seduction chilled into fright, and it took several moments for her to register how hard she breathed.

"I wish... So much..." Olivia gasped. "But I need you to leave. You must go."

"I know."

"I can't..." She didn't dare move. "I need you to see yourself out."

Olivia couldn't even look at her. She sensed the movement of Kate leaving, her shape rising from the chair, the quiet fall of her steps across the rug, then the door clicking to. She sat, blood draining away and dread settling in her stomach.

This was a disaster.

27

Olivia paused with hand raised to the oak-panelled door of Hugo's office. The weight descended again. She never thought she'd have to make this kind of admission. And of all the times to do it. She shook her head.

She tapped her knuckles on a panel, barely making a sound on the wood.

"Come in!"

Hugo's voice came muffled from the other side, and when she opened the door it expanded into the full reaches of his jovial tone and volume.

"Olivia! Come on in." His face held a smile from laughing with Liz, who sat on the corner of the desk.

"I erm...need to talk to you," she said, the perfect clipped edges of her words dulled.

The pair's heightened spirits dampened, because she never hesitated, and she never spoke that tentatively.

"Of course?" His expression dropped into concern, and he gestured to a chair opposite.

"I'll make a move," Liz said as she shuffled off the desk.

"Actually." Olivia's insides hollowed. "You need to hear this too. I don't know the full repercussions here."

"Oh." Liz halted and sobered.

"Do sit down though," Hugo said gently.

And Olivia only realised then that she'd frozen inside the door. This was worse than confessing a transgression to her parents as a child.

She looked at the pair on the other side of the desk. Hugo, managing partner and head of the firm. And Liz, the practice manager who made everything work. The latter a good friend who saw eye-to-eye with her on so many things, the other someone she'd wanted to impress for years. A gulf opened between them, and she wished she didn't have to confess.

"I need to hand over a case," she said.

Hugo's mouth made a tiny 'o', and he rested his clasped hands on the desk.

"I've erm..." she took a breath, "developed feelings for a client and I'm no longer suitable representation."

"Oh," came louder from Hugo, and his brow plunged into a deep furrow. He followed with, "Oh dear," and her heart dropped into that gulf. "You'd better tell us more."

"The client is Kate Woodhouse."

Hugo's eyebrows shot up, and from the corner of her vision she caught Liz pursing her lips. Did she suspect already?

"And how long has this been going on?" Hugo asked.

"There is no relationship," she added quickly. "No impropriety has occurred. But neither am I dispassionate."

"And does the client know? Has Kate realised about your feelings towards her?"

"Yes," she said, almost inaudible. "I've told her I'm unable to represent her given..." All the feelings that had grown without her even realising, until they'd reached over everything, turned all the boxes upside down and refused to go back inside. "She knows."

"Oh goodness," Hugo said. "And would you mind telling us how she took it?"

Olivia glanced up at Liz and she must have pleaded in that look. She feared speaking for Kate, and how she felt, because hope glimmered deep down and Olivia wanted to keep that quiet and restrained.

"I think perhaps," Liz started, "we need to know whether the client is happy to continue with the firm or if there's a bigger issue to handle."

Olivia nodded, half in understanding, and half grateful to her friend.

"I think she'd be happy to transfer to Alec initially. Perhaps after they've talked it over they can decide from there."

"Right, well," Hugo said, "that's a relief at least. I didn't have any inkling she was dissatisfied with our service. So, good, although..."

Here it came.

"I must say, I'm very surprised." Hugo shook his head. "And disappointed."

That sinking sensation hit bottom.

"I didn't expect anything like this from, of all people, you Olivia."

She didn't want to meet their eyes. "I understand perfectly," she said.

That it was the wrong time to make a mistake. Not the behaviour of someone to head the firm.

Hugo continued. "We need to cover the transfer to Alec and ensure we apply fees appropriately for our mishandling of the case."

That jarred like screeching tyres and a crash. She never mishandled a case. It was excruciating.

"I'll chat with Kate myself," Hugo said, sitting back, "but as long as she's happy, I hope the transfer will be seamless?"

Olivia nodded. Of course, she'd do a thorough job, but doubt overshadowed her now, didn't it.

"Kate's divorce has kept a low profile," Hugo continued, "so I don't imagine any questions in public. Liz? Any other issues you need to follow up?"

"Not for now." Liz shook her head. "Olivia, I think you should go home, have a break and get some rest over the weekend."

"Yes," Hugo agreed. "Get some perspective. But first thing Monday, please hand everything to Alec."

Olivia nodded. "Will that be all?"

"That's all for now."

Dismissed by her senior colleagues in a way never done before, she turned from the room a different person, no longer on an equal footing with either. Her youth, drive and fresh expertise no longer counted for anything with this mistake. Feeling lower with every step, the door closed, and she walked away.

She waited for despair to descend in the deafening silence of the building late in the day, but rapid footsteps from behind surprised her. A firm grip took her arm and, before she realised what was happening, Liz tugged her into her own office, switched on the light and shut out the rest of the world.

Liz glared. "You," she pointed, "do not have to be perfect." She didn't blink. "Do you hear me? You do not have to be flawless."

Olivia, slow with swirling thoughts, took a moment to register. "I've made a mistake though."

"Yes, you have. A very human mistake," Liz emphasised. "Like every single other person in this building."

"But I..."

"Yes, you try harder than anyone to make sure that doesn't happen." The defiant glare softened. "But this is a company of imperfect people, including Hugo and me."

Brain fogged with disappointment, Olivia gazed at her friend, who gently smiled.

"You do not have to get it right *all* the time." Liz waggled her finger. "No-one ever does. And I've got you." She plonked her hands on Olivia's shoulders. "I have your back. And I will make damn sure Hugo remembers how many second chances he gives others."

"This is–"

"Something you've now handled appropriately." Liz squeezed her shoulders. "Get it sorted. Hand the case to Alec. After that, you're covered. Just a human who got too involved. It happens."

"I will take care of it," Olivia replied quietly to the practice manager. Then more to Liz, her friend, "I didn't realise how much I'd grown to like her."

Liz's cheeks lifted in an indulgent smile. "I wondered at Hugo's party."

That dance. Olivia's face turned to fire. Of course, someone caught it.

"She is gorgeous." Liz groaned her appreciation.

"Don't you start. Please."

Liz chuckled. "Is that what it takes, hey? To turn your head and make you forget yourself?"

"What do you mean?" Olivia frowned.

"Does it take one of the most beautiful women on the entire planet!?"

"She's..."

It was odd hearing that phrase, even though she'd heard it applied to Kate before. Some silly top-ten list. Because, yes, Olivia thought her phenomenally beautiful, but in a way that was linked to moments they spent together. Kate's face in the evening light while they drifted along the river. When she laughed at Olivia calling her film 'truly awful' and the creases round her eyes turning to stars. Her smile when she greeted Olivia at the Botanic Gardens – a welcome never seen on film.

The phrase seemed banal and artificial for someone so real to her as Kate.

She came to with a gentle nudge from Liz. "You've got it bad." And another laugh rumbled from Liz's chest.

As she opened the door and Liz went out, Alec waved on his way past, coat on and briefcase hanging from his shoulder.

"Alec?" she called, her voice subdued.

"Yes?" The short man spun around, pale face open for whatever Olivia had to say.

"I'm very sorry, but do you have a few minutes?"

"Of course, I can delay if it's high priority."

No, it wasn't. And she wasn't going to pull seniority and make him stay.

"It's more important from a personal perspective," she said, aware that her voice faltered. "Rather than top priority for the firm."

He hesitated, confused a moment, before he looked at her and softened. "Then I can definitely spare you time."

Her heart lurched, grateful for the introduction to Millie's generous friend, and now a respected colleague.

"Thank you," she said. "Please come in."

28

"Shit." Kate put down her book.

She hadn't even opened it this time. Her eyes had washed in blues of the cover as she stared unfocussed and preoccupied with Olivia.

She'd thought of nothing else since leaving the Bentley office. It was dark outside the window of the lounge that overlooked the garden, only the silhouettes of trees visible now against the indigo night sky. The house stood too quiet, with the kids away at Harry's and no distractions to keep her mind from turning over and over.

For something to do, she went downstairs to the lower ground floor kitchen, put on the kettle, then noticed the last mug of tea standing undrunk.

"Shit, shit, shit." She leant on the countertop.

She'd gone in with the best intentions, accepting where they stood and understanding the job Olivia had to do. But as soon as Olivia opened the door, she'd broken and saw it collapse in her too. It seemed like the whole room flooded, and Olivia's presence pulled at her and wouldn't let go. Even when Olivia walked to her desk, desperate to remain the detached lawyer. Even when she told Kate to leave. Kate had to sever herself from the building, knowing Olivia felt as strongly.

She flinched when her phone buzzed on the kitchen top, the screen lighting up with 'Olivia Sachdeva', and she snatched it up.

"Hi... hi... How are you doing?"

Footsteps echoed in the background, from sharp heels on a pavement, and cars streamed by.

"Are you free to talk?" Olivia said, subdued.

"Yes, I'm home. The kids are with Harry. I have all the time in the world for you." Because she couldn't do anything apart from think of Olivia.

"Things have moved quickly," Olivia said. "I... I should give you an update."

The words were formal, the tone was not, and Olivia projected a heavy heart.

"I've told Hugo I can't handle your case. He'll suggest you transfer to my colleague, Alec." Footsteps came through, but no words, and Kate let Olivia take her time. After a deep breath she added, "He's an excellent solicitor and human being. I recommend him without reservation."

"Will you be alright? Are you in trouble?"

Olivia hesitated. The footsteps continued and snatched chatter from others made it through. Kate guessed Olivia passed through the town centre, or perhaps walked home through Jericho's cafes and pubs.

"It's...not my best move professionally," Olivia admitted.

And the hope in Kate's chest crumpled. "I'm sorry."

"It's not your fault."

"But..." She wasn't blameless. "I wish I could have done things differently."

She thought it over, listening to Olivia's footsteps on the other end of the line, her breath catching from time to time, although she didn't speak.

"You," Kate started, "affect me." She sighed. "I shouldn't have said anything this afternoon, but I meant every word."

"I know," came back quietly. "But you need a clear head and heart to get through this."

She listened to what Olivia said. She let it spin round and settle. But it didn't ring true for her.

"It's been over a long time with Nat." She hardly thought of her anymore. "And I had no intention of seeing anyone, because god I realise that I'm a bundle of complicated."

It'd been the last thing on her mind when she'd walked through Olivia's door in March. But the memory morphed into the woman of this afternoon, the prickly, frosty lawyer long gone, and the humorous, charming, vulnerable human being in her place, beguiling beyond anyone for Kate.

"I can't help wanting you," she murmured, unsure if Olivia heard.

She closed her eyes, listening to Olivia's footsteps, unable to pull away, and happier with this small connection than she'd been all evening. There was nothing to say, but she couldn't let go, and kept her eyes shut to hold Olivia nearer.

"I..." Olivia's breath juddered. "I can't help wanting you too."

And Kate caved inside, hearing that need. Her face warmed where she held the phone tight to her ear. It was quieter now, just the two of them on the line, unable to tear away.

"I wish..." Kate paused. She wished Olivia was here, even with everything impossible. Even when everything said this was a bad idea.

Then silence, and she wondered if Olivia had made it home.

"Where are you? Are you ok?" she whispered.

"I'm..." Olivia started. "I know I shouldn't be..." And Kate waited, praying she didn't hang up. "But I'm here, trying not to knock on your door."

Kate opened her eyes and was plunged vividly into where she stood. The kitchen glowed in the cabinet under-lights and the hum of the fridge was the only sound.

"Olivia," she gasped, before striding across the floor, running up the stairs, with quick paces down the dark hallway to the door. She threw it open.

Beneath glowing street lanterns, the central garden trees silhouetted behind her, Olivia stood in the road, phone in hand, eyebrows that could be so imperious now raised as if pleading. Her mouth hung open wordless, as if afraid to ask.

"Please, please, please come in," Kate had no hesitation begging.

She stepped back, allowing Olivia inside, and gently shut the door, so it was only the two of them, away from the world.

"This is a bad idea," Olivia said, pitch breaking in desperation.

"I know," Kate whispered.

She gazed at Olivia's face, those brown eyes softened and her beautiful, silky eyebrows a ripple of concern.

"This can't even go anywhere," Olivia implored.

"I know that too."

"But I want to kiss you."

And to that, Kate could only say, "Please."

Olivia dropped her briefcase and stepped closer, distinctly taller in her heels. Kate didn't waver when Olivia lifted her hand to near her cheek, the heat apparent on her face before Olivia touched her. The gesture was careful, delicate and appreciative of this first intimate contact. Then only fingertips landed, so that Kate closed her eyes to savour the warm places they joined. Everything within her pulled to those pools on her cheek, like she flowed inside.

So used to the harshness of filming and the bodies of random partners, take after take, until she was physically sore, this careful, considered woman was a gentle balm. The two of them stood hidden from the street outside, Olivia taking her cheek in her hand, barely touching. Then came a kiss that was divinity and honey on her lips.

Everything blended, the world dissolved away, her mind melting and body gone. For moment after moment she had no foot on earth. The delicate intensity of the fingertips was nothing compared with the tenderness of Olivia's lips. And when Kate opened her eyes, she soared higher seeing Olivia's face betray the same insensibility.

"Again," Olivia murmured, as if unaware she spoke and the thought made its own way out.

Kate reached up this time, taking Olivia's beautiful lips with hers, then took her deeper, so she felt Olivia's heat on her tongue. The movement to close the gap between them was unconscious, but the vivid awareness of Olivia pressing against her burst inside.

Olivia's lean body, which had moved sensually beneath her hands when they danced, was softer and primed for a different intimacy. She stroked around Olivia's sides, the warm, real presence enthralling, and it was almost with disbelief that she finally held her near.

They parted lips so that their rapid breaths fluttered in the gap between their faces.

Kate didn't know what to say, but they must have shared the same thought, because they kissed again, more eagerly. Hands caressed around her back, and Kate hummed with appreciation without realising she arched into Olivia. This was overpowering, her head swimming and eyes heavy, all clumsy with the swell of desire.

She gulped as she tipped her chin away.

"I erm..." she was almost slurring. "I don't want to presume anything." She had to stop to gasp. "But I test, regularly. And there's been no-one. In a long time." She swallowed again. "Just saying."

Olivia's breath misted her mouth. "Same." She licked her lips as if also struggling to speak. "No-one since. Just saying too."

A moan escaped Kate as she pulled into Olivia again, the admission freeing them both. Her hands made their own way up, stroking and appreciating Olivia's slender neck and taking handfuls of hair as they kissed.

Olivia's touch wandered her body at the same time, so that every bit of her came alive, from the fingers massaging either side of her spine, curving around her hips, then pausing, tentative but clearly wanting more.

"Can we...?"

"Let's go upstairs."

Kate switched the lights low in her bedroom at the rear of the house. She drew the curtains on the garden and quickly checked around – the ensuite door shut, the bed clear, smooth white duvet and sheets open. She turned to Olivia in the doorway, who waited patiently with dark eyes following her every move.

Kate approached and took Olivia's hand, their fingers slipping together enough to light lines of desire again.

"Come in," she murmured, and she pushed the bedroom door shut.

She smiled suddenly, stroking beneath the lapels of Olivia's coat. Familiar with the intimate warmth of that garment from weeks ago, she wondered at the inevitability of them being here now. She slipped the coat away and Olivia's body heat was still perceptible as she lay it on the chair.

Her attention immediately sprung back to Olivia, and she sighed.

"Have you any idea how beautiful you are?" she said, resting her hands lightly on Olivia's shoulders.

Because Kate hadn't appreciated it fully until now. She allowed herself to really, truly look.

She stroked her fingers through Olivia's luxurious black hair, tucking it behind an ear. Gazed at her eyebrows and traced a finger along them; rare that they acquiesced and stayed relaxed, with Olivia's intense gaze entranced. Over her cheeks, proud and prominent, down to her dark lips that opened with warm breath as Kate stroked, so pliable and evocative of other places she wanted to explore. She descended Olivia's elegant neck, fingertips over her collarbone, to the top of her dress neckline and the neat thin zip that ran all the way down.

"Can I?"

The slightest nod, and Kate slowly pulled down the zip, the sound subtle in its suggestion but promising so much that Kate felt it through her whole body. She paused, shy, at stroking the dress over Olivia's shoulders, because the suppleness of Olivia's skin on her palms overwhelmed. She'd never touched this much of her naked, and it was another wave, another step up in their intimacy, and had her reeling.

Kate was only half aware of Olivia undressing her too. The shirt unbuttoning, her chest prickling alive at being exposed. Her arms tingling as Olivia gently stripped the sleeves. A finger stroked beneath the waist of her jeans, and her breath hitched. Everywhere shivered heightened as her garments dropped and they stood close in only their underwear.

"It's almost too much," she whispered, resting her fingers on the black straps of Olivia's bra.

But she didn't stop. She slipped them away over Olivia's shoulders, the cups folding down, and revealing the curves of beautiful breasts.

"My god," she breathed. Her hand swept around their curves, and she delighted inside. And again, as Olivia inhaled at the caress.

She stared stunned, while Olivia quickly undid behind, bra dropping to the floor, and dispensed with Kate's too.

Then Olivia stroked around her back, encouraged her closer, and with the softest touch of breast to breast, she fell into Olivia.

"I... It's..." So sensational she almost couldn't stand it. The naked caress of them together all-consuming.

"Come to bed," Olivia whispered by her ear.

And somehow her legs turned and made it there, her entirety receptive and awake as she lay on the sheets.

Olivia knelt beside her and leant over, her body a captivating vision. Her beautiful brown skin, the line down her stomach, her breasts swaying with the movement.

Sensing Olivia gazed at her, she looked up and found a radiant face consumed with want. It shocked and warmed everywhere. Olivia bent down and, without hesitation, kissed her lips. The sensation on her mouth was loving and liquid. Then the touch of her breasts on Kate's, fire again.

When Olivia leant back, her gaze trailed Kate with hungry appreciation.

"Talk about beautiful." She hummed.

Olivia stroked down her chest, and Kate writhed as Olivia took her breast firmly in her hand. She spread fingers to enjoy their curves and squeezed.

"Oh," Kate breathed, seduced as much by Olivia's intoxicated expression as her touch.

She gasped quicker as that touch journeyed down her stomach, lighting her inside with multiple trails sparking lower. Olivia stopped there, a single finger slowing and teasing its way over the wide band of Kate's bikini briefs.

"These," Olivia murmured.

A finger swept down edges of Kate's underwear and around the curve of her thigh. It flirted between her legs, circled around her lips, over her opening that was wet against the material.

"I want these to come off," Olivia said quickly.

Obediently, because Olivia had always commanded her, she lifted from the bed and pulled them down.

Olivia's face slackened a moment, clearly overcome with what she saw, then quickly stood back, removing her own neat black underwear, never taking her eyes off Kate. Eager, Olivia climbed towards her, careful not to touch in a single place, and knelt between her legs, hands either side of Kate's chest.

Kate lay expectant in the warm shadow of Olivia's body and under the spell of dark longing in her expression. A curtain of black hair fell and swept across her face, and Kate closed her eyes to enjoy the electrifying tickle on her cheeks. It leaped about her scalp and sent her tingling, with everything heightened and sensitive to Olivia.

Vision blanked and body euphoric, a succulent kiss to her top lip came vivid, long and tender. Oh, it was divine. Then a sharp nip at her bottom lip, and she inhaled.

Kisses trailed her neck, one tiny caress at a time. Some like satisfying pin pricks. Others soft blissful droplets of attention that sent pleasure in waves across her skin. She revelled in Olivia's touch, that was as gentle but confident as the woman herself, and Kate gave in to her expertise.

Then succulent warmth surrounded her nipple.

"Oh", she drew out in a moan, caving with the thrill that gripped her breast.

She shuddered as the arousal twinged deliciously, Olivia's lips firm around her nipple. Still thrilling, her lower body fluttered in tune to Olivia's hand, which trailed along her side and swept under her behind.

She opened her eyes to find Olivia with intention burning in her stare and eagerness in the hands that lifted Kate's hips towards hers.

"I want to sink into you," Olivia said, voice low.

Kate pulsed between her legs, her heat craving contact with Olivia. She spread her thighs wide to let her in and watched Olivia carefully lower her body. A tiny touch quickened Kate's inner thigh, then away again with a slight adjustment, so that when Olivia descended, her smooth hip slipped perfectly between where Kate soaked.

She shot back with the intensity of it. When she forced her eyes to stay open, she found Olivia's fixed on hers. She bucked again as Olivia rolled the roundness of her hip bone over where she throbbed. Kate groaned in rhythm, with Olivia circling down into her moisture and rubbing over her clit. It must have overcome Olivia too, her eyes hooded and breaths short. Firmer, Olivia rocked her hips, so she stroked with an exquisite sensitivity that had Kate climbing.

Quicker, Olivia pushed onto her, the rhythm deepening, and Kate held her arms around Olivia, hugging her tight.

"Oh that's..." Kate tried.

Unbearably good. Unspeakably good. The whole sensation of Olivia naked and intimate between her legs, both gentle and raw.

She clasped her hands down Olivia's back, hungrier now to take her in, over the wonderful curves of her behind that moved faster as Kate squeezed her.

Her body took over, urgent to explore, and she slipped her hand between them both. And she was shocked, finding Olivia hot and wet.

"Oh my god," she gasped. "You're so turned on."

Olivia moaned and slackened as Kate swept her finger around her pert desire. Kate circled her in a daze, savouring the sensation, so impossibly tender beneath her fingertips.

"Please touch me," she whispered. "Touch me with your fingers too."

And Olivia urgently rose up her body. She dipped her hand between Kate's lips, immediately becoming slick with moisture. A soft finger found her edges with trembling eagerness. Another sweep, and she shuddered with an incoherent moan. Then with purpose, both firm and delicious, Olivia stroked a fingertip around her centre.

Kate clenched and hung to Olivia without a sound. She thought she would tip.

But she wavered and acclimatised again to a new high. They thrust, shorter and quicker, their fingers slick with the other. Kate groaned, insensible, unsure if the noise was her or Olivia.

Above her, Olivia shook, coming undone. She swayed and a breast stroked Kate's cheek. She opened her mouth wanting to gorge on Olivia's plump softness and swirled the nipple inside with her tongue. With every sweep around her clit, she sucked in time, hard and harder, to an aroused and loud cry from above.

The sensations were too much. And with Olivia's soft breast in her mouth, her slick tenderness swollen beneath her fingertips, her own clit tensing with Olivia's caress, the first tidal wave hit. She clung on and thrust blind in the divine hold, gripped from head to toes, as she exploded at the centre.

Blinding, ferocious, exhausting intensity.

Plunging and riding the waves, one after another. Delirious shaking. Sinking and falling. Slowing and melting.

Then Olivia on top of her, gasping and misted with perspiration. Soft. So soft. And so unbelievably wonderful.

Kate threw her arms around Olivia, and held tight, as their deep breaths rose and fell, her mind and body dazzled, never wanting to let go. She couldn't stop kissing her.

***

Later, when they'd kissed and touched, over and over until spent, Olivia lay serene by her side.

"We probably shouldn't have done that," Olivia said quietly, brown eyes content, lips smooth and fulfilled, utterly unrepentant at what they'd done.

Their legs intertwined and arms rested on each other in a loose, relaxed cuddle, bodies humming and happy on hormones.

"A very good, bad idea." Kate smiled.

Lying here, after being tenderly loved by this woman, was the best of moments. As her, Kate Woodhouse only. No-one making demands. As if they had all the time in the world.

She gazed at those darkest brown eyes, so beautiful it was absurd how much she loved them now.

"I don't regret a single thing," Olivia murmured.

"Me neither," Kate whispered. "And I know it's complicated, but please stay. Just one night. I want you here."

"I'd like that."

And they held each other closer, Kate marvelling at the shape of her, and the beautiful woman flowing down the bed.

"This is nice," Olivia said.

Kate quietly laughed at their shared habit of understating things. Perhaps they always tried to hold back, because being together had been forbidden. And she also laughed because this was pure delight. Kate didn't have many moments like this, and she wanted to enjoy every second.

"Yes, it is. It's incredibly nice."

Because this nice was rare.

29

Warmth bathed Kate's eyelids and she blinked awake in a beam of sunlight through a gap in the curtains. She shifted beneath the duvet, letting the present sink in. This was the most relaxed and content she'd woken up in a long time, with Olivia, naked, beside her.

Her cheeks rose, and she smiled more, because her cheeks glowed too.

Olivia lay faced away, with her shoulders and the sweep of her back exposed. She stirred with Kate waking, took a moment perhaps coming to the same awareness, and rolled to face her.

Olivia in the morning was something divine and beautiful, and silly and wonderful. Finally, a hair out of place with that black silkiness all mussed up and tousled. Kate didn't think she could love it more. At the same time her heart skipped, not used to the woman who'd been her lawyer naked in her bed, having been touched and loved by her the night before.

Olivia smiled too, maybe at the same fantastic incongruity but with a characteristic tilt of her head.

"Good morning, Ms Woodhouse," she said, breaking into a brilliant grin.

That did it. Full on beaming from Kate.

"Good morning, Ms Sachdeva."

Would she ever get used to an Olivia smile? No, not this one.

"Are you OK?" Kate said. "Is this too strange?"

Olivia gazed at her, taking in her face, sweeping around her cheeks and seductively down to her lips.

"It's not my usual morning," Olivia replied, "but I like it."

Kate shuffled closer with the duvet pulled to her chin, a little self-conscious with the daylight streaming through the curtains. Then she lost herself in Olivia's eyes, the pupils merging with the deep brown in the subdued light and the hint of makeup still perfect. Long inky eyelashes blinked, slow and relaxed.

"Me too," Kate sighed, dopey and content.

She wanted to reach out to Olivia. To touch her forehead that was smooth from concerns this morning, only a thin thread and vestige of old disapproval remaining at the top of her straight nose. To stroke the silky black eyebrows, cup her shapely cheeks, take in her light brown skin that had deepened and warmed in the spring sunshine, trail a finger down to her plump lips, where patterns of delicate lines fascinated.

Kate must have dwelled with intention, because one of those silky eyebrows raised with amused accusation.

"If you look at me like that, Ms Woodhouse, it won't be just one night."

Kate laughed at the mix of formal and suggestion. "Sorry. It's nice looking at you like this."

"Same," Olivia said, and she raised her hand as if to touch Kate's face but hesitated, the same urge apparent.

"Do you mind if I shower before I go?" Olivia asked. "I'm," she glanced down, "covered in us from last night."

A flood of images worked on Kate, of Olivia naked beneath the covers and scented with their intimacy, and she burst with memories of how that happened. She baked under the duvet.

"Go ahead," she said, voice turning husky.

Dark eyes blinked back at her with a flash of desire pooling, and the tip of Olivia's tongue moistened her lips apart unmistakably. She swallowed. "I'll get showered then."

"OK," Kate sighed, the longing audible.

Olivia turned away, stretched like a graceful cat – she may have even purred – threw back the duvet, swept her long legs out of bed and stood up naked. She twirled round with the same elegance as when she danced and put her hands on her hips.

"Where's best for me to shower?" she asked.

"..."

"Your ensuite perhaps?"

"Of...course," Kate answered, voice strangled.

Her jaw hung open, because Olivia was ten times more beautiful in daylight. The curves of her hips were more generous naked than when covered in the tight lines of a black dress, with a suppleness that made Kate ache.

Olivia moved with obvious confidence, as if she wore one of those pristine dresses. Kate envied it but was also floored as she watched Olivia sashay into the ensuite. That movement. Those legs. That sway of her chest.

She groaned.

"Did you say something?" came from the ensuite.

The groan had been loud.

"Erm...Would you like a coffee?" she projected to cover the revealing sound.

"Yes please," came back.

Kate sat, brain buzzing and body tingling.

Then, "Strong with milk, please," came softer and nearby.

Kate turned to find a curving breast and dark nipple at face height. Her memory of the night before conjured its imprint on her lips, and the sensation struck deep.

"OK," she said with a throttled whisper.

And Olivia's beautiful physique disappeared again.

She may have sat stunned for several minutes, and at the end of them all she managed was, "Oh wow."

Then, "Towel."

Kate jumped out of bed, grabbed a fresh white one from the cupboard and stomped, much less elegantly than Olivia, to the ensuite.

"Clean towel's on the radiator," she called out, not waiting for an answer.

Because they said just one night. And if she stayed a second longer, she'd be gone for days.

***

Olivia padded down the stairs. She found the front room open and glowing with sunlight from outside, with a fresh green hue to the shadows from the central gardens. She couldn't remember the door ajar before, and peeped inside in case Kate was there.

Books. Hundreds of books. Floor to ceiling cases lined every wall and either side of a cushioned window seat. Irresistible curiosity drew her inside and she ran a finger along a row of spines. Classics, old and modern: Austen, Ishiguro, Woolf. Then a collection of Kuang and Pullman and others, which Olivia guessed at an Oxford setting, because the books were not randomly thrown on the shelves. A set of romances took a criminal turn through Iceland, then *Nimona, Lightening Thief* and *Hunger Games* started a run of novels she assumed were Kate's son's. Lower shelves burst with picture books, and she imagined the whole family used the beanbags and two sofas that were covered in cushions.

"Hi."

She turned to find Kate in the doorway, hair thrown into a messy bun and golden strands falling across her face. She wore a loose white T-shirt, sleeves cut high and neck low, so it was immediately apparent how toned she was. Her upper chest was strong and her shoulders gently defined, biceps rose in soft mounds from holding two mugs of coffee, and the rest of her figure the beautiful curves that she was known for.

Olivia took a breath, because she knew those curves intimately now, familiar with the softness between her thighs, the sensation of full breasts on hers, the pillow of her belly, the deliciousness of descending and rolling between her legs. And the wetness there. That had a vivid seduction of its own. It leaped from her imagination into real flutters over her body, as if she were still slick on her mound.

A sheen of sweat broke on her back and she may, it was entirely possible, have sighed. A smile pinched at the corners of Kate's mouth, and Olivia snapped up her eyes.

"Good morning," Olivia said, some part of her brain desperate to stay polite.

"Good morning again," Kate said. Her smile broadened. She passed a mug forward, putting it on a shelf and twisted the handle towards Olivia.

Olivia sipped at it for something to do that wasn't appreciating curves or reliving moist tenderness, while Kate bit her lip.

Olivia tried to speak several times. But failed. Kate's cheeks betrayed her with rose blooming on them. And Olivia's glow inside was nothing to do with hot coffee.

"I see you found our book room," Kate said, taking a sip of coffee and her face deepening. Perhaps it was from the rising steam from the mug. Maybe at their night in bed. Or just the obvious attraction which persisted and pulsed between them.

"You were right about your passion," Olivia said. A flush of warmth touched her own cheeks. "I meant your book passion."

Kate's eyes brightened with humour, and she glanced away along the shelf, but then returned to Olivia.

"We're a bunch of book nerds, all three of us."

Kate ran her finger down a glossy dark-pink spine on the romance shelf. She stopped, the movement suggestive, and they fell quiet again.

"I'm not used to this, you know," Kate said. Still the smiles.

Olivia opened her mouth in silent question.

"I feel a bit exposed this morning," Kate added, and they quietly laughed.

Olivia wondered, "Aren't you used to undressing in front of people and cameras?"

"No. Not as me." Kate shook her head. "Work is work. It gets to a point that my body's like a tool, shot in a particular way, airbrushed beyond recognition, even when I insist it should be real. It all becomes fiction after a while." She took a sip as if to boost her confidence. "But being with someone, letting them see everything...as truly me, close up, unfiltered..."

Kate gazed at her, a seriousness behind the blushing smile.

"And this," Kate said at last. "I don't do this very often. The intimacy." Her eyebrows twitched into a frown. "I know you think my past is messy but–"

"No. I was being judgemental. I'm sorry."

"It's not accurate, that's all," Kate said. "People are different, and I don't care what they do." Her face softened again. "But this is...a big deal for me."

Olivia peered down at her coffee, then to Kate, because everything drew back to her. "You've probably guessed, but I don't do this often either."

And the air hung so thick between them that Olivia imagined it tickled over her hands.

"Is it the whole not-liking-people thing?" Kate asked, her mouth curving.

"It does tend to get in the way."

And both laughed.

Olivia's heart thudded, and she couldn't ignore the rising of something vital for her.

"It takes time," she admitted, "for me to grow to like someone. But when it does happen, when I find someone, with friends too, they become very important to me." She hesitated. "There aren't many." She was afraid to overstate it or admit it to herself. "And even fewer who have my full respect." She swirled her coffee but succumbed to the ever-present pull and looked Kate in the eye. "But you are one of them."

"You know I like you," Kate said. "And it turns out I find you..." she paused and inhaled deeply, as if to cool herself, "very sexy."

Olivia's cheeks burned too hot not to be visible. "Same," she admitted, even though she didn't know how to say it. She gave up the restraint. "If you must know, you standing there in that T-shirt makes me sweat."

Surprise played on Kate's face, then she bit her lip, holding back both amusement and, Olivia could see, pleasure too.

"To be honest," Kate said, "memories keep intruding this morning, which is inconvenient given the erm..." Kate was, if Olivia wasn't mistaken, sweating, "...time limit on our agreement."

Just one night, they'd said.

Kate's eyes travelled down her body, a subconscious trip, and Olivia thrilled with the attention as keenly as if fingers trailed her.

Kate swallowed just as affected by the journey. "Seriously regretting the time limit of our agreement, Ms Sachdeva."

Olivia didn't want to speak because it might come out a moan. She licked her lips instead and Kate grinned, both blushing with their minds travelling to the same destination.

"I want so much..." Olivia began. It unravelled into a husky groan.

They'd agreed for a reason, the one night already a complication too far. Although Olivia had a hard time holding on to that right now. She couldn't stop smiling.

"I need to leave before we redraft that agreement," she said.

Kate beamed at her. "Walk you home, though?"

Olivia nodded, because she should be safe from succumbing to Kate in the refined streets of North Oxford.

Kate threw on a blazer and large sunglasses as they stepped outside. Perhaps to anyone else she appeared as Kate, the smartly dressed Park Town resident. But to Olivia she was irresistibly curvy and toned Kate. She'd put on a necklace, the pendants and long chain resting in the top of her cleavage. The weight of it captured Olivia's attention and tickled at her own chest in tactile empathy. It teased and thrilled, while drawing her gaze. She wanted to stroke the firm rise of Kate's chest beneath the collarbone before sweeping lower to full breasts.

Not so safe.

"Do you have plans today?" Kate asked.

It was a tentative and leading question. Olivia didn't mistake where it was going, because she still had eyes there too.

"Regrettably," she groaned. "I have friends coming round."

"Shame."

"Huge shame," Olivia gasped.

"Because I wondered," Kate walked closer, "if, you know, our agreement had specified the one night, or..."

Their fingers touched.

"There was ambiguity?"

"Quite."

"Perhaps it could have been twenty-four hours?"

They looked at each other, open lust surely on both their faces. Kate's expression bloomed, the smile overcome with want, both breathing harder than the gentle stroll needed.

Olivia licked her lips again and, for once, had to roll her eyes at herself. Because this level of attraction rarely happened for her.

They didn't live far apart. Olivia cursed and welcomed it at the same time. The sunny morning roasted as they strolled the smart brick terraces of leafy North Oxford. Walking became uncomfortable, and she regretted an earlier decision.

She needed to get inside her house, to cool down and prepare for guests, and later she'd try to put last night in a box.

They quickly crossed the main road into her narrow, quiet street. Olivia stared determined ahead, while hopelessly aware of the heat of Kate beside her. Imagined or not, it didn't matter, because Olivia stripped Kate in her mind, and Kate may as well have been naked and touching her.

Home. The yellow door. She'd nearly made it.

She opened the small white gate, marched to the door and quickly unlocked it. She twirled round, but Kate stood closer than she expected, the warmth of proximity now blazing heat. Those green and amber eyes were shaded behind sunglasses, but passion resided there. And those lips, distinctive curves as always, but plump and red with desire. Those kissable lips with a sheen that made her own mouth water. She wanted to lick inside. Oh god, she needed to get in the house.

"Have," Olivia inhaled, "have a..."

She had no idea what Kate's plans were, or how to engage in ordinary conversation.

"Good night," Olivia said, and she spun on the spot and closed the door.

She dropped her briefcase, leant on a wall and moaned. It was broad daylight, not night. But her head was back in Kate's bedroom with her fingers between Kate's thighs.

"Oh my god, get a grip," she said to herself, as she wiped her forehead and beads of sweat merged into liquid through her fingers.

She stumbled into the lounge and clung to the back of her grey sofa. She trembled, body filled with longing and lust, much greater than the night before. The hunger ached stronger now she'd tasted Kate.

"Oh good god," she murmured again, covering her face.

She was soaking wet. Her upper thighs had slipped against each other while she'd walked and craved Kate. She put her hand to her stomach and it sent a shock through her whole body, the actual physical contact heightened by the imagined.

A knock at the door, and she twitched round.

Dammit. It couldn't be Charlotte and Millie already. She glanced at a clock on the wall. No, still mid-morning. She straightened her dress, ran hands through her damp hair. Whoever it was, they'd have to be quick, because she burned all over.

She tugged the door open and found herself face to face with Kate. She didn't have time to step back and they panted close together, the heavy heat and intimacy intoxicating.

"Hi," Kate said, glasses off, eyes dark and gaze sweeping over Olivia.

"Come in," Olivia stuttered, because Kate couldn't look at her like that in public.

Kate shouldn't look at her like that in private either because Olivia was down to her last drop of will power. She marched into the lounge to get some distance, hearing the front door shut behind her.

But when she turned, she found herself almost nose to nose with Kate again. Those lips were a terrifying lapse away, and luscious breaths steamed Olivia's cheeks.

"I wondered," Kate struggled to breathe, as if she'd sprinted back. "How long until your friends?"

"An hour," Olivia whimpered. "Maybe two?" That last drop of will power? Pure vapour now. "Would you like a cup of tea?" Final futile resistance.

"Olivia," Kate said, low and like velvet.

"Yes?"

"I didn't come back for a cup of tea."

And Olivia gasped, "Oh, thank god."

She didn't know who moved first, but they kissed. Deep, lingering, wonderful kisses. Lips slid over lips, with tongues dipping, wanting and needing. Hands hungered everywhere and her mind turned to some heady oblivion, and she lost where she was.

"Oh," she moaned, as Kate's hand swept over her breast.

Kate squeezed her, and again, and deep instinct had her thrusting into Kate's thighs.

"Do you like that?" Kate whispered, slipping away from her lips, then devouring her between words.

Olivia nodded, quick and easy as if her neck was oiled. Kate squeezed her breast hard in rhythmic pulses that played out between her legs, electrifying pleasure shooting from chest to core.

"I want this so badly," Kate said, hands burning Olivia in a tantalising massage. Kate had reached the hem of her dress and caressed up her thighs.

Olivia tried to speak, to warn her, but nothing formed in her head or voice. While hungry kisses seduced her, fingers stroked higher, hitched up her dress and swept around her naked backside. She groaned out loud.

The hands halted on her buttocks, soft and tantalising and holding her on an edge. Olivia looked down to Kate's astonished face.

"You're not wearing knickers," Kate gasped.

Olivia panted. She'd tried to say. That she didn't have a clean pair at Kate's. That she'd left them off for the quick dash home, which had become a protracted stay and coffee, and had her glowing, then hot, then liquid. But none of that made it from her mouth.

Kate growled low in her throat, "That is so sexy," and fell into her again.

Olivia's head hung back as frantic kisses covered her neck in synchrony to soft hands mauling her buttocks. She rocked against Kate as hands squeezed her behind. The movement teased between her legs in an agonising and gentle massage, her lips nudging over where she tenderly ached. Closer Kate stroked, arousal and anxiety rising, because as soon as Kate found her, Olivia's longing would be hopelessly apparent.

The tips of Kate's fingers dipped at her edges.

"Oh my god, you're so wet," Kate breathed.

And Olivia couldn't say a thing.

Kate teased her relentlessly, playing at her wet lips, delicately kneading them so they embraced her clit.

Olivia stumbled back in a daze under Kate's guidance, and her buttocks nudged into a surface edge.

"I want to strip you," Kate murmured.

Fingers tugged at her dress zip. Hands pulled it apart and tussled it over her arms. An adept movement released her bra, so her breasts thrilled in the open air. But only for a moment because Kate's lips enveloped her nipple and sucked hard.

Olivia caved so intensely she thought she might come, the strength of Kate's kisses perfected from the night before, and hot tingling shot from breasts to core.

Kate was everywhere, clasping around her sides, kneading her body. Kisses and caresses trailed lower and lower, and Olivia twitched again and again, as Kate's seduction reached her belly, turning into a rhythmic pulse as her mouth explored lower.

She cried out as Kate kissed the top of her slit. And again when her tongue parted her outer lips. Lapping at her. Teasing her open.

Olivia arched forwards desperate to let Kate in, frustrated at the awkwardness of spreading her legs to give Kate access. Then she felt light as her leg lifted and Kate's shoulder swept beneath her thigh. All of her ascended onto a surface and her knees spread wide. And for a moment she pulsed in expectancy, exposed, aching and craving contact.

She opened her eyes to Kate kneeling, face pale between Olivia's dark thighs, expression engulfed in arousal.

"You look so good," Kate breathed with complete abandonment.

Kate closed her eyes, relaxed into pleasure, and lapped a soft tongue over Olivia's clit.

Light seared through her head and she cried out. She thrashed back an arm which clattered on a wood panel. Then flashes again, as soft lips surrounded her.

Beyond control, she caved and shuddered with every sweep Kate took. Then she thrust as Kate licked lower and dipped her tongue inside.

Kate held her firm and pulled her into her face, moaning as she pushed deep one minute before a heavenly sweep the next.

Olivia's tension climbed higher and higher. Kate must have sensed her rising to a peak, because she held her clit between lip and tongue, and licked quicker and firmer until she teetered at the top. She hung there, precarious and breathless, before Kate gave one last, decisive, delicious and firm sweep. Then Olivia plummeted, like swooping down a slide, so powerfully she feared she'd black out.

She cried out one last time when she hit the bottom, before gasping at waves that buoyed her high and swept her low, Kate clinging to her all the way.

Olivia couldn't see at first. She blinked, dazed and half surprised to find herself in the kitchen. She shuffled off the countertop, muscles jelly and legs trembling, and Kate stood up to steady them both.

Kate's face. Sigh. An aftereffect rippled through Olivia at the sight of her lover, deliciously hooded eyed with lips hanging open, and incapable of speech.

"That..." Kate swallowed. "Sexiest thing I ever saw."

Olivia trailed her finger down Kate's cheek, the scent glistening there, fresh and clearly hers. Quivering, she threw her arms around Kate's shoulders and held her tight.

"Sexiest thing I ever felt," Olivia whispered.

She couldn't stop shaking and she realised Kate trembled too. She kissed her, and the taste of them mingled tugged at her heart. She stroked her hands through Kate's hair, massaging her scalp and wanting to kiss her impossibly deep.

Olivia gently turned them around, so that Kate leaned on the counter. Still fluttering, she trailed down Kate's T-shirt and over her breasts. She tugged at the metal button at the top of Kate's jeans, pulled down her zip, then slipped her finger between Kate's warm outer lips and into soft depths.

Kate moaned, "It won't take... I'm so..."

Olivia found her, swollen and smooth, and hot and wet. She swept her finger around her slowly, because she knew Kate was sensitive and near.

"I love touching you," Olivia quietly groaned, intoxicated and her breath humid against Kate's cheek. "I can't believe how much I love touching you."

And Kate's head hung, overpowered.

Olivia hugged her tight and deepened her strokes, so she massaged the tenderness that pearled beneath her fingers. She clasped Kate tighter with every moan. And when she came, Olivia experienced it through her own body. Like it hit Kate with an exquisite punch and radiated through every atom between them.

And Olivia held her closer and closer.

30

Olivia covered her face and sighed into her hands. "What am I doing?"

Kate had hurried away with apologies, blushing cheeks and many smiles, and left Olivia here with scent on her fingers.

She inhaled. "Mmm." And her head swirled.

It wasn't every day she found herself naked in her kitchen, and today really shouldn't have been that day, because Charlotte and Millie were due soon.

In the last twenty-four hours she'd run from the office into Kate's bedroom, an enormous leap already for Olivia. Then Kate had buried her face between her thighs, while she sat with her legs spread on the kitchen surface. The woman had her skipping with ridiculous abandon outside her usual lines and areas of comfort and she closed her eyes again, because it had been delicious.

She opened them at a growling sound, and blushed because it was only her in the kitchen – quietly growling and completely naked. Kate, that woman, could make her do anything, and she grinned like a fool. She was throwing career and caution to the wind, fallout surely to come, but right now she felt astonishing.

Her conscience nagged that Charlotte and Millie were an immediate issue, and she and her kitchen were in no way presentable. But she just didn't care as much as usual, because, sigh, and smile, and la la la. Her brain swam in blissful, happy hormones.

Where were her clothes? Her dress lay on the fruit and veg rack over a pair of oranges, which made her laugh. She wouldn't have found it funny normally. Knickers, she'd neatly packed earlier in a plastic sleeve in her briefcase, naturally. Bra? Who knew where her bra had been flung? Kate, that's who. Because she'd adeptly removed it, thrown it away and descended on her nipple with a succulent delight that had Olivia melting at the memory.

"Oh," she sighed. And there was growling again.

She spun neatly on the spot in a last attempt to find her underwear, pausing with her brain going 'weeeeeeeeee' on hormones and centrifugal forces. She scanned the kitchen with her dress over her arm, none the wiser. What was an errant black lacy bra when she had several identical ones in her drawer.

And a few minutes later, she wore a similar black bra, dress and a protective apron. She stretched a yellow Marigold glove over her hand, snapped it to her wrist and hummed a tune while wiping down the countertop. Because hygiene, blah. She shrugged. Then she paused mid wipe, reliving the delicious moment that had happened there. She'd never cook in this kitchen again without recalling it.

A knock at the door shifted her from the daydream.

"Oops." Time was up.

She'd probably bleached everything out of existence. Would it do? A quick rinse was perhaps necessary.

Another knock at the door. The first had been Charlotte's and this noisier rattle was Millie's.

"Morning," she said, opening the door wide. Did she slur? She smacked her lips together, to wake them up for proper enunciation. "Do come in."

"Good morning, you," Charlotte said, with a big sunshine smile and stooping into the house.

Millie followed behind. "Blimey, you look as if you've dressed to give us an enema."

Olivia inhaled, tried to shoot an eyebrow aloft, but even that was sluggish. She shrugged instead. "No enemas today, but would you like a cup of tea?"

Then she smiled, because the last time she'd offered tea had been a very different moment and ended in all kinds of delight.

Millie paused and peered at her. "You all right, Olivia?"

"Yes?" Olivia swallowed.

Millie's eyes narrowed. "Are you sure?"

Suggestion riddled the question. It was like Millie was a mind reader when it came to sex. But, surely, she couldn't tell.

"I'm perfectly fine." Olivia blinked with heavy eyelids and threw her gloved hands carefree in the air. "Come in. Sit down. I will be with you presently."

It was hopelessly obvious something was different if she couldn't muster razor-sharp comebacks to Millie.

"OK then." Millie considered her with suspicion and tongue prodding out a cheek. "You look well this morning, despite being dressed for a medical procedure."

Olivia blinked lazily again. "Why thank you, Millie. You are too kind."

Millie sauntered down the hallway, not taking her eyes off Olivia, and sat next to Charlotte on the sofa.

"I'll just be a moment," Olivia said.

She yawned as she passed and headed to the kitchen to finish tidying, while Charlotte and Millie glanced at each other in question.

She rinsed the surface one more time with a sponge and dried it in circles with a tea towel. She'd stood exactly here, snug against Kate and touching her. She smiled, reliving that rush of wellbeing at hugging her close afterwards.

"You're humming," came Charlotte's incredulous voice.

Olivia glanced over her shoulder and spotted her friend in the doorway.

"I hum sometimes?" Olivia said, back to swirling the tea towel around the surface.

She hardly ever did, but it felt so natural today.

"You're very distracted too, Olivia."

She paused because that had come from right behind her in Millie's unmistakable tones. She turned, slowly, to find the shorter woman biting back a grin.

"It's the weekend?" Olivia suggested. "I'm relaxing?"

"Oh, you look relaxed," Millie said. "I've never seen you so laid back." She stressed 'laid'. "What satisfying activity have you been up to this morning?"

Olivia didn't have an answer, because she might slur if she attempted one.

"That would also require," Millie continued, "an urgent scrub and bleach?"

"Erm." She smacked her lips open with a 'mwah' to enliven them. "What do you mean?" It was light and distinctly too high pitched. There wasn't enough evidence, even for Millie. Surely.

Millie stepped forward, eyes not leaving Olivia's, and reached out. Olivia puzzled for a moment because it looked like Millie might hug her round the waist. But the arm stopped, and it plucked at something sticking from the cutlery drawer by her hip. It slowly withdrew the long black item and raised it in front of her face.

"Anything to do with this?" Millie said lightly.

Her bra. Her black lacy bra she'd been searching for earlier. The strap hung from Millie's index finger, followed by the cups in a long, revealing line. How had that got in her cutlery drawer? Well, because clothes had flown everywhere. But it was very, very unfortunate.

She looked at Millie and swallowed, not only visibly, but audibly. And the smile on Millie's face grew.

Charlotte laughed from the doorway. "That's messy and random of you, Olivia."

"I don't think it's random at all," Millie said, that smile still rising.

"What do you mean?" Charlotte asked.

"Must have got hot in the kitchen." Millie tilted her head. "If underwear had to come off?"

"But Olivia doesn't often cook."

"I think it's Olivia that got cooked."

"Millie, are you being crude again? We talked about that with Olivia. Wait..." Charlotte's nose crinkled at the top because neither Olivia nor Millie denied it. "Do you mean... Have you..." Then a loud inhale. "No. Olivia? You?! When? Who?!"

Oh dear lord.

"Perhaps we could withdraw to the sitting room," she suggested.

"We are withdrawing, and expect to hear everything," Millie said, but she still stood there grinning.

"Yes? Can I help?" Olivia said, heaving up two sluggish eyebrows.

"Your bra." Millie offered.

"Thank you so much" She put a finger through the strap and Millie let it fall.

So. How to explain this?

Charlotte sat on the edge of the sofa, knees high and leaning forwards. Millie reclined, legs crossed, arm around sofa and Charlotte, clearly delighted. How much had she already guessed? Probably all of it, then embellished it some.

"Are you seeing someone?" Charlotte said, squeezing her hands together in prayer. "Have you found a woman you like?"

Olivia drew up a matching upholstered chair and sat down.

"I'm not in a relationship," she said.

"Aw." Her friend's shoulders sank. Perhaps Charlotte wished she'd found a girlfriend, so she didn't have to feel guilty about pairing up with Millie.

"But I have grown to like someone." Olivia paused. "Actually, to like someone very much."

"Well that's promising." Charlotte beamed.

"It's come as a bit of a surprise," Olivia said. "And it's developed over the last weeks..."

She took a deep breath, because it was unprofessional, and not an admission she wanted to make to Charlotte.

"It's Kate. I have feelings for Kate."

Millie smiled, with not a hint of surprise.

"Wha–" made a shape in Charlotte's mouth, and every thought seemed to disappear and her face went slack.

Olivia wanted to pause her like that, maybe forever, but a puzzled frown crept into her friend's expression.

"But if you've... I mean on the counter... Because your hygiene thing...! Are you saying you're...? But she's your client."

Olivia's heart sank having to admit this lapse. Excruciating in front of Liz and Hugo, it felt no better in front of Charlotte, who was a colleague as well as a friend, and had always looked up to her.

"She's no longer my client. I handed her case to Alec, when I realised...there was an attraction."

"Oh my god, Olivia," Charlotte gasped. Surprise delighted her face. "I know professionally you hate this but–"

"Look," Olivia said quickly. "I didn't notice things develop between us."

"I don't blame you at all." Charlotte smiled in understanding.

Olivia continued determined in her defence. "I had no idea this would happen. It changed over many weeks. Everything was above board and professional. And as soon as I realised I'd developed an attraction for her–"

"You dumped her arse as a client and shagged her on the kitchen counter." Millie grinned.

"That, that, that...is an oversimplification." The weeks she'd spent trying to handle this case with respect and professionalism. But there was no getting away from it. Olivia reconsidered her response, opened her mouth, and said, "Pretty much, yes."

A triumphant grin spread on Millie's face as shock slapped itself over Charlotte's.

"I knew sparks were flying!" Millie said, punching the air.

"Really?" Charlotte frowned, confused.

"They were practically a fire hazard at Hugo's party."

"I completely missed that. I mean, of course, you love her films." Charlotte's gaze flicked back and forth between her and Millie. "But I didn't know you liked her too."

"You should have seen her spot Kate at Hugo's party," Millie shook her head and chuckled.

Oh god. Had it been that transparent?

"It was like she froze," Millie carried on, "immobilised in a fight, flight or fuck reaction."

She wanted to object, but honestly, Millie seemed happy for her, and Olivia's mouth twitched wanting to smile.

"You mustn't say anything," she said quickly. "To anyone. Ever."

"Flipping heck, Olivia." Millie laughed. "If you wanted a secret lover, you could have chosen someone with a lower profile than multiple Oscar winner, Kate Laurence."

"That's not the issue," Olivia snapped. "We're not together. It was just the once."

"This morning?" Millie said, with a lilt of suspicion.

And damn it, if integrity and honesty must rear their heads now. "And the once," she added, "that is, the one session," she clarified, lawyer specificity also intruding, "last night."

"You spent the night together?" Charlotte clutched her heart.

"It's still not going anywhere," Olivia said quickly. "Kate has a divorce to settle and absolutely none of this can leak out until that's final."

Millie pursed her lips and her cheeks went pink. She was clearly trying to hold something back, and she failed. "Because you're confining leakages to the kitchen?"

"Stop it," Olivia said. "Stop it now."

"I bet she's hot though."

"Millie. You promised to be less crude." Charlotte nudged her girlfriend in the ribs.

"Yeah, yeah," Millie waved away the objection. "But a thousand pounds says Olivia finds her scorching hot."

Olivia's cheeks burned. The blush spread and roasted her ears. She slapped her hands over her face and couldn't help groaning. "She's ridiculously hot."

"Knew it," she heard Millie cry out. "Oh my god, Olivia. You are so fucked."

And Olivia only blushed more.

"Of all the clients to wander into your office," she heard Charlotte sigh.

When she composed herself enough to peep from between her fingers, they both still grinned at her.

"Come on," Charlotte said. "Let's get ice cream."

"Because," Millie added, "we need to stop that icy lawyer's heart of yours from thawing."

"I think it's too late." Charlotte laughed.

Millie nodded. "We need triple scoop STAT."

31

They sat in G&D's ice cream parlour in Little Clarendon Street, Olivia with her small tub of pistachio on one side of a table, and Millie and Charlotte on the other.

Opposite, Millie devoured a mound of ice cream and whipped topping with so much relish it bordered on obscene. Charlotte chipped at her strawberry tub and held the scoop by her mouth, before getting distracted and saying, "I can't believe it," for the fiftieth time.

"Charlotte, my love," Millie said, grinning with besotted adoration. "You're fixating again."

"Sorry, I really can't though." She beamed at Olivia. "You're seeing Kate L–."

Gah. She needed a bleeper to redact every mention of Kate.

"We're in public. You can't say anything," Olivia whispered, before moving back to, "So, September, are you both free?"

For Geeta's garden party. And although she didn't want to dwell on her mother's social plans, she seized the opportunity to move Charlotte's focus away from actors.

"Was it the dance at Hugo's birthday?"

Oh my god. Charlotte seemed determined to roll out non-sequiturs. Why was it so hard to keep her on topic, except when she was completely obsessed.

Olivia leaned over the table. "Can we please avoid the subject in public?"

"But this is huge," Charlotte gasped into her face. "This is the most monumental and exciting thing to ever happen to you."

Now she had issues with that statement, while conceding the Earth also moved. Head fluffy with the remnants of post-coital bliss, she hadn't processed it yet. But this did feel different.

"Can we *please* talk about something else?" she said.

"You're asking a lot of ADHDer there," Millie replied, stuffing a huge spoonful of ice cream into her mouth.

"What?" she snapped.

"To move on from an area of hyperfocus," Millie said over a mound of dessert.

It went quiet.

She flicked her gaze between the pair opposite. Charlotte blanched, only a speck of pink remaining on her usually rosy cheeks. Millie tongued the ice cream bulge into her cheek.

"I thought you said you'd mentioned it," Millie said from the other side of her mouth.

"Well, it was to Kate, in front of Olivia," Charlotte said, clearly uncomfortable. Her eyes darted everywhere.

"You're..." Olivia started, thoughts stumbling. "You have ADHD? And you told Kate?"

"I kind of hoped you'd heard and weren't mentioning it?" Charlotte's face dropped into worry, as if her mood changed in an engulfing wave.

"But..."

This had her floored. She'd known Charlotte for fifteen years. And yes, her friend was random sometimes and missed cues. And faff was her middle name, given to her by Millie. And do not start on her messiness and clumsiness.

Perhaps there was something there. But she'd told Kate? Charlotte didn't tell her, a best friend, but had mentioned it to Kate?

"Do you really think you have ADHD?" Olivia asked.

And it hurt when Charlotte peeped at Millie for support before she answered.

"Yes, because I'm so distracted." Charlotte's smile twitched, trying to leap up her face but falling before it reached her eyes. "You might have noticed I'm...not with it sometimes. I can be clever, but I don't always look it."

Olivia didn't know what to say.

"It's frustrated me all my life. Knowing that I can do things, but somehow can't. Or finding stuff difficult that should be straightforward."

Charlotte peered at her, clearly hoping for understanding.

"Like time-keeping." Charlotte pointed her finger into the air. "I was told off for being late so often when I was younger. And I thought I'd got over it and was normal. But I didn't realise people found punctuality so easy. They don't even have to try, or stress about it, or need a million alarms to get through the day. They just arrive places." Charlotte shook her head as if amazed. "What else is there?" Charlotte's gaze drifted skywards.

"Forgetfulness," Millie nudged.

"Oh my god, I'm so forgetful," Charlotte collapsed with a smile for Millie. "And clumsiness. I can walk into walls."

"You do walk into walls." Millie nodded.

"So many random bruises. Erm...Procrastination and mega faffing about work, study, chores, actually most things..."

"Then panic and achieving success," Millie chipped in.

"But followed by burnout." Charlotte deflated. "It's like I could be clever, or do things, but I had to try harder than everyone else, and I got so tired." And despair clutched at her whole being.

"Intensity of emotions," Millie jabbed the air with her scoop.

"Especially about injustice."

"But big-time awe at the good stuff."

"I get super excited to chat to people." Charlotte beamed.

"Or really fucking not, and zone out," Millie finished.

"I still clam up when I'm anxious though. I start spiralling, and worry I'll say the wrong thing."

"Yet, despite all that worry, you'll blurt something out at exactly the worst moment."

Charlotte laughed.

"But are you," Olivia hesitated, thrown by this while it also rang true. "Are you hyperactive?"

"Honestly, I don't know." Charlotte smiled but despaired at the same time. "I remember having to concentrate on standing still at school when others didn't. I'd tell myself to freeze and listen, then I missed whatever the teacher said next. And I would twirl around as soon as I forgot to focus."

"And your brain races. All the time," Millie added.

"Yes!" Charlotte turned to Olivia with bright eyes. "Did you know some people can clear their mind of almost everything? I didn't realise that. I thought I did relax, because I wasn't thinking anything useful, but I don't stop. Ever."

"Oh," Olivia said. "Well, that's..."

"A lot already, and that's the tip of it." Charlotte gazed at her, eyebrows in a little roof of worry.

"So..." Olivia breathed in.

"Oh, come on, Olivia," Millie said, swallowing down a mouthful of ice cream. "As if either of you is neurotypical. Charlotte with her head in the clouds. You and your picture alignment, special interest areas, routine and everything having to be perfect. God, even Kate. She does not do numbers. Have you seen her when she pays for things? And honestly, I have impulse control issues, I'm not gonna lie."

She had a point. Several in fact.

Millie took another huge mouthful of ice cream but didn't pause. "There's a lot of it about. Who said we all had to be the same anyway?"

This made Olivia feel odd and out of sorts. "Doesn't mean we'd all be diagnosed," she said, more as an aside.

"I'd bet good money on some of us though," Millie said, scooping in more ice cream. "Neurospicey types find each other."

"But." What really bothered her was, "You told Kate? Before me?"

"It came up," Charlotte murmured. "I didn't mean to. But you're quite..."

Olivia prickled. "Judgemental?"

"I was going to say intimidating," Charlotte said.

Olivia sat tall and defensive.

"Well, you're so good at..." Charlotte waved her hands around, trying to find the word. "Everything! And so many things I'm not." She looked down at the uneaten ice cream. "I try your patience sometimes."

"Oh," Olivia said quietly, the truth piercing the tension. She put down her spoon neatly on the side of her tub. Yes, she knew her patience was limited, and she owed Charlotte more right now. "So, are you diagnosed?"

"Not yet. The waiting lists are huge. And I think it's more than one condition for me, so it might take years." Charlotte shrugged. "But I have so many traits."

Olivia frowned, being the slow one for once.

"Like," Charlotte started, "the number of times people said, 'you don't listen', when I was little...and I had no idea they were speaking. My mother would drag me off to get my ears tested, and they were always fine. But I don't take things in. I don't know if it's my processing, or I get distracted and stop listening, then don't remember anyone even talking, or if it's both... And my clumsiness. Am I uncoordinated, or not paying attention, or is it both? And... so many things."

And Charlotte deflated, exhausted by it.

"So, I've been muddling through, finally getting to understand myself, and finding strategies to help."

Charlotte peeped up and tried a smile at Olivia, one which held an apology while shame pinked her cheeks at the same time. Olivia didn't want her best friend to feel that way.

"It makes sense," Olivia replied quickly, trying to ease her discomfort. "Is it a bad idea to self-diagnose?"

"What?" Millie tutted. "Find strategies to help with areas she genuinely finds difficult? If they help, they help, regardless of the diagnosis in the end."

"But." Olivia wracked her brain. "Has it got worse recently?" Because she'd noticed everything Charlotte mentioned becoming more pronounced. "Might you need an official diagnosis if you need medication?"

"I don't think it's got worse." Charlotte's nose crinkled at the top while she considered. "It might show more because I've relaxed about it." Her smile was uncomplicated. "I've stopped hiding or masking it and have become more comfortable with myself. I am clumsy. And I do get distracted. But it doesn't always matter. So, I don't beat myself up about it, and I save my energy for when it does count."

"Right," Olivia said.

She looked at her friend, whom she'd met at college years ago. You could know someone too well, have an idea of them so firmly planted in your head, that you refuse to see them in any other way. Even though they might have changed, or there was a side they couldn't show – masking it, hiding it, stopping a nugget of themselves from growing – then they simply embraced who they always were and let it blossom through their whole life.

"Don't you do the same?" Charlotte implored. "Sometimes?"

"Do I mask?" Olivia asked.

"Yes."

She had plenty of traits. And labels and names may shift, but Olivia was sure of who she was. Yes, to get her job done. Yes, to be polite. There were all kinds of roles she played. And it was exhausting and aggravating and exactly why she insisted on the rest of her life being just so. But at the same time, she'd always had a strong sense of self. Possibly greater than Charlotte, who bent every direction, considering every view, apparently while her head spun with distraction. When Olivia had been single-minded, determined and confident.

Only Charlotte peered at her right now, asking for acceptance, having more confidence in herself, no matter how tentative it still looked.

"I..." It was Olivia's head that spun.

"I relax most around you two, I think," Charlotte added.

Was Olivia the same? Comfortable and confident with Charlotte. Strangely with Millie too. So different, it didn't matter that they saw through each other. They were going to clash anyway. Then Kate. The layers fell away quickly with Kate.

"I'm sorry I'm more absent-minded," Charlotte deflated. "I just want to relax around you both."

And before Olivia said anything, Millie dropped her spoon, spun in her seat and cupped Charlotte's face.

"Nothing for you to apologise for, sweet cheeks." And Millie gazed at Charlotte with love and support like she always had, even years ago at college.

The whirlwind that was Millie blew Olivia out of the picture again. She could see it clearly now. Millie teased and joked, brash and vulgar, but *always* showed acceptance of who Charlotte was. The recognition hit her square in the chest. She realised she didn't do that for Charlotte, not in the same way, never had, possibly never would. And grief sank in with the punch.

Millie made Charlotte laugh, with an energy Olivia found chaotic and offensive. But it thrilled Charlotte, bringing her alive, all the while cushioning her with acceptance. She'd seen the years where Charlotte struggled most, and it was always Millie who blew the difficulties away.

It was like everything clicked into place. A peg removed and the parts slotted down into a different picture – Charlotte and Millie, the happy couple who understood each other. Not Charlotte, the one that got away.

She'd forgotten to breathe. She coughed to cover it and picked up her spoon. She met Charlotte's gaze that flickered anxiously.

"It makes sense," Olivia said, at last. "I see you struggle. I will try to notice when you're finding it difficult. And," because she did know herself and her fastidious habits, intrinsic to her nature and bedrock to her sanity, "I recognise I can be very particular about things."

"Thank you." Charlotte smiled, a little too much. "I don't try to annoy you."

"I know." Olivia nodded.

Millie leaned forward, chest on the table. "I do though," she said.

Olivia turned to Millie and raised an eyebrow. "That, I also know."

And Millie beamed ecstatically.

***

Olivia's head spun as they left the parlour. She followed Charlotte through the passageway into Wellington Square, with tall terraced town houses surrounding a garden and a towering sequoia.

"So," Millie sidled up, "when are you seeing your superhot girlfriend again?"

"We're not together," Olivia said, staring ahead.

"Why?"

"Because..."

She conjured an image of Kate, naked their first night, then beautiful and half hidden beneath a fluffy duvet in the morning. Heavenly. She took a sharp breath.

"We're simply not suited."

They fit like a silky glove. She remembered slipping between Kate's thighs, as smoothly as Kate slipped her face between hers. She swallowed.

"Having a moment, Olivia?" Millie smirked.

Was she ever. She'd broken into a sweat again. And Millie didn't miss that kind of thing.

"We still couldn't be less suited," she reiterated.

Millie crossed her arms and raised an eyebrow in disbelief.

"But I cannot deny, I find her attractive," Olivia added.

"She's fucking hot."

"She is, as you say," she swallowed, "very hot."

Millie beamed. "I like this level of conversation with you, Olivia."

She glared at the irritating blond.

"I'm not even trying to piss you off," Millie said. "You do your erudite badinage elsewhere, Ms double first. This is my kind of bonding."

"It's demeaning to you and debases your achievements and ability." Because Millie had been an accomplished law student like Charlotte and Olivia.

"But Kate's still fucking hot." Millie grinned.

"She is undeniably, irrefutably," Olivia conceded, "'fucking hot'."

"I couldn't be more happy for you," Millie said, coming to a stop and knuckling her hands onto her hips. "So why aren't you going for it?"

"Because it's messy."

"You don't get to your mid-thirties without being messy. Come on. That's what Marigolds and bleach are for."

Olivia ignored that.

"Isn't this one worth it?" Millie asked. Her expression didn't make fun anymore. "Seeing through a bit of mess?"

But that was the thing. It probably wasn't worth it. Nothing was forever, apart from Charlotte and Millie it seemed.

It was difficult not to be jaded as a divorce attorney, witnessing the basic errors people made when choosing partners. She'd wanted Charlotte because they had so much in common – lesbian, lawyer, same social class, got on with their families, didn't want children. And Charlotte made her heart go pitter patter.

Whereas Kate – actor, not professional, had kids, nothing in common, complicated personal and work life. Exactly the kind of messy situation she advised against as a solicitor. Make it clean cut. Don't get involved until the divorce is finalised. All that.

And yet, her heart went boom.

Olivia despaired at herself. Was this the foolishness others engaged in? That leap of faith people took against better judgement, while their heads spun with sex and hormones. And she was already wading deep into those waters.

She wasn't a prude, but she didn't want people's paws all over her until she was sure those were the right hands to touch her. Then, and only then, she succumbed to sensuality. She closed her eyes because she'd missed that kind of intimacy. It had been a long time since she let anyone near. And once she found intimacy and release, she couldn't turn back. That's why she didn't understand Millie – because once you had sex, once you were that close to someone, how could you do the same with anyone else at the drop of a hat.

Sex was never just sex for her. To let a person get that close was never nothing. When Olivia wanted to sleep with a woman, it meant she wanted all of her. That others rampaged over that in a single night, then turned to someone else, was as devastating as it was vulgar to her.

And here she was, a night and many sensual encounters in, and way over her head.

Millie watched her, as if she read every thought.

"I see you falling, Olivia," she whispered. That Millie saw, was not the surprise. That she said it with friendly awareness shocked Olivia in multiple ways.

Millie was right, and Olivia inhaled realising where she stood with Kate. She needed the brakes on fast. She needed to floor them.

She stared, not knowing what to say. Millie reached out to squeeze her hand, held it tight a few moments and walked away giving Olivia a reprieve.

By evening, Charlotte and Millie headed home and Olivia wandered up St Giles, with her head still spinning.

This weekend had turned her inside out and work upside down, Kate lighting her on fire one moment and Charlotte plunging her into icy water the next. She paused to catch her breath, eyes blurring in the dusk, not taking in students dipping into The Eagle and Child, nor the cyclists buffeting by at speed.

Her mobile buzzed with a message in her coat pocket.

"Hi," it said.

Just two letters and they consumed her whole attention. She cradled the phone in her hands, her surroundings blending in darkness and everything waiting on the dots that promised more.

"How was your day? Can I phone you if you're free later?"

And Olivia hit call without thinking.

"Hey," came the pickup. That voice, so familiar with its deeply mellow timbre. No matter the accents over the years, Olivia would never mistake it for anyone but Kate.

"Hi," she said, unable to lighten the beleaguered tone of her reply. "I'm heading home."

"Did you have a good day?"

"It was..." A rollercoaster, revealing and shocking, and had left her with an aching heart. "Surprising," she said instead.

"You sound tired."

"I am," she murmured, slowly walking again, her neat black trainers quiet on the paving stones of St Giles. "Tell me about your day instead."

"OK," came the voice, smooth and understanding, and so familiar she pictured happiness on Kate's face from the tone. "I woke up to a beautiful woman. Best start to the day in a long time."

That made her smile and soothed in her chest. "I hope she was nice," she said, joining in Kate's play.

"She's incredible," Kate replied. "I've liked her for a while. She's elegant and intelligent. That was always obvious."

Olivia's smile faltered, because the compliments had edges, coming from someone she craved but couldn't be with.

"She makes me laugh too," Kate continued. "I value that very much, especially when it comes from someone so considerate." Kate's tone turned personal and intimate, and the edge cut deeper.

She must have sighed because Kate asked. "Are you OK?"

"I'm tired," Olivia slurred a little. "It's been a big weekend of many things." She was too exhausted to phrase it more elegantly.

"Are you worried about work?" Kate asked.

"That's part of it." But not uppermost right now. She wandered on, swaying as if worse for wear. "I feel like my world's been turned upside down. And in more ways than one this weekend."

"Can I see you?" came a gentle plea.

"I should go home. I've seen too much of people. Need rest. Quiet. Routine." She trailed off, overwhelmed by so many changes.

"I understand that," came gently again. "I'll let you go."

"No. I like you talking to me," she stuttered. "Please talk. I might not reply that well." Her sharp brain fogged with all kinds of fatigue, but Kate's deeply familiar voice comforted.

"OK then, erm," Kate began. "I'll tell you more about my day. After a stunning morning," it still made Olivia smile, "I read emails filtered through my PA, and from my agent who's been nagging at me to look at scripts. And for the first time in months, I managed to scan through a handful." She sounded happy. "I'm even halfway through a full read, and I'm hopeful." Definitely happy. She could hear Kate's excitement. "I was glad, because I needed something to take my mind off a person." Kate paused.

"That woman again?"

"The same one. She's been on my mind constantly. Did I tell you how intriguing she is?"

Olivia breathed out a laugh.

"She's fascinating and surprises me at every turn, from spinning me on a dance floor to the way her kisses melt."

The edges stung.

"Olivia?" Kate murmured.

"Yes?"

"I understand needing quiet and alone time. But would you like to do quiet here?" Silence waited for Olivia to respond, then, "I don't have many evenings free. This is the last for another two weeks, and I really want to see you."

That reached into her chest and pulled hard.

"We don't have to do anything," Kate whispered. "You can lie on a sofa or go straight to bed. I will do everything to make you comfortable. I have missed you all day."

Olivia ached at that.

"This morning was amazing," Kate's voice lifted, "but I missed hugging you afterwards. I want to hold you all night."

Olivia kept walking.

"But I understand if you need to go home."

"I'm here," Olivia said, lifting her gaze to the sleek black door of Kate's Park Town home. Like she could have resisted. "I'm already here."

The door opened to Kate's urgent face and her hand reaching out.

She half registered the door closing behind her and hands cupping her cheeks. She took a moment to focus on Kate's eyes, which were full of care and searched hers.

"I'm exhausted," Olivia whispered. "My world is tipped upside down. But here's where I want to be."

Kate still stared.

"This is what I want," Olivia said again. "I know we said only one night."

"It was never just one night for me." Kate gazed at her. "Not since you stepped through that door on Friday. Not since you lifted my mask away. I couldn't resist after that."

The pretence gone, the barrier removed, nothing but this woman who treated her with consideration and irresistible tenderness. Nothing to stop her from falling.

She had no more words.

And she didn't need them because Kate drew forward and placed her lips gently over hers. Olivia's head spun, light and free, lost in a kiss that understood how to catch her.

32

Kate loved so many things about Olivia. The way she held her when they stood, arms around shoulders, clutched tight, heart over heart, steady and strong but passionate like they could blend.

The way Olivia stripped in the bedroom, without any self-consciousness, and slipped between the sheets that evening, exhausted and beautiful.

The way she murmured that Kate's voice was perfection, the ultimate comfort, and had drifted to sleep while Kate read a script out loud. That she could trust her and read that script because Olivia had integrity written through and through.

And affectionate. The best surprise of all. Although they'd woken apart their first morning, it had been after a night of them finding each other around the bed.

Then this second night. Kate wasn't used to Olivia naked against her yet. She thrummed and tingled with her nearby, slightly frustrated and amused at having to sleep beside this sexy woman. But she did sleep, slipping into seductive dreams which blurred with reality as they surfaced through the hours of darkness.

Olivia sought her out, kisses turning heated and straddling her, unable to resist the movement and riding her mound. Neither spoke, only half surfacing in the dark, and Olivia slipped her leg beneath hers so they merged, and Kate came hard to Olivia stroking her thumb over her centre.

Exhausted again, she drifted into wonderful oblivion, Olivia's embrace plunging her into bliss, with the strength of them pulling together, chest to chest, heart over heart, falling asleep with Olivia on top of her.

Yes, this is what she loved most of all. The affection and tenderness of her. The elegant, reserved, smooth exterior melted into sublime sensuality and care, so delicious it hit deep inside and took hold of her.

She woke to butterfly kisses along her shoulder and a wonderful sense of well-being. She turned, smiling, to find Olivia with hair mussed up, for only moments, lovely moments, before she smoothed it perfect.

"Can you stay for a while?" Kate whispered. "Harry's not bringing back the kids until late afternoon."

Olivia nodded, eyes blinking slowly. "I'd like that."

She ran her fingers around Olivia's cheek. "Is this something you want to do again? Staying the weekend?"

"Very much," Olivia murmured.

And Kate's chest glowed.

"I'm short of clothes though," Olivia said.

"You're welcome to walk around naked." She grinned, because the thought of Olivia slinking about the place nude was aesthetically and lustfully irresistible. "Or you could borrow something?" she conceded.

She left Olivia to shower and dress while she made coffee, she didn't dare make her tea yet, and took the mugs through to the sitting room at the back of the house. Morning sunshine streamed through two tall windows into the already light space, painted a pale stone blue. A white sofa sat beneath an ornate framed mirror along the rear wall, and two large seats flanked a coffee table. But Kate gazed from a window seat into the garden below, mind skipping between Olivia and pondering a script.

"This is a beautiful room." Olivia's voice diverted her from the garden.

"It's actually becoming a favourite..." she started, then her breath trailed away.

Olivia wandered into the room, Kate's pale jeans oversized on her and pulled around the middle with a belt. A short, loose white T-shirt revealed a glimpse of smooth brown midriff and hung low over Olivia's collarbone, so that the sensuous sweep of her shoulders beguiled.

"You were saying?" Olivia raised an eyebrow, gently teasing.

"I..." Her mouth numbed. "I haven't got a clue what I was saying." She shook her head. "How...how do you look so good in that?"

Olivia sauntered towards her, cupped her cheeks delicately, then lit her lips with another of those kisses that rendered Kate ethereal.

"And how do you do that?" Kate whispered.

Olivia gazed at her, eyes huge and dark. "You do the same to me." Then, "What were you saying? There was something on your mind when I came in."

She was still surfacing from the kiss.

"You were preoccupied?" Olivia prompted.

"Oh, I was thinking over this script I was reading to you last night."

"Yes?"

"It's got me hooked. The story captured me straight away yesterday. I can see how it would work on the screen. I'm already casting roles in my mind but," she hesitated, "I don't know if I'm right for the main part."

Olivia listened.

"It's a been a while since something grabbed me like this and I'm..." Scared, she realised. She hadn't thrown herself into a challenging role since she split with Nat. She'd been sleepwalking through minor roles since. No-one had complained, but the life had gone from her acting.

"Can I try something?" she asked. "Do you mind listening to a bit?"

"I gave away how much I enjoy listening to your voice last night."

"You fell asleep." Kate laughed.

"Exactly. Perfect and blissful comfort." Olivia tilted her head. "Is this for me?" she asked, reaching for a coffee from the table and sauntering to the sofa.

Olivia reclined in a move that was quick and elegant, one knee up and holding her coffee, slim brown fingers threaded through the handle, her other leg and foot swept beneath her bum.

Kate stared.

"Yes?" Olivia raised an eyebrow.

Kate licked her lips. "I am blatantly admiring you. And you know it."

A smile from Olivia, divine. "Read to me," she gently ordered.

And Kate obediently reached for her black-rimmed glasses. She checked up to see if Olivia was ready to listen, then paused. Did the authoritative and smooth Olivia Sachdeva blush a little?

She peered over her glasses. "Are you OK?" Perhaps Olivia changed her mind.

"Go on," Olivia said, in a way that didn't convince.

"What is it?" Kate asked, amused and confused.

Olivia took a moment and licked her lips. "I like you in glasses," she said, with still a hint of bashfulness in her voice. "Makes you look studious."

She was going to say she wasn't anything like that, dropping out of exams early. But in fact she was. A book nerd. A conscientious actor. Then it tickled her. "This is what makes you blush?"

Olivia tilted up her chin in question.

"After all the things we've done in bed?"

Olivia bit her bottom lip.

"After strutting through North Oxford knickerless?"

That earned a quiet laugh.

"After standing in your kitchen naked, and stripping with no hesitation when you turn up at my door last night?"

Laughing louder.

"Glasses is what it takes to undo you?"

"Now you know." Olivia's eyes sparkled.

Kate's cheeks glowed too. "You're a big softy on the inside aren't you, Ms Sachdeva?"

Olivia considered for a moment, but her expression remained unguarded. "A complete mush with you."

Oh, Kate's heart beat faster. She looked at her tablet to avoid a response, but her eyes drifted up again, wanting Olivia to see her honestly.

"Same," she admitted, heart beating and butterfly wings fluttering.

And that draw she felt, she could see the same in Olivia, stretching between them always.

"Read to me," Olivia said gently.

"Are you sure?"

"I could listen to you for hours."

Kate believed her, and the permission allowed her to relax and drop into the role without nerves or guilt.

She paced the room, reading from her tablet, marching quicker when she became frustrated with herself.

"I haven't got it," she said, irritated. She looked at Olivia, who reclined on the sofa, face relaxed, eyes attentive. "The lighter parts are fine, but this is the core of the character, so if I can't live and breathe this part of her..."

"Try it again," Olivia suggested, her openness and patience the perfect encouragement.

"OK, OK." She scrolled back.

She began, this time aware of Olivia leaning forward as she fell deeper into the role. The walls of the sitting room melted away into post-war France.

"This world," she said, her throat collapsing with grief. "How can I carry on and pretend I'm the same person when the people who made me are gone?" She stared with her mind's eye over lumpy and unnatural fields. "Nothing's the same," she said, the broken countryside swirling in her vision.

She blinked coming to, eyes landing on Olivia.

"There," Olivia whispered. "You've got her."

She did. She felt the liquidity of excitement and achieving the flow of the character, all mixed with nerves that she might not hold it for long.

"You've found her." Olivia smiled.

And she had butterflies again. This is why she did this work. This was the whole reason for acting. She let out a quiet laugh, tinged with tears, and her breath juddered when she inhaled.

"I'm not sure if you know what a relief this is," she said. "To find I can do this. I genuinely thought I'd lost it."

"It's still there," Olivia said. "You had the story and character last night, but you've dug down to another level now."

"I can feel it, rather than fake it. This is exciting for me."

"Never gets old?" Olivia asked, as if knowing the answer.

"Never get old."

Nerves and excitement leaped again, because sitting in front of her, she'd found someone who got her too. So often, they seemed on wavelengths that resonated perfectly. And although they had much to learn about each other, they slipped along that journey quickly and easily and...

She stopped herself. There were many obvious differences and hindrances.

Then, as soon as she looked into Olivia's eyes, her heart beat low and strong.

33

It was surreal, Kate walking beside her, large sunglasses on and a wide-brim sunhat, looking more like a star than when she wore neither. Another weekend that Kate's children were with their father, and they wandered the buttercup fields and meadows behind Park Town.

They dipped into the narrows of Mesopotamia Walk between tree-lined rivers. The hedgerows bloomed with abundant cow parsley and other couples passed by with a nod, then another glance as recognition startled.

Olivia almost didn't want to look at her. Because this felt huge. After all the times they'd seduced each other, and the hidden nights together, this simple act of walking close in public on a sunny day seemed more intimate. Could this be a real thing? She peeked at Kate with new eyes, then away, fearful she might not find the same in Kate.

Their hands touched a moment, the back of their knuckles lightly stroking, and her fingers tingled with eagerness to touch Kate. Could this be real? Messy, but possible? She daren't ask.

Then Kate slipped her fingers between hers and her whole body lit up with happiness. She blushed, the delicate hold enormous with significance and her heart brimming. Still, she couldn't look. Did Kate feel it too? She started to turn, but Kate squeezed her hand, the strength of it reassuring. Yes, they were on the same page. Yes, they were together.

At last, she peered at Kate whose face radiated the same glow. "Is this OK?"

"This is wonderful," Kate replied.

And the happiness shone bright.

"Do you need to be careful, because people recognise you?"

"I don't want to hide this," Kate said, drawing up their entwined hands. "If that's what you mean. This is nice for me, being with a woman who is publicly out." Kate considered. "I won't announce it to the whole world and send the media to your door, though," she said softly. "Does it worry you?"

Did it? She pondered and they paused in the path. "I don't know," she said, too content in this moment to want to think about it.

"Is this OK too?" Kate asked. "Going to see your friends for lunch together?"

Because, of course, keen Charlotte freely messaged Kate and invited them both.

"I find Charlotte easy to hang out with," Kate continued. "It's relaxing chatting with someone who's open and honest, and I trust her not to talk to the press."

Olivia nodded, because despite all her randomness, Charlotte was loyal.

Kate drew their hands to her lips and kissed her knuckles, so it tingled through her fingers, up her arm and sent flutters through her chest.

"I cannot exaggerate how lovely this is for me," Kate said, and her amber and green eyes glistened their most vulnerable.

"Same," she whispered.

And they continued walking, hand in hand, thigh against soft thigh.

When they arrived in the small, Victorian terraced streets of East Oxford, Olivia knocked on the door and it was wrenched open by Millie.

"Whatcha lovebirds," Millie said with a huge grin, and beckoned them in.

Charlotte stooped through from a narrow galley kitchen at the back of the single downstairs room, large headphones on.

"Sorry," she said, beaming. She removed the headphones and her eyes flicked between her and Kate. "Have you been standing outside long? Had these on. Helps me tidy if I listen to music."

Kate stepped forward. "Ralph's buddy does that. Says it's the only way he can do his chores. Ralph and he body-double when they need to knuckle down to homework too."

"Millie and I did that!" Charlotte said, eyes wide. "I didn't realise that's what we were doing, but I'm sure it helped me though uni. We worked side by side for three years, and I couldn't have done it otherwise."

That disconnect again. The distance between her and Charlotte crept in. She didn't like it. It wasn't that Charlotte bonded with Kate, but that Olivia was the outsider here.

"Come on through," Millie said, and she followed through double doors into the bright sunshine of a narrow garden, trees of a nature reserve beyond a fence at the end and a new picnic table in the middle of the small lawn.

"She's amazing," Charlotte said later, for the hundredth time.

She and Millie sat opposite, and Kate had gone inside the house to the loo.

"Sh," Olivia said. Kate might hear them.

"But she is," Charlotte replied, earnest eyebrows rising above her nose.

Olivia succumbed to agreement with a neat shrug. "She is, I agree, amazing."

"Suits you down to the ground," Millie said.

What did that mean? There was always that edge between her and Millie, with so much difference between them and the historical conflict over Charlotte. Did she want to hear what was coming?

"It's like you're the grownups in the room," Millie said. "Conscientious, considerate, responsible. You always do the right thing, Olivia."

Actually, far more complimentary than she expected. Was there a catch?

"We don't always agree what the right thing is..."

There it was.

"Kate reminds me of Millie actually," Charlotte said, gazing off to who knows what land, and clearly not the same world Olivia and Millie inhabited because they both chorused, "What?!"

"Well," Charlotte considered, "she's taller but they're both fit, I mean muscley, but also curvy. She's a bit sweary and down to earth." Charlotte beamed, clearly convinced by the ridiculous comparison.

Olivia shuffled, unnerved, because rampant amusement electrified Millie opposite.

Millie licked her lips then leant closer with her chest on the picnic table. "So, is that what you needed all along?"

What did she mean? She stared at that dangerously amused face.

"Not your own Charlotte, but your own Millie?"

And Millie fluttered her eyelids in an outright flirty tease.

That sound was Olivia inhaling audibly through her nose. Then her lips betrayed her too by pinching in irritation. And it didn't help that Charlotte practically fell off her seat laughing.

"She's nothing like–" Olivia started, but dammit the two of them were still laughing.

She crossed her arms and glared at the trees, and waited for the silly pair to compose themselves.

"Olivia, I'm not being serious," Millie said. "It's obvious where I stand in your eyes." She threw her head back and cackled. "Anyway, anyone want a cuppa?" she said, standing up. "I fancy a tea."

"No, thank you," Olivia snapped, and glared at foliage until Millie left.

Charlotte's cheeks glowed pink as she watched her girlfriend retreating into the house, then paled when she turned back to Olivia.

Yes, Millie was joking, but it hit a nerve.

And now that Charlotte was paying attention, she must have realised too.

"Sorry," Charlotte said, eyebrows turning up in apology.

"Nothing for you to apologise for," she snapped.

But still that tension and distance.

"Kate's really good for you," Charlotte said, pleading a little.

Was Charlotte trying to persuade her again that they were better off as friends? It lingered between them. It had hung over everything since Millie returned to Oxford, the last nail in the coffin for Olivia and Charlotte as a potential couple. It was obvious what they were talking about.

Charlotte looked away, then said quietly, "I would have driven you bonkers, Olivia."

Would she? Perhaps. Olivia too tidy and Charlotte with her head in the clouds and crumbs everywhere.

Her heart sank again. Not at Charlotte being happy with Millie, but how it left the two of them.

"Don't I accommodate you?" she said. Her throat throttled it, because she couldn't hide that she was upset. "Don't I support you at all? As a friend?"

Charlotte whipped round with surprise blanking her face. "Of course."

"Because it's like I'm out of touch with you. That only Millie understood you, and I missed the mark every time. And that..." Hurt.

"Oh my god, no. You mustn't think that." Charlotte grabbed her hand. "I'm so grateful for everything you do for me and how patient you are." Charlotte's eyes searched hers. "I'm flattered you're my friend, and it means the world you recommended me to Hugo."

That was just as disconnected.

"Olivia?"

Still the distance.

"Why..." Olivia started. She had to swallow to keep her voice even. "Why am I the last person to know about," she waved an arm around, "how you think about everything? That you've been coming to terms with these ADHD traits."

Charlotte's face held many things. Bashful, perhaps at not telling Olivia, anxious about how her brain worked, hurt at this conversation. Everything played openly in Charlotte's expression.

"I felt foolish," Charlotte whispered. "Your opinion means a lot to me, and I didn't want to admit to being different. Or to finding so many things difficult. I try to hide it all the time, because I don't want people to think I'm not capable."

"I've always known though," she murmured, realising.

Charlotte had always been herself. She couldn't hide an elephant in a haystack.

"You're not last on the list," Charlotte added. "I haven't told my mother and sister."

Great, because everyone knew how she got on with them.

"But my mother?" Olivia suddenly realised. Geeta always had a rapport with Charlotte, whereas Olivia and Nicola were the ones with mutual respect.

"I haven't said." Charlotte hesitated. "But I think she intuitively understands, like Millie did. She kind of gets me." Charlotte sighed, trying to find the words. "And I don't mind failing in front of her."

"But you're not failing. You're good at plenty of things, Charlotte." She wished she hadn't snapped it. "I wouldn't have nudged you to join Bentley otherwise. You have an excellent degree. You have a specialist MA. We have clients who specifically sign up because of you."

"It might sound silly to you, but when I bump into a corner, or forget what you were saying, or fail to do something basic like keep the house tidy, it's difficult not to think I'm useless."

"Well," she started, "basic is a subjective term and people's abilities are broad."

Charlotte nodded, but it didn't help.

Olivia raised her hands, struggling to find the right words. "And cleaning is overrated," she blurted.

Charlotte's face sank into a sad smile. "Now you're lying to make me feel better."

"Can you try not to bump into corners?"

Charlotte slowly shrugged. Then shook her head.

"You're...you're... annoyingly agreeable to everyone," Olivia managed. Because Charlotte was. She walked into a room like a ball of sunshine.

"Is that a compliment?" Confusion wrinkled Charlotte's brow again.

"Yes, in a way. OK," she relented. "You get on with everyone. See that sounds much better."

Charlotte smiled. "Why didn't you say that in the first place?"

"Because I don't understand why you want to. In general, people are very annoying."

Charlotte's smiled broadened, and her eyes swam with emotion.

"You can charm anyone, Charlotte. You bumble through life, making friends of Liz, Hugo, Annie you worked with last year. They all have hearts in their eyes when they work with you."

And even Kate took to Charlotte.

"Richard though," Charlotte said. "I didn't get on with Richard and now he's left."

"Richard's an arse. He doesn't count."

Charlotte laughed. "That." She pointed at her. "That's the reason. Because despite all your high standards, you make me laugh and you're always in my corner." Charlotte grinned at her, sadly, gladly, with a full heart. "I love you, Olivia." Charlotte pursed her lips and gazed at her. "I truly do."

Olivia's breath caught. Because more than ever, it was true. "I love you too," she said. "I don't want to be without you."

"Come here," Charlotte said, standing up. "Can I give you a hug. I'd be very grateful."

She wiped at a tickle on her cheek and the wetness on her fingers surprised her. She inhaled and gathered herself. No, she didn't mind the request today.

"Yes. I would like one too."

"Come on," Charlotte said as they both stood.

Charlotte pulled her tight and hard. "Thank you," her friend whispered by her ear, squeezing her again. When Charlotte let go, she left an arm around her shoulder because Charlotte was easy with hugs.

Olivia sniffed and wiped her cheek again before saying. "I'm glad you get on with Kate. It's nice to be able to come out somewhere together. We spend time at her home but..."

Oh for goodness sake. Charlotte wasn't listening. Her eyes were skywards towards the bedroom window, then following a bird that flew overhead.

Olivia shut down the retort, one that habitually leaped to her tongue. She considered her distracted friend, and instead said quietly, "Are you listening?"

"What?" Charlotte whipped her head round. "Sorry. No. I wasn't listening. I'm really awful at that."

"I know," she said gently. "I saw you become distracted. I was only getting your attention back."

And the biggest smile bloomed on Charlotte's face. "Thank you." Really the biggest smile. "I need that sometimes. Hey, are you still worried about work?" Charlotte said, leaping to another subject. "Have Hugo and Liz said anything?"

"No, but I'm in the bad books."

"Is the disapproval all coming from you?"

Hmm. That was unusually perceptive. No, she corrected herself. Just as perceptive as Charlotte often was about her.

"Perhaps it's mainly that," she conceded.

"You handled it." Charlotte said, with her confident business voice that she used with clients. "Liz and Hugo won't let you go. You're a large part of Bentley and bring it credibility. Family law's the consistent income and you're pushing the firm's reach to higher profile cases. They'd be bloody stupid not to support you."

Olivia looked at her.

"And, yes, I'm going to swear about it."

Because Charlotte didn't swear often, but this came out easily.

"I'll be glad when Kate's divorce is final," she sighed.

"Is it submitted to court?" Charlotte asked.

"Alec sent in the agreement this week."

"Good. Well then." Charlotte beamed with pink on her cheeks, and it still made the day sunnier.

Maybe this was going to be OK.

***

Exhausted walking back, she silently held Kate's hand along Mesopotamia Walk, comforted by Kate's warm fingers around hers.

"Is everything OK?" Kate held her hand tighter.

"Sorry, yes."

Distracted and processing the conversation with Charlotte, she hadn't registered the tension in Kate's face and found her expression stoney and failing to hide concern.

She frowned in question.

"Look I..." Kate stopped and turned to her. "I'll just say it, rather than letting it stew." Kate held her hand in both of hers. "Is there anything I need to know about you and Charlotte?"

"Me and Charlotte?"

"I hung back with Millie inside the house while you talked outside. Millie tried to distract me, but it was obvious there was some...history to sort out." Kate squeezed her hand, more a nervous twitch than comforting now. "I don't need the detail. But I appreciate you being open and honest with me. And I hope I am with you."

"It's..."

Nothing. Complicated. Both of those.

"You're allowed to be messy, Olivia. You've seen my baggage," Kate said, with a tiny smile that was trying hard to be understanding. "But I'm in too far over my head if your heart is elsewhere."

The hands lightened around hers, as if afraid now.

"No, it's not." She leant closer to Kate. "I thought we'd be involved at one point." She pulled herself up on the inaccuracy. "For a while, I assumed we'd be together. But I now think we were always better off as friends." She enveloped Kate's hand. "I'm crystal clear on that."

Relief flooded Kate's face.

"Hey." She threw her arms around Kate's shoulders. She tugged her in, loving holding her and stroking around her neck.

"I'm all here," she murmured, sensing Kate relax beneath her touch.

She pulled away a little, to cup her cheeks and kiss her. And she loved that Kate so obviously melted when she did that. It was catching, her insides turning liquid as they lovingly kissed.

"I'm all yours," she whispered and stroked her thumb over Kate's cheek.

"I'm glad. Because I'm getting in deep here."

And they kissed again, reassurance and honesty communicated in their tenderness.

They carried on walking, slowly, hand in hand, a clear couple to anyone watching.

"Is this why...?" Kate's eyes sparkled and her lips pinched together.

"What?"

"Is this why Millie annoys you?"

Olivia raised an eyebrow. "Oh, there are many reasons Millie annoys me."

And Kate laughed.

34

Would this be enough for Olivia, Kate wondered, these snatched weekends? She kissed along her shoulder and up the rise of neck, the sensation warm and blissful to her lips, and Olivia murmured in her sleep. She snuggled closer, luxuriating as her body shaped into the curves of Olivia's back, and smiled as it elicited hummed approval.

Would this be enough for Kate?

She craved Olivia during the week. They spoke on the phone at night, when Olivia wasn't working late or Kate was working on set. Or the kids hadn't woken up, or tried to wrangle some telly, and returned to bed, then the whole routine again, Bea trying tummy ache, and Ralph asserting teens didn't need as much sleep.

She wished she could curl up with Olivia every day. But if this was enough for Olivia, if these weekends were what she wanted, she would take it.

What if she did take a major role? Would Olivia get frustrated when filming took her away for weeks at a time? Could Kate ever accept another significant job and keep the kids in routine and Olivia happy too?

Her head and her heart ached, and she tugged closer again. She held Olivia with desperate appreciation, fearing they might not last.

She'd drifted when her phone rang, and she made out Harry's blurred name on the screen.

"Hey," she picked up.

"Sorry," he said. "I messaged, but you weren't replying."

She sat up in bed, groggily swiped hair from her face and put on glasses. "What's up?"

"Bea didn't settle. She's insisting on having Mum and being at yours."

"OK." Kate stretched her eyes and mouth wide trying to wake up. Bea sometimes got like this, and she didn't change her mind once set. Harry would have tried everything before calling. "Yeah, I'll come and get her."

"We're outside in the car."

"Oh." God. And Olivia was here. "Erm, OK." She rubbed her eyes, nudging her glasses so they skewed across her nose. "Give me a minute and I'll be down."

"I couldn't stop her crying, but at least she fell asleep while travelling."

Ah the magic sedative of a gently rocking car.

"Don't rush." Harry said. "She's still settled."

"OK. See you in a minute."

She put down the phone and gazed at Olivia, still beautifully asleep in her bed. What was the time? Gone midnight from a glance at her phone. She reached out to rock Olivia's shoulder, then stopped. She didn't want to turn her out of bed and house, not in the early hours, and Kate threw on a pair of PJs and padded down the stairs.

She opened the front door.

Harry grinned through a wince. "Sorry." He carried Bea who murmured and drooled on his shoulder. "I tried all the usual. *Duggee* on the telly, warm milk, Winnie the Witch books, the lot."

"I know," she said. "Come here Bumble Bea." She tried to take her off Harry. "Oh goodness, you're getting bigger. Can you walk sweet pea?"

Bea muttered something about lollipops and pigs, and she seemed very annoyed about it.

"What?" Kate whispered in question to Harry.

He threw up his hands. "Not a clue."

Still half asleep and dreaming, Kate suspected.

"Is everything all right?"

Harry froze and stared at Kate with wide eyes. Because the question came from behind her. Usually precise and enunciated, the voice was softened by sleep and pleasure.

"Ah," Kate said.

She glanced back to find Olivia coming down the stairs, dressed in a long T-shirt and gorgeously sleepy. A truly beautiful sight, but not one she could explain away.

"OK," Kate said.

She turned to Harry, who failed to keep a silly smirk hidden. He made no effort at all in fact.

"So, this is Olivia," she tried lightly, "my lawyer."

"Right." Harry laughed. "Late night appointment?"

"Yes," she snapped. "In front of Bea," she mouthed, nodding towards their daughter, who didn't need to know the details.

"Oh, we're being serious," Harry pursed his mouth shut as if reeling it in. "Good evening, erm, Olivia the lawyer." Then he snorted, which really didn't help.

Olivia approached, beautifully bleary eyed and a little dozy. "Good evening, Mr Shaw. Kate's told me a lot about you."

"Good, good," Harry said, relaxing into a blatant grin. "Kate has mentioned you too," he said, nodding. "Not in this context, but..." His grin grew wide.

She was going to kill him.

Harry dipped in front of her, out of sight of Olivia, and whispered, "Hey, it's nice to see this." He pointed in zigzags. "It really is."

No, she hadn't told him, but he'd realise this was unusual and important for her. He wouldn't miss the opportunity to make fun though.

"Right," he said. "I'm gonna head off. I left Ralph asleep with a note beside him. I should get back in case he wakes." He stepped away with a huge smirk on his lips. "Enjoy your...appointment."

"Shut up," she said, failing to stop her smile, and she closed the door on his silly face.

She heaved Bea onto her hip, her daughter's head lolling on her shoulder. It wouldn't take long to settle her.

She turned to Olivia, who stood there drowsy, lovely and relaxed at the encounter.

"I need to get this one to bed," she murmured. "Do you want to stay?"

"If that's all right," Olivia replied, slumber still softening her face.

"Feels wrong to send you home."

"And I don't want to go." And Olivia gave her one of those subtle smiles, that was all in the eyes and said she meant it. "Although, you may need to clarify what lawyers do at some point."

Kate giggled, then couldn't stop, because Olivia was always Olivia even when dozy with sleep.

"I'll see you in a minute," she whispered.

By the time she'd settled Bea, with a night light on and favourite toys beside her, Olivia was fast asleep in her bedroom.

She eased into bed, leaving on her PJs. She snuggled tight behind Olivia, slipping her hand around her belly, soft under the T-shirt. She stayed wide awake, nerves jangling in her limbs and churning inside her stomach.

Not at the unfortunate meeting with Harry and Bea, and Olivia padding down the stairs looking all kinds of loved up. But because what if this could work? What if the two sides of her life she valued most could exist together? She screwed her eyes tight. The chances were so small, Olivia needing things in a certain way and it being a big ask of anyone. She'd asked Nat, and the answer had been a disaster.

She snuggled tighter again, because she didn't want to lose this. She breathed Olivia in, the natural scent of her skin, enjoying the soft hair against her face, taking in every centimetre she touched from head to toes, realising now how much she wanted her.

***

The child, Bea, was doing that staring thing. Like the time in her office.

Olivia sat at the kitchen table, morning sunshine beaming through the end windows and shining in swirls of steam from her coffee. Kate had taken an urgent call from her agent and had left them alone to talk upstairs.

The child waited, unblinking, on the other side of the table.

Olivia pursed her lips with a smile of acknowledgement, then dipped her head to read a headline on her phone. Perhaps Bea would toddle off and play with the pile of toys in the corner.

She became engrossed in the article, then swiped to another, glancing up as she did so.

Good god, the child was closer.

Bea had crept around the end of the table and now stared with huge eyes from a metre away, only her head and shoulders showing above the surface.

Perhaps the child was passing by. Maybe Olivia should carry on reading. It was worth a try. She swiped. She read a paragraph. A small shadow fell across the screen and eclipsed her coffee.

That clearly hadn't worked.

"Yes?" Olivia said, looking up and raising an eyebrow. "Can I help?"

The child, Bea, blonde and silent, stared some more, then slowly raised her narrow shoulders. Arms appeared above the table, a large book hanging from one tiny hand, and a tin of pencils from the other.

"Colouring books," Olivia observed.

No response.

Olivia was flummoxed. "Do you want to colour in?"

A frown.

"Do you want me to help colour in?"

Oh, a smile. That was it.

"Very well," Olivia said.

Then Bea dropped the book and tin on the table with a clatter, pushed on Olivia's shoulder and climbed onto her knee.

Olivia sat upright, startled, because it was presumptuous, frankly. But fine, she'd cope with being a seat for a while. Kate wouldn't be long.

Bea popped open the tin and flung back a pencil.

"Do the blue."

Bea pointed a short pale finger to an area of sea fractured into patterns, surprisingly complex for a colouring book.

"Right," Olivia said. "All of these areas?"

Bea nodded and indicated the parts she wanted completed in...Olivia twisted the pencil round...aquamarine.

They began.

The pencils were good quality, the grain fine and soft, and she shaded areas with a pleasing evenness. She hadn't done this for years and it was actually quite satisfying.

"What next?" Olivia said, sitting straight to admire her work.

Bea passed another pencil over her shoulder and Olivia moved to put the other away. Bea looked back, eyes unblinking and accusatory.

"It has to go in order," she said, pointing to the picture on the tin lid. Graduated shades of different coloured pencils ran from left to right.

"Well, of course." Olivia smiled. "I wouldn't dream of doing anything else."

Bea frowned.

"Do you like the label facing up or down?" Olivia asked.

Bea's face blanked, like she hadn't thought of it before. "Down," she said.

And Olivia ran her fingers over the set of pencils in a rattle and flourish, so they faced down in clean lines.

Bea beamed, happy with the result.

"You're good at this," Bea said.

Olivia almost laughed, complimented at something so simple, but at the same time, was inordinately pleased.

"Thank you. You are doing well too." For a small child, Olivia guessed. Because colouring neatly within the lines didn't seem the most important element right now.

They carried on, shading the sea in blue, Bea passing back pencils and pointing at where Olivia should colour, the blend of tints satisfying. This was a relaxing activity, not having to think particularly, and filling in colours, one after the other. Actually, very relaxing indeed. She should get herself a book to do at home.

***

So, they were doing this. Today. The two sides of Kate's life colliding with no preparation whatsoever. And Kate had to acknowledge she didn't like winging this, at all. Her stomach and heart seemed to have swapped places.

She rushed back from her phone call with her agent, cursing that she'd left Olivia and Bea together for so long. She barrelled toward the kitchen from the stairs and stopped dead in the doorway.

Bea sat on Olivia's knee. Her girl leant to the left, colouring with her favoured hand, and Olivia leant the other way and coloured in with her right.

"That one now," Bea said, blunt and matter of fact and pointing. And without a word, Olivia continued working on the piece.

They sat neatly, concentrating and engrossed in the activity. Her very particular daughter, happily colouring in with Olivia, who was also very particular.

Kate peeled away from the doorway. Her heart thudded, from the run and from surprise. That had not been what she expected. Not from Olivia, or from Bea. Hope rushed in. Could those two get along in some way? Actually, did they have a wavelength in common too? Then fear ravaged at that hope.

"Finished," said Bea from inside the kitchen. "I'm hungry."

"Let's tidy these up and see what Kate has in for you."

Followed by the sound of pencils, a tin closing and a book sliding on the table.

Kate stood out of view. They were colouring in. Something tiny and insignificant. She shouldn't read too much into it. She waited while her head spun, trying to let the scene settle into some kind of proportion, while the terrifying hope swirled in her chest.

Except Nat had done nothing like that. She'd never sat with Ralph, she hardly looked him in the eye, and she'd only hold Bea for seconds before finding another set of hands.

She trembled and pushed her fingers into her jeans pockets to hide that she shook, before stepping into the room.

"Here she is," Olivia said lightly, glancing up.

"Hi," she replied, wandering towards the table.

"Food," Bea cried, because once Bea realised she was hungry, nothing else existed except that hunger.

"Come here sweet pea," she said. And Bea barrelled into a leg and sank her face into Kate's belly. "Shall we make a banana milkshake?"

There was a grumble and a nod from the bundle of warmth.

Kate's thoughts and feelings tumbled while Bea stood on a step. Her daughter threw large pieces of banana into a liquidiser, spilt milk down the equipment and over the surface and covered her ears while Kate whizzed up the drink.

Still without a word to Olivia, she passed Bea a tumbler of shake and watched her scarper out the back door and into the garden. Which left just her, still trembling and avoiding Olivia's gaze. She rinsed the machine. She wiped the countertops. And with no more excuses, finally turned to Olivia, with no idea what to say.

"Is everything OK?" Olivia whispered.

No, everything was in motion, like she was the one spinning round in that processor.

"With your agent?"

"Oh," Kate said. "Yes, kind of. He's pushing for an answer on that script I was reading." This was too much. Too many good things all at once. "I want to."

"Then?"

But where would it be shot? What was the schedule? Could the kids stay in Oxford? Would it fit Harry's plans? Would Olivia still be there afterwards?

Olivia stepped towards her and slipped arms around her waist. Immediately her body sighed, soothed in Olivia's hands. She held her close, resting foreheads together, so the warmth and comfort built between them.

"You seem overwhelmed," Olivia whispered so it tickled on her face.

"I am." But she didn't want to say why, because this was a lot – the kids and Harry and acting and the media and divorce. It was all a lot.

"Look, erm..." She pulled her head up and gazed into Olivia's sympathetic eyes. "Harry's bringing Ralph home soon. Do you want to stay for lunch so you can say hi properly."

Olivia nodded. "Yes, I'd like to say hello again, dressed in more than my underwear this time."

Kate laughed. She covered her mouth because it was loud from the release of tension.

Olivia's lips curved and dark eyes softened, and Kate must have gazed at her with stupid and open adoration. Olivia smiling got her every time. She knew those rare smiles weren't for everyone.

The appreciation built in her chest again. Oh, this wasn't good. She hadn't realised how much was at stake for her and how big it had all grown. Was she heading for a fall here?

Too late, even if she was, because things were in motion, with Olivia close and warm with her arms around her. And she didn't want to turn away from this.

"I'd like you to meet my son," Kate said.

***

Late afternoon, Kate sat on the patio steps into the garden. Harry sat beside her as they peered down into the kitchen. The kids had disappeared inside, dragging Olivia with them and she wasn't sure what Ralph had planned.

A hand pressed on her knee, and she only realised then that she jiggled her leg up and down.

She snapped round to Harry.

"Relax," he whispered. He squeezed her knee and withdrew his hand. "They're getting along great."

She breathed in, then blew out long and noisily. This was fine. Nothing to be worried about. What could possibly go wrong?

Her knee started bouncing again.

And she knew she shouldn't ask, because it was early and unfair to put him on the spot, but, "Do you like her? I like her. Please say you like her," came out in rapid fire.

The hand returned to her knee and nudged her.

"Of course," he said. "She's similar to you."

"What?" she blurted.

He sniggered. "Haven't you noticed?"

"No?" she said, as if she were a grumpy teen.

"OK." He shuffled and leant back. "From what I've seen and what you've said, you're both super dedicated to your jobs. Didn't you say she's practically running a solicitors in her mid-thirties."

"Yeah. Which is nothing like my work." What was he getting at here?

"But you're both dead serious and conscientious about what you do."

She rolled her eyes. "As if people think that about actors."

"Kate, you are the most boringly responsible actor I know."

"Thanks, Harry." She gave him a look. "Is this why you think we're the same, because we're dull and grown up to you?"

"Yeah."

"Fuck you."

He laughed. "I don't blame you. I know what it's like with upheaval all day long. It's acting. It's the business. So, I can see why you, the most boringly normal actress, would want a professional, cool, responsible lawyer."

"What?" Kate stuttered in disbelief. "She is so far from boring."

Olivia had a glow that was low-burning and ever present. It steadily burned brighter the more Kate knew her. More like the sun, always there, not a firework that's loud and startling for a moment, then gone. And the sun wasn't boring. It was everything.

"I said you were boring, not her," Harry retorted.

He laughed again when she punched him on the arm.

"Doesn't mean I don't think you're fun," he said, putting up his arms. "She reminds me of you there too. You've both got this dry, deadpan sense of humour. If anything," he peered into the kitchen, squinting into the shadows, "I reckon Olivia Sachdeva has a wicked side to her. And sexy." He sidled closer and lowered his voice. "Definitely sexy."

"Not appropriate," she said, sharply.

He tilted his head with a mischievous smile. "Don't you think she has this hot headteacher quality?"

"No."

"Crisp posh voice, perfect posture, strict but naughty thing going?"

"Nope, can't see it."

She was getting annoyed, because yes she saw that, and liked it a lot, but didn't want to tell him.

"She definitely has though."

They both dipped their heads, trying to see what was going on in the kitchen.

"So," he said, sitting up again. "Why aren't you snatching her up then?"

"What do you mean?"

"She's practically perfect for you. Why didn't you tell me about her?" He said it without jesting this time.

She hesitated. "I think it scared me." She quietened her voice at the admission. "If I told you about her, I'd be admitting how important she is to me. And if I'm serious about this, I need to ask a lot of her."

"Like?"

"Fitting in with our lives, Harry. It's not easy, you know that. And with the kids," she paused, "I'm not looking for someone to parent them, they have us, but..."

"A partner can't not be involved either," he finished for her.

"Exactly. And our kids are very particular individuals and fussy about who they spend time with."

Music pulled their attention back towards the kitchen.

Kate recognised the track. "He's not letting Bea watch *Wednesday* is he?"

"Nah," Harry said, leaning forward. "Just a clip on YouTube of the dance."

"Oh god, is he calling her 'Little Wednesday' again?" Ralph's favourite nickname for their serious, small girl.

Harry sat back. "No?" he said, way too high.

"What does that mean?" She pinned him with a glare, because there was more to that no.

"He's calling her Tuesday instead."

She snorted through her nose. "That–!"

Harry clutched his belly.

"Stop it," Kate said. "You mustn't find it funny." She covered her mouth to hide the smile. "At least don't encourage him."

"I won't." He waved her concern away. "What are they doing?"

They leaned further, peering into the kitchen. Ralph propped his tablet on the table, tapped the screen, and he, Bea and Olivia stood in a line.

Kate pulled back, not believing her eyes. Because her nearly teen and determined boy, her grumpy, very particular girl and Olivia, were all doing the Wednesday dance. Her boy, who despaired at having a young sister, but still performed magic for her every day. Her wee girl, limbs loose and face serious. And Olivia, killing it with a floppy elegance that was perfection.

"Oh my..." Harry said, grinning. He leant closer. "You realise they're going to dump us and go home with Olivia?"

But Kate couldn't speak at that moment and stared at them all.

"Perfect," she whispered.

35

What was that noise? Olivia paused from misting the ferns on her office window ledge. She smiled. It had been her, humming.

Happy, she sat at her desk to enjoy her tea before the first meeting of the morning. And to maybe indulge in a daydream about Kate.

Every passing day there was more to love about Kate, but she dwelled on their kisses. The moment of anticipation before they touched, the way Kate's lips melted over hers, the warmth that slipped inside, deeper and deeper as her body succumbed, loving what she did to her. Had anyone ever done that like Kate? Olivia gave in to her, revelled in it, because she saw the same trust and surrender in Kate.

She'd started staying a couple of nights during the week, arriving after the kids had gone to bed and hanging out with Kate, who didn't mind if the children came down and found Olivia now that they'd met. Surprising. Bea and Ralph were a fun pair. Who'd have thought.

She finished her tea. Time for her first meeting of the day.

She opened the door to the corridor but had to step back from a tall man blustering past.

"Morning, Olivia," came a gloating and recognisable voice.

What on earth? Richard? What was he doing here?

Then followed a woman with long brown hair, light skin and a face that scratched at familiarity. Alarm bells rang when she shot a venomous glance at Olivia. The two visitors and another man behind marched along the corridor and Richard blasted into the large meeting room, as if he still worked here and owned the place.

Dipping inside her office, she grabbed her phone from her desk and tapped in 'Natalie Marks and Kate Laurence' into a search.

Pages and pages of images returned going back years. Promotion stills from films where they'd co-starred. Informal shots at events. A rare picture of Nat's arm around Kate's waist. Easy to gloss over with the pair flanked by men as their partners, but it made her feel ill. Physically ill.

She'd avoided this, especially when things developed between them. But that was definitely Kate's ex in the office, right now, with Richard and another lawyer.

Why was Richard here? How had he teamed up with Kate's ex?

She looked at the wall clock and grabbed her phone, tapping in the extension for the admin team.

"Sorry Liz," she said when it picked up. "Could we delay our meeting? Something's come up."

"Of course. Anything I can help with?" came Liz's calm reply.

Oh god. What the hell was happening? This was the kind of fallout she'd dreaded. "I may need to talk to you later."

Olivia darted out of her office and along the corridor. Then staying in the shadows around the door, she peered through a pane into the meeting room, leaning until she could see who met inside.

Alec sat on the far edge of the long table, a little dishevelled as if he'd been called in without warning. And by his side was Kate: pale, shocked and face knotted with distress.

Olivia inhaled and stood back. She took several quick breaths to catch up from freezing still.

"What the...." She covered her mouth to stop any more words and retreated into her office.

She paced. She needed to make sense of this. Then she sat at her desk and tapped her laptop alive. Where had Richard gone after leaving Bentley? She searched her email for the announcement from Liz, wishing Richard well on his new venture in London. There it was. Ferriers, a mid-size independent with a wide range of specialities, including divorce and family law.

She sat up. That hadn't been Nat's solicitors. Had Richard gone fishing on purpose? Or, at least, encouraged someone at his new office to pursue the case, then strode in here to stir things up. This was a more high-powered firm than Nat's original solicitors – better resourced, higher-profile cases, solid reputation.

Dammit. Dammit. Dammit.

She tried to push down her panic and keep a clear head, but every time the image of Kate, distressed in the meeting room, intruded.

After a soft knock at the door, Alec's face peeped around. "May we come in?" he said. "In a personal capacity?"

Kate followed, looking as shell-shocked as before. She didn't so much as avoid Olivia's gaze, but seemed unable to look at anything.

"What's going on?" Olivia asked quietly.

Alec took a seat in front of her desk while Kate remained standing and stared through the window.

"Kate's ex..." Alec started. He pinched his trousers at the knees and tugged them up.

"Natalie, yes?" Olivia prompted.

"She's changed lawyers, rejected the financial agreement and is demanding complete renegotiation."

"On what grounds?" Olivia said, almost laughing.

These were new tactics, and the first interest Natalie had shown in pursuing negotiations face to face.

"She claims..." it came from Kate, painfully quiet and subdued, "that her earning has been severely affected by the secrecy of our relationship. And that her freedom to choose work was hampered by supporting me and my family."

"But..."

That was the complete opposite to what Kate had described. And Olivia hated that doubt intruded for a moment.

"She claims," Kate continued, "that at a crucial age as an actress, she's missed out on lucrative roles for younger women."

Her head spun.

"And that she remained faithful and hoped we'd stay together until a few weeks ago and therefore has a claim to recent earnings."

Which was impossible, because if Kate had time to maintain any sort of relationship with Nat she would have known.

"It's complete fiction," Kate said.

Olivia's stomach turned again, and she covered her mouth with her fingers as if to stop herself from being sick. Because no matter how much she knew it was a lie, she couldn't help imagining Kate and Nat together.

"She hasn't spent a single night under the same roof as me or my family for over two years."

And Kate looked at her then, eyes pleading to make Olivia believe. Perhaps even to stop her own mind from being swayed from the truth.

Olivia pursed her lips into a reassuring smile, but Kate turned away.

Her heart sank. This was why, Olivia's lawyer head said. This was why you didn't get involved and why she advised clients to keep their lives simple until divorce was finalised.

But her heart still broke.

She breathed in, letting it cool her inside, and allowing her mind to settle again. She needed to put Kate to one side, as an upset client, and to consider the political move by the opposing team.

"If there's no substance to this," Olivia started.

"There isn't," Kate said sharply, and Olivia had to take a moment not to let it cut.

She nodded, trying to smile. "Then," she continued. "They must have something else planned."

Alec grimaced. "Richard's being transparently revengeful here."

Olivia was glad he saw it too.

"I agree. Richard's indulging in a vendetta. But the rest of the team? That firm wouldn't escalate this if they didn't have something to back it up."

There were too many things at play and suddenly everything was unpredictable, with a solicitor with a grudge and an ex who looked at Olivia with vicious jealousy.

Nat knew. That's what had changed. She deflated. Nat had heard there was something between Kate and Olivia. How though? Did Richard spread a rumour? But why did he think it had any basis?

Then she deflated further. Of course, Hugo's party. They'd all been there: Richard about to leave, Olivia baring her crush for all to see and leaving a trail of evidence on the dance floor.

"She knows," Kate said, her eyes tired and the shine gone. "I don't know how, and she didn't say so, but Nat knows about us."

Perhaps it hit them all in the same way, like the world tilted off balance and everything became unstable. No-one said anything.

"Where are they're going with this?" Alec asked, shaking his head.

And still they said nothing, and a weight settled over the room.

Kate moved from her position at the window, her steps lethargic and heavy, and Olivia stood to join her.

"I have to go," Kate said firmly. "I'm due on set."

Olivia halted and her heart lurched as if a chasm opened between them. She hated the chill that descended inside. She remained standing, wishing she could hold Kate, talk to her, anything. But Alec was there.

She couldn't help asking gently, "Can I see you later?"

Kate paused then, different feelings settling in her whole demeanour, and Olivia must have sighed when she said, "Please," because the look Kate gave her reached out across that chasm.

It was late when Olivia arrived in Park Town, the summer sky faltering into dark blue. Kate's face appeared pale at the door, clearly exhausted by it all.

"The kids are awake," Kate said. She pushed strands of hair behind her ear. "I'm all over the place. I haven't stuck with their routine, and they're still up in front of the telly."

"That's OK," Olivia said, gently.

She closed the door, put down her briefcase and drew Kate slowly into a hug. She let Kate sink into her until she had her safe beneath her arms. It's how they always shaped together, with no gap between. She held on, sensing Kate relax and release some of the tension of the day. When Kate raised her head, she kissed her gently on her lips and cuddled her again.

"I'm going to say hi to the kids, so they know someone's visiting," she said. "How about we talk in the front room afterwards?"

Kate nodded, and Olivia strode further into the house and poked her head around the living room door.

"Hello, Ralph. Hello, Bea."

The two looked up from being snuggled together on the sofa. Ralph only half-surfaced from the film they watched, sending her a goofy grin and lifting his hand to wave. Copying her big brother, Bea did the same. Then their eyes drifted back to the screen and *Coco*, their cheeks going slack as they became immersed again. They seemed happy at least.

She joined Kate on a small sofa in the front room, under a soft beam of lamplight and surrounded by books.

"I'm glad you came," Kate said, cuddling up. "I'm a mess and I'd understand if you don't want to stay."

"I wouldn't be anywhere else tonight." She wrapped an arm around her.

"It's so surreal," Kate said, clasping her jumper to her neck, as if to protect herself. "It's like somebody's rewriting my history. I'm doubting myself when I shouldn't. I was there for the past two years and saw it with my own eyes, for goodness' sake."

She had the same dissociation earlier, suddenly unbalanced, unnerved and everything not right in the world.

"It's a deliberate tactic. A horrible one. Unfortunately, I see it a lot." She squeezed Kate. "People always have different perspectives on an experience, but sometimes they dig down into fiction to suit their agenda. It's plain gaslighting."

"I'm so sorry," Kate murmured. "This should have been over."

"Yes, it should." She stroked Kate's forehead, smoothing back the long ribbons of hair that kept falling over her face.

"Nat knows I need a quiet life for the kids."

"You've always been clear about that." She tucked another strand behind Kate's ear. "Unfortunately, she's probably using that against you to press for a better deal."

Kate nodded and fell silent. She sensed Kate didn't want to talk about it anymore, perhaps with her, perhaps with anyone, but Olivia stayed to hold her. And the world kept tilting.

36

'I've lost the love of my life,' blazed the headline on Olivia's phone. 'The story of Natalie Marks and Kate Laurence's secret romance,' said the Sunday media byline.

Shocking. Chilling. A daily news notification about matters that were often distant, but this one shot straight to her heart. Olivia sickened the more she stared at it.

The same woman who'd walked into Bentley with eyes that could kill gazed mournfully from the top of the article.

So, these were their tactics. And although they were tactics, her stomach writhed in knots, because it also rang true. Damn her crystal-clear memory, because in an early meeting, Kate described Nat as the love of her life, and that comment between client and lawyer now stabbed at her heart.

She hated this. But she made herself read on.

Natalie spun a tale of living in the closet for the sake of Oscar-nominated Kate, the road to marriage a rocky one of sacrifices for the overshadowed actor.

Olivia threw down her phone on her sofa. Walked away. Took a breath. Reminded herself about Kate. The woman who wandered hand in hand with her along the river with no hesitation. Kate, who made friends with hers with no self-consciousness in queer company. Who didn't have to explain Olivia's gender to her kids or their co-parent. Someone completely at ease with her sexuality. And someone who'd understood Natalie's need to stay in the closet, only to have it thrown back in her face.

She read on, finding the rest of the article a similar inversion of the truth. Then her insides turned colder at a 'new lover for Kate and heartbreak for Natalie'.

Olivia covered her mouth. The shot was indistinct, zoomed in digitally several times, but clear enough to her. She and Kate kissed. From the narrow pathway surrounded by greenery, she guessed at Mesopotamia Walk returning from Charlotte's, when they'd talked and hugged and kissed without a care.

Did it say anything about this lover? Nothing. No names. Not yet anyway.

She dipped into social media. Oh god. Kate was trending. People piled on with every take from the outright homophobic, to condemnation of hiding her queerness, to questioning how she identified, the validity of her bisexuality, all views so equally vehement it spun her head. She swiped it away and Natalie's article and face stared at her again.

She almost dropped her phone when it rang. Kate's name flashed across the screen, and she couldn't help the unpleasant jealousy that curdled from switching from the ex to Kate herself.

This was hard. Her grasp on reality and the truth stretched thin at that moment, and she let the phone ring out.

She wasn't ready to talk to Kate. But she didn't want to ignore her either. Olivia knew what that would do to her.

She rang back and Kate immediately answered with, "You've seen it, haven't you?"

"I have." Her voice came out heavy, even though she tried to stay afloat.

"Do I need to say it's not true and–"

"No, you don't. Not to me." Olivia clutched the phone closer.

"Should I counter this publicly, do you think? Is this going to hold up my case? I... Sorry. I can ask Alec." And Kate fell silent.

Olivia gathered herself, pushing her mind into a professional perspective, the shift sluggish and sore today.

"They'd be foolish to use this line of argument in court," she started, "if they wanted to go that far. But..." So hard to keep a clear head. "This is what I was afraid of. This kind of tactic is all about pressure and influence outside the court. They're pushing you to agree to their terms early and unfavourably."

"It's Nat's jealousy lashing out. It's all about that too."

Olivia's own jealousy stirred, and she blinked back tears.

"You're..." Kate's voice was quiet. "You're finding it difficult."

"Yes, I am," she whispered. She wasn't going to hide that from Kate.

"Do you want to come round?"

"I..." She felt the weight of that pause. She heard what it did to Kate too. "I do, yes, but I need to see my parents. They might catch news of this, and I want to tell them first."

"Of course."

She closed her eyes, sorrow pooling hot behind her eyelids.

***

Olivia hesitated before stepping outside. She was potentially recognisable now. She slipped on sunglasses, the world feeling surreal and tilting again at being in the public sphere and no longer just another Jericho resident.

She took the river path, delaying tactics perhaps, to walk off her nerves and steel herself ready for her parents' reaction when she admitted her unprofessional behaviour and its consequences. And after all these years of pulling away from Geeta, insisting she'd outgrown and didn't need her, Olivia found she wanted her advice.

Actually, who better than her mother? Not even Nani. Because Geeta would listen to her mistakes and always come round. Because the love that annoyed her so much was a critical safety net, she realised.

Olivia wandered the towpath beyond the Isis Tavern, across the lock bridges and up the trail into the village. She knocked on the door of her childhood home and waited for the familiar outline of her mother to come closer through the frosted glass. She might fall into her arms today if she offered a hug.

Her black clothing warmed as she stood outside in the sunshine. Perhaps they were in the garden and didn't hear. She checked down the side of the house and tried the gate that Geeta left unlocked far too often. The latch clicked up and the door pushed in, and she slipped through beneath the rambling roses and rampant clematis.

The garden seemed empty, and she turned to check the house. And that's when she heard them.

Her mother's voice carried, strange and upset. Olivia stepped back with the surprise of it. It was hardly ever raised like that, and it reached deep down and twisted with unnaturalness.

She saw them through the full height windows of the extension living area. Her mother stood faced away and her father stared at the floor as if he hoped it might swallow him up.

Oh god. This was the worst time to call. She should go.

"None of you are ever home," Geeta cried. And Olivia hesitated. "You're in the department every day."

Her father must have said something, but she couldn't make out his quieter tone.

"Of course, I understand," Geeta replied, upset. "I always did and admired your dedication. But there's nothing here for me anymore."

Their old argument, practically the only one, that would surface again and again. She encountered it first when she was ten, before her brother was born.

"Adam has left home," Geeta said, her voice raw. "He's even left the country."

Sumit said something indistinct.

"You need me for bouncing around research ideas, that's all," Geeta snapped. "But you don't have the time and, let's face it, the inclination for anything else with me."

She winced, always uncomfortable and destabilised when her parents argued, especially when it trespassed into areas of intimacy, or the lack of it.

Sumit must have mentioned her name, because Geeta said, "Olivia visited once in six months, and I can't rely on her best friend for company."

Ouch. The guilt struck deep and resonated more than ever. Either Geeta sounded more upset today, or Olivia was sore and sensitive.

"I don't understand the intricacies of law or the environment Olivia works in. That all goes over my head. And she doesn't want to talk about anything else. Not with me anyway."

And it cut deeper. She would have shrugged it off as unfortunate but true usually. But not today.

"What am I meant to do?" Geeta croaked, like she broke inside. "I stay here, the same, wanting to love you all. But none of you need it. None of you want it. But I can't be left with nothing."

That hit hard. The admission and Geeta's loss weighed colossal. The moment hung heavy with devastating inertia, the realisation deepening. Her parents were in trouble this time. She looked back at her father, who sagged perhaps with the understanding too.

Of all the times.

She shouldn't have brushed this off for so long, or dismissed her mother's need for company as part of her strange extroversion like her brother's. She'd rejected every invitation to meet, and it was coming home to roost now. She finally listened, just when her mother was beyond helping her. Just when her life had become more than law and work, and she wanted her advice.

Yes, her parents were in trouble here, and Olivia's world lurched again.

She stumbled back to Jericho, the same thoughts circling. Exhausted she slumped on her grey sofa, too shocked for it to make any sense.

Why were relationships and divorce so complicated? Why was it so hard to find someone and make it work?

Her parents had it sorted, she'd thought. And Olivia had assumed that if she found someone suitable, she'd make it work too. Maybe with Jaipreet, if they'd both wanted to live in Oxford. With Charlotte, if she hadn't been so set on Millie.

Share things in common. Talk to each other with respect. There were obvious factors that increased your chances every time, but people stubbornly ignored them.

But then forever was a long time, with so many changes to navigate. Her heart lurched, losing its grip on the belief that it was possible with the right approach. Because not even her parents had managed. How could you avoid getting lost on the way? It was impossible.

And yet she still she wanted Kate. Despite everything, she wanted Kate.

She dropped her head into her hands and whispered, "Oh god, what a mess."

She'd despaired at clients who made their own lives a misery with ill-advised decisions, and here she was, in the most hideous tangle, not knowing which thread to pull to untie it all.

The sun sank lower in the sky and she thought on, trying to put her thoughts in order, even though it hurt to sort them. Friends, parents, cases, lovers, colleagues, laws, courts, and media. There was little she could control now. Two things remained though, one hard, one desperately harder.

She made a call.

"Liz, I'm sorry to disturb you on a Sunday with work. I'll be phoning Hugo too." She took a deep breath. "You need to be aware of a few things."

37

It exploded overnight.

Kate cursed because she didn't have a chance to call Olivia back. She'd been in conference with her agent, PR firm, personal assistant and the studio, warning them to increase security on set with her name trending again.

In some ways, the scenario was familiar. This happened for all kinds of reasons from time to time.

Then it hit her in the gut when Ralph showed her his phone. He hadn't had free access to the internet the last time she'd trended so widely. Messages flew around his school group. Gossip first, and teasing with the photo, then outright homophobic bullying.

A wave of shame drenched her, leaving her cold and shaking. She hated that it did. She'd brought all this upon her son by being who she was. He was paying the price for her very public job, high profile and queerness. And understanding that homophobia was at fault didn't help right now.

Abuse poured in through every electronic device in the household. Well-meaning friends and relatives contacted her, all requiring more consolation than they gave. She prioritised school and called the headteacher first in the morning and asked for the bullying to be addressed. Not that it would make Ralph's day any easier.

Then she settled Bea at nursery and raced up to Bentley.

"Kate!" yelled a deep voice.

Several men with cameras who'd loitered around the lawyers' entrance swarmed down the street. Shit. So, that information was out – the firm who represented her. Did they know it was Olivia in the photo too? It had been a matter of hours, and they were hurtling towards disaster.

"Who's the new woman then Kate!?"

"Since when were you into birds!?"

"What does Harry think about all this, then? Who's taking the kids?"

She put on sunglasses and ducked her head. She narrowly avoided a camera lens from being shoved in her face. Bodies crowded round her, and she couldn't see a way out until a large man in a dark security suit pushed through the crowd and helped her to the lawyers' doorway. Inside, Liz Oduwole, the practice manager and Olivia's friend, beckoned her in and took her arm. The door swung to and the voices became dull behind her.

"Go straight up to Alec's office," Liz said. "It's quiet up there." And she gave her arm a squeeze.

Kate took a moment to recover her breath and let her heart rate settle. Shit, she hadn't been ready to be ambushed in the streets. What if they'd done this to Olivia too? They were not prepared for this at all.

She climbed the three sets of stairs, round and round again in the bright stairwell. As she ascended to the top floor, the noise of the street receded. She took another breath to calm herself before seeing her solicitor.

Alec's door was open to his long attic office, desk in the corner, two chairs opposite, a dormer window casting in grey light from the overcast day. But no Alec.

Instead, Olivia stood in the room.

The woman she adored stared out of the window, hand on the sloping ceiling and resting her forehead against it. When she turned, her face was paler than usual and her eyes betrayed fatigue and the weight of the world.

"Hi," Olivia whispered, the regret loud in the quiet space. Her smile didn't rise above her mouth, and the air hung solemn. "I asked Alec if I could see you first."

Kate's heart plummeted. No. Please, not this.

Olivia dipped her head, gathering herself. "Hugo and Alec will be along soon. They have a lot to discuss with you, so I don't have long."

Kate knew what was coming.

"Will you come in and sit down?" Olivia asked gently. She gestured towards a chair, movement slow as if her arm weighed twice what it should. She walked elegantly and carefully, as she always did, but with a slowness that betrayed sorrow. She sat with her hands clasped on her lap.

Kate mirrored her, so they remained a couple of metres apart. And a silence descended. She didn't want to hear what was coming, although she knew it must.

Olivia tried to meet her eyes, but failed. She opened her mouth, but no words came out.

It was obvious what their next step was. In the end, Kate said it instead. The phrase that needed saying and the only thing they could do.

"We need to stop seeing each other, don't we?" she murmured. "We need to break up."

Grief washed over Olivia's beautiful features. She attempted to regain her composure, but her eyes remained collapsed in heartache.

"Yes, we do." Olivia's voice broke.

They gazed at each other in understanding, with resignation and longing mixing thick between them. Kate held her breath to keep it from overwhelming her.

Olivia must have done the same because she breathed out heavily before saying, "I was up most of the night, trying to think of another way. But we're pouring fuel onto this case. With their current tactics, they will prey on our relationship and be relentless in the media. You...we... can't afford that."

Kate didn't refute it. She'd seen the glint in Nat's eyes. She hated to imagine what she and her team had planned.

"The press are on Bentley's doorstep," Olivia said quietly. "And although they don't seem to realise about my involvement yet, rumours are flying around lawyer circles and Bentley is under scrutiny."

Shit. "Are you going to be all right?" Kate asked quickly.

"I don't know," Olivia said. "I need the rumours to stop." She pursed her lips and her eyes pleaded with her.

No more pictures. No more gossip. Nothing.

"We have to smother this beyond doubt," Olivia murmured.

"Can't be seen together?"

"No."

"Can't... have any communication?"

"No," Olivia whispered. "It needs to stop completely."

"Do I....?" Her heart was racing, and thoughts spinning. At the same time, she grasped at clarity because her feelings would catch up soon and cloud everything. They were building powerfully already.

"Hugo and Alec..." Olivia took a breath. "They'll be along shortly to talk you through your options. You may want to drop Bentley for another firm."

"Wouldn't that leave Bentley...?" Exposed? Under more scrutiny and subject to more rumours?

"It's not good for Bentley," Olivia replied, her voice heartbreakingly quiet. "But if this case gets worse, that would be damaging too. We're trying to avoid a situation where I'd have to resign to draw blame away from the rest of the firm."

"Fuck."

"It's a distant option at this stage. But it's something I need to consider if it escalates."

And it had already spiralled beyond control and anything Kate had imagined.

Olivia's voice remained subdued but held a gentle consideration. "And it's for your sake too. Just as much." She even smiled a little, with fondness for Kate. "You should deny you're involved with anyone until your divorce is through. You need to nip this in the bud and not let it complicate your case. Otherwise, Natalie and her lawyers will milk this for all it's worth."

Her heart ached doubly watching Olivia, who was so clearly trying to keep a level head while hurting inside.

"It's leaked into the public discussion now," Olivia continued. "You, me, Bentley. And that leaves us short of options. I can't endanger Bentley's reputation. A dip in clients puts people's jobs at risk. And the last thing you need is rumours that have substance."

"I know." Kate loathed it, hated it, but it was true. "Ralph's already having us thrown at him. The photo's shot round all his friends."

"Oh god, no." Olivia's demeanour fractured, and she looked at her with desperate sympathy. "I'm so sorry. I..." She gathered herself. "I wish there was more I could do for him."

Kate nodded, knowing Olivia meant it.

Yes, they needed to do this. To prevent any more fuel on this fire. Then maybe Olivia would be OK. And Ralph. And her.

But breaking up with her? Never seeing her? It hit like a train, and she reeled.

"This," Olivia said, "is the last thing I wanted."

"Same," Kate gasped.

That draw and need to be together was as strong as ever. She saw the same in Olivia's whole being.

"I wish..." Kate started. There was some way to escape this.

"I wish too," Olivia said.

Kate's breath caught in her throat suddenly. It was catching up with her now, what Olivia had been mulling over all night. The realisation was leaking in through the cracks, and flooding in deep and cold inside. Shit. This was going to hurt.

She closed her eyes, as dread overwhelmed. It sank concentrated and heavy as she sat in this private space while chaos swirled outside. When she opened her eyes Olivia was still there, patient and respectful while clearly hurting like hell. And tears began to burn.

"Do you know what the most stupid thing is?" Kate said in a rush, because a rising sob threatened. "What the most frustrating thing is for me?"

Olivia didn't reply.

"That splitting up, us talking like this, is the single most considerate handling of a crisis I've had with any partner. That you're showing me, right now, why you're so good for me... And... it's frustrating as fuck." Her voice broke over the last words.

Because this could have worked. They would have been great for each other.

She swallowed several times.

"I wasn't looking for someone. If anything, I was determined not to. But I found you. And every glimpse has me dazzled." She smiled, even while tears blurred her eyes. "I'm completely infatuated."

Because my goodness, Olivia was gorgeous and witty and a sensual delight. She'd turned her head round and round and it had been magical. Her heart soared for a moment at the memories of their time together, before sinking once more into realisation.

"I'm so sorry," Kate swallowed. "You told me the whole time it was a bad idea. But I got carried away. I couldn't resist."

"You're not the only one," Olivia whispered.

And they both smiled the saddest smile, before Kate's heart dropped again.

What would Olivia think when she looked back at this? Would she judge them both as rash and irresponsible? With disaster striking, would she sober and realise this had all been a crush that got out of hand? Some infatuation with an actress?

But Kate just didn't see them as a mistake. If anything, she saw them with greater clarity. Chaos churned outside. But in here, with the pair of them sheltered together, she only felt the rightness of them even more. Oh fuck this hurt.

"I don't think I've been foolish with you," she started. She had no idea if Olivia wanted to hear this, but her heart was bleeding. "Because after everyone telling me to crave whirlwind excitement," all the things that were celebrated in her youth and in film circles, "I need you." Wonderful Olivia, sitting in front of her. "Someone who can take a moment seriously when necessary, but make me laugh out loud when not."

She shook her head in disbelief that she'd found someone so incredible, to have it all whipped away.

"I admire so many things about you. And I hoped..." She had to swallow. "...I had started to really hope, that you saw the same in me."

She blinked back tears and looked up at the ceiling, not wanting to meet Olivia's gaze. Because she would crack. And it was too late to ask if she shared the same longing anyway.

Dammit, this was shitty timing. Hopes of them being together had steadily built with every encounter. All to be swept aside for nothing. She wanted to shout at it all to stop.

"My head is spinning from everyone's takes. Yet it only makes what we have clearer. Because I thought...I really believed...we made a great couple." She faltered, realising how large her hopes had grown.

"Because we spark," she whispered. My goodness they sparked. "We share interests and an attitude. You are sensual and considerate," she couldn't help smiling, "sexy and funny. You're responsible and sympathetic. You even understand where my kids are coming from, and they are two of the most perplexing human beings on the–"

"And I love you."

She stalled at Olivia's words, the rest of her thoughts left hanging and eclipsed. Her strident breath was loud, and she slapped a hand to her mouth. The room disappeared in white, watery swirls, and she clasped her lips tight to close down the sob that hiccupped inside. Her chest heaved, beyond any control, and when she inhaled it hid nothing.

She blinked and blinked. And when her vision cleared, Olivia stared at her distraught, hands gripping the seat arms, as if she had to stop herself from going to Kate.

Oh my god, this sucked. The timing of this fucking sucked. Finding a woman like this, in the middle of a divorce, from someone who'd played her for years and should have been long gone.

"Shit," Kate said. "Shit and fuck it all."

"That," Olivia said. She swallowed hard over an obvious mound of regret. "Same."

Kate had to cover her face and eyes. Because it was too much. She breathed into her hands with hot humid breaths until her palms were wet with tears.

She coughed out a laugh and swiped at her face. She must look a state. Fuck it though, because she was in a state.

"When you've finished with Alec," Olivia whispered, "we can take you out another exit to avoid the press."

And there she was, reading her mind, anticipating what she needed. She was tempted to let the cameras catch her like this. But it was fuel and headlines, and a picture in a teenage message group to taunt her son.

She nodded. "Thank you."

They sat silently a while, both exhausted.

"This must feel like the worst mess for you," Kate whispered.

Olivia must hate this. Had they been doomed from the start? This private and reserved lawyer, and a public figure who was bound to bring in a hurricane of exposure.

"You know..." Kate started.

Yes, it was futile, but she might never get another chance to speak to Olivia.

"My life isn't always like this. I'm not going to lie, it gets frenzied at times, for all kinds of reasons, and I go to ground. But it will pass.

People's attention moves on. And I'll be a wreck for a while..." She stared at nothing, anticipating the toll it would inevitably take later. She'd have to be careful with herself. Manage her stress and steer her family through.

"This though..."

It had been truly awful. And, of course, it was too much for someone like Olivia to stand. Why would she want a life like this?

But Kate couldn't give up.

"This *has* been the worst," she said. "Because it's reached the people I care about most."

She looked at Olivia, unable to let go yet. "But it will be over. The divorce will end. The media forgets and moves on to their next feast." The feelings rose in her chest. "But I'll still be here. And I will want you." She was certain of that.

Olivia didn't say anything.

"I understand if..." If Olivia had seen enough to decide this life wasn't for her. Not many stood it for long. God, the trail of broken marriages the industry left. And the relentless public pressure. Shit. The same realisation descended again. Of course it was too much.

"I'm all in," Olivia whispered.

"What?"

Olivia blinked slowly, as if she had no strength left. "I'm all in." She shrugged with the tiniest movement of her shoulders. "I'm already all in, Kate."

She stared at her.

"I have been for a while," Olivia said quietly. Those considerate brown eyes, which saw everything, said everything too. "Maybe it's not the same for you. Maybe you're not there yet. Your life is complex, and you're still mid divorce. You have many people to consider. And we haven't seen each other for long." A tightening in her slim neck. "But I'm all in, Kate. I can't help it. You have this hold on me and I'm not going anywhere."

It was Kate's turn to lose words. They looked at each other. Olivia as gorgeous and refined as the first time they'd met, but brimming with love for her, and shining as the one Kate wanted most of all.

"Really?" she gasped.

Then one of those Olivia smiles. Subtle and beautiful. She didn't mistake the depth of feeling behind it.

Olivia swallowed, then answered. "Couldn't help it if I tried."

"But..."

"This is my worst-case scenario," Olivia said. "It's everything I feared when I took you on as a client. The media on Beaumont Street. Handing you over as a client... But I still want you. All those things you've said. Goes for me too."

Was that true? Was Kate the one just catching up now?

She sat stunned, gazing at this considerate woman, composed but breaking inside, and telling her she was all in.

"I love you," Kate said, before she realised she was even going to say it. "I love you." She shook her head. She was already there too. "I am in love with you, and I think I have been for a while. I'm all in for you as well."

And they stared, shocked at it, like finding a diamond when everything else had burned to the ground.

Kate breathed in quickly. Because was this possible? Was there a chance here? Because she wanted it more than ever.

"Would you–?"

A knock at the door.

No. Not yet. Please.

"Could you wait?" Kate whispered desperately.

Would Olivia do that? But where would the next few weeks or months take them both? That's what hung between them.

"This is going to be rough," Kate said quickly. "This article...the press against me..." she waved her hand because she didn't want to mention that person's name. "It's just the start. But it will go away. And the person you know, me," she touched her chest, "I will still be here."

Would Olivia? Would the love and longing and consideration that overflowed endure?

Kate paused, because what she asked was a lot.

"Can you try not to build a wall?" she said, her voice uneven. "Can you give me a chance before you turn away and try to get over me? Because I won't be getting over you. I will be waiting and waiting, until the first moment I can come back."

How could she not.

"Please?"

Olivia's lips trembled and those deepest dark eyes swam with tears. Then she whispered, "Of course." Then a smile. The tiniest of smiles. "The same."

Oh god, Kate begged, more to the universe than anything. When everything is settled, please still be here.

And she lifted from her seat. One last hug, please. Olivia in her arms one more time.

But another knock at the door froze them apart.

The hope faltered, and sadness descended. Because there were weeks, maybe months, looming ahead of them, and god knows what would happen over that time. Would Olivia keep her job? Would Nat drain every penny from Kate? What kind of state would they be in?

"This needs to stop though," Olivia murmured, her hands raised to keep them apart. "Completely. We can't be seen together. There can be no relationship. No trail at all. Nothing to link us."

"I know."

And she felt the cool absence of the hug she'd craved all down the front of her body.

Olivia hesitated, as if she wavered, then she turned to answer the knock. She wiped her eyes, pulled the handle, nodded to the person outside and let Alec in. She looked back once, then was gone.

38

Liz gently suggested Olivia leave early and promised to rearrange her appointments. Olivia took the back door and wandered home, hardly noticing where she was. She set down her briefcase in her hallway, slipped off her trainers, her movement slow when lining them up on the shoe rack, and she changed into leggings and her comfy top from Nani.

She sat on her sofa and put her arms around a cushion.

One of the hardest things she'd had to do – quietly face Kate and tell her all the reasons they couldn't be together while wanting her the most. She'd kept it all inside. Last night while she thought every scenario through, separating the threads and tidying her life into compartments. This morning when she discussed it with Hugo and Alec. And when she waited for Kate to arrive, then supported her through it. All the while knowing it would hit her later.

Then Kate said she loved her. Would wait for her. And Olivia had to walk out, perhaps never to see her again. So now it was going to hit ten times harder.

She gripped the cushion so tight it hurt. A sob leaped out of her, and she didn't hold it back any longer. She buried her face in the material and let herself cry until it soaked.

Olivia lay down and hugged the pillow to her belly, like it was the compartment with hope and Kate inside. She squeezed it tighter and tighter as she shuddered with tears.

She must have drifted at some point, her sleep-deprived body shutting down, and she roused to a familiar quiet knock. Olivia wiped her cheeks, grainy with dry tears, blinked swollen eyelids and got up to answer the persistent visitor.

She opened the door to Charlotte, and her friend's expression dropped without subtlety.

"Oh, Olivia," Charlotte said, shoulders sinking. "Sorry. You weren't answering your mobile and messages. I wanted to check you were OK."

She nodded, her neck aching and head heavy. She'd ignored her phone and the incessant notifications before switching it off.

Charlotte stepped forward. "I'm here, if you want company." Her cheeks twitched, trying to smile. "Always for you, Olivia."

And that hit her in the chest too. The loss of Kate and the endurance of Charlotte's friendship.

"And if it's OK with you," Charlotte murmured, "I'd like to give you a hug."

Olivia's eyebrows gave her away, damn them, rising in the middle, because she was touched that Charlotte was here. And yes, a hug was essential right now.

"Come here," Charlotte whispered.

Arms wrapped around her back and pulled her close. She rested her forehead on Charlotte's shoulder and a hand swept through her hair. Charlotte said nothing but stroked her head, comforting relief under the weight of her sadness.

She lifted away and found all those readable feelings that played on her honest friend's face – sympathy, empathy for love lost, hope that everything might be all right, and despair because it wasn't right now.

"Shall I," Charlotte said, "make you a terrible cup of tea?"

Olivia laughed then sniffed. "Charlotte, you make a perfectly," she breathed in, "adequate cup of tea."

"High praise indeed." Charlotte grinned. "One mediocre mug coming up."

Her friend would find everything in the kitchen, and Olivia slumped in the corner of her sofa, drew up her knees and hugged the cushion to her belly.

"Here you go," Charlotte said, placing two cups in the middle of coasters on the coffee table. She even aligned them today, the square coasters parallel to the edge of the table and mug handles a perfect one hundred and twenty degrees.

"You're coddling me, aren't you," she realised.

"Yes, I am." Charlotte slumped down beside her.

"Have the press left Beaumont Street?" she asked quietly.

"Yes. Liz took Kate out the back, and they disappeared eventually."

"Good." She nodded.

"I had a chat with Liz," Charlotte said. "Hugo's encouraging Kate to stay with Bentley and brazen it out. He doesn't think we have anything to apologise for and that confidence is key right now."

"And Kate...?"

"She's happy to stay apparently. Liz said she was determined for it to work out with us."

Oh god, she hoped it would.

They were quiet a while.

"Geeta's asking after you, by the way," Charlotte said gingerly.

"Oh." Olivia deflated.

"She rang me when you weren't answering messages."

"She's heard then?"

Charlotte nodded. "She's heard."

"I was going to tell them but..." Her heart sank deeper, remembering the despair in Geeta's voice and the conversation she'd overheard. She drifted through all the times that Geeta had said she was lonely, that Sumit wasn't home enough, before they'd all carry on again, hoping it would somehow get better without doing anything about it.

Olivia paused before saying, "Mum's unhappy, isn't she?"

"Desperately," Charlotte replied.

Her friend looked shy about it, because Olivia should have been the one to know that. But Charlotte had always shared the easy rapport with Geeta, sometimes joking that they should swap mothers.

"Geeta's cheerful when I see her," Charlotte said, "but the minute she thinks no-one's watching, it's like the life disappears from her."

She felt that. Charlotte didn't mean it as a blow, but Olivia still reeled from it.

"It hangs in the balance for her and Dad," she said, picking up her tea and hugging it for comfort. "She's lonely. You were right. And I may as well have dropped off the planet for her."

"She needs others too," Charlotte said.

"Of course. But I've blamed her for how badly we get on, except..." She sighed. "I can't spend time together without her annoying me."

Charlotte smiled. "I don't blame you for that. You've seen me with my mother."

"What should I do though? How do I help her?"

"I...erm...well..." Charlotte got stuck in thoughts and Olivia realised now how many raced round for her. "I think, even if you don't know what to do, keep showing up. That might not impress you, but I appreciate the people who do for me. Even if they don't get it right every time."

Olivia nodded, too tired for any other solution. They fell into silence, while she sat appreciating that Charlotte was one who always showed up for her.

Her friend reached out and squeezed her knee. "She seemed good for you."

She didn't need to say they talked of Kate, because there was nothing else on Olivia's mind.

"Yes, she was." She hugged her cushion and drink closer.

Charlotte watched her.

"Kate's my person," she admitted, having to swallow down a lump. "Amazingly, bizarrely, she's the one."

Charlotte pursed her lips, eyes betraying the deep empathy she always had with people, like she felt everything they did.

Warmth tickled Olivia's cheek. "Oh stupid," she said, as a hot tear ran down her face and she swiped it away.

"Not stupid. So not stupid." Charlotte squeezed her knee again.

She had to take a moment, breathing in and out several times. "She's...everything." Especially right now. "Kate's my comfort zone," Olivia realised. "She's where I want to be. She's where my mind and body go when I'm tired, or distressed, when I'm happy, or sad. I find my way to her."

Even now, awareness of Kate tugged at her, her mind wandering to her house.

"And at the same time, she inspires me to step out of my comfort zone."

To dance in front of the world. To strip off and give in to passion. To leave everything behind.

"Kate's someone who I..." How to explain this?

"You do mess for her."

"Yes." Olivia nodded. "I will go through mess for her."

Because despite everything. Despite the whole terrible untidy situation. Something that would have had her running from anyone else. She still wanted Kate.

"I'm sorry I don't have patience and energy sometimes," she said, feeling guilty about those she accommodated less.

"No-one does," Charlotte said, as if she were being silly. "Speaking as a seriously limited human being, I know you can't have energy for everyone, all the time."

"Kate is someone I want to spend my energy on though. I want to be there for her."

"And family?" Charlotte asked gently, because they'd both always been adamant about not having kids, Olivia despairing with her baby brother when she was a teen and Charlotte a huge softy for babies but horrified by her niece and nephew.

"Actually, they're a rather fabulous pair." Olivia laughed quietly. Something that had completely taken her by surprise. That instead of running for the hills, she slipped into family time when the kids were around. And she realised, "Apparently, kids are just mini people – mainly annoying, but I like some of them."

Charlotte smiled indulgently. Then her face slowly turned preoccupied. "It's funny. Turns out I agree with you. It seems that I..." Her thoughts seemed to haunt her. "Well, I'd like a family. I want a family with Millie."

This was a change, and she put down her drink and shuffled to face her friend properly.

Charlotte sat upright, tea balanced on her knee, staring into her cup, the importance of this clear.

"I never had the strong urge to have a baby," Charlotte said quietly. "Maybe it scared me, because everything seemed so difficult just looking after myself. But I understand how I function better now. And with Millie coming back to Oxford and into my life, having someone who always intuitively understands me, and supports me, and..." Charlotte breathed in, a glow building in her face, "loves me like she does." She turned to Olivia. "I'm suddenly happy about who I am. And even something as huge and daunting as having a family is actually what I want."

"Oh." She couldn't help the smile and raise of an eyebrow. "Are you going to try for a family?"

"It's erm..." And all the happiness fell from Charlotte's face. "Complicated."

She let her friend recover.

"Millie..." Charlotte started, then she glanced at her. "Can you promise to never mention this to her?"

"Yes?"

"But I have to talk to someone."

"You're my friend, Charlotte. Yes, Millie and I," she begrudgingly admitted it, "are friends, but not in the same way."

Charlotte's fingers tightened around her mug. "Millie wanted a baby once." She paused, clearly uncomfortable at telling Millie's story. "But she can't have kids. She told me last year before we got together and it's a very painful subject for her."

"And you?"

"Well, I always said I never wanted them, so it didn't even come up for discussion. She couldn't have kids. I didn't want them. We got together. But now..."

"You do."

"Very much, and," dread hung in Charlotte's expression, "I don't know how to tell her."

Olivia reached for her hand.

"It would be hard for her I think," Charlotte said, "to consider it all again."

She didn't know what to say. Perhaps there was nothing she could say. And a silence fell as they held hands. She squeezed her friend. Because she really needed her, and it was clear Charlotte needed her too.

"Thank you," Olivia whispered.

"What for?"

"Everything."

Charlotte smiled. "Same."

They stared out at the small leafy walled garden, shadowy in the overcast day. Although one ray of sunshine was that she felt closer and stronger with Charlotte than ever before.

"Is there a chance?" Charlotte asked. "Later? That you and Kate can get back together?"

Olivia twitched, and she squeezed Charlotte's hand while she fought the tears again.

"Kate wants to," she said.

Amazingly and wonderfully, Kate wanted her. She listened when Kate said to wait. And she believed Kate meant to as well.

"Her divorce has turned very messy though. And I don't know how things will play out for Bentley."

And neither of them could make promises with that ahead.

"If the divorce goes to court, it will drag on and then..." She didn't want to imagine, because the longer it took, the harder it would be for both of them.

But yes, she would wait. Because how on earth would she get over Kate?

39

Kate stepped into the Bentley building and immediately thought of Olivia. She almost sensed her as she climbed the stairs to the attic offices, but it didn't feel right today. Behind his desk in the corner, Alec must have spotted she was preoccupied.

"Olivia's taken a few days off," he said with kind understanding.

She nodded. "Thank you for telling me."

The temptation to call Olivia was huge, but she respected why they stayed apart and how she needed to handle this.

Kate took a seat on the other side of the desk. Olivia had recommended Alec, and she saw why. He proved knowledgeable and honest and she trusted him. A steady hand was needed if Bentley and she were going to pull off a show of confidence.

But when he sat up and straightened his tie, his face was grim. Oh god, more bad news was coming already.

"Your wife's team has geared up with a barrister," he said.

"OK?" What did this mean?

"It's complete overkill for this case. I don't know if they're serious about going to a trial or are simply applying more pressure. But their choice of barrister suggests they're willing to push all the way to court."

"Go on," she said.

"A man called Blake Hudson. There's no reason you should have heard of him, but he's well known in law circles. Early forties, experienced and has a history of pulling things out of the bag at trial. Usually nasty things."

"Shit."

"Yes." Alec nodded. "They're getting ready to sink their teeth in."

Oh. There was that honesty anyway.

"And how are things looking on our side?" she asked.

He paused. "Not great."

"OK," she said, letting it sink in, then nodding to prompt him on.

"I'm having trouble finding a barrister at short notice. We need to level up as well. Blake is intimidating and, I'm not going to sugarcoat it, Olivia's involvement, alleged involvement," he put up his hands, "with you has spread among lawyers and probably isn't doing us any favours."

He really wasn't sugarcoating it.

"What's it going to take?"

"To settle quickly?"

"Yes."

"A lot of your money."

"Shit," she breathed. And thoughts of financial stability disappeared.

She wondered where she'd take the kids and whether she could balance lucrative work with family before the roles dried up. It had been a risk, stepping down into minor characters the last two years, and there were no guarantees in her profession. She may never get another major part. That was the risk for every actor.

"Like Olivia said," Alec continued, "they're pushing hard because they know you don't want a bruising court case."

With a long case, she'd lose the role her career needed and the money to set up a permanent home in Oxford. If she settled and gave Nat too much, she'd also lose the opportunity to buy the house, couldn't afford the PA, would lose track of opportunities, miss the roles. It all spiralled after that, and with a family she couldn't drop everything and start from scratch again.

"I should have pushed back earlier. I should have followed Olivia's advice."

Alec politely pursed his lips.

"At this point, I'm fucked either way, aren't I?"

"We are short of options," he confirmed. "I can represent you in court and I'm trying to get advice and consultation to prepare to face their team, but..."

"Everyone's avoiding Bentley," she finished, seeing the big picture. She shook her head and muttered, "Even though Olivia acted professionally before we got involved? Even though she passed on my case?"

"Gossip takes on a life of its own. Any hint of transgressing boundaries and people stay clear."

Exactly why Olivia insisted on a clean split now. She'd told Kate to see through this divorce without them clouding the issue. And Bentley needed them to stay apart too, so there was no further implication of impropriety from their lawyers with clients.

Kate got up and paced in front of the window.

"Shit, shit, shit."

Damn, Nat. This divorce should have been over by now. They'd had the financial agreement ready to submit weeks ago. And at the last second, Nat had seen an opportunity to screw her over. Again.

She stared outside, Oxford blurring in her vision. Her head taunted her with a game of memory, sliding back through time and reflecting on all the opportunities she'd had to steer a different course. Back and back, wishing she'd never met Nat, then forwards again, because with different choices she may never have had kids or met Olivia. Then she was in the present, still without a solution. They seemed such simple things that she wanted. A home, her kids happy, and to see the woman she adored. And yet it was impossibly complicated.

Her heart ached. What she would give to settle this, see Olivia and quietly get on with her life. And that was the point, wasn't it. Exactly what Nat was preying on.

"Fuck," she whispered, and even that broke in her throat, because she craved Olivia so much it hurt.

She half registered Alec's phone ringing and him answering. He tilted his head towards her. "Erm, Charlotte wanted to pop in. Is that OK?"

"Yes," she said, breathing in and dabbing a threatening tear with the base of her palm. "Of course."

She took a seat, sniffed and composed herself, and it was only moments later that a soft knock disturbed the door.

Charlotte poked her head around with waves of hair flowing. "Hi," she said, cheeks pink and face full of sunshine. It even made Kate lift for a moment.

"I erm..." Charlotte paused. "I may have found you a barrister."

Kate glanced at Alec. He perked up at this.

"I mean, if you're still looking for one?" Charlotte finished.

"Definitely," Alec said. "Who have you got?"

Charlotte turned back outside the door and said something Kate didn't catch. Then a moment later a woman strode in, with a very similar appearance to Charlotte, but with a hundred times the attitude.

Striking, broader shouldered than Charlotte, ribbons of grey streaking through long mahogany hair, the woman filled the room with sheer force of personality. Chin aloft, powerful smile and with eyebrows that could command a judge.

"Nicola Albright, KC," the woman said with a voice that demanded to be heard, and she struck out a hand to Kate. "I hear you're looking for a barrister."

Kate obediently raised her arm and said a prayer for her metatarsals crushed in Nicola's fingers.

"It happens that I have an opening at the moment," Nicola said. "Are you interested in my representation?" An accompanying eyebrow lifted, and Kate felt compelled to agree to anything this woman asked.

Kate checked towards Alec. She'd been convinced by the woman's presence alone, but she'd defer to his judgement.

He, though, looked like Christmas had come early. He stood up quickly and stretched over the desk to shake hands with the woman who towered above him.

"We are very much interested. I cannot emphasise how much we," he checked towards Kate, and she nodded, "are pleased to see you."

***

"Is she good?" Kate whispered.

Were they finally getting a break?

Alec leant closer as they stood by the window. Nicola sat in Alec's seat, scanning through files and flipping through pages she'd printed out.

"I wasn't looking forward to facing Blake Hudson," he said quietly, "but I would choose a showdown with him every time over Nicola. Our chances of getting this sorted have just improved tenfold."

She had the jitters, because her hopes leapt with the arrival of this woman. Honestly, Kate had no idea if she'd like Nicola ordinarily, but she wanted this barrister in her corner right now.

"Is she related to Charlotte?" The physical similarity was too obvious not to ask, although their personalities and attitude seemed complete opposites.

"Her mother."

"Ah." She nodded.

Kate had guessed at something like that, Nicola's age likely mid to late fifties and owning every one of those decades. The imposing woman currently sat, striking out large sections of a document.

She wondered how much she owed Charlotte for her mother's arrival, and how much personal intervention she'd made on behalf of Bentley, Olivia and Kate.

"Right," Nicola said, and Kate and Alec stood to attention. "I have an overview at least, so let's talk this over."

Kate and Alec sat on the other side of the desk like obedient children.

"This is all well documented as I'd expect from Olivia and Alec. There is nothing that anyone could complain of."

Nicola was perhaps covering herself or Bentley or both. She didn't need to for Kate's sake.

"Now," the barrister continued, "early on I believe Olivia informed you that your spouse likely has assets left undeclared on the prenuptial agreement."

"Erm, she did," Kate confirmed.

"And in the interests of a quick case, you chose not to pursue any course of action against her."

"Yes," Kate said, "I think."

"Honestly," Nicola took off her glasses, "there are a lot of ifs and buts. And it depends on which judge oversees the case. But with these hidden assets, the prenup would likely be invalidated. Without that, and taking into account the protections it afforded against your funds, then overall you're likely left with what Olivia drew up as your original agreement. A fair-minded judge would likely split them along the same lines, if it went that far, even considering your spouse's claims that her potential to earn has been hampered by supporting your family, which Alec says is fiction and you have plenty of witnesses who can back this up."

"Right. Yes," Kate said. Oh god. She did not want a court case. Her brain did not like this.

Nicola leant forward on the desk. "I'm saying, that if you went to court, you'd probably end up with the split Olivia showed you, but you'd incur larger fees."

"OK," she said. That sounded reasonable to her.

"It would take time, which you don't want, but your position is secure if that happened." Nicola sat back. "Your case is solid."

Kate tried to smile. But Nicola wasn't finished.

"The rest is theatre and psychological warfare. And that," Nicola fixed her with sharpest blue eyes, "you're losing."

"Oh," Kate said.

"If you want any chance of settling this quickly, you need me, and you need me to take the gloves off," Nicola said, her expression serious.

There was a steel about the woman that had Kate agreeing without hesitation.

And later in the day, after some discussion between Alec and Nicola and reassurance from the first, Kate descended the stairs to the main meeting room.

She and Alec sat on one side, backs toward the windows. Opposite and already in position were Nat – Kate could hardly look at her – a man she'd seen before, and their barrister. Blake stood tall, shirt and suit over a firm frame, with a practiced smile on his face.

"Good afternoon," he said. "Glad you could join us."

The door swung open with a blast, and Nicola strode into the room. Blake, opposite, did a double take.

"Good afternoon gentleman and client," Nicola said, in that cheerful way that sounded like she might stab them the next second. "Glad you could join us too."

Blake's mouth hung open for a moment, surprised by her entrance, then he buttoned his suit jacket and slipped into toxic cordiality again.

"Nicola, what a delightful surprise. Still printing out documents?" he said, eyeing the papers in her arms.

It was a clear dig at her age. Kate imagined he was twenty years younger. They were also clearly familiar with each other.

"Indeed," Nicola said, pinning him with a look over her glasses. "They make a satisfying slap on the table when I throw them down."

He put on a laugh. Theatre indeed. But the other team were caught out by Nicola's involvement.

"So, what do you have for us?" Blake said.

"Let's start at the beginning, shall we?" Nicola slipped out the first pile of papers from her arms. "This shoddy prenup."

She slapped it down in front of him.

"You might not be up to speed on the case, Nicola, but we're all familiar with that."

"Pretty shaky, don't you think?"

His face remained polite. "Regardless, it's a little late for your client to complain."

"And also late for your client to be forthcoming about her assets," Nicola hit back. "All of them, that is."

He paused, then tucked the hesitation beneath a supercilious smile. "Nicola, if you need clarification regarding the financial statements of my client and her assets–"

"I certainly will need clarification. Starting with these. Funds omitted from the prenup and which would invalidate that agreement."

She threw down another document with a slap.

This one echoed. While Nat didn't flinch with any surprise, Kate knew her well enough to catch the smirk afterwards. Yes, she'd been caught. Those suspicions about her hidden funds were correct.

It clearly disturbed her representation though. Blake's expression fell, and he remained serious and silent. Nicola was right. This would attack the lawyer's confidence in their client.

Nicola took her time, happy to dwell on the reaction of both client and lawyer.

"Ms Marks," Nicola said lightly. "You seem unfazed, but the potential penalties for fraud might surprise you. Your team," Nicola smiled at Blake, "can clarify for you."

That earned another smirk from Nat.

"No?" Nicola purred. "Then perhaps this will worry you." She lifted out another document. "A libellous interview you gave about my client, who will be pursuing a claim. Not with me," she paused, "but I look forward to referring her to a colleague. And of course, I know all the best defamation barristers."

The document slapped onto the table, and it spun to a stop in front of Natalie. This she did blanche at. She clearly didn't expect Kate to push back on that. Nat turned to her team, but no-one reassured her.

Blake cleared his throat. "Of course," he said, recovering and smoothing his tie. "We are here to negotiate, obviously, and we can review–"

"You misunderstand," Nicola shook her head with disarming nonchalance. "Negotiations are over, gentlemen. My client has been patient enough. And you will agree to this financial split."

She threw down the final document, which slapped and spun to land in front of him.

"Or we go to court." Nicola smiled. "My favourite playground. Simple as that."

And Blake's expression completed its journey into a grimace, because the prospect of Nicola standing in court resonated with them all.

"I think we're done here," Nicola said to Alec and Kate.

"Nicola–" Blake started.

"Do get in touch," the barrister said over her shoulder.

Kate followed her from the room, and she bounced with every step.

40

Geeta appeared at Olivia's house with a Tupperware box in her hands filled with ice cubes and jewels of silvery kulfi cones.

"I made your favourite." Geeta beamed. "Pistachio."

Her mother smiled, but Olivia didn't immediately turn away this time. She lingered to appreciate that Geeta turned up. To see the sadness beneath her smile and not ignore it. And to remember that her mother went through things too.

"Come in," she said, closing the door behind Geeta.

She took the box and put it on the stairs, then turned to wrap her arms around her mother's shoulders.

"Oh!" Geeta said.

Olivia drew her in and pressed a cheek to her mother's head. "Thank you," she whispered into a warm cushion of hair.

Initial, rigid surprise beneath her arms abated, but then a fierce hug replaced it, as if this were her mother's only chance. She couldn't blame Geeta for that and Olivia didn't let go. Her mother tried to stifle a sob, and Olivia kept cuddling her through the judder and noisy inhalations. And longer, while there was a sniff and another deep gasp, and only when Geeta pulled back to wipe her face did she release her.

"Goodness," Geeta said. "You gave me a surprise." She wiped her cheeks with both hands and smiled through her tears. "But thank you, because I needed that."

"I know," Olivia said.

She didn't expect her mother to expand on it but was glad she'd taken the time today. She intended saving more energy for her from now on. It wouldn't be possible always, but she would remember to keep trying.

"Would you like one of these in the garden?" Olivia asked.

And Geeta nodded.

She slid open the glass panel into the tiny courtyard, the low maintenance space still tidy despite neglect this year. The walls were covered in neat leaves of ivy on the shaded side, and a profusion of vine in the sun. She sat next to her mother on a small bench, their hands freezing around two of the silvery moulds to release the frozen desserts.

"This is very much appreciated," Olivia said, admiring the smooth, light-green cone and the sprinkle of nuts that decorated around the stick. "Especially with how long it takes to prepare." Because her mother reduced the milk to make it.

"My pleasure," Geeta said. "I listened to an audiobook while stirring. I wanted to make something nice for my daughter." Geeta reached out and patted the air above her knee.

Olivia sat in silence, licking and enjoying the kulfi, and her mother did too, the day not too hot so they could savour the firm dessert at leisure.

"You don't have to talk about her to me," Geeta said, still sampling her kulfi, "but I wanted to say that I liked her." Geeta didn't look towards her, perhaps assuming she didn't want to be watched and preferred to keep her reactions private. "It was a wonderful surprise that she's so down to earth and open." Geeta spun round her dessert. "It was obvious she liked you too."

Heat struck her cheeks. Yes, she was grateful her mother averted her gaze.

"Hmm," Olivia said.

And yes, Geeta was right. She wasn't ready to share everything about Kate with her.

"She's," Olivia paused. Her feelings about Kate could fuel an entire speech. "She's very nice," she said, aware her voice clipped tight over her words.

Her mother smiled though. It was enough information for her to run with.

"Have you heard from her?" Geeta asked, her eyebrows dipping into seriousness.

Alec had said that Kate moved to London for the summer. The kids were off school, and Kate apparently had a full shooting schedule at Twickenham Film Studios. Nicola handled the case and negotiations in central London with Alec travelling down.

It had drawn attention and the press away from Bentley at least.

"She messaged," Olivia replied.

That morning in fact. A short note that held sorrow and longing, and asked Olivia to call if she ever wanted to talk about anything and everything.

"I haven't replied yet," Olivia managed, before swallowing over the lump in her throat.

Her chest filled whenever she contemplated talking to Kate, so she could hardly speak and calling would end in silence while her heart broke and throttled her words.

"By the way," Geeta said, pulling her mobile from her jeans. "Adam sent this."

Geeta tilted the screen with a message from Olivia's brother and link to a clip from some news channel. The still showed Nicola Albright frozen at the front and Kate and Alec behind, in a street somewhere in London she guessed.

"So, he's knows..."

"As much as I do," Geeta said.

Geeta pressed play.

The quality was poor, the camera tracking back as Nicola marched towards it and Kate and Alec followed.

"Is it true you've been lovers for years?" a man said in between breaths. He pointed the camera over Nicola's shoulder at Kate.

"When did it start?" he yelled. "Was it in front of your kids?"

Olivia winced at it, but the camera shook too violently to see how Kate reacted.

"Kate! Kate!" he kept yelling. "Will this bankrupt you? How much is she taking you for?"

The screen suddenly filled with a blurred blazer before bouncing out and slowly focussing on the face of Nicola Albright. Her eyes and smile were friendly. It was deceptive though, because her stance threatened to pounce with claws extended from her designer suit.

"My client will not be answering questions," Nicola said. "Queries regarding the case can be directed to me." She tilted her head, the smile suggesting she was open to conversation.

"Erm... erm... Are you worried about this going to court? Is Natalie Marks going to tell all and leave Kate bankrupt?"

Not a flicker on her face, Nicola pierced the man with her gaze, one that held him captive second after excruciating second.

Finally, she said, "No," with such a firm sense of conviction you could hear the words dying on his lips. "Good day," she said, with genuine enjoyment at seeing every syllable wither. Then she walked away, the screen and street empty, with Kate and Alec long gone.

Geeta tucked her phone away. "Kate looked good to me," she said. "Tired, but less stressed than I anticipated."

Olivia nodded. She avoided snippets like this. It made Kate feel distant and unreal. She didn't want the vivid memory of her to fade into fiction again.

"And I have to admit," Geeta sighed. "That woman, Nicola, is impressive." She stroked up a rivulet of kulfi that threatened to drip.

Olivia waited for it, the follow up, and her mother's usual irritation with Nicola and her attitude to Charlotte.

"That's all," Geeta said, putting up her hand.

Olivia raised an eyebrow.

"You know my thoughts on the woman," she added.

Did she though? Olivia wasn't sure why they wound each other up so much. Yes, they were very different people, women, mothers.

Nicola a force in the law world and a barrister at the top of her profession. Geeta just as clever and studious, who'd graduated in molecular biology, but started a family with Sumit. Geeta had never gone back into the field but acted as a sounding board for Sumit throughout his career in the same subject, and he never would have risen to head of department without her support. She'd always been there for her family, and Nicola, according to Charlotte, had remained mainly absent for hers.

My god, Geeta had been young when Olivia was born. She flinched at the prospect of having a family at twenty-one. By the time Geeta had reached Olivia's age, she'd been a mother most of her adulthood. Understanding descended again, just how much Geeta put into Olivia's life, and her father's, and brother's, and now for Nani too, and how they all formed her world, but took her for granted.

They sat there. Her mother not talking about Olivia's father. And Olivia, glad her mother had visited, but not talking about Kate.

Charlotte had suggested trying a film night with Geeta, but that would only remind Olivia of Kate. She'd lost herself in books lately instead.

"Would you," she started, suddenly thinking. "Could you show me how to make your samosas sometime?"

Geeta twitched round and stared at her, eyes large and unsubtle with both eyebrows lost in the waves of her smoky black hair.

"I do cook sometimes," Olivia said, returning a look.

"Yes, I know." Geeta nodded. "Actually, do you?"

"I..." Olivia inhaled and raised her shoulders, "arrange fruit, yoghurt and oats together. I've perfected all kinds of Bircher muesli."

Her mother smiled too much. "I would love to show you how I make samosas," she said, grinning. "They're not difficult, or too time-consuming, especially if you have left-over potatoes and veg handy."

Olivia jutted her chin and looked at her.

"Which you probably don't, despite your finesse and expertise at yoghurt breakfasts."

She pinched a smile back at that.

"A bit messy though," Geeta warned. "Deep frying? Making the pastry dough?"

"I will," Olivia said, squirming a little, "manage."

"Come on then," Geeta said, putting down the stick from her kulfi. "Shall we get ingredients from the Co-op?"

"Yes," Olivia said, standing and smoothing her top. "That would be very agreeable."

****

They made a ludicrous number of samosas. They had a whole assembly line going.

She found it satisfying: making the tidy pouches, filling them and folding them into shape. She was determined to make the neatest samosas in all of Oxford. When they'd packed Olivia's freezer compartment with pastries to reheat another day, Geeta had a box left to take home and one to drop off for Charlotte.

Olivia didn't fool herself they'd do this every week. But, on occasion, it would be nice and was a life raft when they both avoided talking about heartache. And if you were going to clean and air the house after deep frying anyway, you might as well make the most of it and cook a hundred samosas.

It was still light in the extended summer evening after Geeta left, and Olivia took a book upstairs to read in bed. She stared out of the sash window of her bedroom, the sun setting over rows of Victorian houses and trees.

She missed Kate. Nothing took her mind off that for long. Her small and neat room, with a double bed covered in smooth ironed sheets and a soft duvet, seemed empty because she craved Kate there most. Olivia closed her eyes and longed for Kate so hard, she almost nuzzled into her.

She still hadn't replied to the message. She picked up the mobile to call, and her throat constricted, heart too swollen in her chest to speak. Because Olivia would say she missed her, and Kate wouldn't be able to reassure her, because neither knew the future. Then Olivia's mind would burrow into all the possible ways that life might keep Kate away, and grief would strike.

She hadn't found a way to manage her feelings yet. To open the lid on how much she yearned for Kate without it overwhelming and spiralling into fear that she'd never come back. So instead she'd been carrying on, as if holding her breath, hoping she would surface one day and avoid taking the lid off and looking at it all properly.

But she couldn't hold her breath forever.

She sat up in bed and began to tap out a reply with care.

"I want to call you, but find it hard to speak, because I miss you so much. I'm afraid my conversation would be a painful silence. So if I tell you something small instead, a snippet about my day, please know it's important to me. I can't dwell, but when I say I walked by the river and the meadows were full of buttercups, I spent the whole time thinking of walking there with you. If I mention that I read a novel, I wanted to talk about it with you afterwards. And if I heard music, I thought of dancing in your arms. I miss you more than I can say."

Olivia rested a finger on the send button and closed her eyes as it made its way to Kate. She kept them shut, comforted that Kate would read her words, until her phone buzzed in her hands. She opened her eyes to a burst of happiness that was a reply from Kate.

"Any word from you makes my day better. Tell me anything, from what you had for lunch to which black dress you're wearing today. Just your name appearing on my mobile made me happy. And I love you. I love you. I love you. And I wish I'd told you every single day we spent together."

Olivia covered her mouth. She laughed at the dress comment and a hot tear trailed her cheek. She read it over and over, then held the phone to her chest, aware of Kate's presence somewhere feeling the same love for her.

41

Things stayed quiet for Olivia over the summer holidays. Tourists took over Oxford from the students and Olivia concentrated on smaller cases already on the books. To her surprise, two new high-value clients seeking amicable divorces signed up. Then came referrals from other lawyers. It seemed her reputation might stay intact.

She was careful and gentle with herself though. She resisted the urge to swamp her hours with work to distract herself from missing Kate and kept herself ticking over by dipping into books and seeing Charlotte, Liz and Geeta.

Alec's schedule was busy too, his calm understanding and association with Kate as her solicitor doing no harm.

It could have been worse. It could have been a lot worse.

Late Friday afternoon at the end of September, she headed to Hugo's office, joining Liz on the way.

"Hugo wants to talk to both of us," Liz said as they approached his door. "I think he has a proposal." Liz nudged her, eyes wide with innuendo and excitement.

The three of them met regularly, but this was an unscheduled meeting. She guessed at the subject and prepared herself. Had he found someone new to manage the firm?

Her heart sank. The timing was awful. She'd worked indefatigably for the partnership, just to trip at the wrong moment.

And, if by some slim chance he offered it to her, right now she didn't have the energy to step up to a higher role.

The days she took off after splitting up with Kate had revealed how much she valued free time. She wished to spend that occasionally seeing her mother, and giving herself brain space, and if Kate never came back she still wanted a life with a better balance between career and friends and family.

"Good afternoon both," Hugo said, getting up from his large partner's desk. "Come in and sit down."

He closed the door behind them and indicated two seats in front of the desk. He drew up a third for himself.

"I've drinks ready for you," he said. Three mugs steamed on the coffee table. "Don't worry, Zain brought them. He knows how you take your beverages," he said, mainly to Olivia.

He seemed at ease and faced them both, crossing his legs and resting an elbow on the desk.

"Do you know," he said, "my daughter has decided to study law." He chuckled. "After all my encouragement as a teen, which she ignored, she's retraining as a solicitor now she's in her thirties." He tutted. "Children. Sent to confound and frustrate us while being so lovable we can't turn away."

For a moment her sympathies lay with Geeta.

"It was a dream of mine when she was growing up," Hugo continued, "that she'd join the firm that my father established. But she's years from qualifying and may not want that anyway."

He frowned and gazed into his coffee.

"I don't want to retire yet," he said, "but neither am I in a position where I should head the partnership. I'm struggling, frankly."

What on earth was he going to propose? Who had he found? Olivia tried not to look at Liz, who already rankled with tension from the corner of her vision.

"I'd like to focus on the technology side of things. I'm very excited about the organisations Charlotte works with and I'm thrilled how that department is taking off."

She practically read Liz's thoughts. Get on with it, man.

"Family law and high-value clients are the other areas at which we excel," he said, with eyebrows shooting up. "Then everything relies on the smooth running of the whole organisation."

He looked up at them.

"This is the core of our business," he indicated the three of them, "and I have relied on the pair of you for years. So, I wondered if you'd find the following suitable? The three of us," he suggested, "we head the firm together?"

That wasn't what Olivia expected, and neither did Liz given the quick questioning look she threw her.

"We've effectively been working as such anyway." Hugo shrugged. "I wondered if we should formalise it. Important decisions would have a majority vote. That way, you might stop me from making god-awful ones like hiring Richard."

He looked directly at her. "I'm in no doubt why the situation escalated this summer. No doubt at all. I do believe in second chances, but Richard was undeserving and brought us no end of trouble. And while the whole situation did impact the firm, we seem to be weathering it." He sighed. "We have Nicola Albright to thank in part for that. But I think it does us credit that we've stayed afloat and largely untarnished."

She opened her mouth but didn't know what to say.

"I can see this working well," Liz said. "As you've pointed out, Hugo, it's how we've been operating for several years. Olivia? I think it's you who it affects more?"

Liz knew heading a law firm was her ambition and sharing it hadn't been her plan.

"I'm..." Olivia started. "This is something I've worked towards." But right now? She deflated. "I'm sorry Hugo, I can't work any harder." Because even though he claimed it required no changes, she didn't have the energy to head her team and adjust to new duties too.

"I don't want you to," Hugo replied. "You have worked hard enough already. I propose you make another hire for the family law group to relieve your workload, so you can take on the relevant responsibilities in due course. You're clearly a better judge of character than I am. Alec has proved himself a safe pair of hands. Other than that, I'd prefer not to expand further. I'd rather focus on quality of service and a sustainable workload for the entire firm. I'm enjoying having grandchildren, but still have an interest in Bentley. I'm sure everyone in the company has similar considerations. What say you two?"

"I think it's an excellent proposal," Liz said. "We work well together, with the odd hiccup." She tilted her head to consider Olivia. "We could talk through the practicalities next week? Let the idea settle over the weekend?"

Olivia nodded. "I'd appreciate that."

"Good." Hugo beamed. "Because I'm very keen on the idea. Besides, a new firm name of something along the lines of 'Bentley, Oduwole and Sachdeva' has a nice ring to it."

***

Olivia's life was up in the air, with nothing how she expected, not even a year ago. Her parents, Charlotte, work. How did life keep churning everything up when it should be neat and tidy?

She walked slowly up St Giles towards home, with Oxford in September its most charming – warm late summer days with fewer people, tourists sparse and undergraduates not yet arrived. And right now, she could do with something to steady her.

Her coat pocket buzzed and buzzed, likely a recipe link from Geeta, who had run with their cooking sessions, or multiple random thoughts and messages from Charlotte. They were wonderful, the pair of them. She was glad of them in her life. But, oh my god, they were going to have to wait while she de-peopled for a few hours, and Olivia ignored her phone.

She cut across into Jericho, the café crowds quiet and relaxed in the evening sun. She paused outside the blue-painted Phoenix Picture House, because the poster of Kate Laurence had gone. The season of her films was over, and the blank space waited for a new face. She watched while an attendant filled the frames on the cinema front with posters of movies coming soon, but none featured Kate.

Had she dreamed these past few months? Olivia's head swirled, her life inextricably changed but still in motion and chaotic. Was she delusional about Kate's love? She juddered a breath out, afraid to hold on to the hope she'd clutched all summer.

Eyes unfocused and mind tumbling, she wandered down the narrow residential street of neat, terraced brick cottages, thoughts about everything spinning up in the air. Until one came to land.

She blinked.

A figure stood outside her house, hand resting on the short fence, about to unlatch the gate and stride up to the door. A figure nearly as tall as Olivia, with streaked honey hair, a white shirt open at the top and necklace pendant dipping into her cleavage. A woman with strong shoulders and curving chest and hips, and a walk that was very ordinary, which made Olivia smile because it was extraordinary it should be for someone like this.

Olivia slowly approached, still in a daze, as the woman removed sunglasses to reveal piercing eyes, which looked worried right now. Lips with a curve beyond mere mortals pinched anxiously together before trying to speak.

"Hi," Kate said. The tone of the one word asked many questions.

"Hi," Olivia replied, the same small word breaking. She only then realised that her throat was full. "Are you...?"

Divorced? Back in Oxford? Still in love with me? So many big questions.

"It's done," Kate said, her expression pleading with Olivia. "It's over."

And the relief Kate showed was profound. She tried to smile, even while her eyes searched Olivia's. She breathed in, chest expanding. "I'm back and..." They gazed at each other, the space between filled with so much, always. "So, if you still want me and–"

Olivia dropped her briefcase, stepped forward and flung her arms around Kate's shoulders, and as Kate's body fitted into hers a flood of relief washed over her.

"I have missed you," she gasped, pulling Kate as close as she could, chest over chest, heart over heart, cheek to warm, wet cheek. "I have missed you so much."

She hugged her tight, as if she filled herself up again with Kate. She nuzzled into her hair, inhaled her scent and held her head close, so she had all upon her.

"I have been waiting for this," Kate whispered beside her ear. "Ever since I last saw you, I have needed this hug."

Olivia leant away to cup her face.

"I have missed you." Olivia couldn't say anything but that, because it was the biggest thing she felt and nothing else would intrude.

She kissed Kate's forehead, warm to her lips. Then her cheeks, the salty tears vivid and the sense of taking her in greater. Then deeply, fondly, without holding back. A kiss of longing and happiness and tenderness.

"I love you," Olivia gasped as they broke for a moment.

Kate sniffed and looked into her eyes, gently stroking her fingers through her hair. "I am completely and utterly, bowled over, head over heels, besotted and in love with you, Olivia Sachdeva."

Olivia laughed between gasps. She covered her mouth and nose. "Sorry," she said.

Kate kissed her fingers gently to encourage them to drop, then took in every inch of her face in delicately desperate kisses. Kate trailed her forehead, eyebrows, the tears running down her cheeks, the sensitive corners of her mouth.

"No need for sorry," Kate said, smiling and gulping down her own tears.

"Are you...?" She tried to catch her breath. "Are you back here? Living at home?"

"Arrived this afternoon after dropping the kids with Harry for the weekend. And I came straight here." Kate's eyes sparkled and travelled Olivia's face, as if she wanted to take her in as much as Olivia did her. "I did call," she added.

"Oh." Olivia laughed. "I'm avoiding calls and people."

"Can you cope with the company of one?" Kate asked, smiling.

"I would very much like the company of just one."

She slipped her fingers between Kate's and drew her through the gateway and into her house.

****

"How have you been?" Kate murmured when they stepped into the hallway.

But Olivia dropped her briefcase and immediately hugged her.

"How are you?" she asked again.

"Better now," Olivia said, voice muffled into her shoulder.

Oh my god this felt good. She'd been craving this for weeks, into months. She'd thought she remembered how Olivia fit against her in one of these cuddles, but reality sank in a hundred times more deliciously.

She squeezed her tight, Olivia's slim physique tense, warm and vivid with that suppleness that had Kate's body both soothed and sensitive.

She kissed Olivia's cheek, intending to console her, but the cherished scent of her near engulfed and turned her head with desire. It hit deep after yearning all summer.

They should talk. Kate had so much to tell her.

She pulled back to say, but Olivia's lips were soft on hers and she swayed with the powerful intimacy.

"Oh," she moaned. This she had forgotten; just how sweet Olivia's kisses were. And when they landed mingled with salty tears, she melted inside.

Kate trailed over her cheek then lower. How Olivia tasted came back to her in force, and she couldn't resist the compulsion to know her with her lips. She descended her neck, the tenderness and vulnerability there squeezing at her heart, while every contact flooded her body with passion. Without thinking, her fingers fluttered down Olivia and unzipped her dress.

She stood straight, breathing hard. "I'm sorry. We should talk."

Olivia quietly laughed. "Don't be. I can't keep my hands off you either."

They seemed on the same page again, like they took off from the last time they saw each other. When Olivia said she loved her, that she was all in, and Kate said she'd wait for her. And she'd waited and waited and now it felt like she could burst.

Olivia smiled, the fullest and most gorgeous one. "Come upstairs."

Kate didn't need asking twice. She hurried up the narrow steps, Olivia ahead with her beautiful back exposed by the half-open dress. She entered a small bedroom with autumn sunshine glowing through a window onto a double bed.

They stripped without hesitation. Olivia took off her dress, tugged free her underwear, and flung it across the room with a laugh. Kate threw her shirt to the floor and kicked away her jeans. When they were both naked, they paused to look at each other, eyes large, smiles wide, reacquainting and appreciating.

"Somehow you are even more beautiful than the last time," Kate whispered.

And Olivia's eyebrows raised, imploring. "Come to bed."

Kate took her hand. "Lie down. I can't wait to know all of you again."

Olivia lay back, while Kate sat beside her. She drew her fingers closer, admiring the neat shape, her pale pink nails, and smooth brown skin.

"I have missed you right down to your fingertips," Kate said, laughing. She couldn't quite believe she was here.

She kissed along their length, dipping her tongue between the sensitive joins to a quiet gasp from Olivia. Joy and passion leapt all over her body at that sound.

She turned over Olivia's hand and traced the dark lines on her palm with a fingertip, wanting to memorise them forever. Then caressed beneath her wrist with her lips, the skin impossibly soft there. Explored down her forearm, the tenderness inside her elbow, the rise of her firm upper arm, breasts gently nudging into Olivia's as she travelled.

Olivia gazed at her with large, dark eyes.

This was working fast on them both.

"Is this OK?" Kate whispered huskily, her smiles giving way to arousal.

Olivia nodded and pinched her lips tight, as if holding in a moan. The struggle playing on Olivia's face was erotic and beautiful, and Kate was vividly aware of how she quickened and became wet, even at this beginning.

"Oh my god, I want to taste all of you," she said, running a finger down Olivia's chest which had her collapsing.

Trembling, she covered Olivia with kisses; down her cleavage and gently around her breasts. She had to pause between each caress, hovering a fraction above her skin, Olivia succumbing almost to the edge, then recovering a little, before dabbing her with another touch to keep her high.

Kate's head filled with the scent of her. She nuzzled into the shape of her tummy, feeling soft invisible hair against her cheek, and leaned back to appreciate the dip of her neat belly button and the descent down between her legs.

"I have longed for you," she murmured, as she bent down to kiss her again. And then thoughts of conversation disappeared entirely.

She kissed the top of her thighs, silky smooth, back and forth, giving each due attention. Then her mound and outer lips, her kisses filled with both love and desire as she trailed over Olivia's quivering sensitivity. The familiar and irresistible flavour drew her in, and she lost awareness as her tongue slipped inside. Nothing existed except Olivia on her mouth, taste filling her head, soft legs embracing her cheeks, a deep moan an overwhelming seduction to her ears. There was nothing except them, her lips surrounding Olivia's tender bud, and moving in waves and waves.

She was incapable of speech when Olivia sat up and encouraged her to turn in the bed. She was already whimpering as Olivia descended her body. Her head spun and her heart beat so deep that she didn't even know if Olivia in fact touched, because everywhere thrilled with their coming together after so long.

Then came the most intimate sensation of Olivia's lips on her. And, quiet at the peak, Kate caved harder, longer and deeper.

Eyes still closed, she sought Olivia and they collapsed in each other's arms, gasping, kissing and laughing. Talking at last, and touching again. Then falling asleep through dusk, and never letting each other go.

42

The door opened, and Geeta beamed from the hallway of Olivia's childhood home.

"Hello! Come in!" Geeta threw her arms in the air. "Can I give you a hug?"

Kate leant forward. "Of course, and thanks for inviting us."

"It is wonderful to see you again." Geeta gave her a squeeze.

"This is Ralph," Kate said, reaching for her son beside her.

"Hello," came her son's deep voice, which still took her by surprise.

"And Bea," she said, turning towards the car in the driveway.

Her small girl was checking the contents of her bag. Olivia patiently held it open for her while she rummaged.

"All in order?" Olivia asked.

Bea nodded. "All in order," she copied.

When Kate looked back, the expression on Geeta's face held a complicated happiness, but she covered it swiftly with a simple welcoming smile when Olivia and Bea walked towards them.

"Hello, darling," Geeta said to Olivia. "Come in, all of you."

Geeta led down the hallway, through the open-plan kitchen and dining room and into the garden. It glowed with the reds and yellows of sunny autumn trees and the bright green lawn that flowed down the slope towards the river.

"Luckily the weather's stayed dry and we're all outside," Geeta said.

A group of perhaps twenty people milled around near the house. Two long, cloth-covered tables displayed a spread of savouries and cakes that must have taken Geeta days to prepare.

"Is this all right?" Olivia asked, slipping her fingers through hers and standing close.

"This is lovely," she murmured. "I'm already a big fan of your mum," she added, grinning.

Many things clearly threaded through Olivia's brain, all those complications of family, but she smiled afterwards and said, "Good, I'm glad," and nudged closer so they touched all the way down their bodies. It was an exquisite comfort, and Kate hoped she'd never take it for granted.

Olivia's father made a quiet appearance. There was a stiff exchange between him and Geeta. Sumit asked if she needed any help, and brief instructions passed between the pair, while maintaining a polite melancholy distance. It wasn't common knowledge yet, but Olivia said they were separating and shared the house while they worked out how to manage things.

Sumit was a tall, slim man and introduced himself to Kate with a quiet friendliness. He took time to talk to Bea and Ralph and seemed pleased that her son liked chess. The two bonded over an old set which Sumit brought out from his study.

Millie and Charlotte arrived late, with pink cheeks and full of smiles, and it wasn't difficult to guess the reason for their lack of punctuality.

"Oh, my goodness, your hair!" Charlotte said to Geeta as soon as they spotted her. She reached forward impulsively, stopping short of touching Olivia's mum.

Geeta ran her fingers through the waves of black and grey and tucked it behind her ear. She'd had it cut shorter above the shoulder and the waves bounced around her head in a way that suited her.

"I'm pleased you like it. I fancied a change."

Kate was glad that Charlotte said something, because Kate didn't feel familiar enough to pay the compliment. But Geeta looked good.

Perhaps it was the new hairstyle, perhaps new clothes. A soft jumper in a deep yellow ochre flattered her curves and heightened the colour of her skin so that she glowed.

"It's beautiful!" Charlotte said.

"Fworr." Millie knuckled her hands onto her hips. "You look gorgeous!"

Beside Kate, Olivia prickled. "Just not appropriate," she said under her breath. "For god's sake, that's my mother."

But Geeta laughed with Millie and Charlotte, and looked as if she appreciated the admiration. It didn't take long for Geeta's lingering sadness to descend. Kate glanced at Olivia and caught the same realisation in her eyes. She squeezed her hand and Olivia returned the same in acknowledgement.

Bea and Ralph took off down the garden with cousins of Olivia, and Sumit slowly followed to keep an eye on them by the river.

Kate sat back on the cushioned sofa next to Olivia, and Millie sat to her right.

"Thank you for inviting my mother," Charlotte said to Geeta, as they passed around drinks to them.

Nicola Albright KC was an addition that surprised Kate, although not unpleasantly.

"My pleasure," Geeta said. "You mentioned she was house viewing this weekend, so I thought she might appreciate it."

"Yes, she's finally looking for houses again. She's been busy with work since the divorce with Dad, and living in a chamber's flat. It was very kind of you to include her." Charlotte said it so emphatically that something surfaced in Kate's memory suggesting the two mothers didn't get along.

"I believe," Geeta drew air between her teeth, "she's put an offer on a cottage further up the road."

Millie chuckled quietly beside Kate, and she wondered how much effort it took Geeta to remain polite when she talked about Nicola.

"There have always been tensions between those two," Millie whispered to Kate.

"Right," Kate said. Yes, her nagging memory was correct.

"Anyway," Geeta carried on to Charlotte, "I'm going to take some nibbles down to the kids by the river."

Kate squinted down the long garden. She could see Ralph and Bea were safe with several adults with them, but it was a habit she couldn't shake.

Geeta flitted through and obscured her view while heading towards the food table. Nicola stood there with her back towards them.

"Excuse me, Nicola, I need that plate of cardamon cookies." Geeta reached around the tall barrister and stretched across the table. She almost lost her balance and instinctively put her other arm round Nicola to steady herself. "Sorry, nearly landed face first in the trifle." Geeta laughed and took the platter down the garden.

But Kate's attention stayed on Nicola, because the taller woman had reacted to Geeta's touch. Not a flinch, or withdrawal, but an ever so slight easing in her stance when Geeta held around her waist. The barrister stared ahead, her hand hovering above a plate. And Kate was about to dismiss it as nothing, except for the turn that followed.

Nicola's gaze was drawn after Geeta, who sauntered down the garden. It was a gaze that thought itself unwatched, mouth open a little, and it lingered too long. Then Nicola stiffened and altered her balance and moved away to find company.

Kate blinked.

Olivia chatted with Charlotte to her left, the world apparently continuing unchanged for everyone else. All except for Millie, who seemed to have caught the moment too.

They looked at each other. And Millie's eyebrows shot up. Yes, they'd both seen it – Nicola and her intake of breath and compulsion to follow Geeta with her eyes, while the other woman walked away completely unaware.

Millie coughed out a laugh. "Now, that would be something."

"What?" Charlotte said, leaning around Olivia.

"Just a silly idea," Millie waved off her concern, and stuffed a biscuit in her mouth.

"Are you all right?" Olivia asked.

"Yes," Kate replied. "I was just wondering about something you said ages ago. How does your mother get on with Nicola? Are they friends?"

"No. Absolutely not. Couldn't get two more different people."

"Oh."

"Why?"

"Ah, no reason," Kate replied lightly. "Just a silly thought," she echoed Millie's dismissal.

Then Olivia squeezed her hand and drew Kate's full attention.

She trailed her finger up Olivia's bare inside arm, still unable to fill up enough with her since they'd been parted over summer. A flutter shivered up Olivia's arm and she knew she craved the same.

"Later," Olivia whispered, with a delightful tickle of warmth beneath her ear.

Then Olivia rested her head on Kate's shoulder and everything was comfort. Soft hair against cheek. The warmth of her snuggled beside. Wonderful.

It felt incredible just to exist – on an early autumn afternoon, full of sunshine, food, good company and the woman she adored by her side. Very simple things, but the very best. What a world she'd stepped into. Changing, no doubt evolving, but she loved these people and never wanted to leave.

THE END

Acknowledgements

I'm really enjoying writing a series and living in Oxford in my head, a city that was my real home for over ten years.

Writing a series, though, involves a large and varied ensemble of characters and I'm hugely grateful for the broad experience of the people who read early versions of this book and gave me feedback. And although some key facets of the series fall within my own lived experience, I am a white writer and I'm very grateful for the work of a sensitivity reader towards trying to ensure the British-Indian characters are realistic and avoid harmful tropes.

Thank you hugely Di, Sue, Gabby, Georgina, Jay and Cindy, for insightful comments, encouragement, even more support when I wobble and so much patience. It's appreciated no end and has critically improved the book.

I, however, have had the final say on the words, and all remaining issues are solely my responsibility.

About the Author

Clare Ashton is an award-winning author of sapphic romances and mysteries with German translations of her work published by Ylva Publishing and Verlag Krug und Schadenberg.

Clare grew up in Mid-Wales, one of her favourite settings for novels, with sunny romance Poppy Jenkins and fiery family drama The Goodmans set on the Welsh-English borders. The darker mystery The Tell Tale is also set in the Welsh hills.

Setting is like another character in her novels, and her new romance series is based in the beautiful city of Oxford where she adored living for more than a decade. Book 1, Meeting Millie, kicked the series off.

Her books have won several awards. After Mrs Hamilton, Finding Jessica Lambert and The Tell Tale are Golden Crown Literary Society (Goldie) award winners. That Certain Something and Finding Jessica Lambert were Lambda finalists. And her most popular novel, Poppy Jenkins, won the Rainbow Award for Best Lesbian Contemporary Romance.

Clare now lives in the Midlands, slowly working her way back towards Wales, with her wife and son and daughter who are a lovely distraction from writing.

Printed in the USA
CPSIA information can be obtained
at www.ICGtesting.com
LVHW021151071224
798596LV00043B/1164